Hidden Voices

Deborah J. Hughes

Deborah J. Hughes

Copyright © 2012 Deborah J Hughes

Cover Design by Anya Kelleye
http://www.AnyaKelleye.com

This book is a work of fiction. Names, characters, places and incidents are either the product of the author's imagination or used fictitiously. Any resemblance to actual persons, living or dead, business establishments, events or locales is entirely coincidental.

All Rights Reserved

This book contains material protected under International and Federal Copyright Laws and Treaties. Except for short quotes or brief excerpts for purposes of reviews, reprint or use of this material is prohibited. No part of this book may be reproduced or transmitted in any form or by any means, electronic or mechanical, including photocopying, recording, or by any information storage and retrieval system without express written permission from the author..

First edition published by WoolysWagon

ACKNOWLEDGMENTS

So many people are involved when it comes to getting a book ready for publication and though every single one of them are important, I have to give highlight to a few. To Stephanie Foote for her editing advice, thank you so much! You certainly challenged me to make this story more credible as well as entertaining. To another dear friend, Katrina Norwood, thank you, thank you! We've known each other for "ages" (no I shan't say how long!) and I've always admired your wit, humor and intelligence. Your critical approach to this story helped me see it from a different perspective. To my daughter April Hughes, my mom Judy Patten, my dear friend Bonnie Smith and another dear friend Riquita Carpenter, thank you so much for being my critique group! Your enthusiasm for this story fired my own. I also must give credit to my friends and family for being the best support-group ever! Every writer needs "peeps" like you in their lives!

CHAPTER ONE

As I entered the small town of Bucksport, Maine, a feeling filtered through me that was unlike anything I've ever experienced before. I could only liken it to a sort of low-grade static vibration, though that wasn't quite right either. Maybe a strong suggestion of it would be more accurate. In any case, the sensation was so peculiar it made my skin sensitive, enough so that the tiny hairs on my arms almost tickled. The closer I got to the town center, the stronger it became and I was put in mind of an old television show called the *Twilight Zone*. Perhaps I'd just entered something like that.

What a tantalizing thought.

The Tri-State, that mysterious place between Heaven, Hell and earthly life, was abuzz with excitement. Expectation fluttered through the ranks of the spirit world and it made me jittery enough to put me on alert and yet curious enough to encourage my interest.

Since I was here to see a witch's cursed gravestone, I wondered if that was the cause for these unusual sensations. Thinking it quite likely, I took it as a good sign that Bucksport's infamous legend was about to make my life a bit more interesting than it already was. Even back three weeks ago (when I first heard about the infamous legend) I'd known it was something I needed to look into because the sensation of madly fluttering butterflies had erupted in my belly. It was something I sometimes experience when spirit activity is involved.

So here I was, about to see this cursed stone and (depending on what happened when I got there) preparing to investigate the story's validity. A good thing too for now that my vacation to Sea Willow Haven was over, I needed a diversion from the depression beginning to take hold. I seriously hated it that my time in Maine was coming to an end. A short stay in Bucksport seemed just the thing.

As for this legend, there were several stories in circulation and the one I was told entailed a witch cursing the town's founder Jonathan Buck. She did so in retaliation for his having her condemned to death for practicing witchcraft. The story goes that many years after his own passing, his family erected a monument to honor him and a mark of her curse soon appeared upon it.

To what extent spirits were involved I didn't know but I did believe they were part of the mystery. If it turned out I was right, then my stay in Bucksport could be a little longer than anticipated and that was fine by me. Most fine indeed for my reluctance to return to New York was growing stronger by the minute. Besides, having just left another of Maine's famous haunted places, it was quite exciting to now be entering another.

Of course, Sea Willow Haven Resort may no longer be haunted but that sure wasn't the case when I first arrived there. And it wasn't the case here either. This I knew for my suspicions were no longer in doubt, not with the hairs on the back of my neck standing on end and goose bumps rising on my arms. Oh yes, I was in for a new paranormal adventure.

The air hummed silently with spiritual flutter and it seemed the Tri-State was waiting in anticipation of my response. Given how strong their presence was here, how did mediums live in a place like this? Surely they blocked or siphoned the psychic noise for how else could they handle it? As for me (when spirit activity is roused), I can block things to some extent but I am not always successful at it. Right at this moment, however, I didn't intend to block anything. In fact, I was open and willing to communicate.

It was Monday and late morning. Traffic was minimal but steady, the sky dismal with a promise of imminent rain. It was fitting atmosphere for a graveyard visit to be sure. Were this a movie, the scene was aptly set and when the cemetery came into view, I imagined the shrill of music building to an eerie crescendo.

Caught up with anticipation and responding to the images taking place in my head, I slowed the car as I neared and an icy shiver slithered along my spine, turning my blood cold. It was a chilling sign and one that told me I'd be staying longer than a week. Kade would be happy to hear that and honestly, so was I. Though in truth I must confess to being more than happy.

Despite that uplift of joy, the mention of Kade caused a pang of loneliness to pierce my heart. The time wasn't right, however, to think of him and so I brought my focus back to the situation at hand. Later, when there were no other distractions, I'd indulge in thoughts of him. In fact I'd do one better and call him. As for right now, the monument was in view and it engulfed all of my attention.

The tallest stone in the cemetery, it was easy to spot, especially as it faced the street and was close to the fence enclosure. Although its size suggested prominence for the one in which it was erected, there was something else about it that oozed mystery.

Since Nancy told me to park on the side street adjacent to the cemetery, I was able to slow to a crawl as I prepared to make the turn. That gave me plenty of time to get a good look at the infamous image emblazed upon the stone. Seeing it made me impatient to get a closer look and once I was parked, I had to take a moment to settle down.

My heart was pounding so hard it was loud in my ears and the fissure of unease riffling through my body gave me pause. The cause for this physical response required careful handling and I figured it best to ensure my protection before going any further. So I closed my eyes and took in a few slow, deep breaths. As my excitement settled down, I used the imagery of immersing myself in a bright, white light to ensure my physical and spiritual protection. Calm and reassured, I opened my eyes and stepped out of the car.

Whatever mystery surrounded that gravestone, I didn't sense it being dangerous. Even so, I intended to proceed with caution and with the help of my trusty spirit guide, I felt pretty confident in dealing with whatever might come up. It would be great, though, if she'd just tell me what I wanted to know. But, alas, it didn't work that way. Sheila was hardly ever forthcoming and clear with her messages to me. Subtlety was a major talent for those residing in the spirit world and especially so with spirit guides. Given that, the best thing I could do was stay in touch with my feelings and aware of what was going on around me, physically and spiritually.

Filled with purpose and fully engaged in the moment, I slipped on a lightweight jacket and set out to investigate this mysterious legend.

Although the cemetery, which was smaller than I'd expected, was closed to the public, it didn't matter. What I came to see was easy enough to view from the sidewalk and once I was standing directly before it, I was immediately mesmerized.

Even had I not heard the stories, I would have known there was something special going on here. Before I explored that on a deeper level, however, I felt it only right to pay homage to Jonathan Buck and his wife. They were buried a few feet behind the monument and from all I'd read about them, both were esteemed as upstanding citizens. On their behalf I felt a stirring of indignation. It just wasn't right that their good name was sullied in such a way. How terribly unfortunate that the images marring the otherwise perfect stone had effectively trumped the purpose for which it was placed here. Though it was meant to venerate Buck's contribution to the town, it had become instead a horrific legend of the most unflattering kind.

Though I felt it a betrayal to Buck's honor, I finally turned my full attention towards the cursed stone. It was an impressive monolith. Made from a single granite rock, it had a square base and an obelisk-shaped top. It was on the base and right under the Buck name that the image was located ... the supposed witch's foot. Its dark outline was clear and distinct and did indeed resemble the bottom part of a leg. It was prominent and unmistakable and it practically demanded notice. As there was no sure explanation for its existence, I could see why it had inspired so many bizarre stories.

The legends were somewhat varied but most held the common theme of Jonathan Buck, town founder and acting magistrate, being the one responsible for the condemnation and sentencing of death for one purported to be a witch. Her heinous crime was the practice of witchcraft (and yes I was being quite facetious about this part because, naturally, I held no such opinions about witches and their craft). As one might expect of a sorceress, she returned his dastardly deed by cursing him. Some stories even had her cursing the entire town! There were other tales, though, that delved deep into the gruesome realms of horror. To those I paid no mind. Their invention, to my thinking, was purely for the benefit of those who indulged in the macabre.

What I found most interesting is that in most all variations of the legend, there was one part that remained quite consistent. It involved the claim that the image appeared shortly after the monument was erected. There was also an agreement about the stone being replaced several times. But, to the dismay of the family, the image soon reappeared.

There was no record of those replacements or of anything at all involving this interesting mystery. Even so, the stories persisted and no wonder.

The image existed. That couldn't be disputed and it was a definite recognizable shape. Even I had to wonder at its purpose for being. There had to be a reason for its creation. Things don't just happen without a purpose. So what was the reason for the appearance of this particular image and why did it trigger so much supernatural controversy?

Though I wanted to stand there and study it with a clear and quiet mind, my thoughts would not be still. Instead of waiting for information to come through, I sought to reason things out on my own.

In the end, all I did was repeat the questions over and over in my head. What did it mean? Why was it there? Why that particular image?

Getting nowhere with the questions, I looked up toward the top of the obelisk where another stone defect marred the smooth gray surface, this one in the shape of a heart lying on its side.

How odd for two oxidized stains to appear in such recognizable shapes on the same piece of stone. No wonder there were so many stories floating around to explain the anomalies, some of which suggested that Jonathan Buck, a married man and the father of several children, had an affair with the witch in question. Again, there was no validity to the story but that didn't seem to matter.

I conducted some research and found no record of witches being put to death in Maine. Not that it didn't happen, after all, not everything was recorded, especially stuff meant to remain a secret. So what was the story here? Why those particular images on this particular monument? And here I was, right back to the same questions.

A chill shook through me, prickling the top of my head and pulling me from my thoughts. It was a good indication that paranormal activity was afoot.

Knowing it was best to be still and stop crowding my head with thoughts, I quieted my mind and waited to see what else might happen.

A wind kicked up and my hair, which was tied back in a loose ponytail, pulled free and blew across my eyes and into my mouth. I tried to capture the wayward locks but the wind grew stronger and made the task a fruitless one. I finally abandoned the effort and dropped my arms to my side. Since the air was becoming heavy with the threat of rain, I needed to get on with it.

Although I didn't like being rushed, I closed my eyes and opened my mind to spirit. Almost instantly it felt as though I was no longer in my body but that of another. She was someone taller, younger, and her hair was even longer than mine. In fact, it felt nothing like my hair, which was dirty blond, thick and naturally wavy. The hair I now felt on my head was feather-light and it fluttered in the breeze like wisps of silk. It also felt black. Strange that, feeling a color, but there it was.

The preoccupation with my hair was soon circumvented by a sudden pang of regret. It stabbed like a sharp piercing pain into my heart and I had no problem relating to it. I'd felt it often enough over the past couple years. Tears sprang into my eyes and I had to fight the urge to throw myself to the ground and sob in despair. What in the world was going on here?

Injustice. Betrayal. Those were the main feelings that surged through me and I had to clench my hands in order to control myself. The need to toss back my head and scream in frustration was so strong it was all I could do to resist it.

Uneasy and yet curious, I opened my eyes and stared at the monument, focusing my attention on the Buck name. "What have you done, Jonathan?" I spoke the words softly and the air went still, as if it too waited for an answer.

With bated breath (a cliché I suddenly understood very well), I waited to see what would happen next. All I got was an increase in agitation. Her discontent was so strong it affected my emotions, causing me to empathize with her. Our connection, however, was severed when I opened my eyes. Despite that, though I no longer was one with her, I continued to feel the disturbance of her presence. She was not a happy person and I had a very distinct feeling she was different somehow. In what way I could not say. Just different.

"Everyone is always fascinated with that stone."

The voice came from right next to me and it startled me so much I nearly jumped out of my skin. Another dang cliché but it suddenly made a lot of sense why someone would use it. That is exactly how it felt!

Swinging around, I looked with surprise at the elderly gentleman standing right next to me. Considering how close he was, I couldn't believe I didn't hear his approach.

Although I was of average height, standing at five feet four inches, he was considerably shorter. Of course, that might be due to his being so thin and leaning on a cane.

Sitting obediently at his feet was a small, wiry-haired brown terrier of some sort. Although the small dog wasn't interested in me, I did notice that he was staring at the monument with almost as much interest as I'd been giving it.

The old gentleman gave me a smile of apology, his regret for startling me genuine. "Didn't mean to scare you."

I waved off his apology. Given how hard I was staring at that stone, a herd of elephants could have been charging towards me and I probably wouldn't have noticed. "I'd heard about the cursed stone and had to come check it out." Without trying to be obvious about it, I eyed the kindly looking man with interest and wondered if he could shed some light on the witch story. I was pretty sure he was a local and his being here at this precise moment had to be of some significance to me.

It was no coincidence he was out walking in this particular area at the same time I was here having a spiritual connection. After all, who goes for a walk when rain is about to pour from the sky? No, he was here because he had an important role to play in my life. I just knew our meeting mattered in some way.

"It's just a story, you know. In fact, that isn't even his gravestone." The old man nodded toward the two headstones behind the monument. "He's buried back there next to his wife."

"Yes, I heard this was just a monument. His grandchildren must have been very proud of him to put this up."

The old man smiled. "Well he was a war hero you know and he was the founder of our little town."

"Have you lived here long?" Who better to talk to about this than a local?

"Born and raised."

A few drops of rain began to fall and it was our warning that something more substantial was about to let loose.

The old man pulled his long grey jacket closer around him and looked down at his dog, a slight frown of concern deepening the wrinkles on his brow. "I used to run the library but my tired eyes have a hard time seeing these days. Me and Teddy here," he gave the dog leash a gentle shake and Teddy looked up at him with adoring eyes. "We just live to take walks. Now they have that nice walkway along the river, we do it more often. Today, though, we wanted a change of scene." He turned and pointed toward the direction of town. "You go that way and below the bridge is a parking lot. You can walk all the way to the mill from there. It's a nice walk. You should check it out."

I nodded my thanks. "I certainly will. Thank you." Was this the purpose for our meeting on this dismal morning, his directing me to the riverwalk? There was no way I was going to ignore the suggestion. Once I was settled in at the B&B and the rain had cleared, I'd be going for that walk.

Satisfied, the old man made to move on. "I better hurry on home before Teddy and I get drenched. Going to be a hard rain. You better be going too, young lady."

"I will. Thanks." The old man followed the path around to where my car was parked and started up the hill. I watched him through the fence spokes until the rain came down a bit harder. He was right, it was time to leave and as I hurried to the car, I wondered if I'd make it to the B&B before the sky really let loose.

Now that I was here, I was eager to get myself settled in and call Kade. He would be interested to know my first impressions of Bucksport and I couldn't wait to share them with him. This town, I believed, was going to be just as interesting as my last stay. Well maybe not "just" as interesting, after all, Kade wouldn't be involved (sadly).

Ghosts were in abundance here. I felt their presence as surely as I felt the cold raindrops pelting my face. But it was the girl I connected with earlier whom I was most interested in. Who was she and what did Jonathan Buck have to do with her?

CHAPTER TWO

Just as I reentered the main street leading through town, the sky opened and the rain came down in a torrential fury. I thought about the old guy and his dog and hoped they made it home okay.

Since nearly everything is a sign from the heavens, I wondered if this downpour meant I was about to get flooded with supernatural activity. Water, after all, is associated with all things spirit related.

Although a possible spiritual onslaught was rather daunting, it eased some of my sadness for leaving Sea Willow Haven and left me looking forward to a new adventure. It would surely keep me too occupied to miss Kade. Or rather, it would diminish how much I missed him. Besides, after all that's happened in the past three weeks, I was quite ready for more spirit interaction.

Right now, however, I needed to find the B&B and get off the road. Until the heavy rain passed I'd just sit in my car and use the time to call Kade. I missed him. Only two hours since I left the resort and how many times have I thought that? About once every minute or so, that's how many. How on earth was I going to get through the next couple of days? Wednesday seemed like a long ways away. He said his current painting would be done by then and he would need the break. I felt like telling him to pack the painting into his car and bring it with him. He could paint here just as well couldn't he?

Giving myself a mental scolding for thinking about him yet again, I returned my attention to my driving. The issue of Kade could be handled later. First things first and that was to find the B&B, which was somewhere near the center of town. Nancy said it would be on the right side of the street.

As for the single row of buildings on my left, they lined the banks of the Penobscot River and right behind them was the riverwalk the old gentlemen had mentioned. For sure I was going to check it out. Just as soon as I was settle in and the rain was gone.

Since I was told to start looking soon after going through the town's one and only traffic light, I scanned the buildings to my right and spotted the cute wooden sign almost immediately. It said BARB'S B&B and hung from a wrought iron post just outside a yard enclosed by a white picket fence. A paved walkway led from the gate facing the sidewalk to the front door. It was a charming Victorian house and its view of the river was unhindered by the small office building directly across the street from it.

There was one parking spot available along the sidewalk directly in front of it and I pulled into the spot with a sigh of relief. Since I wasn't sure how long the rain was going to continue, I wasn't relishing the idea of dashing through it for any amount of distance.

The charming décor of the house and the carefully tended flower gardens told me the person who owned the place was going to be very friendly. A fact I already figured since Nancy told me a little about the B&B owner when she suggested I stay here.

Without being gossipy, Nancy related only the facts. Barbara Taylor was a widow in her mid-sixties. She bought the house a few years back, not long after her husband's death, and turned it into a B&B. As Nancy explained it, the place gave Barbara something to do and provided company to a lonely woman.

Nancy also told me that Barbara grew up in Bucksport and married her high school sweetheart. He joined the Army right after graduation and she spent the next thirty years moving with him from base to base. After he retired from military service, the Taylors moved back to Maine and bought a small family campground in Orland, a small rural town I'd passed through before entering Bucksport. They ran it for almost ten years, up until Thomas, Barbara's husband, was diagnosed with testicular cancer. The couple decided to sell the campground and concentrate on fighting the disease. He managed to do so for three years.

"You must stay with Barbara, Tess!" Nancy enthused. "You'll love her, she's such a character and her B&B is so charming."

"Is it haunted?" I remember asking because it seemed to me that most of the Bed & Breakfast homes were large, old and full of history. It wasn't unusual for places like that to be haunted.

Although I asked the question in jest, Nancy took it quite seriously, her smooth brow wrinkling in deep thought. "I don't know. She's never mentioned that it was." Then Nancy said something that lingered with curious tenacity in my mind. "Although given the history that's taken place in the area, I wouldn't be surprised if the whole town is haunted."

I had to ask. "What's that supposed to mean?"

Nancy laughed and waved away any serious consideration of her ghostly suggestion. "I speak in jest, Tess. I can imagine you've had enough of ghosts after everything that's happened here."

It was nice to see the tension gone from Nancy's face. Thanks to the supernatural activity going on when I first arrived at the resort, she'd been quite tense and worried. But, thankfully, we'd taken care of the problem and my last couple of weeks there were quite free of ghosts.

What I really enjoyed about those ghostly issues being resolved was the freedom it gave me to immerse myself in Kade's company. Though, to be honest, I did miss the spirit activity. Well some of it anyway. Truth be told, I was ready to get involved with the spirit world again and judging from the feelings stirring within me, I was going to get plenty of action.

The rain let up as suddenly as it started and I eyed the sky with distrust. The weather here was quite versatile. Nancy and Jack often joked that if I didn't like it, then I need only to wait five minutes and it would change. I didn't want to tell them we said the same thing in New York! Still, keeping that thought in mind, I stepped out of the car and hurried up the walkway. The sky was still heavy with rainclouds and I wasn't convinced they were done relieving themselves upon us.

The welcome sign above the door said *"Come on Inn, Stay a Spell"* and I had to smile a little at the wording. Considering I was here to investigate the legend of a witch's curse, it seemed somewhat prophetic.

With the feeling that I was doing exactly what I needed to be doing, I entered an enclosed porch and hung my wet jacket on the coatrack next to an elegant set of French doors.

Through their square panes of glass I could see the front desk and a sitting room off to the right. A woman was standing there waiting for me to join her. Figuring it must be Barbara, I opened the door and smiled in welcome.

"Hello."

"Hello, dear." She stepped forward and held out her hand. "You must be Tess. I'm Barbara."

Her grip was warm and firm and there was an aura about her that was very pleasant. I didn't doubt that we were going to become good friends and once again I knew I'd done the right thing to come here. Not just to the B&B but to Maine. The state's welcome sign said that Maine was *"the way life should be"* and I was beginning to think it had the slogan right.

"Hello, Barbara, it's nice to meet you and I'm excited to stay here for a spell." She laughed at that last part and I followed her to the front desk where I proceeded to fill out a registration form. In the meantime, Barbara kept up a steady stream of chatter.

"Sorry about the rain but it's due to clear up soon and tomorrow's forecast is calling for a warm, sunny day. We've needed the rain though so can't really complain about it. Better than snow, that's what I say." She leaned over to see where I was on the form and waved her hand. "Don't worry about filling all that out. I just need the basic info."

"Ok then." I turned about and waved toward the street where my car was parked. "I'll just go get my luggage and settle in. If the weather is going to clear, I'd like to take a walk along the river later."

Barbara followed me to the door. "Do you need some help?" When I started to protest she brushed away my objections. "I may be getting old but I can still carry luggage. Surely you aren't going to be able to handle it all alone." Shorter than me by a couple inches and with a frame that could easily be described as 'pleasingly plump', Barbara did not look like a frail old lady in the least. She had a healthy vitality about her and I did not want to insult her by refusing her kind offer to help.

Between the two of us, we managed to get all of my suitcases in one trip. My room, however, was on the second floor and that took two trips between us to get everything up the carpeted stairs. Situated in a corner room, my bedroom windows offered a great view of the river and I could see Fort Knox across the way. I had forgotten about the old fort and now that I was seeing it, I put it on my list of places to visit during my stay.

Pushing the lacy white curtain aside, I took in the view with an exclamation of delight, playing it up a bit for Barbara's benefit for she was clearly waiting for my reaction. "This is a lovely view, Barbara. I love that I can see the bridge and the fort."

"Have you been to the fort yet?"

I drew away from the window and glanced around the room. "No, this is my first time to Bucksport. Other than when I passed through on my way to Sea Willow Haven that is."

"Well you should try and get there during your stay. It's a charming place to walk around and explore." Barbara walked to the door and paused. "Have you had lunch, dear? I was about to make a sandwich and there's plenty if you'd like to join me."

Touched by her thoughtful invitation, I was regretful at having to turn her down. "I ate a large breakfast at the resort and I'm just not hungry. But I do thank you for asking."

Barbara nodded with understanding. "I stayed a weekend at Sea Willow, they had lovely food there I remember." She paused for a brief moment and I got the impression she was trying to decide what to say next. "I heard you had some interesting developments while you were there."

Wondering what Nancy told her, I kept my reply vague but polite. "Yes it was a memorable stay." I waved my hand toward the window. "Can I access the riverwalk from across the street? It looks like the rain is about done and I think I'll take that walk once I've finished unpacking."

"There's an access point to the right, at the end of the building across from us. It's a lovely walk. I try to go at least two or three times a week. Me and Max."

"Max?"

"My dog. He's a Schnauzer. Right now he's at the groomers but my daughter should be bringing him back any time." She stepped out of the room. "I'm usually in the sitting room if you need me. Feel free to come and chat whenever you feel like it." She nearly had the door pulled shut when she quickly opened it again and caught my eye. "Oh, in case I forget. I do have one other guest right now. Ted Kendall. He's staying in the room downstairs. It's the only one with a private bath. Yours is across the hall, second door on the right. The three rooms up here all must share a bathroom but it's usually not a problem and for the moment at least, it's all yours."

A small twinge of unease tugged at my psyche. A lone male guest was staying here? How was Kade going to feel about that? Though he had nothing to worry about, I was concerned he might not see it that way. The fact this guest and me would be sharing close quarters meant we'd probably see quite a bit of each other. Such was the case at Sea Willow with Kade and it led to the new and exciting relationship we were now exploring. Given that, he might not like to hear I was now in a situation similar to what had brought us together. Surely he knew me well enough to know he could trust me in that regard? Though we'd made no pledges, we were definitely in the "couple" stage (despite not yet taking things to a sexual level) and considering my struggles to move on from my husband's death, our relationship was a major deal for me. "Will he be here long?"

"Until Wednesday. He checked in last night. He's here to evaluate the Tenney house. The people he works for are interested in purchasing it." Barbara gave a satisfied nod, letting it show how happy she was about such a possibility. "I hope they do so soon or the whole building is going to go to waste and ruin."

That information made me ping with excitement. If she was talking about the building known as the Tenney Inn (now closed for several years), then I definitely was interested in whatever she could tell me. I'd conducted some internet research in preparation for this visit and I'd learned that the building was in existence during Jonathan Buck's time. Not only was it built during his reign as the town's top citizen but the house was on one of the stops in a stagecoach route. Given that, it was quite likely Colonel Buck had been inside the building and that meant a connection between the two was formed. If the connection was a good one, I might be able to pick up his spiritual imprint. "You are talking about the Tenney Inn?"

"Yes, it used to be such a nice hotel at one time. Fancy place. A shame for it to go unused for so long."

"I wonder if the gentleman staying here would let me check it out." From wanting to keep my distance to now seeking his company. That's how it happened with Kade. Only I wasn't the type of woman to run from man to man. After all, it took me two years to move past my husband's death and get to this point with Kade (which wasn't far, not for this day and age). Still, for all intents and purposes we were developing a solid relationship.

"I'm sure he could arrange for you to tour the place," Barbara said, her eyes lit with curiosity. Though she clearly wanted to know the reason for my interest, she didn't pry. "Mind you, it's been closed for quite some time so I'm not sure it will be pretty to see." When I shrugged that I wasn't concerned about that, her curiosity deepened, but again she refrained from asking my reasons. "He should be here sometime in the late afternoon."

"Thank you, Barbara."

"Well I'll let you get on with it then. See you later, Tess." And this time she pulled the door closed.

Glad to have some time alone, I placed one of my suitcases on the bed and started the task of unpacking it. With nothing to distract me, I thought about the girl I connected with at the Buck monument and wondered who she was and what part she played in his story. Did she have anything to do with the witch's curse? Wanting to discuss it with Kade, I started to look for my cell phone but an urgency to "hurry up already" put me back on the task of unpacking my clothes. Seconds later, I turned away from the suitcase and headed for the door.

I needed to go on that walk and I needed to do it now.

Though I hurried on down the stairs, it was like I couldn't move fast enough. It made me anxious though I had no idea what was spurring on the feelings. I knew, however, not to question it. I learned the hard way (as did many of us when it came to life lessons!) not to ignore my feelings. If I was being urged to take a walk, then take a walk I would do.

So with that, I picked up my pace and practically ran down the stairs, my heartbeat increasing with each step.

What, I wondered with anticipation, was going to happen next.

CHAPTER THREE

Barbara was on the phone when I reached the bottom of the stairs. Though she seemed curious as to why I was in such a hurry, she indicated with her hand that whoever she was talking to was quite the chatterbox and I gave her a sympathetic wave as I headed out the door. Good. I didn't want any delays and I wished to heck I knew why!

The clouds were clearing enough for the sun to poke through them and its glorious rays made the world glisten with vibrancy. The air smelled crisp and refreshing and I drew in deep, appreciative breaths. Though invigorating, it was nothing compared to the sense of anticipation that loomed over the town. What had everything all stirred up? Did it always feel this way around here?

Perhaps my presence was causing the excitement. The idea of it gave me a bit of a jolt me and I immediately attacked such a notion. Surely I wasn't important enough to generate this level of psychic energy. Spiritual excitement fluttered everywhere and even at Sea Willow Haven it hadn't been this way. No, this wasn't normal. For whatever reason, Bucksport's ghosts were stirred into something of a tizzy and I wasn't leaving until I knew why.

The urge to call Kade made me reach for my cell phone. If there was one thing I needed right now, it was to hear his reassuring voice. Despite only knowing him for less than a month, he had the remarkable ability to calm me. There was a solidity about him, a sense of comfort and security that I needed and welcomed. It was a little disturbing how much I missed not having him around. Funny how a few weeks with a person can seem like a lifetime.

My cell phone was not on me. Then I remembered tossing it on the bed while attempting to unpack my suitcase. Aw well, no matter. It would have to wait. There was no time to go back and fetch the phone. Though what that meant I had no idea. Why did I feel like I would 'miss the boat' if I did not hurry the hell up?

Pick up the pace, Tess, for goodness sakes!

Not only did I feel like I needed to hurry, I was now telling myself to do so! Taking heed of my urgent suggestion, I quickened my steps and ran across the street, glad for the lack of traffic to delay things even more.

When I saw the stairs leading down to the riverwalk, I heaved a silent sigh of relief. Great. Almost there. Maybe this puzzling sense of urgency would calm down and allow me the luxury of an easy pace.

Once on the brick-paved walkway, however, I wasn't sure which way to go. After a quick glance in both directions, I headed right towards the town's marina. Further on down was a paper mill, its smokestacks sending plumes of smoke into the air. It looked like the path ended at a pier just outside the facility's fenced border.

Though it appeared far more interesting in that direction, I took only a few steps before it hit me that I was going the wrong way. Wondering what was driving that thought, I turned around and went in the other direction.

The view was lovely, especially with the impressive expansion bridge stretching in majestic splendor from the island of Verona to the mainland across the river. Another bridge, one like many others, functional and unimpressive, connected Verona to Bucksport. It was toward that bridge that I headed. I had a vague memory that a park of some sort was located on the land below the end of the bridge and this path should lead right to it.

Along the way were plaques that offered information about the landmarks nearby. I started to stop and read one but knew immediately that I must not. No time! Must go. So I kept walking.

Wondering if my trusty spirit guide could shed some light on this compelling urgency, I calmed my questing mind enough to summon her. Sheila glided into my thoughts almost immediately, bringing with her the sensation of cobwebs brushing across my face. Though I didn't know why this phenomenon occurred, it was my signal that she was indeed with me and my harried psyche began to calm, slowing my steps to a more reasonable pace.

What's going on, Sheila? Why the hurry?

Most of our communications were done mentally and a good thing. Otherwise, people would probably wonder why I was talking to myself all the time! She mingled in my thoughts like a separate presence, her voice distinctly different from mine.

Be calm, Tess. Be open and aware.

Nice advice but not all that helpful. Surely she could do better? *Is that all you're going to give me? Is Jonathan Buck stirred up because I'm here to investigate his curse?*

Sheila's laughter was warm and light, making me smile. She always brought with her a feeling of security, much like I felt with Kade. There was also a strong sense that I had nothing to fear. That did not, however, calm all my fears. It was a human trait to be afraid and one I was determined to conquer.

Fear also helps to keep you safe, Tess. Sometimes, fearlessness spurs careless actions. Fear not, but fear enough.

That's pretty cryptic, Sheila, thanks. I heaved a silent, heavy sigh. Although I loved our communications (she was such a loving spiritual being), she spoke often in riddles. Why couldn't she just be frank for once?

Understanding must come from within you, Tess. My telling you all you seek will not bring with it the understanding needed to learn the lessons you wish to master.

I could no more stop the scowl than I could contain my admiration. *You are a clever guide, Sheila, but I seriously think I could learn just as much from information you give me as I can from self-discovery.*

Her tinkling laughter once again rang through my mind and I couldn't help but laugh with her.

When told things you don't understand, the knowledge is useless. If you are not ready for the answers, then understanding will elude you, leading you to reject what you are told. It has always been this way. So now we let you discover things on your own. It's the only way.

Feeling a tad bit glum for the stubbornness of the human race, I had to agree with Sheila, though I did so with reluctance. Still, it didn't hurt to try one more time. *I would believe whatever you told me. Just so you know.*

Believing and understanding are two different things and both must be accomplished to not only learn but to also accept what you learn. Two years ago you did not accept what you learned. This is the only way, dearest. You must understand that.

The reminder of my ignorance sent a ripple of displeasure through my nerves. When Mike and Tootsie were killed, it wasn't only Mike and God I was mad at. I was also angry with Sheila for not warning me. Had she done so, I reasoned, I could have saved them and her silence was looked upon as a betrayal of my trust.

Feelings of betrayal do nothing more than feed anger and I had plenty of it to go around. Sadly, the negativity of my feelings had shut off my communications with the spirit world. Sheila, I thought, had abandoned me. The loss of it all was too much to bear and I held a terrible grudge for two whole years. Not only did it eat at my heart but it also blocked my conscious connection to my soul. It was a very dark, lonely period.

Now I understood things a little better, it really bothered me that I let anger throw me into an abyss of sorrow. Leaving my house of memories and going to Sea Willow Haven was the best thing I could have done for myself. Much as I hated to admit it, I had quite the pity party going on and the beautiful resort, ghostly inhabitants and all, helped pull me out of it. I was determined to never allow myself to fall that low ever again. No matter what.

Sheila's sudden withdrawal drew me from my thoughts and I felt chagrined at not thanking her for coming to me. Though I was tempted to call her back, I became distracted by the fact that I was approaching the small park. A monument of some sort was located there and since several flags fluttered in the light breeze, their poles standing high and proud behind a curved granite wall, I knew at once it was a veterans' memorial. Even from this distance I could see the flags represented each branch of the armed forces, the State of Maine and our great country.

A subdued but dignified air hung over the memorial and once I was close enough to read the plaques, it was to discover that the impressive monument honored those from the local area who had served in the military. Although veteran memorials certainly were connected to death and sacrifice, that wasn't why the air had a heavy feeling to it.

A woman sat on a stone bench to the left of the monument wall. She looked to be in her mid to late thirties though I wouldn't stand behind that guess. Sorrow had a way of making one look older than their years. Since her head hung low over hunched shoulders and she didn't appear to realize I was approaching her, I knew she was lost in deep, soul-wrenching thought. A dark aura of sadness surrounded her and I wondered if she'd lost someone whose name was stamped on that wall. Or, perhaps she was suffering from a traumatic event related to her own service. She could well be a veteran herself.

Since Kade had served in the Marine Corps, I thought about him and all he'd endured. The lone survivor of a roadside explosion, he suffered not just from the loss of his comrades but from injuries that ended his career. When I first met him, his despair was similar to what I sensed in her, though it wasn't quite so poignant. Thank goodness he was now at peace with the tragic events of his past. That being in part because we'd made contact with one of the men who hadn't survived the explosion. It's what I loved most about my gift ... bringing people from here and "there" together. It helped ease some of the grief and stifling pain.

So what to do about this woman? She could clearly use a friend right about now and yet I didn't want to intrude. It was a tough decision for me. Do I bother her or not? Could I help her? Would she even want my help?

Again I thought of Kade and how that connection with Humphry, his deceased comrade, had done wonders for his peace of mind. If her issue was the loss of someone she cared about, then I could possibly help her. Although such communications didn't heal broken hearts, it mended them enough to help them deal with the loss. It sure made a huge difference for Kade and me. We'd had so much healing to do and together we were getting it done.

So. What to do? As much as I wanted to help her, I had no idea how this woman would react to such an offer, particularly of the kind I had in mind, and I wouldn't give it without her consent.

So I stood there, a few feet away, silent and indecisive. Then the woman lifted her head and looked in my direction. Our eyes met and the pain in hers called out to me.

Giving a small apologetic shrug for interrupting her solitude, I offered a smile. "I don't mean to interrupt. So sorry." I turned to go but she stood and held out a hand in entreaty.

"No, please. It's fine." She swept an arm toward the monument. "Did you come to see the wall?"

No. I came to see you. I knew instinctively that she was the reason for my urgings to come here. "I just arrived in town and had no idea this memorial was even here." Though I should have noticed it and realized what it was when I drove past earlier, it was raining hard and I was looking for Barb's place.

Making a visible effort to shake off her sad thoughts and concentrate on me (a welcome distraction no doubt), the woman gave her best impression of a smile. "You just arrived? Are you visiting relatives then?"

"No. I'm passing through actually. I just finished a vacation in Poke Harbor and am making my way slowly back home to New York."

The woman's eyes, which I must add were disturbingly black, widened just a tad. "Poke Harbor? I just read something in the news about that place. What..."

Not wanting to discuss what I knew very well she had heard in the news, I hurriedly cut in. "I heard about the Jonathan Buck curse and had to come check it out."

More of the sadness let up as she uttered a small chuckle. "The witch's cursed tombstone? Everyone is always so interested in that old legend." She turned slightly away, her thoughts having gone elsewhere. Seconds later she gave herself a mental shake and stepped away from the bench. "I should go. My mom wasn't expecting me to be gone so long."

Ah, perhaps her mother was ill and the cause for her heart-weary persona. My expression must have given away my thoughts for instead of rushing off, the woman continued to stand in place. As she was worrying her bottom lip, I figured she was contemplating a decision. Should she stay and explain or leave it be? Not wanting to interfere with her decision, I waited quietly and looked away, giving her the space she needed to think.

Finally her poised-for-flight stance relaxed. She'd decided to stay. "She's not doing so well right now. I needed some fresh air." Her dark eyes glistened with the threat of tears and after giving an impatient sniffle, she shook her head vigorously, an attempt, no doubt, to shake free of the thoughts charging through her mind. "I'm sorry..."

I took a step toward her and the air thickened between us. It was a mixture of heavy thoughts, strong feelings and the flutter of spirits. The Tri-State was in a flux and that told me I needed to keep her here for just a little longer. "Please don't rush off. It helps to talk sometimes. I'm a great listener. My husband died two years ago and I talked the ears off anyone who would listen. Now I'm in a better place emotionally and I am all ears." Giving her a gentle smile I gestured toward the bench. "You want to sit and talk a bit?"

I watched her changing expressions as she fought the need to rush home against the need to talk and when she settled back down on the bench, I breathed a sigh of relief. Thank God. Now to find out what this was all about.

Since I was still standing, she patted the empty space beside her and scooted back to give me even more room. "Please sit with me."

I settled next to her and sought to keep things light and undemanding. "Are you from Bucksport?"

Since she didn't answer right away and was back to staring at the monument again, I wasn't sure if she heard my question. As I knew thoughts were often sluggish when in an emotional funk, I decided to wait a minute or so before repeating it. In the meantime, I studied her profile. Although her head no longer hung with the weight of the world, her thin shoulders were slightly hunched and I knew her strength was nearing its end. Hopefully she would open up and tell me what this memorial had to do with what was going on in her life.

"Yes I'm from here. I think my family probably helped Jonathan Buck build Bucksport." Hearing my mutter of surprise, she gave me her attention and managed a genuine laugh. "I'm just kidding." Then giving a slight frown, she added, "I think." When I lifted my brows in inquiry, she went on to explain. "The Rowans, my family, have lived here forever it seems. I'm not all in the know on my ancestral history I'm afraid." She thought about that for a moment then went on thoughtfully, as if she found the idea appealing. "Maybe I should look into it. It's so much easier these days with the internet."

Glad to see that she didn't seem as sad as she was earlier, I rejoiced quietly. Every victory, however small, was worth celebrating. But I hoped to do more. Although some of her melancholy had lifted, there was a heavy aura around her.

It wasn't something I could see but I could very well sense. Dark thoughts loomed in her mind, blotting out her spiritual light. Having suffered as much myself, I wanted to help her get through it.

There was certainly nothing to lose and everything to gain by making the offer. So I turned a little to better see her and took note of her long dark hair. It was tied back in a loose ponytail and that was my style of choice during my two-year mourning period. I just hadn't cared enough to do anything more. Now, however, I let it fall loose about my shoulders because Kade loved long hair and I loved being on the receiving end of his admiration. A pang of longing hit me but I pushed it aside. I'd deal with that later. Right now I needed to concentrate on the woman sitting beside me.

"I think looking up your family history is a great idea, especially if you have strong ties to the area. You'll probably find a lot of information right here in town. The local museum would be a good place to start. I hear they have a great collection of stuff. My name is Tess by the way."

"I'm Mary Rowan."

She flashed a brief smile and I was at once ensnared within the dark depths of her eyes. They were the blackest eyes I'd ever seen and disturbing only in the wealth of secrets brimming there. I suspected a lot was going on behind that gaze, more than even she could comprehend. It made me want to know her better and that told me she was indeed the reason I was compelled to be here.

"Did you lose a family member in a war?" I indicated the memorial and Mary's eyes flashed with remembered pain.

"No."

Hmmm. I wasn't expecting that answer. "You just seemed so sad while you were looking at it...?" I let my explanation drift off in a silent question. Yes I was shamelessly prying for information and for good reason. Now that I knew the Tri-State had orchestrated our meeting, I needed to know why.

"I was in the military. I retired earlier this year." Mary closed her eyes briefly then continued on. "I swore I was never coming back to Bucksport and yet here I am. My mother is here and ... well things aren't going well. I had to come back."

"Is she ill?"

Mary gave a short bark of laughter. "As pathetic as I'm acting, you might think so. No, she's not ill thank God." Her mouth firmed in an effort to control her emotions. "She's financially broke and losing her home." Mary's head bowed under the weight of a future she feared and resented. "It's been in the family for generations, since Bucksport's inception in fact. It will kill her to lose it." Her voice wobbled with the effort it took to keep her emotions in check. "It will kill us all."

"I'm so sorry. It's tough times for many people right now."

Mary closed her eyes and sucked in a slow, deep breath. I knew she was trying to keep from dissolving into tears and so remained quiet while she collected herself. Although I wanted to reach out to her, I knew how fragile a hold she had on those threatening tears. Sometimes a caring touch was all it took to break the dam. She wasn't ready for a good cry and to encourage it would only make things worse for her right now.

"It all just seems so hopeless, you know? I keep wondering what the point is."

"The point?"

Mary's eyes opened and narrowed on the monument, her expression tightening with contempt. "Life. What's the point with life? We work our asses off, we fight stupid wars, we kill…"

My heart did a little lurch. "Kill?"

Now the tears started falling, spilling in rapid succession down her pale cheeks. "You'll have to forgive me, Tess, but I'm a mess right now. I'm dealing with post-traumatic stress disorder. PTSD. Have you heard of it?"

"Yes I have. I'm sorry. Is it from your military experience?" Again thoughts of Kade sprang into my mind. The military life was hard on those who served it, especially for those who fought in a conflict. Although I couldn't truly understand what they went through, having nothing in which to compare the experience, Kade was helping me with that, explaining some of the challenges and difficulties they all endure.

Mary pressed her hands to her eyes. "I can't stop thinking about it, the deaths…" She broke down for just a moment, drew in a breath then continued on, her voice shaking with emotion. "I was part of a medical team. We often accompanied troop movements or were sent in after an attack." She lifted tortured eyes to lock with my sympathetic gaze. "I killed a man."

"What happened?" She needed to talk about it and get it out in the open. I kept my regard of her steady and unwavering, knowing how important it was that I not appear appalled or disgusted. As I was neither of those things, it was easy to do. Of course I was appalled that those things occurred but I was not appalled with her.

"Our convoy was attacked. We all were armed and well trained on the weapons we carried. Shooting at a paper target is nothing compared to lifting a gun and aiming it at a person." Her hands dropped to her lap and twisted together in nervous tension. "He was carrying an explosive device and I just couldn't let him get near us. I didn't even pause when I lifted my gun and shot him." Her hands went to her head, pressing against her skull as if trying to push out the memories. "I can't get it out of my head, the way he looked when he realized he was shot."

"Was it a quick death for him?"

Mary's head bowed low, as low as it was when I first came upon her. "He died almost instantly. Just that split second and then it was over."

"I'm sorry you had to experience that. He's in spirit now and I can assure you, he harbors no feelings of resentment for what happened. He knew the score when he started at you with that explosive device. He knew what could happen and he accepted those conditions."

"But he was someone's son, maybe someone's husband or a father to some child who no longer has a daddy."

"Yes he was someone's son and it's sad for them to lose him. But he chose to be there that day and do what he did to bring about the result that he experienced. Perhaps it was even his life mission and now he's done."

"His life's mission?" Her curiosity roused, the tears halted and Mary lifted her head to look at me. "What does that mean?"

"For whatever reason, it was his fate to take part in that horrific drama. Maybe that was his reason for being born, to go through that moment in his life. Maybe it was God's plan for us to experience the things his actions have caused us to experience." Since Mary was staring at me so intently, I knew I had her complete attention and I did not want to waste it. "Think about it. His actions and his death have affected many people. Not just his family, friends and comrades but you and your family, friends and comrades. That awful, terrible experience has made a profound affect on all of you and what you get out of it ... whatever it is you've learned from it ... that is what makes his sacrifice worthwhile."

"Are you a therapist or something?" Mary eyed me critically, trying to process what I was telling her and yet not sure if any of it mattered.

"No." I had to make a face over my next admission. "But I underwent a year of therapy. Does that count?" I'd hoped that would lighten the heavy atmosphere and it seemed to work. Mary actually gave a tremulous smile.

"Why were you in therapy, if you don't mind me asking?"

"My husband and dog were killed by a drunk driver two years ago. I had a hard time accepting it, especially since it could have been avoided. If that man hadn't been drinking and driving, my husband would be alive." Old resentments wanted to raise their ugly heads but I was done with it and let the feelings go. "I've since come to accept it was his fate that day to do what he did. I learned from the experience and others have learned from it as well, especially his wife and kids." The man was 43 years old when it happened and he had two children, a ten-year-old son and a twelve-year-old daughter. And now, two years later, I finally wondered how they were doing.

Though I wanted to stay in the moment, my mind went back to Mike's funeral. Foggy though the day was for me to remember, I could recall meeting the family of my husband's killer with crystal clarity. They didn't stay long because I couldn't deal with it. I'd been icy and unresponsive and it stung me to recall how awful I was. The worst part was they didn't know the reason for my deplorable behavior. Though it was no excuse, my heart had gone out to them, responding to the pain stamped all over their faces.

Much as it shamed me to admit it, even to just myself, I couldn't face their pain and deal with my own as well. I especially couldn't handle the sorrow stamped on the faces of his kids. Seeing it made me furious that his thoughtless actions had robbed them of their father.

The memory sent a surge of anger charging through me and I closed my eyes to temper it down. How was it that I'd blotted out that memory until now? Not even during therapy did I remember it. Then again, I was stuck in the past, back to when Mike was alive and I was busy resenting the fact that he was no longer with me. If there is one lesson I've learned very well, it's that wallowing in the past does nothing in the way of good. It keeps us from living in the present and looking forward to the future. It keeps us engulfed in sorrow and resenting everything.

Another lesson I finally came to learn was that good memories are to be enjoyed and savored then released for another time to enjoy and savor. What one should not do is cling to them as I had done. It kept me anchored to a past that cannot be relived, the memories no longer bringing joy but sorrow. It also kept me from experiencing new joys, ones to be just as treasured as those of old. It was a painful lesson but one I finally was getting a grasp on.

"Tess?" Mary touched my arm in concern. "Is everything okay?"

I opened my eyes and smiled at her. "I'm fine. Just thinking." Grateful for the return of that memory, painful though it was, I sent warm regards to his family and asked the angels to engulf them in a shower of love. From now on I would focus on the present, look forward to the future and stop wallowing in the past. Much as I meant it, I found I had to constantly reinstate those intentions. It was a hard one to do. Despite its difficulties, however, I would prevail. Eventually.

"I'm so sorry about your loss, Tess." Mary sniffed, pulled a twisted tissue from her pocket and wiped her nose. "Life sucks."

"Well it can but it's also pretty awesome." Kade once again came to mind. Oh how I wanted to call him.

"My father died of lung cancer three years ago," Mary said. "His health insurance wasn't much help when it came to paying for his care. My mother never worked because they had five kids to take care of. Our whole family has struggled all our lives." Her eyes drifted down to the stones paving the ground in front of us. They were stamped with a service member's name, the military branch in which they served and the dates involved. "Two of my brothers live here in the local area and another one lives with my mother. My sister lives up north near the Canadian border. She and her husband are struggling. So are my brothers. If mom loses the house, I'm not sure who of the five of us will be in a position to help her."

"Are you only here to help out then? Do you actually live elsewhere?"

"I've separated from my husband. He's in Georgia with our two sons." Her voice deepened with hurt and bitterness. "They are fourteen and sixteen and they have sided with him." Her voice broke. "I've lost everything and now my mother is about to do the same."

"I'm so sorry, Mary." We were silent for a moment and then I felt compelled to share with her a saying that often comforted me, even if only briefly. "There's a saying that says 'All obstacles are but stepping stones to a brighter future' and I firmly believe in it. Don't ask me where I heard that, I don't know, but it's something I've always believed. Of course, right after my husband's death I didn't believe much of anything for a while. Now I know better."

Mary's eyes lifted to mine, curiosity now more prevalent than pain. "How is it that you now know better?"

"Well I never thought I'd be happy ever again and yet I am definitely happy with my life right now. It took me two years to get to this point and I'm disappointed with myself for taking so long. The problem was that I'd turned from my faith and that is not conducive to being happy."

Mary nodded with understanding. "It's our faith holding us together right now, for me and my mom anyway. My siblings couldn't care less. They are too angry to be giving much thought to God."

I covered Mary's twisting hands with one of my own. They were cold to the touch and stiff with tension. I did my best to infuse some warmth into my gentle squeeze. "Things are going to get better, Mary. I just feel that so strongly right now."

"Are you psychic?"

I laughed at that then regretted it when I saw the brief flare of hope in her eyes. How to explain? I bit my lip, thought about it for a moment then decided to just put it out there. "I'm a medium. I talk to the dead. I also converse with a spirit guide named Sheila. I feel her right now and she's urging me to tell you that things will get better."

They would get better, I now believed, because the two of us had come together. Though how our meeting was going to solve Mary's problems I hadn't a clue.

"You talk to the dead? That's amazing. I don't think I've ever met anyone who can do that." She stared at me as if trying to find evidence of my claims. "Doesn't it scare you?"

"No. Spirits do not scare me. They are people like us after all."

"But aren't some of them bad?"

"I suppose so but I rely on God to protect me. My faith keeps me safe."

Mary nodded, accepting that answer. "I can understand that. I keep trying to hold the faith that God will help us through this mess but so far nothing." She heaved a long, heavy sigh.

We were both silent for a few moments, reflecting on our discussion, when a wind kicked up and shook us from our reverie. Mary gave an exaggerated shiver, her thin sweater not holding up to the cool afternoon weather, and rose to a stand, her expression filled with reluctance. "I need to get home." But she made no move to hurry off. "Are you staying in Bucksport long?"

"About a week I think. I'm staying at Barb's B&B right here in town."

"Oh yes, I've always loved that house. Never been inside of it though."

"Then stop by some evening when you can and chat with me some more. During the day I suspect I'll be out and about but once the evening hits, I'm going to be a free agent. Any restaurants around here you care to recommend? The B&B comes with breakfast obviously, but lunch and dinner are up to me to find."

"There are only a couple of restaurants available and I recommend them both." She paused for a long moment and I could see that she was struggling with a decision. "Maybe you would consider having a meal with us one evening? I know you don't know me at all and that might make you feel awkward but I do cook a pretty decent lasagna."

"That sounds lovely, Mary, thank you." I handed her a small card that contained my name and cell phone number. Since I'd planned to dig around for information, I'd made them up in advance. You just never knew when you needed to ensure people had a means of contacting you. I hadn't thought it would be to arrange for dinner with a new friend but that was one of life's many pleasures ... meeting new people who you just knew were going to become important.

Mary glanced at the paper with a smile and tucked it into her pocket. Her eyes, when they rose to meet mine again, were not as heavy with sorrow. At least, not like they were when I first met her. Even her aura was lighter. "Great, I'll call soon and we'll figure out when." She held out her hand to me and I grasped it gently, sending her loving, energized thoughts as I did so. "Thank you, Tess. It helped to talk to you. I feel hopeful now." She smiled again, gave a wave and hurried away.

I watched until she disappeared up the hill and around a building situated next to the memorial (I think it was public restrooms but I wasn't sure and didn't care enough to find out) then turned and headed for my temporary home.

Now that my mission was accomplished, I figured I deserved a little time to call Kade. I had a lot to share with him. Bucksport was turning out to be just as interesting as Sea Willow Haven. Maybe it wasn't teeming with ghosts but spirits lurked here. If they had anything to do with that witches curse, I intended to find out how and I wasn't leaving until I did.

CHAPTER FOUR

Barbara was in the sitting room when I entered the B&B and since I didn't pause other than to offer a quick wave, she gave me a smile and returned her attention to the open book on her lap. Glad I was not to suffer any further delays, I rushed to my room and snatched up my cell phone.

Kade answered on the first ring. "Tess, how's it going?"

It felt so good to hear his deep, rumbling voice that I let the pleasure of it seep through my senses as I sank onto the bed. "I meant to call earlier but I've been pretty busy since arriving. How goes the painting?"

I wanted him to say, "What painting? I'll be there in a jiff" but I knew it wasn't fair to expect such a thing and pushed those thoughts firmly away. Expectations could kill a relationship and I didn't want to ruin this.

"It's coming along fine." A pause, then his voice lowered, making my stomach jump around in response. "I miss you already."

"I miss you too." Silence. We both reflected on what that meant to us then I decided I better start talking or this was going to get awkward. "I saw the tombstone. It definitely has a story behind that marking. A female spirit visited me while I was there. She wasn't very happy, more so resentful than anything. Like some sort of injustice has been done."

"Well the stories do say she was burned for being a witch. I would think that's reason enough to be resentful."

I shook my head in response, feeling that wasn't the case here. "No, I think the story is skewed somehow. It feels more like a grave injustice has occurred."

"A grave injustice?" Kade laughed. "Now that sounds appropriate considering what we are discussing."

I laughed with him. It was one of the things I loved about our relationship. For two years I went without laughter in my life, feeling I had no right to be happy, and now it seemed I did it all the time. Thank God those dark, awful days were behind me. How they'd gotten as bad as they had, I just couldn't fathom. To say I was disappointed in my reaction to Mike's death was an understatement. I'd really gone off the deep end, delving the depths of despair and wearing it like a mantel of sorrow upon my soul. It made no sense that I'd reacted as I had. Me, a person who dealt with the dead on a regular basis, and I become unhinged when my own husband crosses over. Two long years to recover. Why? Then again, if I hadn't taken that long, I wouldn't have gone to Sea Willow Haven and I wouldn't have met Kade. For everything there is a purpose. But honestly, why did the universe have to take two years to bring us together? Of course, two years ago Kade was in the military and engaged. Heck even one year ago the circumstances weren't right for us to meet. Timing is everything and the universe is an excellent timekeeper. Thank God.

"You lost in thought? You got awfully quiet."

That's another thing I loved about him. He accepted my constant slippage into thought and usually left me to it. But as we were on the phone, long stretches of silence were not quite appropriate. "Sorry. I was just thinking how glad I am to get laughter back in my life." It was a wonder I even got the words out for my throat had tightened up and I had to pull in a breath to calm the emotion filling my chest. If I didn't know any better, I'd think my heart was expanding. In any case, the sensation was enough to make me take another breath in order to accommodate its need. Would I be an emotional mess for the rest of my life? I used to be so calm, cool and collected. Since Mike died, I was none of those things.

"You deserve to laugh, Tess. We both do. Everyone does." He started to say something more but stopped. I heard him give a little sigh and wondered what was on his mind. Before I could ask, he put our conversation back on point. "So you think there's some merit to the story about the curse? Does that mean you might be staying there a little longer than a week?"

Smiling at the hope in his voice, I sprawled across the mattress and twisted onto my stomach. After bunching one of the pillows under my chin, I bent my knees and swung my feet in the air, giggling at the picture I made when I realized what I was doing. I felt like a kid again, a teenager talking to her first crush. Only it was a woman's feelings that charged through my body. "I think it might take longer than a week. I need to talk to Barbara but I suspect the room will be available for as long as I need it."

"Good." He didn't bother to hide how much that answer pleased him.

Now to tell him something he might get uneasy about. "There's another man staying here who's evaluating the Tenney house. His company is thinking of purchasing it. You remember me telling you about the Tenney house?" By keeping the subject on the house and not the man, I hoped to keep this conversation going in a direction that didn't lead him towards worry. The very last thing I wanted Kade to do was become concerned about me and other men. In fact, I didn't even want it to be the "last" thing. I wanted it to be no issue at all.

"A man? Have you met him yet?"

The pit of my stomach plummeted with dread. The only thing I could do was treat this situation as nothing more than an opportunity to get where I wanted to go. "No not yet. Barbara said he will only be here until Wednesday so I'm hoping to meet him tonight and politely beg him for an invitation to view the building. Colonel Buck was probably in that house several times and I want to see if I can pick up on his energy." Please, I prayed, please don't concern yourself about a man who is nothing more than a way in to a house I want to visit.

"I see." Several quiet seconds went by. "What else do you plan to do to figure out the curse?"

He was letting it go, but I knew it would eat at him. Kade had trust issues. It was understandable considering what happened to him with his ex-fiancée.

Feeling the need for some spiritual help on the matter, I closed my eyes and made a silent plea to Sheila, one that required no words. She knew what I needed. We had so much baggage, Kade and I. Could we overcome it and make us work?

"Tess?"

Oh right, he was still waiting for me to answer him. "I'm not sure what I'm going to do. I think I'll just walk around the town and see what happens. The universe knows why I'm here.

Hopefully it will work its magic and lead me to where I need to go." So far that method had worked well for me. It brought Rid and Mary into my life. I could only anticipate what else would come of it.

"Nancy said to remind you about the historical museum there in town."

"I haven't forgotten. We talked about my going there when I read about it on the town's website." The internet was a wealth of information but I loved discovering things first hand.

"I shouldn't have any trouble coming up on Wednesday like we planned. Maybe you could ask Barbara if she'll have an extra room available and I'll stay a day or two." A short pause and then, "That's if you want me to."

He sounded so uncertain and that wasn't Kade. One of the things I noticed about him when we first met was his self-assurance. Of course that was a demeanor he presented to the world. Inside he was as vulnerable as I was. Well maybe he wasn't as bad as me. I was much worse. "I would love that, Kade."

He let out a barely audible breath, telling me he'd been holding it while waiting for my reply. I wanted to reassure him that he had nothing to fear when it came to me but held my tongue. Maybe it was too soon to start sounding like I was going to stick around for a good long while. Maybe he wasn't ready for that and even if he was, our relationship wasn't yet at a point where I could voice such a thing out loud. Besides, he wouldn't really believe it. Time and action would show Kade what was happening between us.

"Good. Sounds like we have a plan." And then his tone lightened and I knew he was making an effort to get our conversation onto something less personal. "Have you met anyone else of interest?"

"Yes, actually, I have. Mary Rowan. She was at the Veterans Memorial not far from here. It's located at one end of a nice walkway along the river. I was going to stay in my room, unpack my things and call you but suddenly I had this overwhelming urge to take a walk. When I got to the memorial and saw Mary, I knew why."

"So what's her story? Any significance to the witch's cursed tombstone?"

"It's not a tombstone, it's a monument and no I don't think so." And yet a sudden little twinge made me wonder.

"I stand corrected".

"She was in the military too, Kade. She retired earlier this year. She's suffering PTSD and her family is going through a lot of financial strain."

"What branch was she in?"

"You know, I didn't ask but I get the feeling it was the Army."

"What's the PTSD in relation to, did she say?"

"Her convoy was attacked. She was a medic or something." I paused for a moment and wondered if Mary would be okay with me sharing her story then figured I might as well. It wasn't as if it was a well-kept secret. Well not the military stuff anyway. "She had to shoot one of the attackers and she's having a hard time dealing with that."

"Yeah it's a tough thing to deal with. We grow up being told not to kill then we're sent off to war and expected to do that very thing." He heaved a heavy sigh. "It's a screwed up world, Tess, but we are not going to spiral down into the pity party we've managed to achieve in previous discussions."

"I agree. I don't want to get into a heavy, deep and real discussion about the military and war. We have done that a time or two and as important a topic as it is, I want to talk about my current mission ... solving the story behind the curse of Jonathan Buck's stone monument."

"So why do you feel you were led to the Veterans Memorial to meet Mary? Are you going to contact the spirit of the guy she killed?"

I had to laugh (though quietly to myself) at the question. When Kade first heard about my ability to talk with the dead, he was quite skeptical about it. Even so, despite his misgivings, he kept an open mind and for that I was grateful. Not everyone did. It seemed amusing now to have him automatically go there ... asking a question like that. "No, I don't think so. Besides, he probably doesn't even speak English. That would be interesting to interpret."

"Don't laugh, you never know. Maybe we all speak a universal language when we die."

"Maybe." It was an interesting thought. Kade's observations were sometimes a pleasant surprise to me. I wondered if Sheila would enlighten me on the matter if I were to ask and made a mental note to bring the question up in a future communication with her. "I'm not sure yet why I had to meet Mary unless it was to help her in some way, though how I'm to accomplish that I don't know. She did seem to feel a little better after we talked though."

"Well there you go. I know I feel better after talking to you."

Smiling, I buried my face into the pillow. If only he was here beside me. "Come early on Wednesday."

His soft laughter made my breath hitch and then he spoke in that deep purr of his that I so loved. "Bet on it."

Now I was laughing softly. It put joy in my heart to know he was as eager as me to be together again.

The sound of voices in the reception area downstairs told me that Ted Kendall may have arrived and since I wanted to be sure to meet him, I figured it best to get off the phone. Besides, if I stayed on any longer, I might say something I wasn't ready to voice out loud. "I think the other guest just came in. I hear him talking to Barbara. I don't want to miss meeting him and worming that invitation to see the Tenney house. I'll call you tomorrow, okay?"

"Okay, Tess." The tension was back in his voice and I wished I had time to reassure him. "Have a good night."

"If I can get an invite to that house then I will. Tell Nancy and Jack I said hi and fill them in on what I've got so far. Okay?"

"Will do. Bye, Tess."

"Bye, Kade." I tossed my cell phone on the nightstand then took a moment to gather my thoughts. The problem here was the distance between us. If we couldn't get to each other via a quick walk then we weren't close enough. It might only be two days away but Wednesday wasn't going to get here soon enough.

Losing Mike so suddenly made me realize how precious our time is. Now that I'd met Kade, I didn't want to waste any of it in getting to know him better. Maybe it wouldn't work out between us, but I didn't believe that. Our current living arrangements, however, was going to be a big issue. He lived in Maine and I lived in New York. In the schematics of distance, that was unacceptable and moving to Maine didn't seem like such a bad idea.

The fact I was already thinking about moving told me that I was invested in this relationship far more than I thought. Was it too big a step to take at this point? We met a mere month ago. Not long at all. And yet, strangely enough, it felt as if I'd known him forever.

More sounds of commotion sounded from downstairs and then I heard a dog's excited yapping and knew Max was home. Time to get down there before I missed my opportunity. And so with that, I pushed off the bed and hurried to join the fray.

I found Barbara cooing to a black schnauzer who was literally lapping up the compliments by showering her face with appreciative licks. "Max, you look so handsome. Yes you do. Just look at you. What a pretty boy."

I smiled at the picture they made but thought having a dog bathe my face with his tongue was not something I'd enjoy. Tootsie was never a licker. She had been a nose-nudger.

Barbara looked up at my approach and stood to greet me, her dog doing the same. He went into immediate investigative mode by sniffing about my foot, my shin and then my other foot. Satisfied with my scents, he sat down on his hind legs and gave me a greeting by way of a tongue-hanging yap. I was at once charmed and knelt to give him some attention, doing what Barbara had been doing just moments ago. "What a cute little dog you are! Yes you are. So handsome." I scratched him behind the ears and Max's stubby tail began to thump enthusiastically on the hardwood floor.

"I've had Max for almost five years now. Got him a couple years or so before my husband died. He's been such a comfort to me." Barbara watched our exchange with a fond smile. She was proud of her baby and showed it.

The stab of pain that pierced through my heart took me a little by surprise and my eyes filled with tears in response. Losing Tootsie still saddened me and I'd not allowed myself to get close to any other animals since. In fact, I wasn't sure I wanted to be in a position to become that vulnerable ever again. Then what of Kade? A niggling voice of worry made its way through my thoughts. What if I fell madly in love with him and he died? I just couldn't go through with that again. I couldn't. The sudden depression that followed such thoughts was swift and merciless. Oh God.

"Tess? Are you okay, dear?" Barbara's worried voice penetrated my spinning thoughts and I looked at her as if she was my lifeline back to sanity.

"When my husband died, I lost my dog Tootsie as well. She was with him when it happened."

Barbara's face scrunched in sympathy. "Oh my dear, I'm so sorry. Bad enough to lose your husband but then not to even have the love of your dog to help ease the pain..." Her voice drifted off and she looked at Max with an expression of heartfelt gratitude. I knew she was thinking how lucky she was to have him and I was glad for her. "Max is a comfort to me. He pulled me through the dark days."

A man stepped forward at this point and patted Barbara's shoulder in sympathy. "Well I for one am glad you had such a good dog to help you through that, Barbara." He then looked at me and offered a smile. "I'm sorry, though, that you did not." He held out his hand in greeting and I took it without hesitation, noting the positive energy swirling around him as I did so. "My name is Ted. I'm staying here as well. You must be Tess?"

A tall thin man in good health, Ted looked to be in his early thirties. His well-cut, dark gray suit fit him perfectly and it had not a wrinkle in sight. His dark hair was slicked back with just enough gel to do its job but not cause an unnatural shine and he had a nicely trimmed goatee that covered his narrow jaw line. It met a mustache that was also nicely trimmed and the whole look gave off one of good character. He was a handsome man and (much to my delight) he had a gold ring on his left hand. Good. Married.

"I am indeed Tess. Tess Schafer."

Ted pulled his hand away and motioned toward Max. "He's a very well behaved dog. Last night he sat obediently at my feet the whole time I chatted with Barbara. I felt quite welcomed." As if on cue and knowing he was being spoken of so favorably, Max barked once and started prancing from one foot to the other. Ted laughed and reached down to scratch his ears. "He's a shameless beggar of scratches as well."

"I didn't see the new collar anywhere, Mom." A woman came out of a room behind me and I turned to smile a greeting. She was short, plump, somewhere in her mid-forties and well on her way to looking just like her mother. "Hi, I'm Nellie." She shook my hand and nodded to Ted. "Hi again, Ted. How goes the purchasing talks?"

"Nellie, that isn't any of your business." Barbara shot Ted an apologetic look. "Sorry. Nellie has always been the nosey one."

Ted laughed as Nellie drew in a breath with exaggerated flair and splayed her hand over her ample chest. "Well really, Mother. How can you say that?"

Barbara smiled at the theatrics and turned toward the sitting room behind her. "I need to sit down. My hip is acting up today. Must be all the rain from this morning that did it." She dropped into a comfortable looking rocking chair with a satisfied sigh and motioned for the rest of us to join her. "Come on in and sit a spell. Nellie, are you going to stay for a bit? Don't worry about the collar, I'll find it later."

Nellie shook her head, her blond bob bouncing about her shoulders as she did so. "Can't, sorry. Dix has a swimming lesson in about an hour and I haven't pulled anything from the freezer to thaw for dinner." She waved at me as she headed for the door. "Nice to meet you! Enjoy your stay in Bucksport. Bye, Ted. I still expect an update before you leave. Just fill mom in on the details and she can pass it on to me." And then, without giving any of us a chance to reply, she was gone.

Once again Barbara gave Ted an apologetic glance. "Sorry about that, Ted. She's always made it a habit to know everyone else's business. No amount of talking to her is going to change that."

Ted waved away the apology. "No worries, Barbara. I imagine she's only expressing an interest that everyone else is curious about as well." He stretched out in the recliner he chose to sit in and sighed with appreciation. "It feels so good to sit down. I've been on the go all day." After a few seconds of silence, Ted looked at me. "So what brings you to Bucksport?"

Here was the opening I needed. "The witch's cursed tombstone."

Ted's hazel eyes widened and the thought passed through my mind that they were similar in color to George's. And why, I wondered, did I have to think of Sea Willow Haven's talented chef. Along with it came thoughts of everything that happened there and I just didn't want to deal with any of those memories right now. So with determination, I pushed them away. Now was a time for new adventures. Besides, didn't I just remind myself earlier that I was not going to get caught up in the past again?

"Witch's curse? What's this about?" Ted turned to Barbara as if I suddenly wasn't reliable enough to believe.

Barbara smiled with a pleased-as-punch expression and spoke proudly of the town's little supernatural mystery. "Well it's not actually a tombstone, it's a monument, but it is in the graveyard so most people think it's a tombstone. But anyhoo, our town's founder, Jonathan Buck, is buried in the graveyard down the way a bit and it's believed he had a woman put to death for witchcraft. Just before her death, she cursed him and his family and her booted foot now appears on his monument."

Ted turned back to me, his expression suggesting that Barbara sounded sillier than I did, though he did so without coming across as condescending. "Really? And you are here to do what exactly?"

His baffled 'I can't believe this but am interested anyway' expression made me smile though I did my best to keep it a small one. I didn't want to offend him. "It's an old rumor that the town can't seem to shake. The image on the stone doesn't help. I was there this morning and it's clear as day."

"How interesting. So what do you plan to do?"

I shrugged and spoke in a manner that suggested what I was about to impart was quite normal. "Contact the witch's spirit if I can and find out the truth. Or maybe contact Jonathan Buck. Whoever of the two is willing to come through and chat."

Ted's mouth compressed thoughtfully, his eyes narrowing as he looked first at me then Barbara. She nodded her head with the air of one who was part of the whole scheme and proud of it. His gaze finally settled back on me. "You are going to contact them? Are you a medium then?"

A little apprehensive, I decided to be honest. It was a risky move because he could get up and leave the room, deciding to stay as far from me as possible. Of course, such a reaction would probably end any hopes of seeing the Tenney house up close and personal. "Yes I am." And since he wasn't making any move to get up and leave, I decided to put out there what I wanted. "I am hoping to see the Tenney house. If I'm lucky, I might be able to contact Buck's spirit. Or maybe even the witch's. If there is a witch, that is."

"I see." Ted's manner became somewhat guarded. "Okay. Not sure if I'm creeped out by the fact that you want to see if the house I'm trying to secure for my company has anything to do with a witch but, well, I guess we'll have to just see if that's the case before I freak out about it." He offered a smile to show he was okay with my revelation. "We can't all pick our gifts now can we?"

I let out a quiet breath in relief, not realizing I was even holding it until that moment. "No we can't. But I'm not sure I would change it to something else even if I could."

Ted leaned forward now as growing interest began to take hold. "So do you actually see dead people?" He gave an exaggerated shiver. "I'm pretty sure I couldn't handle anything like that."

"Well if I do see them, they aren't usually in the same state they were in when they died, despite the Hollywood depictions to the contrary." I gave a small shrug, like what I did was as normal as Barbara's job, though it wouldn't surprise me if even she ran across strange situations at times. "Some spirits are a little spookier than others but in the end, they are all people. Without bodies certainly, but people just the same."

"So how are you going to contact the witch or the other guy, what was his name?"

"Jonathan Buck," Barbara supplied, not wanting to be left out of the conversation. And then she too was looking at me for an answer to Ted's question. "So what are you going to do, Tess?"

I shrugged in answer then expanded my explanation as best I could. "Not sure. I usually play it by ear. I've put my intentions out there and now I'll wait for spirits to guide me along." Hopefully they'd be willing to help me out. It might be that the people involved didn't want the truth coming to light. And if that was the case, well darn. But I wasn't going to think about that.

"Are you going to hold a séance or something?" Ted asked.

Barbara looked slightly alarmed at the suggestion and I spoke quickly to dispel her unease. "No, I don't think so." Again I shrugged. "I'm really not sure how I am going to go about it." Now was the time to make my appeal so I looked at Ted and gave him an earnest smile. "The building you are looking at, the Tenney house, was built around the time that Colonel Buck was still alive. He being the town's founder and the builder of that house being someone of prominence, I imagine Buck visited there several times. I'd love to go in and check it out. See if I can sense anything." With nothing left to do but wait for his answer, I met his eyes and waited patiently for him to decide.

Ted stared back at me with a thoughtful expression and I knew he was giving it some serious thought. I also knew when he made his decision before he even said it. "Well I can help you out with that but I do have one request." His expression was firm and I knew I'd have to accept the condition or it was a no-go. "If the place is haunted, I need you to keep it a secret. My boss is very superstitious and he's terrified of ghosts."

I held out my hand. "Deal." Ted gave a short laugh and shook my proffered hand, this time his grip a little uncertain. "Don't worry, Ted. You won't suddenly be haunted with spirits because you touched me. I promise."

Laughing at himself, Ted gave a small, sheepish grin. "Am I that obvious or are you psychic too?"

Smiling, I stood and made to leave, deciding it best to go before he regretted his decision. "No, unfortunately I'm not. Not usually anyway. Sometimes things come through from the Tri-State but not very often."

"The Tri-State?" Barbara and Ted spoke up at the same time and I stopped my backwards retreat to explain.

"The place between our physical world and heaven and hell is what I call the Tri-State. When we die, we cross into another state of being but are still connected to..." I shrugged trying to come up with the best word they'd understand. "Earth, I guess you could say. Our spirits can roam freely among our loved ones or wherever. This place where our spirits reside before moving on to other spiritual adventures is what I call the Tri-State. But at some point we must move on ... to hell or to heaven or whatever."

Ted nodded in acceptance of the explanation though it was one he'd probably never heard before. "Well then, when I get to the Tri-State and it appears I'm getting shipped off to hell, I think I'd just hang around there. Maybe that's what all the ghosts who haunt us are doing? You think?"

I kept my expression serious though I wanted to smile. It sounded logical and maybe to some extent he was right, but it was all so much more complicated than that. "I don't think we really have a choice. We must always be moving forward. Some get stuck for a while but eventually we must move on. And if it is to hell, well, I really don't think it's for eternity. That just seems so unforgiving to me."

Barbara's face was earnestly serious. "Oh but some people deserve it, Tess!"

Not wanting to get into this discussion because it would go nowhere, I simply nodded. "That's true, Barbara. It's hard to argue against that." Now it really was time to take my leave and I waved my hand toward the stairs. "Well I best get to my room and finish unpacking my things." But I only took a step before turning back for a quick question. "Any recommendations for dinner?"

"There's a nice restaurant just down the street, about a two-minute walk from here. They serve just about anything and they are quite reasonable." Barbara stood and followed me to the stairs. "Breakfast is served at eight but I can arrange for it to be earlier if that's too late."

"No eight is fine, Barbara. I imagine nothing is open until nine so that works." I glanced at Ted who was standing now as well. "When would be a good time to meet you for a tour of the Tenney house?"

"We can go right after breakfast if you like."

"Sounds perfect. Thanks. See you later." And I bounded up the stairs, feeling buoyant and excited. I was practically walking on air, I was so happy. Things were working out just fine. What kind of luck would have me staying in Bucksport and in the same place as the only guy around who could get me into the Tenney house?

Preoccupied though I was, that didn't stop me from detecting someone approaching from behind and I paused at the door to my room. Though it was so strong a feeling I entertained that it could be Barbara or Ted, I knew almost immediately that it was not. No, this was definitely someone from spirit and their approach halted the moment I became aware of it.

Although I send out psychic feelers and tried to bring its presence into clearer focus, I couldn't really get a fix on anything. It felt more like an observance from the Tri-State than a spirit hoping to make contact. How interesting. Someone in the spiritual realm was interested in my investigation. Now why, I wondered, was that? The shiver that raced along my spine gave me hope. It was a good sign that I'd attracted someone who could help me out. All I had to do was bring them into my sphere of awareness. But not now. Maybe tomorrow.

So with that decision being made, I walked into my room and turned to shut my door. "Not now. Later. I promise." It was a welcome relief to feel the presence vanish from my awareness. Satisfied, I closed the door.

With so much going on and so much to look forward to, how was I ever going to be patient enough for tomorrow morning? A look at my luggage and I knew I could somehow keep busy until bedtime.

As I unpacked the rest of my clothes and put them neatly away, I kept glancing at my laptop sitting on the desk. Would another story come to me? Shortly after arriving at Sea Willow Haven, I had the strongest compulsion to write and was soon in the midst of a story. I thought at the time that it was a fictional work from an active imagination, especially as none of the names corresponded with actual people. But the story turned out to be real enough. Somehow or other I'd picked up on the energy of people who had lived (and died!) at Sea Willow Haven and managed to channel their story. Would the same happen here? Something told me it just might.

Although I really did want to get my room in order, the anticipation of writing took hold and I couldn't wait to get to it. As I only had my toiletry bag left to unpack, I let it go and headed for my laptop. Who was I to argue with spirit?

CHAPTER FIVE

My heart pounding in anticipation, I put my fingers to the keyboard and waited for the words to come. Although traffic was busy outside my windows, the sounds were muted and didn't hinder my concentration. I was too focused in any case to pay it any attention.

Wondering what sort of story was going to form next, I could barely contain my impatience. Luckily, it wasn't long before the words started flowing, the images that accompanied them clear and vivid in my mind.

The meadow Isi had found while gathering kindling for the ritual fires was nearly overrun with the plants needed to save her brother. Now she was back to gather them, she prayed the Knowing One kept her safe and went about her task in quiet efficiency. She didn't have much time and every second counted. Her people would come when they discovered her missing and she didn't doubt that had already occurred. As they were excellent trackers and she'd done nothing to hide her way, they'd be here soon.

Though their displeasure with her would be great, it wasn't her people that worried her. It was the strange men who stalked the area, picking her people off one by one and sometimes village by village, that gave her the most concern. They'd seen none lately, however, and so she'd dared this mission. Hopefully the elders sent to fetch her wouldn't arrive until her satchel was full.

She worked with quick, sure hands and stayed low to the ground, feeling safe enough considering the danger. Since the Knowing One had shown her this location as a gift (she stumbled upon it almost within seconds of having made her request), she felt justified in defying the elders' orders to never leave the village alone. Although she could have let one of them come in her place, she didn't want to be responsible for anything happening to them. Besides, with the risks so high they might have decided against it, and then she too would have been honor-bound to obey the decision.

Since a growing unease began to filter through her, she took less care with her gathering technique and bemoaned the fact that at one time this task was a mundane routine. Now it was fraught with danger. The strange men who steal spirits were increasing in number and showing up everywhere.

Although she was well hidden by the tall grass, it wouldn't be hard to know something was about if anyone should observe the meadow for any length of time. Luckily she was efficient and quick and her satchel was filling fast. Soon she'd be on her way back to the village. Soon. But soon enough?

An urgency to get going spurred her on. No time, no time. Hurry. Hurry. The litany rang through her head until she felt she had collected enough for their needs.

After closing the flap on her leather pouch, Isi went still and in a flash of knowing, she became aware of the fact that she was no longer alone. Her heart pounding loud in her ears, Isi flattened to the ground and waited in silence, her rapid breathing mixing with the breeze blowing in gentle whispers through the grass.

She heard nothing, but they were there. Somewhere. Close. So close. Time slowed to a crawl then came to a point where she had to make a move. Her people, she knew, were also near but it wasn't them causing the prickle of alarm, the sense of pending doom. They, too, knew she was not alone and so they stayed hidden.

What to do? Since a run for it entailed standing and thus would make her an easy target, she began a quick belly crawl instead, slithering through the grass with an economy of movement. It would not bode well to cause too much of a disturbance among the grass and plant stalks. If she could make it to the woods, then she might have a chance.

The fear racing through her made it difficult to move but she made slow, agonizing progress. With each bit of ground gained, she became hopeful. Almost there, she could see the thicket just ahead.

Then someone grabbed her arm and yanked hard.

Gasping with pain and shock, Is was pulled upright, her captor raising her so high her feet barely touched the ground, making the gain of sure footing impossible. Before she could even think to pull herself free, her other arm, flailing madly, was captured in the same biting grip. The move brought her around to face the one who held her.

Isi stared in horrified awe.

He looked like no man she had ever seen. Where did such a person come from and why did the Knowing One bring him to her? Why show her the meadow, knowing she would come, then allow this to happen? Why allow her to think she might actually provide the means to save her brother? She thought of Siem, normally so big and strong, now lying weak and still on his pallet, and her heart hurt for him. His illness worsened each day. He needed these plants or his fever would continue to rage.

Her spirit heavy with the realization of her predicament, Isi knew she had failed him and pain lanced through her heart, its agony increasing as a dawning understanding began to take hold. She would never see him or the rest of her family again. The elders were clear in their telling of the danger they faced. "If the strange man who stalks the woods raises his magic stick and points it at you, he will steal your spirit and you will go into darkness."

So many of her people, she thought sadly, one by one ... gone. They suffered so much already, hiding, moving, trying to survive in a world gone hostile.

Their difficult survival was nothing, however, to the dangers they faced with this new threat amongst them. They did their best to minimize the danger by moving often, never staying in one place for more than a few days. Though the world was large, it was becoming more and more difficult to avoid the men who suddenly appeared in their land. And if found by them, it was impossible to avoid their magic. They'd learned quickly that the strange stick the strangers carried took their spirit and ended their time of growth and learning.

She'd understood this was a possibility, that her decision to gather the medicines on her own might lead to her demise but she'd had to do it and even now, dangling before this strange man, held fast in his biting grip, she didn't regret her decision. Her tribe needed her brother. She needed him. But soon, she would need no one. Not if this beast-like man before her had any say about it.

Fear clutched at her chest and tightened her throat, making it hard to breathe. She could only hope her failure did not mean her brother would pass into the land of darkness.

Though only a few seconds had passed, it seemed so much longer as she stared into the disturbing eyes of the man scowling down at her. They were a strange color, like that of the sea when angry. Isi lowered her gaze, unable to look at them any longer. What did it mean to have eyes that color? Was there magic in his gaze as well?

His skin coloring was just as strange. It was a lighter shade than hers and covered in hair that was the color of the grass during the late fall. It seemed to cover his entire body, even his face, though it was longer and thicker there. If he were not shaped like a man, she would think him some sort of animal. Did the Knowing One send him? If so, why? Should she prostrate herself at his feet and beg for his mercy? If only he would release her she would give it a try, but his biting fingers held her steady.

Neither of them spoke and time continued to stretch on. Why was he staring at her so intently? It was as if he found her stranger than she found him! Then he started making strange noises and his hold on her arms tightened, his grip like that of the big bird's talons. As she was not sure if he was invoking the spirits, Isi bit her lip to keep from crying out. What more magic did this man have?

The sound of another voice coming from behind him made Isi look up and she was shocked to see another of his kind come rushing towards them. This one, however, was a female and her expression was anxious. Isi stared in fascination for the woman's head was wreathed in hair that shined like the sun, the color similar to the little flowers that bloomed brightly in early spring. Her eyes were the color of the sky at dawn.

Although they both wore strange material on their body, the likes of which Isi had never seen before, the female's *covering was loose and flowing compared to her captors. His clothes were wrapped close about his big body.*

Although they spoke in a language Isi did not understand, it was quite clear that she was the topic of their discussion. Her fate, she knew, was being discussed and she bowed her head in silent communication to the Knowing One. If she had displeased him, she asked for a chance to once again make him happy with her.

After a quick length of time, one in which each took turns speaking and gesturing, Isi was thrust toward the woman and the man of the light colored hair that covered his body began to walk away. It was then she noticed his magic stick slung over his shoulder. She was told that it thundered loudly when stealing the souls of those it was pointing at.

The woman took a firm hold of Isi's hand and pulled her along with them. Though Isi wanted to resist, the man's thunder stick frightened her and she knew it was best not to anger him. Besides, her people were watching and she would take no chances of having them discovered. So she went with them in meek compliance.

Since she would not be returning to her village, Isi hastily slipped the pouch from her shoulder and allowed it to fall to the ground. They would fetch it once it was safe to do so and they would track them to see where they took her. Her people would not risk their discovery, however, and so she knew the sacrifice that must be made. Her only hope now was that the medicine she'd gathered would be enough to save her brother. Surely it would, otherwise, why would the Knowing One bring her here?

As they entered the woods on the opposite side of the meadow, away from where her own people stood hidden, Isi glanced back in their direction. Sadness engulfed her as it hit her hard that she would see them no more.

Gripped with apprehension, I stopped writing and pulled myself out of the story. So what was this about? Now that I was somewhat familiar with the process, having done it at Sea Willow Haven, I knew this story was significant to what I was about to discover here in Bucksport. But was it significant to the cursed monument? And if so, how?

What I found strange about this particular piece of writing was the fact that Isi did not know how to label the things she saw and felt and experienced. She acted more on instinct and knowing than specific knowledge. It was me, as the writer, who put her thoughts into the appropriate words. Writers do that anyway but this was different.

For instance, I knew the plant she was gathering was yarrow but Isi did not call it that. In fact, I wasn't even sure if she called it anything. Despite my lack of knowledge about plants, I did know a little about some of them and somewhere along the line, I'd learned about the healing properties of yarrow. So when Isi mentioned her brother suffered with a fever, it triggered a memory of someone telling me that the yarrow plant, a weed to most people, and something that grew all over the northeast, was used to reduce fever.

What I wasn't sure about was why Isi found the man and woman she encountered so strange and unfamiliar to her. Since the story most likely stemmed from the local area, Isi had to be from Maine. If this was indeed the case, then the man and woman who took her must have been from elsewhere.

Since I was investigating a curse that took place during the time of Colonel Buck's colonization of Bucksport, I would make a guess that Isi was a native Indian. The state was teeming with them when the colonists started arriving. After all, explorers were coming to Maine long before Buck and his people settled here. What I found somewhat puzzling is the fact that the timeframe for the story was much earlier than Jonathan Buck's lifetime. It had to be. Isi's reaction to seeing her captors was a pretty good indication that the story took place during the time when the Native Indians and the Europeans first began to encounter each other. That had to be the case for the magic stick Isi referred to was nothing other than a rifle.

I found the story a bit confusing because I'd always thought the native Indians were friendly toward the European settlers at first. Some, like the Iroquois, were never quite friendly, resenting the white man's advancement into their world, but I didn't recall reading about there being a problem in Maine. For sure I was going to have to look it up. My knowledge of history was pretty bad. Practically non-existent.

Considering all the unknowns about the story, it really puzzled me that it was coming through so clearly. What did the Indians have to do with the witch's curse? Perhaps nothing and yet I felt sure there was a connection. All I could do at this point was hope the story developed enough to give me some answers. For now it remained an intriguing mystery, though there was one other benefit as well ... it gave me a place to start on my investigation. Just what was the relationship between Colonel Buck and the Indian tribes local to the area? Learning those answers would surely lead me to more.

In any case, my heart went out to Isi. I could picture her very clearly in my mind and she was quite young, twelve or thirteen at the oldest, and my fear was that this story would not end well.

Heaving a sigh, I had to accept the fact that in light of my ability, death was usually involved. And though it wasn't supposed to be sad for the one who died, it sure was sad for those left behind. And besides, how one died was not always pleasant. It was the violence of those particular deaths that I did not like learning about. How frightening to go through the last moments of life in violence.

Giving a shudder, I glanced at the clock on the nightstand and grabbed my sweater. Maybe I'd just go for dinner. I needed a break and I was getting hungry. Besides, I needed to do something to lift my spirits. My sadness for Isi was casting a pall over my feelings and robbing me of my enthusiasm to uncover the truth behind the monument's curse.

* * *

Bucksport really was a small town and the B&B stood right smack in the middle of it. As I only had a couple choices for dinner locations, it only took a moment or two to decide where I wanted to eat. To my right was a restaurant about two minutes away. To my left and about ten minutes away was a Chinese place. Then, of course, there were the convenience stores with pizzas and subs but I was in the mood for a quiet dinner and so I went right.

Barbara said it was an upscale restaurant with booths that helped hide one's lack of company. Why it bothered me to eat alone, I don't know. It wasn't me that was bothered by it so much as I worried about what other people might think. Or perhaps it was because I'd never had to eat alone and it felt strange to be doing it now. So strange that I figured others would think so too and I was uncomfortable with the idea of being the object of speculation. But then again, what did it matter what anyone thought?

With my self-confidence bolstered by those brave words, I walked right up to the restaurant and stepped inside, determined to show total unconcern for my lack of companionship. And that's when I spotted Ted. He was emerging from what I presumed to be the restroom and our eyes met almost immediately.

"Hey, Tess! I wondered if you'd end up here." He broke into a smile and came over to shake my hand. "I should have just asked if you wanted to eat together. Would that be okay? Would you care to join me?"

"Hi, Ted. If you want the company then I'll be happy to join you but please don't feel obligated to ask." Although he appeared genuine in his pleasure to see me, I felt somewhat awkward and uncomfortable though I couldn't really say why. It wasn't like we were going on a date. And yet I had to wonder what his wife would think about him eating with a woman she didn't know.

"I really would like the company. I was just sitting there a few moments ago asking myself why I hadn't asked you earlier. I should have done so when you asked Barbara about a place to eat but I didn't want you to ... well..." Now he looked uncomfortable. "I wasn't sure if you'd think..." Again he stuttered to a stop.

"As long as you are sure your wife won't mind, Ted, then I will be happy to have dinner with you. I don't want to upset anyone though." His very actions told me he wasn't out to score anything but companionship with dinner.

"I'll call her right now and let her know what I'm doing if it will make you feel any better. She'll be very jealous, though, because my wife loves anything to do with the paranormal and when she hears you are a medium, she's going to be mad that she didn't come with me." Ted grinned and waved a hand toward the dining room. "My table is there by the window." He turned to the waitress who stood a respectable distance away. "She'll be joining me at my table."

The waitress gave me a smiling nod. "I'll be right over to get your drink order."

As soon as we were settled, Ted pulled his cell phone from his blazer pocket and called his wife. I listened as he told her that a new guest at the B&B checked in today and that I was a medium looking into a story about a cursed tombstone. He gave a dramatic pause then added with a teasing smugness to his voice, "And now I'm having dinner with her because neither one of us dug the idea of eating alone and I'm going to pump her for information about ghosts. How about that?" I heard a squeal and then rapid talking. Ted listened with a grin split all over his face, twirling his finger at the phone to indicate how excited his wife was. "Yes, honey, I'll ask her. Yes, dear. Okay, honey. I said okay." The waitress stopped at our table and Ted said hastily, "Honey, hey, I gotta go, okay? I'll call you later. Love you." He set his phone down and folded his arms over his chest in a self-satisfied manner. "She's going to be all over me tonight when I call her for she's going to want to know every detail of our conversation." He then waved a hand toward the waiting waitress. "I already have my drink so go ahead and give her your order."

"I'll just have unsweetened iced tea, thank you."

The waitress smiled in acknowledgment of my order and handed me a menu. "I'll be right back with your drink and take your dinner orders."

Once she was out of hearing range, Ted leaned on the table with his folded arms. "Do you think the Tenney house is haunted? Is that why you really want to see it? Do you think Colonel Buck is haunting it?"

"I can't say one way or the other, Ted, as to the place being haunted for I haven't been there yet. I explained why I want to see it and I assure you, there is no other hidden agenda. I truly believe I might be able to pick up on some of Colonel Buck's energy because he actually walked on the floors and put his imprint in the woodwork."

Interested though skeptical, Ted's gaze did not waver from mine. I think he was looking for any telltale signs that I was pulling one over on him. "How do you leave an imprint?"

"We are all beings of energy. In fact, all things exist as an energy form. When energy meets energy, a transference of some sort takes place. It is either conducted, repelled or absorbed. Wood absorbs. So if Colonel Buck was in that house, as I'm sure he was, some of his energy was absorbed into the wood. I'm hoping to tap into that and get some impressions from it."

The waitress returned right at that point and I stopped for a moment to concentrate on the task of ordering dinner. Clam chowder was the soup of the day and both Ted and I ordered it. I then selected broiled scallops for the main course and Ted ordered fried clams. Once our selections were given, the waitress collected our menus, told us it wouldn't take too long and hurried off to the kitchen to place our order.

Ted didn't waste any time getting back into the conversation. "So you tap into the energy left in the house and that's how you do your psychic thing?"

"Well in the sense that you probably mean, I am not a psychic. I don't make predictions or foretell the future in any way. I can't read minds or see ailments or anything like that. I just pick up on the energy people leave behind to try and connect with them." I gave a small shrug because I just wasn't sure how I was to explain this. "Physicists believe the past, present, and future all exist at once." When Ted nodded to indicate that he had heard that, I went on with my explanation. "Well if that's the case, then Colonel Buck could be in that building the same time as we are. I'm hoping to pick up on that and maybe make contact." It was my theory and my hope anyway. Ted was clearly fascinated by the idea.

"So what do you plan to do? Are you going to ask him about the tombstone?"

"I'm not sure what will happen. I like to play it by ear."

"Can you summon anyone you want from the spirit world?"

My stomach muscles tightened slightly with apprehension. Here was the gist of my problem. When people learned I was a medium and believed it, they often wanted me to contact someone for them. A perfectly normal reaction to be sure, but here I had to tread carefully. I wanted Ted to let me into the Tenney house and if he wanted me to make contact for him and it didn't go the way he wanted it to go, would he then be less willing to help me out? I would not lie to him, not even for my own ends, and so I answered his question. "Usually."

Ted stared at his drink. It was a beer, a dark ale from the looks of it and nearly gone. "My wife thinks she can do that but I'm not sure I believe her." He let out a heavy sigh. "The fact is, she hasn't brought anyone through that anyone recognizes and most everyone thinks she's faking it. Finally she stopped talking about it but she's always watching shows on it and reading about it. I want to believe her when she says she's getting messages from beyond but..." He looked up at me and searched my face, his own expression carefully blank.

He was looking to see if I was going to confirm his wife was a phony. I was not going to do any such thing. "The thing about being a medium is fighting the doubt that what we are getting is coming from anywhere but our own imagination. Your wife might actually be getting better information but she's filtering it. It's normal to do that. To not trust what you hear and so you tailor it a bit thinking you are doing a favor when you aren't. The key to getting a good message is to not worry about being wrong. It was tough for me at first also. I thought my imagination was running wild. Either that or I was schizophrenic." I smiled then to show him that his wife's experiences were nothing to be ashamed about. "I'll be glad to talk to her sometime, Ted. But right now I want to focus on what I'm doing without any other distractions." Because he perked up at my offer, I went on with more confidence in having made it. "Ask her if she wants to talk with me about it and if she does, give me her number before you head out of town. Once I'm done here, I'll give her a ring and we'll figure it out. Okay?"

"That's awfully kind of you, Tess. Thank you."

Our meals arrived at that point and the rest of the dinner was filled with discussions about Maine, his job, the plans for the Tenney house (a hotel, what else?), my stay at Poke Harbor (with a brief sketch of the haunting I'd dealt with while staying there) and the weather.

The meal was delicious and after we waved off dessert and finished our coffee, we headed back to the B&B where we parted ways and went to our respective rooms. He was off to call his wife and I was off to bed. I'd stayed up late the night before because I wanted to spend as much time with Kade as we could fit in and that meant staying up to the wee hours of the morning. I was quite tired and I wanted to be all rested up and alert for tomorrow morning's tour through the Tenney house. Already I could feel some stirrings from the Tri-State. They were as excited about my tour as I was. The very fact of it made me quite hopeful. Tomorrow was going to be a great day full of surprises. I could feel it. And now to try getting some sleep with that on my mind.

Minutes later, I was out.

CHAPTER SIX

My dreams were a jumbled mess. Images of plants, fields of them, filtered through my mind like a film reel moving slowly, showing frame by frame one plant after another. I saw people, old and young, male and female, and their nationalities mixed. None of it was clear and none of it made sense. I woke up feeling tired and worn out. My mind's all-night activity, working on something I could not tap into consciously, made for a very restless night. The information would sort itself out eventually. It usually did.

Not in any hurry to rush out of bed, I lay still for a few minutes longer and thought about the dream's images, trying to lock on one or two and possibly identify them. It was a fruitless endeavor. Then I remembered that today I was to go into the Tenney house and came wide awake. A glance at the bedside clock told me I had just over a half hour to take a shower and prepare myself for the day.

As I went through my morning routine, I couldn't help but notice the chill in the air...and I'm not talking about the temperature. The cold went deep into my soul and I wondered if I was being warned to tread carefully? After my experience at Sea Willow Haven, I knew enough to take note of how I was feeling and pay heed to it. I needed to stay on heightened alert. So be it. I'd stay very conscious and aware of what was going on around me. In both the physical world and in the spiritual one.

I made it downstairs to the breakfast room at five minutes to eight. The tantalizing smell of bacon and fresh-baked muffins permeated the air. The breakfast room faced the back of the house with windows on two sides of the room allowing lots of warm sunlight to filter in. A large square table of shiny mahogany wood took up most of the room. Ted was already seated and halfway through a stack of pancakes. He had a crispy piece of bacon in his hand and was about to stuff it in his mouth when he saw me.

"Morning, Tess. Ready for your tour?"

"Yes, I am." I sank down in a chair opposite him and grabbed the coffee carafe. Barbara walked in with a plate of freshly made blueberry muffins. She set them on the table and smiled at me in greeting.

"Morning, dear, did you sleep well?"

"Yes. The bed is very comfortable, thank you." No sense in telling her that despite my physical comfort, my dreams plagued me most of the night and robbed me of a restful sleep.

"So what will you have this morning?" Barbara took the carafe as soon as I set it down and poured a cup of coffee. She sank into the chair next to me, cradled the warm cup in her hands and waited for me to decide.

Unable to resist the hot muffins, I grabbed one, pulled it apart and buttered it. "You know, I don't normally eat a big breakfast. If you could throw together a breakfast sandwich of egg and cheese and some of that crispy bacon I see Ted enjoying, then that would do me just fine."

Barbara stood up and headed for the kitchen. "Be back in a jiff."

I sank my teeth into the fluffy muffin and closed my eyes in pure enjoyment of the succulent taste. "Mmmm. I think I've put on a few pounds since coming to Maine. The resort I stayed at before coming here had the best food and I ate more in one day there than what I used to eat in a week."

Ted just forked a large pile of pancakes into his mouth so he had to chew for a minute before he could answer. His eyes looked me over in a purely impersonal but critical assessment as he munched. "You must have been a skeleton before then, Tess, because you still look pretty skinny to me."

Feeling a little embarrassed, for I wasn't fishing for any reassurances on my weight and now it felt like I was, I simply smiled my thanks and finished off the muffin. "So, is this Tenney house far from here?" Best to get the conversation onto a less personal topic.

Ted shook his head. "Nope. About two minutes' walk." He picked up a wad of keys that were sitting next to his plate. "Got the keys right here. I figure once we've eaten breakfast we could head right on over. There are a couple things I need to check out that the boss asked me to look at. You can wander around all you want. I'll probably be there awhile so you don't need to stick with me if you don't want to."

Barbara came back in the room with my breakfast sandwich and an omelet for herself. "Here you go, my dear." She handed me a small plate with my sandwich on it then resettled in the chair next to me. "So, are you two planning your trip to the Tenney house?"

Ted finished off his coffee and poured another cup. "Soon as Tess finishes breakfast." He indicated his empty plate. "I'm going to miss your breakfasts when I leave, Barbara. I'll have to bring the wife here for a vacation sometime." He glanced at me and I knew before he asked that he was going to mention Sea Willow Resort. I'd be willing to bet he'd checked into a few things last night on the internet. "What do you think, Tess? Should we book a vacation at Sea Willow Haven as well? I hear the place is overrun with ghosts. Might be a good place to take my wife."

Barbara turned in her seat to look at me and it was quite obvious that she was just as interested in my answer as Ted. "Is that true about the place being full of ghosts?"

I had to tread carefully here. I didn't want to give away any more than the newspapers did. Nancy and Jack had enough to deal with and I didn't want to add to the rumors. They were such a nice couple and I wished them nothing but success with their beautiful resort. "Well, I'm not so sure there are any ghosts there now. But it did have a few at one time. You might have better luck, Ted, bringing your wife here and letting her go roam around that fort across the river than to expect any encounters at Sea Willow Haven. But, if you are looking for a great place to stay while visiting Maine, then I would highly recommend the resort. It's beautiful there."

"So, did you get rid of the ghosts for them?" Barbara was not going to let the topic drop. I wondered about that considering she and Nancy were friends. Had Nancy confided in her at all?

"I hope that I was beneficial regarding the haunting problem." I made quick work of finishing off my breakfast sandwich and chugging down my coffee. "Are you about ready then, Ted?"

Ted pushed away from the table. "Sure am. I just realized I forgot the camera, let me go fetch it from my room and I'll

69

meet you in the entranceway." He rushed off and left Barbara and I alone.

"Nancy was so vague about what happened there that I thought it might be because it embarrassed her. But, the truth is, you all would rather let the subject drop wouldn't you?" Barbara looked a little disappointed not to be filled in on any juicy details but there was understanding and acceptance in her gaze.

"The less we talk about the past, the less influence it has over our lives. Don't you agree, Barbara?"

She nodded her head and heaved a sigh. "Yes, I do. But, I hope you keep me in the loop on your investigation here. I promise nothing will make it into the papers. Just as Nancy and Jack did for you at Sea Willow Haven."

I had to smile because Barbara was letting me know that she knew I had more to do with what took place at the resort than what was mentioned in the papers. She was also offering her silence and I thought it fair. "Okay, agreed."

As we stood up and headed for the entryway, Barbara asked me with some trepidation, "You haven't detected any ghosts here have you?"

Max joined us in that moment and I bent down to pat his head. He'd been waiting patiently in the sitting room for us to come out of the breakfast room. He was not allowed in there when people were eating and I thought it pretty obedient of him to honor the rule. "What a good dog you are, Max." I ruffled my fingers around his ears and Max shifted his head this way and that to get scratches in wherever he could. After a moment I straightened up and looked at Barbara. She was still waiting for my answer. "Not really."

"Not really? What does that mean?"

"The spirit world knows what my intentions are with this visit. Those involved are in a bit of a tizzy over it. Not sure if they are happy or apprehensive. I think both reactions are involved depending on the spirit. I think one of them followed me to my room last night but I told them to hold off until today. If I'm to confront any spirits, I'll do it at the Tenney house."

"Will they follow you back here?" Barbara suddenly looked very doubtful about the whole business.

"I will do my best to ensure that they don't. If they do, however, it is me that attracts them. They won't hang around your house bothering anyone else. So please don't worry."

Ted joined us at that moment. He looked from me to Barbara and back to me. "What's up? What is Barbara worried about?"

"I just want any spirits Tess makes contact with to stay right where they are and leave my house out of it." Barbara smiled then to show she meant no ill will and headed for the sitting room. "Let me know how it all goes down."

Laughing at Barbara's phrasing, I waved for Ted to proceed out the door. "Lead the way."

When Ted said it was a two-minute walk, he wasn't kidding. It might have been less than that. The Tenney house was located on Bucksport's main street and right in the middle of its epicenter. Built on a rising hill above the street, it loomed majestically over the town. Three stories high and of a simple Colonial architectural style, it looked both dignified and appealing. The front and left side of the house was outfitted with a wrap-around porch in need of repair. Wide steps leading up to it were located in the front facing the street and stretching to meet the paved sidewalk. The house had side and back entrances as well. Ted headed for the one in the back.

"We'll just enter through the kitchen. What I need to check into is there. You can go on through the house and explore all you want. The electricity isn't on, however." When we stepped into the darkened interior, Ted grabbed a couple flashlights off the counter and handed one to me. "Hope you aren't afraid of the dark?"

Smiling, I took the flashlight and made my way across the massive kitchen toward a set of double doors "Nope. Not usually anyway." As soon as I stepped into the hallway outside the kitchen, I was immediately enshrouded in darkness. No windows here. I stood for a moment and said my prayers then imagined a protective light glowing around me. This was how I protected myself and it seemed to work just fine. There was no reason to doubt it and so I didn't. I made my intentions clear to the Tri-State that I was looking for anyone involved in the Jonathan Buck curse and almost immediately I detected another presence hovering a short distance away. It loomed in the shadows drawing near, making me shiver as it did so.

Some people believed that spirits drew energy to themselves to manifest into our physical world. An easy form of energy to draw from was heat. Light was another. I was beginning to wonder, though, if their energy, which moved at a much higher rate of vibration than anything on the physical plane (our level of existence), was actually drawing our energy to them inadvertently. After all, did they really need to use our slower form of energy to manifest in our world? It was a theory I'd have to consider later. Right now I would concentrate on the fact that the hallway was getting quite cold. More than one spirit was with me. There were several in fact and I wondered what I was supposed to do with them all?

Not wanting to stay in such a dark spot, I moved cautiously down the hall toward an area where I could see lots of light. It turned out to be the front entrance area facing the street. There were several windows here and the sunny morning spilled in. Chilled to the bone, I walked into a spot of sunlight and switched off my flashlight. I set it down on a windowsill and rubbed my cold hands together to warm them up. A large oak counter elaborately carved in fancy designs took up most of the area. The few pieces of furniture scattered about the lobby were covered in dust blankets. I walked over to the long, narrow counter and put my hands on the smooth wood. Echoes of times past whispered through my mind. It was like tuning into a bunch of radio stations at once and having none of them clear. I closed my eyes to focus better and tried to put a lock on the jumbled noises. I heard laughter and loud boasting and soft whispers and anger. Taking my hand off the counter, I gave a long sigh. So many people had passed through these doors and all of them had left their imprint.

There was a set of carpeted stairs on both sides of the front reception area. A peek up them showed darkness. I grabbed the flashlight and went up the set of stairs on the left. It led to two long hallways. One went straight toward the back of the house, and the other went to my right, turning at the end to also go toward the back. I went straight. Another set of carpeted stairs was located at the end of the hallway. They went up three steps and turned right going out of view up to the third floor. Letting my hand run along the papered wall and over the various doors I passed, I walked the hallway and waited for a sign...some sort of signal from the Tri-State. I let thoughts of Jonathan Buck fill my mind. I had no idea what he looked like and wished that was not the case for it would be nice to have an image to concentrate on. Spirits followed behind. I didn't pay them much attention because it seemed they were more curious than anything. A medium was in their midst, that always got them excited.

I was almost to the stairs when the hairs on my arms went on alert. I instantly went still and waited, listening intently for any sort of sound be it physical or spiritual. Nothing. I took another step forward and as I did so, I heard the unmistakable sound of someone descending the stairs ahead of me, the tread heavy and slow. So distinct was the sound that for a moment I wondered if someone else might be in the building with us. I continued forward, but the footsteps ended when they reached the landing facing me and I too came to a stop. Whoever it was, he did not come down the last three steps. I could feel his energy easily enough. He stood on the landing, some sort of imposing force field, and waited. I had a very strong feeling that a challenge was being issued. Would I approach him? I flashed my flashlight beam toward the stairs. Of course I saw nothing. Heart pounding, I took a couple steps forward. Though I wasn't afraid, I was a little apprehensive. The spirit before me felt large, his spirit very strong. He obviously wanted me to know he was here and he clearly wanted my attention.

When I was within a couple feet from the stairs, I imagined the white light around me getting stronger. Just in case, it didn't hurt to protect myself. I wasn't sure if the entity was friendly or not and I knew he couldn't penetrate my light. Imagined or not, it existed because I made it so and the spirit would honor it. Still I saw nothing. No stirring in the shadows, no dark shape. Although I wasn't afraid, I decided that I was not going to get any closer to the stairs. So here we stood. I held out my hand and felt cold air move around it. The hotel wasn't warm but the cold that swirled around my hand didn't seem natural. Now the skin on my back began to prickle. I drew my hand back and clenched it against my chest. Heart pounding, I wondered what to do. "Who are you?"

The wooden landing creaked. My heart jumped. The spirit, for whatever reason, was enjoying my discomfort. Eyes narrowing, I dropped my hands to my side and relaxed. "Tell me."

Impressions filled my mind. I saw a big man, very tanned...no that wasn't right either. He was a different color but it wasn't brown. He appeared unnatural to me. The image was somewhat frightening because I wasn't sure what I was encountering. Why the strange color? I tried to focus more. He was bare-chested but his legs were encased in a soft dark material. He had a large chest and big arms. He was not happy to be dealing with me but felt he had no choice but to do so. Wondering what that meant, I lifted my hands, palms out, in appeal. "I mean no harm. I just want to talk."

As soon as I got the words out, there was a loud cracking noise, like he just stomped down hard on the stairs. The noise was loud in my ears, sounding similar to a lightning strike, and reverberated in my head even louder. I took a step back. Another booming sound and now I did think it sounded like thunder. I began to retreat, moving slowly backwards, my eyes fixed on the stairwell that was obviously filled with a very large, angry male. What was he doing? Why force my retreat? I felt quite strongly that he wanted to communicate with me but he didn't trust me. So how to get through?

"Tess? What in the heck was that noise?" Ted's voice nearly made me and my skin part company for I came darned close to jumping out of it! I swung around and motioned for him to stay right where he was and to be quiet.

When I turned back toward the stairs, the huge angry spirit was gone. But I didn't think he had gone far. Heaving a sigh at the disappointing first encounter, I turned to Ted. "Sorry, but I was trying to communicate with a spirit."

"By banging the floor so hard it cracked the old plaster below?" Ted shook his head. "I think part of the ceiling came down." He frowned at that and I knew he was wondering at the supposed instability. It surely wasn't a good sign for someone interested in buying the place.

"That wasn't me, Ted."

The poor guy's face went white. "It wasn't?"

"No. It was the spirit. A big guy. Weird color." Frowning, I wondered about that. What other color could he be if not black or white?

Ted took a step back. "Maybe we should go?" Another step back, one foot dropping to the last step of the stairwell behind him.

"Not yet." I turned and headed toward him, determined to check down the other hallway. I had to stop at the juncture though for Ted stood in my way. I pointed at the other corridor. "What's down there?"

"All these rooms up here are bedrooms except the corner room at the end of the hall facing the street. I think it was a study or something."

I nodded with intent and brushed past Ted. That was the room, I felt sure, where I needed to go. Ted heaved a resigned sigh and followed close behind. No doubt he was quite ready to vacate the premises.

I glanced back at him and smiled with reassurance. "He's gone, Ted, and I can assure you that he's not following us at the moment." We stopped at the closed door at the end of the hallway and as I made to turn the knob, Ted touched my hand and jiggled the keys he was holding.

"Locked. Let me." He rifled through his huge assortment of keys and finally selected one which he slid into the lock. A blast of cold air rushed out at us as soon as I opened the door. Ted gasped and took a step back. I stood still and made haste to envision Ted and I encased in light. "Don't be afraid, Ted, but there is someone in here. He means us no harm." It wasn't the big strange-colored guy I encountered on the stairs though. This entity seemed older, almost austere. His spirit felt agitated and disturbed. I had a pretty strong impression that he stood near the window facing the street. The sheer white curtains hanging there suddenly began to sway back and forth and Ted made a choked sound behind me. I lifted a hand to quiet him. "Please, Ted. There's nothing to be afraid of."

"But the curtains…"

"Won't attack you. Please, Ted, just trust me. Okay?" I took a step toward the window. If I kept my gaze slightly off to the side of it, I could just make out a shadow. It was hard to keep myself from looking head on but I knew it wouldn't do any good. For some reason, our peripheral vision was better at picking up spiritual entities. Though this wasn't always the case. Something else I'd discovered recently. The room was very spacious and empty of furniture. Two windows faced the street and another faced the right side of the building. The room had plenty of light and it was buzzing with spirit activity. I wondered why? What was the historical significance of this room? The man near the window seemed to detect my presence and it puzzled him greatly. I had a pretty strong suspicion that I wasn't going to be able to communicate with him. His aura was weak and I had the distinct impression he was nearing the end of his physical life. Since he was already quite dead, I wondered why he would come across that way. Surely there was no illness in the spirit world? Was I picking up on his energy as it was when he was alive? Maybe I was just detecting the man's ghost and not his spirit. Then again, he did seem to be aware of me which was something ghosts couldn't do. They were too caught up in their own drama to notice anyone or anything not directly involved in it. The other spirits whispering in the room made it seem like I'd stumbled upon some sort of secret meeting and the thought made my heart pound with excitement.

"They used to plot things in this room."

Ted didn't budge from the doorway. He kept his back against the doorjamb so he could keep an eye on both the hallways and the bedroom. "Wouldn't be surprised. It's a large room and used to be the one reserved for important guests."

A fireplace made of granite bricks was located on the wall to the left of the doorway. I walked over to it and put my hand on the mantel. Immediately I was thrown into a vision. Men surrounded me. They were agitated and arguing. I couldn't bring them into focus enough to understand their words but the tone was clear enough. Someone was gripping the mantel with me and he was in deep turmoil. For a moment I connected with him and could feel his anguish. Before I could try and make the connection more clear, I felt as if someone a little more threatening was suddenly standing next to me. I turned my head and gasped in shock. A face completely covered in blood stared at me, the whites of his eyes in stark contrast to the deep red of the blood. It was a fierce and terrifying face and I let go of the mantel and fell back. Immediately the vision went away. With my heart knocking painfully against my chest, I turned and fled for the door. It seemed my protective light had somehow weakened. Although I knew no harm would come to me, I still felt violated. The bloody faced man had come too close. Without pause, I rushed past Ted and headed back to the stairs wanting to get down to the lobby and into the bright sunlight. The dark pushed behind me, following my path. So much negativity, what did it all mean?

Ted followed close behind. "What's going on? Did you see something? Did you hear anything? Should I be scared? Tess! For God's sake will you say something?"

I couldn't catch my breath. It felt as if I'd just run a marathon. Gasping for air, I leaned down, resting my hands on my knees. What was going on here? Frightened a little more than I was comfortable with, I closed my eyes and asked Sheila to come and help calm me. Just her presence alone would help ease the fear and eliminate the panic. I felt the brush of cobwebs across my face and almost cried out loud in relief. Thank God. For a moment I focused on her loving energy and let it calm me from within. Once I felt in control and safe, I straightened and looked at Ted who was standing next to me with a terrified look on his face.

"I'm sorry, Ted. It's okay. There's nothing to fear. It just got too close. It startled me but I'm okay." I wouldn't tell him the face I saw was covered in blood. Ted wouldn't handle that well. Of that, I had no doubt. Even I was freaked. It was something I have never encountered before. I had a sinking feeling in the pit of my stomach that the entity was the same one I encountered on the stairs. He was big and different and now I knew why. What did the bloody face mean? Was it just symbolic that his face was covered in red? Colors had esoteric meaning and I was trying to remember what the meanings were for red. Passion for one, but that wasn't it. Anger? Perhaps, but that didn't feel right either. I made a mental note to check it out when I got back to my room and pushed it away for the moment. Right now I had to calm Ted and see if I could make sense of what was going on here.

"Why did you run?" Ted wasn't convinced by my assurances and honestly, I didn't blame him. He glanced nervously around him. "When a medium goes running, I'm thinking it can't be good."

"One of the spirits got a little close and it startled me. But there was never any danger." Because he looked skeptical, I gave a sheepish shrug. "Okay, I admit it, even I get a little spooked." I glanced around the room and held up my hands. "All clear for the moment."

Ted's gaze wandered up toward the ceiling. "You think the room up there is haunted?"

"Not sure. I think I was picking up on some energy imprinted there because of the high emotions involved. Some serious plotting and discussion took place in that room."

Ted visibly relaxed. "Was it the same spirit that was on the stairs?"

"Yes. At least...I think so." My curiosity was definitely roused. Who was he and what did he want? The really puzzling question is what was he?

"So what else do you want to do here?" Ted glanced meaningfully at the door. He was ready to leave. I wasn't.

"Is there a dining room here?"

Ted waved a hand toward the room to the lobby's right. "Through there. Why?"

"Well, Colonel Buck was probably in that room as well...I'd like to check it out, see if I get anything." Ted gave a reluctant nod, agreeing with my logic but not liking it. As I headed off toward the place he indicated, Ted stuck close to my side. I didn't much blame him. More than likely he didn't want to be alone and he probably felt responsible for me. I couldn't help but wish that Kade was here with me.

We walked through the empty room to the right of the lobby reception desk and went through a set of double doors to a large spacious room filled with tables and chairs covered in dust cloths. I walked slowly, my mind open and alert as we moved deeper into the room. I could almost hear the echoes of patrons past and the clink of utensils on plates. The atmosphere was generally pleasant. I turned back and headed at a brisk, determined walk for the front lobby. Ted rushed after me.

"Where are you going?"

Determined not to falter, I marched steadily up the stairs and headed straight for the large room at the end of the hall. That was where I needed to be. Something was there. I just knew it!

Ted grabbed my arm before I could cross over the threshold. "What, are you crazy? You aren't seriously going in there again?"

"Ted, all the psychic energy worth exploring is in there. A lot took place here. Whatever happened to cause the strange markings on Buck's monument is somehow attached to that room. I need to figure out what. Especially as I only have today to do it." I gently removed his hand from my arm. "Seriously, it's fine. I know what to expect now so I won't be startled. You have nothing to fear, Ted. If something menacing was about, it would have chased us down the hallway." Truly, I didn't believe menacing spirits would chase us but Ted did so I thought I'd just go with it. Once again Ted took a position near the doorjamb. He waved a hand for me to go ahead in though his expression was still registering wariness. "Be my guest then."

I smiled at him to ease his fears and show him how calm I was then stepped into the room. Butterflies fluttered with nervous anticipation in my stomach. I stood still and once again envisioned a strong white light around me. I said a quick prayer, asked Sheila to stay with me and walked again to the fireplace. This time, however, I did not touch the mantel. Instinctively I turned toward the spot where the red-faced man had stood (it felt better to say "red" rather than use the word "blood"). An air of anticipation crowded the space around me making it difficult to breath. My heart sped up and my pulse jumped wildly in my veins. Calm, Tess, you must stay calm. Fear invited all sorts of problems. It lowered my protective strength and left me more vulnerable to the darker forces lurking in the spiritual realm. For some reason the Psalm 23:4 came to mind and I was glad that it did for it calmed me instantly. "Yea, though I walk through the valley of the shadow of death, I shall fear no evil". God's powerful might would protect me. I truly believed that and relaxed even more. "Bring it on, red man." I whispered the words under my breath, but Ted heard some of it.

"What's that? Bring what on? Don't go inviting anything, Tess!" Ted's voice nearly ended in a squeak.

I gave a silent sigh and wished I could be in here alone. This was why I didn't like to have people with me when I was trying to communicate with the other side. At least, people who weren't of like mind. I turned to Ted and lifted a quieting finger to my lips. "Shh, Ted, please. I need to concentrate."

Ted nodded, his face going a little pink. "Sorry."

I returned my attention to the fireplace. It had been here since the building's inception. Somehow I just knew that. It was made of granite and rock. The mantel was wood; it was very old, smooth and worn around the edges. Wood was a great absorber of energy. If trees could talk... I often thought that as I walked through the woods. Those tall silent sentinels had witnessed much. But, it wasn't the mantel I was interested in. My attention was now drawn down toward the grate. One of the oldest organizations in the world was the Freemasons. A collection of educated men, it stood to reason that a Freemason helped to construct this fireplace. Why this popped into my head, I don't know, but it felt a worthy clue. My eyes moved slowly about its construction. The outer hearth particularly. I looked down where I was standing. Bricks of the same width and length made up the hearth. Dropping to my hands and knees, I looked closely at the bricks where the red man had been standing. One of the bricks was slightly off from the others. It wasn't anything you would notice unless you were looking for it. My heart thumped loudly in my ears as I pushed on the brick. There was just the slightest give.

Ted forgot his apprehension and came to join me, crouching down to better see what I was doing. "What are you looking at?"

Just at the corner of the brick was an etched symbol of some sort. It looked like an arrow. Excited beyond measure because I knew I was about to discover something spectacular, I followed the direction of the arrow to the inner hearth where the ash pit was located. The fireplace hadn't been used in years from the looks of it. I turned to Ted. "Is this fireplace still up to code for functioning?"

Ted shook his head. "No. It's more for looks than anything. Because the house is on the registry for historic buildings, there's not much we can do with it in respect to closing it up or removing it."

I crawled into the inner hearth and looked in the ash pit. The side that opened to the door for ash removal looked off. I felt around it until my fingers encountered a small catch of some sort. I gave it a gentle push and the side of the ash pit fell open. Oh my! Heart pounding furiously, I reached in the opening and pulled out a blackened metal box.

Ted gave an exclamation of disbelief. "What the ...? How did you know that was there?"

I sat back on my haunches and examined the box. The metal hummed with energy, its vibration making my fingers tingle. "I don't know how I find things sometimes, Ted. I just go with my gut feeling and here we are!" I crawled backwards from the fireplace and into a spot of sunlight coming through the windows. The lid would not come open and looking at the front of it, I saw a keyhole was present. "It's locked."

"Let's smash it open."

I looked at Ted and tried hard to keep my exasperation from showing. "What if we damage what's inside?"

"But don't you want to know what's in it? How heavy is it? Shake it."

I gave the box a gentle shake and what sounded like a bunch of small objects rattled in muted sound. I handed the box to Ted. "Hold this, I have an idea."

I crawled back to the stone with the arrow etched on it and gave it another push. It definitely had just a slight give. "This stone is different from the rest and it has a slight give. Do you have anything we might use to pry it up?"

Ted crawled next to me and pulled a small Swiss Army knife from his pocket. "Try this."

I opened the switch blade and gently moved it around the crevices of the brick, carefully removing fine dust and dirt. After clearing enough out of the way to wiggle the blade down a ways, I began the tedious task of working it free. It took time and patience but finally I managed to pull the brick up from its position. Beneath it, laying in a slight indentation in the mason work beneath the brick was a small skeletal key. For a moment I just stared at it in disbelief. Although it shouldn't surprise me anymore, I still found myself astounded by the things spirit helped me do.

Ted gave a small whoop. "Holy sh... crap, Tess! I can't believe this." He motioned for me to pick up the key. "You found it, you do the honors."

I lifted the key out of its hiding spot and wondered how long it had been there. Let's see....Jonathan Buck died in 1795 and why I felt this was connected with him I wasn't sure but since my current quest was to discover the mystery of his cursed monument, it felt right that this all fit somehow. I would just have to trust in spirit to help me figure it all out. So back to my calculations. If the key has been in its hiding spot since the time of Colonel Buck then it had to be well over 200 years old. It certainly felt old. I took the box from Ted's hand and compared the two items. "What kind of metal would you say this is, Ted?"

"Copper." Ted motioned again for me to open the box and I gave a small laugh at his boyish eagerness.

"I don't know why I feel so nervous." My hands were actually shaking but I think it was more from pent up excitement than anything. Although it couldn't really compare, I thought that this must be how it feels to be an explorer making new discoveries. Drawing in a calming breath, I rested the box on my knee and fit the key into the hole. Despite its age, the key turned easily and the lid popped free. I glanced at Ted, noting the shine of excitement in his eyes and knew my own reflected the same. Giving an impatient nod, Ted prompted me to open it already. I lifted the lid.

It was nearly full of beads of some sort. They were mostly red in color although some of them were darker with shades of brown. Most of them were multifaceted although others were perfectly round. They were no bigger than a pea. I put my fingers in the beads and felt a zing of energy charge through me. The hairs on my arm actually stood on end. Startled, I gave a small gasp and scooped some of the beads into my palm for a closer look. Ted leaned in as well. Although most of them were red to reddish brown, some of them were black and smooth, reflecting almost like silver.

"Hematite." Ted said, nodding with sudden understanding. "Indian beads. Have to be."

"Hematite." I was vaguely familiar with the name for I'd studied the mystical properties of stones and gems at one time. I'd let it all go when I married Mike because my life was just too busy to do more than I already was doing. Besides, although Mike was somewhat tolerant of my communications with dead people, he did not like me getting into anything more.

Ted seemed quite sure they were Indian beads and although I have never seen an Indian bead before, it made sense considering how old they were. "They are in perfect condition." Ted reached in and scooped up a handful and when he did, a large flat stone about the size of my palm was revealed.

I immediately reached for the stone and as I picked it up, the hairs on my arm, still standing mind you from the earlier reaction to the beads, now tingled. The feeling of cobwebs brushed across my face and my heart began to pound in earnest. If Sheila was here, then something really important was going on. But how in the world did a box of beads and a smooth flat stone have any significance to the Buck curse? I returned the beads to the box and examined the smooth stone in my hand. It was oblong and of perfect spherical dimension. It was only about a quarter inch thick and it was smooth as glass. As my thumb rubbed over its surface, it actually began to shine up more. I continued to rub the stone, noting how fast it warmed in response. The smooth surface became almost reflective. Mesmerized, I could no more pull my gaze from that stone than I could make my heart slow its pounding. I heard Ted say something but it sounded far off and then suddenly I wasn't in the room with him anymore.

My consciousness became merged with that of a young girl and I found myself crouching low in a thicket of brush. Her heart pounded loud in my ears as we peered through the branches at the scene before us. An expanse of grass led to the edges of a rocky coastline. Beyond that was a stretch of mudflats and then the ocean itself, stretching on into forever, it's gently rolling surface reflecting the bright sunlight as if a million diamonds floated upon it.

Small row boats dotted the rocky shore wherever it was possible to land one. Men dressed in heavy dark clothing that was not typical of today's fashions were scattered everywhere. Whoever I was sharing this vision with, she was not happy with what she was seeing. Trepidation ran rampant and it was all she could do not to turn and run. The stone in my hand was nearly too hot to handle and I looked down at it curiously. The hand holding it was of a dark complexion and very slender. The rock suddenly heated to such a degree it made me gasp and I pulled from the vision.

"Tess? Are you okay?"

Ted's worried voice penetrated the fog cluttering my thoughts and I blinked several times to ground myself back to the present. "It's okay, Ted. I think I was connected with whoever owned this stone."

Ted looked nervously around him. "Are we surrounded with ghosts?" His voice cracked and he visibly tried to man up. "If so, they are friendly I'm hoping?"

It was hard not to laugh because he really looked a contradiction of emotions. He eyes looked terrified but he was trying to hold himself as if he weren't afraid of a damned thing. "No ghosts, Ted. Relax."

Ted stood up and I did the same. He nodded toward the box. "Keep it. Indian beads aren't going to bring in much money. There's a gazillion of them around." He indicated the flat stone in my hand. "Although that's interesting, I can't imagine it being worth anything either. Hematite is common enough."

I wanted to hug him, I was so excited he was going to let me keep what we'd found but I refrained from doing so and instead gave him a beaming smile. "Thank you, Ted. I promise if they do turn out to be valuable, I'll let you know and return them." Then I remembered that they hadn't even bought the property yet and he really had no say in the matter. "Who owns the building now?"

"Mr. Owens owns the building, but we'll be taking it off his hands very shortly."

"Mr. Owens? And where can I find him?"

"He lives out of state...Florida. It's his uncle who is overseeing the sale of the property. Why?"

"Well, I probably should let him know what we found. It's only right."

Ted gave an unconcerned shrug. "I don't really think they'll care." He reached in his jacket pocket and pulled out a business card. "Here's the numbers. The uncle's name is Ridley Truman. The other name is the nephew but Rid is the one you need to call."

I tucked the card in the back pocket of my jeans and motioned toward the door. "I think I'm done here."

Looking much relieved, Ted waved a hand for me to precede him from the room. I thought it very gallant because he looked like he wanted to make a run for it. Despite his enthusiasm to quit the premises, Ted forced himself to walk sedately beside me as we made our way down to the front door. Once we were out on the porch, I could easily see Ted's overwhelming relief. He looked very much like he was surprised and happy to have made it out alive. He caught my eye and grinned sheepishly, knowing I wasn't fooled one bit.

"Well, that was interesting. I'm heading off to meet with Rid now. I'll let him know what we found but I'd appreciate you waiting to contact him either later today or maybe even tomorrow. I'd like to clear up our business before you go distracting him with beads."

I was okay with that. It gave me more time to figure out the mystery surrounding their existence before Mr. Truman decided to take them from me. Despite what Ted said, I had a very strong feeling that Rid was not going to want to part with this little treasure, worthless or not.

CHAPTER SEVEN

Ted and I no sooner parted ways when I felt my cell phone vibrate. Knowing who it was before I even looked, I hastily pulled it out of my pocket, glanced at the caller ID to confirm my suspicion and began smiling with inner joy. It was going to be so good to hear his voice again. "Hi, Kade."

"I know I shouldn't call in case you are busy or in a trance, but I was feeling…I don't know how to describe it, but I felt I needed to call." His voice was low, deep and sexy and I had to stop walking to better enjoy it. Chills of pleasure raced from my ear down through my spine and out across my skin.

"That's fine, Kade. I was about to call you anyway. We just left the Tenney house."

"How did it go? Did you get to chat with the long dead Colonel Buck?"

Laughing because I knew he still thought it strange to be having conversations like this, I sank down on a short brick wall that shored up the front lawn of an old house now converted into business offices. "No, I didn't talk to him but I do think he was there."

"So? What happened? Are you going to make me ask for every detail?"

I could tell he was smiling and it made my grin widen to the point that I actually wondered if it looked unnatural. A discreet glance around didn't offer up anyone staring at me as if I had gone off the deep end but I toned down the smile and lowered my head in an attempt to blot out the world and enjoy our connection. "Well, I might if it means listening to you talk."

There was a silent pause then Kade's voice went gut-wrenching, toe-curling deep. "Tess Schafer, you are making this time apart very difficult. Especially when I hear that teasing tone. What makes it worse is that I can pretty much picture the look on your beautiful face right now and that alone drives me crazy. I miss you."

I couldn't breathe. I couldn't. Two years I went without hope of forging a loving relationship with a man ever again and now it seemed to be happening. I wanted to take the feelings and hold them tight. But, as always, the bone-chilling fear that soon followed those thoughts took over. What if I lost him in a freak accident? My body stiffened in reaction to the question and I knew I was going to jeopardize this relationship if I allowed those sorts of thoughts to manipulate my life. "Why don't we discuss the Tenney house and talk about…other things when you get here tomorrow?"

"Of course. No problem. But the fact is, I've been asking you for details and you've yet to tell me a thing." Kade's reply was quick, the low rumbling quality gone. He understood my fears and even had some of his own. The easy way he allowed us to be was one of the things that made him so endearing.

Clutching the phone and wishing it was him I was holding, I tried to focus on the topic I'd just insisted we restrict our discussion to. The vision of the bloody face came to mind and suddenly I had no problem getting back to the matter at hand. "I encountered a male spirit, a big guy, not very friendly but not threatening (blood wasn't threatening though it usually indicated something along those lines). He was covered in…red."

"Red?"

"Well, it looked like blood but I can't be sure."

"What?" His voice rose on mild alarm. "Well, I don't like the sound of that at all." He paused for only a second and then rushed on before I could reply. "Maybe I should come out there today."

"As much as I would like to see you, there's really no need to change your plans. Besides, I will feel guilty if you don't finish that painting. I told you he wasn't threatening. I think he was trying to show me something." Remembering the box now resting on my lap, I could barely contain my enthusiasm for its find. "You'll never believe what I found, Kade!" When I paused to see if he'd make a guess, he expelled an exasperated breath.

"Well? Are you going to hold me in suspense forever? I'm not getting any younger, Tess." He laughed.

I laughed with him and thought how good it felt to do so. I really believed, on that day when Mike and Tootsie died, that I would never laugh again and yet with Kade, it happened often.

"Indian beads. At least that's what Ted says they are, and a flat smooth stone that's very shiny. It makes my body tingle when I rub it, like an invisible electric current is stirred up or something. It's the strangest thing. It also sent me into a vision. I connected with a girl. I think she used to own the stone."

"Wow, Tess, that's really interesting. Where did you find them?"

"Hidden in a secret compartment in the fireplace."

"And how is it that you found it there? Let me guess...you used the same technique that helped you find the entry to the tunnel we nearly died in?"

Remember the incident to which he was referring, a shiver passed through me. I still felt bad about that. "Yes, and let's not talk about that, Kade. I don't like to think about it."

"Well, I mostly focus on how cozy it got in there anyway. The almost dying part is pretty much forgotten when my mind wanders down that avenue."

His voice had gone sexy again and my breath caught in my throat. For a moment I closed my eyes and tried to reign in my raging hormones. "Kade," It was supposed to be a warning to behave and stay on topic but it came out sounding breathless. My face turned red, I knew it because I could feel it. The last thing I wanted was for him to think I was sitting here getting all hot and bothered for him. The fact that I was in fact feeling that way made me a little uncomfortable. We weren't there yet in our relationship and I didn't want to encourage him to think that we were. I wasn't ready.

"Sorry. Please tell me more about your find and your vision." All impersonal and businesslike. Thank God.

"She was holding the stone in her hand." And a very young hand (early teens?) it had been, too. Was it the girl at the cemetery that I encountered the day before? "The stone got really hot which I found interesting. But anyway, she was hiding in the trees and watching a bunch of boats land on shore. There were a lot of men there, about thirty or so, I would think. She was not happy to see them. That's all I got."

"Were the men armed?"

"It wasn't a military raid, Kade." He being an ex-Marine, it figured he'd go there. "It wasn't like they were storming the beaches."

Kade laughed. "Okay, so what did they look like?"

"Not sure. I'm going to make a guess that it was during the first explorations of Bucksport. At least, I think we were in Bucksport." Frowning, I thought about the shoreline in my vision and then realized that I hadn't seen anything like that around here. Bucksport was located along the Penobscot River and although it emptied into the ocean eventually, I didn't think that occurred anywhere close by. My vision clearly showed a beach on the ocean. I think I saw islands in the distance but for the most part, it was a vast endless ocean that stretched in the background. I had focused so much on the men that I didn't think to pay much attention to the surrounding area. Darn it.

"So they were British?"

"Kade, really I'm pretty sure it was American colonists. Not the British." I had to laugh then because I could just see his face turning slightly red.

"Oh right. Well, colonists then. They must have had muskets on them, I'm sure they didn't leave home without them."

More laughter but now Kade joined in. "Maybe but I didn't really notice."

"So how does any of that tie in to Colonel Buck and his curse?"

Sighing, I shook my head. "I have no clue. But, the universe is helping me out. I'll figure it all out eventually."

"So you are sure you are okay until tomorrow? The bloody face guy won't haunt your dreams or show up in your bedroom?"

His concern was genuine and it touched me deeply. He was so understanding about me and my gift and how it affected me. Mike didn't like for me to talk about it. "I'm fine. As I said, I think he wanted me to find that box filled with beads."

"So that Ted fellow didn't take the box?"

"He told me to keep it but I think I should clear that with the actual owners of the building. I'm going to call him later this evening. Ted wanted me to wait because he was headed over there to discuss the sale and he didn't want there to be any distractions."

"Understandable. Okay, sounds like you have a plan. Maybe the guy can shed some light on the box and what the objects might mean."

"Maybe." We both went silent for a moment and then a crowd of teenagers started coming my way on the sidewalk. Probably headed to the ice cream parlor as it was actually getting quite warm. I stood up and finished the short walk to the B&B. "I'll call you later and let you know how it went with Mr. Truman."

"Okay, Tess. I'm nearly done with the painting, a few touches here and there. We'll discuss tomorrow later on tonight."

I didn't want to end the call but I was now entering the B&B and Barbara was waiting. "Until later then, Kade. Bye." I put my cell phone in my back pocket then looked at Barbara. "Got anything cold to drink?"

"Just made a fresh pitcher of iced tea, how does that sound?"

I pulled my sweater off and hung it on one of the hooks in the small entryway and headed for the sitting room. "Sounds perfect."

"Hang tight, I'll be right back." Barbara rushed off toward the kitchen and I sank into the rocking chair beside the one Barbara seemed to prefer. The sitting area was cozy, the wall space containing lots of shelves filled with knickknacks, animal figurines, angels and Victorian teacups. Pictures of people and beautiful scenery were hung in every available spot big enough to hold one. And books were everywhere. The bookcase on the wall next to Barbara's chair was crammed full with many more stacked on the floor. Small braided rugs were scattered here and there and a couple hassocks were available for weary feet. I slipped my shoes off and propped my feet up on one of them. Feeling relaxed and happy, I cradled the small copper box on my lap and waited for Barbara to rejoin me.

"Here you go, my dear." Barbara returned carrying a tray with two full glasses of iced tea and a plate of freshly made cookies. She set the tray down on the stand between us and handed me one of the glasses.

"Thank you, Barbara." I drank half of it down and then set the glass back on the tray so I could pick up a cookie. "These smell delicious."

"They are lemon cookies, an old family recipe." Barbara watched with satisfaction as I gave the cookie proper appreciation. "So how did it go at the Tenney house?"

I finished off the cookie and gave her a thumbs up. "If you share that recipe with me, I'll be forever grateful."

Barbara smiled. "Consider it done. I'll copy it down for you later today. Now spill."

I tapped the box on my lap and Barbara's gaze lowered to it. Her eyes widened with curiosity and flew back up to my face for an explanation. "We found a little treasure."

"No way!"

"Before I show this to you, let me tell you the story first."

Barbara leaned forward in her chair, her gaze fixed on me as if I was about to provide her with the secret to the universe. Although I was pretty excited with my find, I hoped Barbara wasn't disappointed when I told her that I didn't make much contact with spirits. Seeing one wasn't the same as having a bona fide interaction.

"The house has lots of memories embedded there...old energy. There might be ghosts hanging out but I didn't really feel like any of them were attached to the place, you know what I mean?" At Barbara's nod that she did in fact know even though I didn't really think she did, I went on with my story. "Well I encountered the spirit of a man on the stairs going up to the third floor. I don't think he's haunting the third floor, though, or any floor for that matter. I think he came because I was there. But anyway, he didn't much like me or maybe I should say that he doesn't trust me though he knows he has no choice but to deal with me if he wants my help." Though why he should have need of me, I hadn't a clue. Perhaps this box and its contents would eventually lead me to that discovery. The niggling feeling that he wanted something from me was too strong to ignore. I'd be seeing him again. Even though my insides tightened up with apprehension, I told myself to relax and let it be. A bloody face wasn't great to look at but viewing a little blood never hurt anyone. Surely I could deal with it? "We didn't communicate with each other. Ted showed up and he went away."

"Do you think it was Colonel Buck?"

"No. He was...different."

"Different? In what way?"

Now here I had to be careful because although Barbara was fascinated with the idea of ghosts, she was also afraid of them. "I'm not sure how to explain it. He didn't seem to be of a type I am familiar with. He had an air about him that was...different." I shrugged my shoulders because honestly, I didn't know how else to describe it. "Maybe I'll learn more as time goes on. But for now, we'll leave it at that. We then went into a room on the second floor that Ted said was used for dignitaries or VIPs. I knew as soon as I entered that a lot of plotting and important discussions took place there. This is where I felt Colonel Buck's energy though I wouldn't go so far as to say it was his ghost. But anyway, I went to the fireplace and suddenly the big strange man I encountered on the stairs is back. It startled me and so I have to admit here that I turned tail and ran."

Barbara sank back in her chair, her hand splayed across her chest and her expression one of horrified fascination. "Why? Did he threaten you?"

"No. I just wasn't expecting to see him suddenly standing so close. He was like, right next to me. Had he been alive, I would have felt his body heat."

"You saw him? Did Ted see him too?"

"I saw him very strongly in my mind's eye. The vision was so clear it blotted out what my physical eyes were seeing. I don't know how to explain it, I'm sorry. It's like my brain switches focus from my outer eyes to my inner eyes." It was hard to explain this process but I thought this a good explanation and Barbara seemed to understand it as well.

"So if he wasn't threatening you, why did you run? Why didn't you just step away so he wasn't so close?"

She was an astute woman, this Barbara was. "He ... he's a big man who was dressed strangely and looked strange, I just needed to get out of there to calm myself so I would be better prepared to confront him again."

"So you went back?"

"Yes. And he was gone. But I went back over to the fireplace and started studying the hearthstones where he'd been standing. One was a little different than the others and on closer examination I noticed it had an arrow etched into one of its corners. I followed the direction of the arrow and," I lifted the box like it was a trophy I'd just won. "Ta da! I found this."

"So what's in it?"

I opened the lid, removed the smooth stone and handed her the box. Barbara exclaimed over the beads and picked some of them up to better look at them. She examined them closely and oohed and aahed. "This is just so wonderful, Tess. Can you imagine how long they've been there?" She looked at the stone I held in my hand and nodded toward it. "What's that?"

I held my palm out so she could see the rock I held. "I'd let you hold this, Barbara, but it will absorb some of your energy and I want to try and see what I can pick up from its previous owner."

Barbara leaned close to get a better look. "It looks like its smooth as glass. What is it?"

"I don't know. Ted says its hematite and so are the beads."

"Oh yes, now that you mention it, I'd say he's right. My brother Leroy is a rock enthusiast. He travels all over the place to find them. He has a huge collection, travels to all the rock shows. He started collecting rocks when we were young and I got lectures about them whether I wanted to hear them or not. But I did find some of his rocks to be very pretty. He has quite an assortment of hematite and yes, that is what these are. I think." She laughed. "Too bad he's in Arizona right now, on a dig actually, or I'd ring him up and have him come take a look. He'd go ape over these beads."

"Although Ted told me to keep them, I thought I better clear that with the actual owners first. He told me to call a Ridley Truman and talk to him about it."

Barbara put the beads back in the box and handed it to me. "You'll enjoy talking to Rid. He used to be the librarian here in Bucksport but is retired now. He reads extensively and is especially interested in Maine history. You probably should talk to him anyway since you are so interested in the Jonathan Buck story."

"He was the librarian?" The man I met on the sidewalk in front of the cemetery had said he used to be the librarian. It had to be the same man. It was no coincidence that the first person I interact with after entering Bucksport would turn out to be an important contact! The universe was working its magic. "I think I met him then."

Barbara's eyes widened with a "tell me more" look and reached for her glass of iced tea. "Oh?"

"Just before checking in yesterday, I stopped to look at the Buck monument and he was walking by with his dog. He was the one who told me I should take a walk along the river."

"Rid walks that dog just about every day. His wife died two years ago. They were married for forty-six years. He's very lonely." Barbara shook her head in sad commiseration. "He comes in here every now and then to enjoy a cup of coffee with me or to see if I've made anything sweet. He has a sweet tooth and he loves my coffee." She leaned forward as if to impart a great secret. "I add a dash of salt to the coffee grounds. Makes a big difference."

"Really?" I reached for another cookie. "And what is your special ingredient in these?"

"Lemon curd but don't tell anyone."

I laughed because Barbara really was a treasure and I liked her a lot. She reminded me a little of my mother. "Does Rid live far from here?" I couldn't imagine that he did if he was walking around Bucksport every day with his dog.

"About five minutes by car. He lives near the churches up on the hill and has a beautiful home. His son and daughter-in-law live with him. They moved in shortly after his wife died.

His son Sidney was worried about him and rightly so. Sid is a lawyer and has an office here in town and in Bangor."

"Sid and Rid?"

Barbara laughed. "Cute isn't it? Rid's wife's name was Bridget but everyone called her Brid."

I joined in with Barbara's laughter. They sounded like a nice family. I looked forward to meeting Rid again and talking with him. Hopefully I could convince him to let me hold onto the box of beads and the stone for a couple more days. I didn't think it right to expect him to let me keep them. My iced tea finished and two cookies polished off, I figured it was time to head to my room, open my laptop and do some research. "I really need to go hop on the laptop for a while, Barbara. Thank you for the iced tea and cookies and great conversation."

Barbara stood and gathered our empty glasses onto the tray. "You run along, dear. Just come on down and give a yell if you need me for anything."

Though my intention was to head straight for my laptop as soon as I made it to my room, I didn't follow through with that plan. Instead, I went straight to the bed and sat down, the box in my hands holding too much of my attention to concentrate on anything else. I took the smooth rock out of the box and rubbed it between my fingers. It was cool to the touch but as I rubbed my thumb across it, the rock began to warm up. Not quite ready to be thrown into another trance, I set it down on the nightstand and put the box beside it. Research first and then I'd explore the interesting properties of the stone.

I no sooner opened my laptop and started it up when my cell phone began buzzing. I forgot that I had it on vibrate so it was a good thing I'd set it on the desk next to me or I wouldn't have heard it. The caller ID said Mary Rowan. "Hello."

"Hi, Tess Schafer?"

Mary's voice came across sounding uncertain, as if she wasn't sure she should even be calling and I wanted to put her at ease right away. "Yes, I'm Tess. This is Mary who I met at the Veterans Memorial, right?"

"Yes." Her tone relaxed and continued on a more sure footing. "Are you all settled at Barbara's place now?"

"Yes I am. Thank you for asking. How are you doing?"

"I'm doing okay, thanks. We, my mom and I, would love it if you could come to dinner tonight? I know it's short notice so if you've already made plans we can do it another night."

"Oh, Mary, I would love to come to dinner. Thank you for asking." I could feel Mary's trepidation through the airwaves. She wasn't sure about me coming and yet she'd made the invitation and was keeping to it. I felt an overwhelming sense of compassion for her and her family's situation and very much wanted to lend them my support. She gave me directions that seemed quite simple even for me. I liked a town with a simple layout. Getting lost was something I easily managed to do which made this whole trip to Maine quite a feat for me. It was the first time I'd ventured anywhere on my own. After exchanging a few more pleasantries that helped to ease Mary's reserve (something told me she was typically quite talkative when not hung up on worries), we said our goodbyes.

I set my cell phone down on the desk and rubbed my hands together in anticipation. Things were moving right along. The universe at work. And it was just the beginning. I had a strong suspicion the hours ahead were going to uncover a few more exciting things. The box of beads being just the tip of the revelation iceberg.

CHAPTER EIGHT

Two hours of internet searches and my neck was stiff from leaning over my laptop. Beside me I had a bunch of notes scribbled. Bucksport was rich in history for such a young town. Not so young if you included its history before colonial settlers landed on her shores. The place was teeming with native Indians when Jonathan Buck and his cohorts began to establish their townships. A sad part of our American history occurred in the years following our arrival on America's shores. The takeover of Indian territories did not go well. It hadn't been possible for everyone to live together in peaceful harmony. No, of course not. Instead, the Europeans, arriving in droves, took and took and eventually the Indians pushed back. Unfortunately for them, we had guns and they did not. At least not at first; it was survival of the fittest at its worst. Still for all that, it seemed that Buck had a pretty good reputation with the local Indians. He was quite respected among all his peers as well. Certainly he didn't seem like the sort of man to condemn a woman to death for witchcraft. In fact, his entire family sounded like a pretty decent lot with most of them quite devoted to their religious faith.

I closed my laptop and stretched up my arms in an attempt to relieve all the tight muscles in my shoulders. Because the beads I'd found were Indian beads, I was now very interested in local history concerning the natives. What really caught my attention during my internet search was the mention of the Red Paint Indians, an extinct tribe believed to be specifically prominent in this area. Very little was actually known about them because they died out several thousand years ago. In fact, the only reason we knew anything about them at all was because several of their burial sites had been found. Apparently this unknown tribal clan used to be heavily concentrated in Bucksport and the surrounding area. In fact, one burial ground was located where the huge paper mill now stands. The thing that particularly excited me about this tribe was the fact that they had a fascination with red ocher! Their dead were buried in the stuff. It was speculated by some historians that the Red Paint People were related in some way to the long extinct Beothuk of Newfoundland because the Beothuk also loved red ocher. In fact, they used to cover themselves in it. The man at the Tenney house was covered in red. Although I naturally thought it was blood, I now wondered if it was actually red ocher covering his face. And if he was, in fact, a Red Paint Indian, what did he have to do with Jonathan Buck's curse? Especially considering the fact that they were believed to have disappeared from existence several thousand years before Buck and his crowd ever landed in Bucksport!

I glanced at the rock lying on the nightstand and thought about the smooth tanned hand that had been holding it in my vision. Reason told me that if the red-faced guy was a member of the Red Paint Indian tribe then the stone and beads couldn't possibly have belonged to him. The girl holding the rock in my vision was probably an Indian but from which tribe? Was there a connection between her and the red-faced guy? It just didn't make sense. She had to have been from a more recent tribe, one still in existence today. Hopefully this little mystery would resolve itself as more information came to light.

To tell the truth, I found it all pretty fascinating and now that my interest was aroused, I wanted to learn more. Especially considering what I learned when I looked up red ocher. It was a byproduct of hematite, the very stone from which the beads were made. The hematite stone had history I found particularly fascinating. Egyptian pharaohs were buried wearing hematite amulets because it was supposed to protect their energy and guarantee survival into the afterlife. A stone right up my alley! Additionally, American natives believed the war paint made from the red ocher rendered them invincible in battle. As if those beliefs concerning the stuff weren't interesting enough, the stone was also supposed to help with divination and acted as a protective shield for whoever wore it. And still there was more. It was believed by some ancient societies to have healing qualities as well. How interesting that I now had a small stash of beads that could possibly do all that! The question uppermost in my mind, though, was what were these beads used for? And the stone? What was its purpose?

Suddenly the hairs stood up on the back of my neck as the temperature in the room dropped. I was no longer alone, it seemed, and I quickly imagined my protective light. Once I had that established firmly in my mind, I stood to face my unseen visitors. Goosebumps rose on my flesh as unease prickled the surface of my skin. Whoever now shared the room with me was not very happy about the circumstances in which we found ourselves—me in physical life aware of their presence, them (for I did feel there was more than one) in spirit and just as aware of me. I didn't think the anger was directed at me, however, and that was a tad comforting. Their discontent was in the fact that I was the only one at present to pick up on them and our connection was tenuous at best.

"I'm here to help." I thought I should get that out right away. It might help matters if my intentions were clear to them. I tried to feel out their location but it seemed they were everywhere. The idea that my room was crammed full of spirits didn't sit well. Even for me. "Give me some space." The air was so stifling I could hardly breathe. This distracted me so much that my focus on the imaginary light fell away and began to slowly extinguish. As a warning shiver raced through me, I pulled my focus from my struggling breath and closed my eyes to better imagine the light growing strong again. What was this? Were they out to attack me? This would be a first. Never having dealt with Indian spirits, I wasn't sure what I was up against. Surely they couldn't be any different than non-Indian spirits? The cold air grew frigid and when I opened my eyes, I could see my breath coming out in puffs of white fog. All around me I heard the whispered echoes of chanting. The metal box on my nightstand began to vibrate and shimmy across the surface. I stared at it for a moment and then again tried to talk to them. "I want to help you. I'm on your side."

The box rattled harder across the nightstand's surface and then the lid popped open just before it flew onto the floor. In complete fascination, I watched the beads scatter in an almost controlled manner, as if some sort of force were directing their movements. What happened next was really quite unbelievable, even for me. The beads started banding together to form a shape. The lightest shade of beads, an almost pale yellow in color, began to take on the shape of what looked like some sort of bird. Then another shade slightly darker, not quite pink, not quite red, formed a solid circle around the bird. After that, the varying shades continued to band together and form circles about two layers thick around each other until there were about seven layers of circles in all, each shade getting darker and darker until the solid red ones formed the final layer. The remaining beads, the ones made from black hematite, began to form a single layered circle considerably larger than the solid design just finished. Once it was completed, I knew what I was looking at. A necklace. For a moment, all I could do was stare, the cold forgotten, my focus on the light gone. I have never witnessed anything like this in my life and honestly, I didn't quite know what to make of it. You think you've seen it all and then you realize you've seen nothing. Who, I wondered, was going to believe this story?

Once the last bead rolled into place, the cold temperature vanished and the room was once again comfortably warm. Released from my paralysis (which I hadn't even realized I was in until that moment), I dropped to the floor on my hands and knees and looked at the beads in complete fascination. What on earth did this mean?

A rapid knock sounded on my door and I glanced up. No doubt Barbara heard the box drop to the floor and came to investigate the noise. "Come in."

Barbara opened the door enough to poke her head through and peak in. "Is everything okay, Tess? I heard something fall and then I got the strangest feeling. Max started growling low in his throat and he never does that. It made me worried."

I waved her into the room and beckoned her to come join me. "Come look at this, Barbara!"

Barbara came into the room and around the bed to where I was crouched on the floor. I waved down at the beads. "Look."

Barbara looked and shook her head as if what she saw was more a mild catastrophe than anything spectacular. "Oh dear, did you drop the box? Do you need me to help you gather them back up?"

Puzzled by her response, I glanced down and stared in shock and dismay. Disbelief chased doubt as my thoughts raced to consider the situation. Had I imagined it all? The beads were no longer forming a symmetric design. No. They were now scattered all over the place. "But...just a moment ago they were all formed together."

Barbara knelt down next to me and began to gather the beads. "What do you mean?"

"The beads were just formed into a necklace with the most interesting design. I was looking at it when you knocked on the door."

"Well, they aren't in any sort of design now." Barbara looked at me with doubtful eyes and I knew she was wondering if I was going bonkers.

"No, they aren't. But I'm going to put them back together as I saw it." Even as I said it, I knew that I probably wouldn't have the patience to do it. There were hundreds of beads and it would take me a deuced long time to accomplish. What was the point anyway? "I could draw it." Although I was speaking more to myself, Barbara gave an enthusiastic nod.

"Please do, I'd like to see what you saw."

Realizing that I was not helping Barbara pick up the beads, I immediately began to do so. "The Indians who owned these beads wanted me to know what they were used for. The design was of a strange looking bird inside a circle. The beads made several layers of circles around it and then these black ones," I picked up a couple of the shiny hematite beads, "made up the chain from which to hang the necklace around the neck."

"Why do you think the beads were taken apart and put in this box?"

"I don't know. But I think I need to find out." Thinking back to the emotions flooding the room, I would say that finding the beads had stirred up old resentments. The only way to calm them was to get to the truth. Kade was going to love this.

Once the task of gathering the beads was finished, Barbara stood up. "So, did you find anything interesting in your research?"

"I've been reading up on the Indians that were here before and after Bucksport was first settled."

Barbara nodded as if she were familiar with the stories. "Yes, there were quite a few. Maine still has a small population of Indians but none here in Bucksport that I'm aware of. Mixed descendants maybe but no tribes. We didn't treat each other very well for a while there."

"From what I gather, there has been quite a large assortment of Indian artifacts discovered all over Maine, particularly along the coastal areas and other waterways."

"Yes there have." Barbara pointed at the copper box now resting once again on the nightstand. "And you have a few more."

I glanced at my watch and said with some regret, "We'll have to discuss this more later, Barbara, but right now I've got to call Mr. Truman and then I've got to get ready to head out as I've been invited to dinner."

Barbara's arched gray brows rose curiously. "Oh? I didn't realize you knew anyone around here."

"I don't really. I met Mary Rowan during my walk along the river yesterday. She's invited me to dinner with her and her mother."

"Mary Rowan." Barbara's brows now came together as she sunk into thought. "I believe she just got out of the military not too long ago. Her family has lived here in Bucksport for a long time." Her forehead wrinkled as her thoughts continued to dredge up what she knew of the family. "Her mother's name is Dawn. She's a very dear lady. You are going to like her. She's about to lose her house, though. Very sad."

"How do you know this, Barbara?"

"You forget, Tess, that this is a small town. I grew up here before my travels with my husband and I've lived here for over twenty years since returning. Dawn and I went to school together. She's a couple years younger than me but the schools were small back then and we knew everyone. Her husband Night Rowan also attended school with us though he was several years ahead of us. He was a good man."

"Night? As in night time when the stars are out?"

Barbara nodded. "They are a strange family but very nice." She laughed as if years of remembered amusements filled her thoughts and turned to head out of the room. "You have a good visit with them. Give Dawn my love and tell her that I'll be stopping by soon for a visit. Whenever I can get that scatterbrained daughter of mine to stick around long enough to keep an eye on the place for me."

"Will do, Barbara." Once she was gone, I sank down on the bed and thought about what I'd just learned. Dawn and Night Rowan? It was almost as bizarre as Rid, Sid and Brid! Another thing that puzzled me was why Mary kept her family's last name? She said she was going through a divorce, which meant that the divorce was not yet final. Did she not take her husband's name when they married? If not, I couldn't help but wonder why? Not that it was all that important, really. I was just curious.

My gaze fell upon the alarm clock next to my bed and when I realized how late in the day it was, I pulled the business card from my back pocket and grabbed my cell phone. If I wanted to see Ridley Truman today then I needed to call him ASAP. Moments later, his familiar voice answered on the second ring.

"Hello?"

"Hello, Mr. Ridley Truman?"

"Yes, this is Rid."

"Hi, I'm Tess Schafer. Did Ted tell you I was going to call?"

"Yes he did! Hello, Tess. It is so nice to be speaking with you again."

So he knew I was the woman he spoke to outside the cemetery yesterday. "Did Ted tell you about what we found?"

"Yes he did and I am excited to see them. He said you'd probably come around this afternoon?"

My heart sank a little at the excitement in his voice. I really was hoping to hold onto my find for just awhile longer but it didn't sound like that was going to happen. "I've got to be somewhere at six, can I come around five-ish?" It was ten minutes before four, which gave me about one precious hour with my little treasures. Darn.

"Yes, any time will be fine." He hesitated and I waited to see what more he would say. "Ted said he told you that you could keep the box. I'm too old to be holding onto artifacts so I'm okay with that. My nephew won't care either. But I would like to see them."

The breath whooshed out of me. Oh my God. How awesome was this. "Mr. Truman, thank you so much. Of course I'll bring them with me. I have lots of questions. Barbara said you know a lot about the area."

A chuckle filled my ears. "Yes I do as a matter of fact, and I love to talk. You might want to show up a little earlier or an hour isn't going to be long enough. Do you know where I live?"

"Barbara can give me directions."

"Good, dear, then I'll see you around five."

"Thanks again, Mr. Truman."

"Not sure why you are thanking me, but you're welcome. And please call me Rid. Everyone does."

"I'll see you in an hour then, Rid."

After I disconnected from the call, I immediately dialed Kade. He answered on the first ring. It made me smile how quickly he always answered my calls. "Hi, Kade."

"More has happened? Did you have another run in with the bloody guy?"

The concern in his voice made my smile widen and once again I felt like a grinning idiot. "Actually yes. The most bizarre thing happened. The beads fell onto the floor and formed into a design. They used to make up a necklace."

"They rolled around on the floor and formed into a design all by themselves?"

Although his voice was incredulous, I knew he believed me. And that made him all the more endearing. Pushing down the swell of emotion in my chest, I managed to speak in a normal voice and not give it away that my insides were a quivering mess of excitement. "They did. Although it might have been a vision because when Barbara came into the room and I waved her around the bed to see it, the beads were a scattered mess."

"Oh, sorry. I know you would have liked for her to see what you saw."

Again he was saying all the right things. I closed my eyes for a moment and tried to tamp down the surge of emotion that wanted to well up and burst from my chest. "I'm going to draw what I saw, that will be almost as good. Luckily the design is pretty simple. I wonder what it means and who the necklace belonged to and why it was hidden in a box in a secret compartment in the fireplace?"

"Sounds like we have ourselves a new mystery to solve." Kade actually sounded excited about that. But then I knew he would be.

"Yes, I'd say so."

"So, how early can I come tomorrow and do you think there is a bedroom open for the next couple days?"

Laughing at his eagerness to join me, I headed for the door. "I know there are plenty of rooms free at the moment. I'll let Barbara know right now to hold one for you. Ted is leaving tomorrow so you probably won't get the chance to meet him. Oh, and before I forget, Rid said I could keep the box and its contents!"

"That's great, Tess. Maybe you can have the beads restrung into the design you saw."

"What a wonderful idea, Kade." I trotted down the stairs and found Barbara sitting in her chair reading a book with Max lying next to her feet. He lifted his head and began to thump his stumpy tail as I made my way toward them. "Hi, Barbara, I was wondering if I could book a room for the next few nights for my friend Kade Sinclair?"

Barbara stood up and walked brusquely to the reception desk to grab her reservation log. "Certainly, Tess. Will he be arriving tomorrow then?"

"Yes, early though, if that's okay?"

"He can come any time he likes. He'll probably like the room across from yours. It's a bit more geared toward the masculine gender."

"Thank you, Barbara, that would be perfect." I gave her a little wave, pointing at my cell phone so she could see that I was still on the phone and ran back up the stairs to my room. "So it's all settled. You come as early as you like."

"The crack of dawn too soon?" He gave a low laugh that made my breath hitch then went all serious on me before I could succumb to the lure of his sensual appeal. "So, what are your plans for the evening?"

"Well I'm going to visit with Mr. Truman for a little bit, he wants to see the box and its contents and I want to pump him for information on Bucksport's history and then I'm going to Mary Rowan's house for dinner."

"Mary Rowan? Oh yes, the woman you met yesterday."

"Get this, Kade, her parents' names are Night and Dawn."

Kade laughed softly. "How odd."

"I thought it interesting."

"Well I hate to cut this short, Tess, but I need to get some things here squared away before I head out tomorrow."

After giving him directions to the B&B, we ended our conversation and I fell back on the bed to enjoy the feelings of contentment wafting through me. It felt so good to feel good. I thought back to the angry bitter person I was only a month ago and shuddered with revulsion. How could I have allowed myself to sink so low? However, I couldn't regret it. It was those negative emotions that led me to Sea Willow Haven and brought Kade into my life. Strange how life worked out sometimes.

A glance at my watch told me I had just over a half hour before it was time to head to Rid's place and then Mary's. I set my cell phone on the nightstand, picked up the smooth rock then settled myself comfortably on the bed. Holding the stone in the palm of one hand, I rubbed its smooth surface with the thumb of my other hand. Closing my eyes, I focused on relaxing my muscles and when I felt I couldn't possibly get any more comfortable, switched my focus to my breathing. Drawing in deep, slow breaths, I concentrated on the air entering and filling my lungs. As my chest expanded with breath, I imagined the oxygen enriching my blood and circulating throughout my body. With the exhale, I noted the feeling of my chest deflating and imagined my breath mingling with the air around me. Relaxed and focused, I switched my attention to the stone and noted how warm it felt in my palm. In fact, it almost felt as if it were pulsing along with my pulse.

And then I felt my consciousness expand to awareness of the room around me. My body lost all form and became light as air. Then I was part of the air and soaring through it. Exhilarated by the sense of freedom, I let myself go and soared higher. Just when it felt as if I had become the atmosphere surrounding the Earth, I found myself rushing down and plunging beneath it.

Everything went dark and the sensation of warm damp earth enveloped me. It wasn't a smothering feeling, though. It felt nurturing and embracing and I luxuriated in the sensation. Before I could really wrap my head around those feelings, it suddenly felt as if I were shrinking and shrinking, becoming so small it was a wonder there was anything left of me. And yet I didn't feel insignificant. Quite the contrary. As I marveled over this, the thought popped into my head that size really doesn't matter and before that could pull my mind off in other directions, I suddenly became aware of the fact that I now was nestled within a small shell perhaps the size of a pea. I felt comfortable and safe.

Content. I could have stayed there and enjoyed the feeling a little longer but suddenly I was filled with restless longing for more. I burst free and began to grow. Little tendrils sprouted from me in all directions and expanded through the earth, drawing from it nourishing nutrients I readily enjoyed. And then I was moving up, up and up until I burst free from the earth in joyful exhilaration. I continued growing, moving ever upwards toward the sky. I grew bigger and firmer and stronger and realized with wonder that I was now a tree, part of all, the earth and the air. I grew to such a height it should have made me dizzy. But it didn't. I was very much aware of the land below me and loved the connection I felt to it. My branches danced with the wind and swayed to currents of air that moved around me in loving caresses. I drew in the oxygen-rich air and soaked up the sun's rays. It was all so majestic and beautiful. For a while, time seemed quite irrelevant and I enjoyed the feeling of being part of everything.

But as with all things, time moves on and I began to pull away and separate from the tree. A gentle sensation of floating down, down and then I was once again aware of the bed beneath me. I said a prayer of thanks for such a wonderful experience and opened my eyes.

The bedside clock said that only fifteen minutes had gone by but it seemed as if I'd just experienced a lifetime. It was the strangest vision I'd ever had. A nice one to be sure. One that gave me a new appreciation for the world around me. The rock was cool in my hand. I sat up and stared at it in curious wonder. Just what sort of power did this rock have? Invigorated, I jumped off the bed and set it back in the box with the beads. I'd have to puzzle it out later. It was time to freshen up and prepare for the evening ahead. I couldn't wait to get on with it and see what was going to happen next. I felt pretty certain tonight was going to bring about even more interesting revelations.

CHAPTER NINE

The drive to Rid Truman's house was a short one. Anyone living within the town's epicenter was relatively close by since Bucksport's business district was quite small. The main drag followed along the riverbank on level ground but the rest of the town was built on a hill that I was told eventually leveled out again. Barbara told me to turn right just after the Tenney house. I would come to a stop sign with the police and fire stations ahead and to the left. She said most of the town's churches were located on this street and anyone not told that would figure it out anyway for I saw several within easy view. I turned right and followed the street until it went up a steep hill. Barbara said Rid's house was at the top on the left and to slow down after passing the Catholic church on my right. "You can't possibly miss it," she said. "He has the nicest house on that street."

Barbara was right. Rid's house was indeed impressive. Built in typical Colonial style and painted white with black shutters framing large windows, it was two stories high and had two large chimneys facing each other from opposite ends of the roof. A small cupola took center stage between the chimneys. I pulled onto a paved driveway ending in a three-car garage. A black BMW was parked closest to the house and I pulled in next to it. When I stepped out of the car, a door at the side of the house facing the driveway opened and there was Mr. Ridley Truman himself. He stood waiting with a smile on his wrinkled face. His pure white hair was combed neatly across his head to one side and it somehow made him seem gentle and engaging. Sitting at his feet was the dog he'd had with him during his walk the day before. The dog didn't bark.

A memory of Tootsie rose to mind. She loved company and used to get so excited whenever anyone stopped by for a visit. It took a lot of work to train her not to jump all over everyone and she turned out to be very well behaved towards the end. My throat felt tight as I allowed that memory in because such memories were always followed by a pang of sorrow. I missed her. I missed having a dog. I pushed the thought away as I stepped around the car and waved in greeting to my host.

"Hi again."

"Hello, young lady. Welcome. Come on in." Rid ushered me into the house and I entered a wide hallway where an antique coat rack took up most of the wall to our right. I slipped my sweater off and hung it on a hook then indicated my sneakers. "Would you like me to remove my shoes?"

Rid waved the offer away. "Don't worry about it. If it was winter and they were covered with snow and mud, I might take you up on the offer." He walked ahead of me down a short hallway and I followed slowly behind. To the right we passed a door that revealed a huge kitchen. On my left was a bathroom. The next door we passed on the left was closed and then we entered the main living area, which was very spacious by today's standards. Windows facing the front were to my right and on the left was a huge brick fireplace. Rid indicated I should take one of the comfortable-looking chairs placed near the windows. "I like to enjoy what is left of the afternoon sun if you don't mind."

I sank down in the chair nearest to Rid's obvious preference and he took his seat carefully, his back seeming to give him problems. As soon as he was settled, the dog jumped up to snuggle beside him and rest his head on Rid's lap. He immediately went to sleep. Closer inspection revealed that the dog, a terrier of some sort, was probably older than Mr. Truman. In dog years anyway.

As if reading my mind, Rid patted the dog's head affectionately. "Teddy here is older than I am. The two of us are just biding our time until we move on to our next big adventure."

Although Rid's voice didn't sound sad about it, I felt a surge of sorrow well up within me. Was that how it would be when I got old? Would I just bide my time? It seemed so sad to me. I wanted to enjoy life until the very end. Like Mike had done. "How old is he?"

"Well, let's see...I got him when my son turned thirty-five. He's going to be fifty next month so I guess that makes Teddy about ninety or so in dog years. Not bad for a little fella. I think he sticks around just to keep me company. I do appreciate it."

I had to drop my gaze to the box nestled in my lap while I did my best to bring my emotions back under control. The devotion between the two touched my heart. I would have loved to have had Tootsie in my life longer than the two years I had her. But it wasn't to be. She was with Mike and I was here. "He's lucky to have someone who loves him as much in return."

Rid continued to gently stroke Teddy's head, his own bent down as if lost in thought. He wasn't completely with me at that moment. I wondered where his mind had taken him and then he spoke. "My life has been so quiet, the spark for life having faded when my wife died. I love my son and his wife is a wonderful daughter-in-law. The two grandsons they gave me, they are the best. But I'm ready to get on with it." He gave a soft sigh and shook his head in an effort to bring himself back to the present moment. "I still feel her near sometimes. It's the strangest thing. I would swear to you that I can smell her...the perfume she liked to wear, the lotion she was forever putting on her hands, the shampoo she used..." He drifted off for a moment, once again lost in his memories.

The room swelled with a buzz of quiet excitement. I sat up a little straighter and looked around curiously as the light tickle of cobwebs brushed across my face. Sheila was bringing someone near and I knew immediately who it was. I felt her love warm the room and cocoon around us. Teddy lifted his head and focused his eyes over Rid's left shoulder.

"He does that sometimes. Acts like he sees something. I often think he can feel her too." Rid's voice was quiet and reverent of the moment. He knew as I did that she was here.

"She's waiting for you, Rid, but she isn't in a hurry for you to join her. She worries about your son. He works too much."

Rid glanced at me, his hazel eyes faded but sharp in their focus, fastened on mine and stayed there. "You can feel my wife's presence? My son thinks I'm being fanciful." Rid gave a small grimace. "Although we didn't raise him that way, he hasn't much faith in God or the afterlife."

"Has he always felt that way?"

Rid shook his head. "No. He attended church with us and took part in their youth ministries but this job of his..." Rid shook his head, his expression troubled. "He sees so much ugliness. It's pushed his beliefs away. He's a lawyer and he's seen it all. It's hard to hang onto the belief that there is good in the world when you are constantly dealing with the ugliness."

Now I understood his wife's concern. It was practically bombarding me. "Your wife feels that you keep him from losing what little faith he has left."

Rid's eyes narrowed slightly as he continued to hold my gaze. "Ted told me you speak to spirits and I figured this would come up...I pretty much steered us to it, but are you really talking to my wife?"

"We aren't having a discussion like you and I are, Rid, but I can feel her emotions, her concern. I can't see her but I can feel her." I nodded to Teddy who had once again lowered his head to Rid's lap though his eyes remained fixed on the spot above Rid's shoulder. "Teddy probably sees her. Dog's eyes are different from ours. They see what we cannot. They also can hear what we cannot."

After a moment, accepting that I was being honest with him, Rid gave me a wide smile. "I thought I was just being an old fool thinking that. It gave me comfort to think of Brid being near me still."

"I think it's wonderful that you are aware of her. It shows how open and sensitive you are and I must tell you, that in itself is a gift."

"I am what I am in part because of her. She was a wonderful woman. She still is." He turned his head toward his left shoulder and closed his eyes. I knew he was talking to her and waited quietly, fascinated at how close they were. Death had not separated them. Some, like Mike, moved on in the afterlife. Where they moved on to, I couldn't say for sure...heaven? Another life? We'd all find out someday. But some people stayed close like Brid with Rid. And as soon as that thought went through my head, I had to fight to keep from smiling. It was cute how close their names matched. I had no doubt that when his time came to join her, she'd be the one to help him cross over.

Rid opened his eyes and looked at me curiously. "Are you a Spiritualist, Tess?"

It was a good question. Given my spiritual beliefs and mediumship ability, you'd think that I would be involved with just such a church. What other religion would I be better suited to? "I've been to Spiritualist churches a time or two but I'm not a member. Why?"

"I was just curious. You know, we used to have a pretty strong spiritualist community right here in Bucksport. There used to be a prominent Spiritualist camp located across the bridge on Verona Island. Of course, that was many years ago."

"When?"

Rid waved a vague hand. "Oh about the time the spiritualist movement was sweeping across Europe I image. The late 1800s."

"How interesting that they were prominent in this area." Was there something about Bucksport that drew people like me here? How many ghosts had I encountered since arriving? The place practically oozed spiritual activity everywhere I went.

Eyes twinkling, Rid smiled, pleased with my interest. "I knew you'd find that tidbit of information interesting." He gave a small puzzled shrug. "Not sure why they moved on. There aren't any Spiritualist communities here anymore" We both went silent for a moment then Rid leaned forward, his eyes focused on the copper box I held on my lap. "So, is that the box you found?" He gave a nod towards it and held out a hand. "May I see it?"

I handed him the box and watched his reaction as he lifted the lid then parted his lips to draw in a breath. "These are exquisite." He scooped some of the beads into his deeply lined palm and examined them closely. "Such workmanship. The Indians really knew what they were doing, didn't they?"

I leaned forward as my enthusiasm for the pending conversation increased. "I believe they used to be strung together to make a necklace."

Rid let the beads fall through his fingers into the box then lifted the smooth stone. He held it between his thumb and forefinger on its rounded edges and turned it this way and that. "It's slightly reflective isn't it?"

I leaned forward to see what he meant and he held it tilted toward the window and the late afternoon sun streaming through it. The light danced across the surface of the rock but did not reflect a glare as would a mirror. Something niggled at my mind. When I was researching the magical properties of hematite, one of the things I read was that it was often used for divination or fortune telling. The flattened smooth surface of the stone was held near a candle flame and the idea was to stare at the flame's reflection, which would then reveal the future. In other words, it was used for scrying and when I said as much to Rid he asked me to explain.

"Well, scrying is sort of what one is doing when they are looking into a crystal ball. Bodies of water are often used as well. Actually, any smooth, reflective surface is sufficient. The idea behind scrying is that when one stares at the surface long enough, eventually it will reveal things. Answers to questions, the future, a past event." I shrugged, "It just depends on what the scryer is trying to accomplish."

"Interesting."

"Yes." And then just like that, I knew it was for this purpose that the rock was used. Since only a tribe's spiritual leader, typically known as a medicine man or woman, was the only one to perform anything like this, then it stood to reason these items must have belonged to one. Was it possible the red- faced guy at the Tenney house was a spiritual leader? The idea was an exciting one because it might explain a few things. But it also created many more questions. As Rid and I stared at the rock, admiring how it captured the light of the sun that danced across its surface, I worried that he was going to change his mind and keep it. But then he suddenly stretched his hand toward me and when I held out my palm, he dropped the stone onto it.

"I imagine you will get a lot more use out of it than me."

I curled my hand around the stone and sat back in my chair. "Are you sure, Rid?"

He nodded his head decisively. "Quite. Now tell me how you found them."

I explained to him about my vision of the bloody face and how I now wondered if maybe it wasn't blood but red ocher, and then how I noticed that one of the hearthstones was different where he'd been standing, and so on until I ended the story where I pulled the box from its hiding place. Rid listened without comment and seemed quite fascinated with the whole tale. When I finished, he glanced down at the box he was holding in his hands as if to remind himself that the story had to be true and closed the lid. He handed the box to me then nodded towards it.

"So you think the beads used to make up a necklace? Why?"

Now here I wasn't sure what to say. The truth of it was just too fantastic. Besides, I was now more inclined to believe that I had been having a vision and hadn't really witnessed the beads move themselves into a pattern. "I had a vision." It seemed the easiest explanation.

"What did it look like?"

I looked at the table that sat between our chairs. It was cluttered with notepads, books and a cup full of pens and pencils. "Maybe I should draw it for you?"

Rid waved a hand. "By all means."

I took a pen and a small notepad and drew the necklace as best as I could. My talents did not run in the art department. Not at all. I closed my eyes for a moment as I tried to remember how many layers of circles I'd seen. I was pretty sure it was seven. When I finished, I handed Rid the drawing. He stared at it for a long quiet moment then he looked up at me. "Is that a Thunderbird in the center or an eagle?"

"I have no idea. Why?"

Rid returned the paper to me then resumed petting his dog's head. He thought for a long moment and I knew he was thinking everything over and trying to piece it together. "Well, thunderbirds are very symbolic to the Native Americans. As is the eagle." He went quiet again and frowned, thinking hard. "It could be those beads were hidden away because of who they belonged to. If the stone was used for...what was the word? Scrying?" When I nodded, he went on, "Then I'd be willing to bet the Indian that owned them was a spiritual leader in his or her tribe. They are typically known as either a Medicine Man or Woman though I refer to them as Shamans. Since these are Indian beads then it is pretty logical to accept that assumption." His lined face tightened with displeasure. "The fact they ended up in our hands...well, I'd say something unsavory must have taken place. I'm quite sure spiritual articles were not given or bartered away. They were considered sacred."

My heart pounded with excitement that his thoughts were matching mine on this issue. The fact Rid came up with the same conclusion was surely proof I was on the right track. "I was just thinking the same thing." And then, because I was really curious, "Do you know what the eagle or thunderbird symbolize?"

Again Rid's face pulled together in thought. "I believe the thunderbird was a messenger of God or the Great Spirit or whatever it is the Native Indians called him. Such birds were thought to have supernatural strength and power. Thunderstorms are connected to them obviously, which is why they are called thunderbirds. I just can't remember much about it, I'm sorry."

I thought about the red-faced guy on the stairs at the Tenney house and how he made a booming noise which I likened to thunder. It wasn't a coincidence that these beads used to make up a necklace with a thunderbird (for now I was sure that is what it was) as its centerpiece.

Rid continued with his theory. "If those items in that box are indeed sacred, they would never have been given to anyone not of their culture. They wouldn't even have shared them among themselves. Seeing as the box was found in the house of a colonist and was obviously hidden away, I'd venture a pretty strong guess that whoever hid it came by the contents in a way that required discretion. How they ended up staying there for so long, I can't say. Perhaps the person who hid them died before he could tell anyone about them. It certainly makes you think." His eyes regarded me curiously. "You haven't been able to pick anything up on that?"

"No. But I'm not a sensitive in that area. At least, not a very good one."

"A sensitive?"

"Some people are sensitive to energies left in items. Picking up past energies by someone sensitive to that is called Psychometry. Sometimes I can pick up impressions but I'm not really good at it. I think my own thought processes get in the way."

"I see. So you haven't a clue concerning them?"

"Well, I had a vision while holding the stone that I was standing in the trees looking out at a rocky shoreline dotted with boats and lots of men walking around dressed as Colonials. At least that's who I think they were. I'm not totally sure how they dressed back then but from pictures I remember seeing in high school history books, I'd say that is who they were. Although my vision showed a girl holding the stone, it was a man who inadvertently led me to where the box was located. So, I'm not sure what to make of that. As for the girl, I'm pretty sure she was an Indian. I know she did not like seeing those men and was afraid of them." I decided not to tell him about the second vision I'd had in which I became a tree. It didn't seem to have any relevance to our current discussion.

"How interesting. You are quite a fascinating young lady, aren't you?"

I laughed at the remark, finding it most amusing to be called fascinating. I'd been called many things over the years, and that wasn't one of them. After a moment Rid laughed along with me. Even Teddy lifted his head and wagged his tail as if he too found our discussion amusing. "I'm different, that's for sure."

Getting all serious again, Rid frowned as he puzzled over our discussion. "Do you think there is any relation between the girl in your vision and the man you encountered at the Tenney house?"

"I'm not sure. I do think the man I encountered at the Tenney house might be a Red Paint Indian. I'm sure you've heard of them?"

"Certainly and I seriously doubt he was a member of that particular tribe. They died out a long time ago. Precious little is known about them but they were pretty exclusive to Maine.

Matter of fact, a Red Paint Indian burial site was found right here in Bucksport."

"Yes I know. In the area where the paper mill now stands."

"You've been doing your research," Rid nodded with approval, his eyes meeting mine and twinkling with mutual enthusiasm for the topic at hand.

"I have."

"There were no Red Paint Indians still in existence when settlers began arriving in Bucksport so I can't imagine the Indian you saw at the Tenney house was one of them." Cocking his head to the side, Rid regarded me for a long quiet moment. I couldn't help but wonder what he was thinking. "Why would you think the spirit you encountered at the Tenney house was a Red Paint Indian?"

"Because he was covered in red. When I first saw him, I thought it was blood. Soon as I got back to the B&B, I looked some stuff up on the computer. As you say, there isn't much written about them but when I read that they were buried in red ocher and were thought to be connected to the Beothuk who liked to cover themselves in the stuff, I just figured that was who he was."

"As far as them being connected to the Beothuk, that is quite disputed. But in any case, if he was a Red Paint Indian, I find it curious that you would encounter him at the Tenney house. How odd." Rid lapsed into thoughtful silence. After a moment he heaved a sigh. "The Indians didn't fare well as our numbers increased. We started taking more and more land and they eventually had no recourse but to start fighting back. You know, there was a period of time in our history when it was ordered that all Indians be shot on sight." He shook his head sadly, "It was quite a sorry mess. Very tragic."

I agreed with him whole-heartedly but didn't want our discussion to fall into a quagmire of gloom about the tragic circumstances of times past. "Do you know anything more about the Red Paint Indians?"

Rid shook his head regretfully. "Not much, I'm afraid. As I said and you know from your research, the only reason we know about them at all is because of the gravesites we found.

You know, there were three other burial sites for them found in Orland, the next town over."

I nodded that I did know that though I didn't find it particularly important. "So obviously they were prominent in the area at one time. I just can't help but wonder why the spirit I saw at the Tenney house had a red face if he wasn't a Red Paint Indian?" It was a rhetorical question and Rid understood that, making no attempt to answer. Instead, we both lapsed into thoughtful silence.

The moments ticked quietly by. I stared out the window, my gaze inward, as I once again allowed the images of the red face to fill my mind. The more I thought about it, the more convinced I was that it wasn't blood I saw on his face. But then again, I was being swayed by the whole Red Paint Indian idea. After a moment I shook my head, giving it up for now. "I'll just have to wait and see what else I uncover."

"Ted tells me that you are looking into the mystery of Jonathan's Buck's cursed monument."

"I am."

"Why?"

Wow. That was a good question. "I heard about it and it caught my attention and so I thought I'd come check it out. When I was standing outside the graveyard yesterday looking at that monument, just before you arrived actually, I detected the spirit of a girl. I was thinking she might be the same girl I had the vision of holding the rock and staring at those men scouring the shoreline but now I am not so sure."

"If it was an Indian girl you connected with at his gravesite, I can't think why. It could be that Buck might have killed some Indians but I highly doubt it. He had a pretty decent reputation with them. Most of the town settlers traded with them and there was really quite a bit of tolerance. At least until we started taking more and more of their land. But why they would curse him and none of the others makes no sense."

"Unless he was the most prominent figure involved with her death and she was a medicine woman! I could see people back in the day calling her a witch if that was the case." The very idea filled me with excitement because it felt like I was on the right track. Rid nodded that he thought it a sound theory though a doubtful one. We both lapsed into thought again. After a quiet, reflective moment, I looked at Rid curiously. "Do you believe in the curse?"

"Not sure what I think. It seems quite far-fetched. But since Brid died then began to come around and keep me company, I'm suddenly open to possibilities that I never would have considered before."

"Piecing together what I have so far, I really think Buck was involved with a girl's death and that's why this curse legend was born. If the red guy I saw at the Tenney house is connected to her somehow, then it could be he is a distant relative or something."

Rid frowned and shook his head. "I've certainly never heard of Indians casting spells and giving out curses."

"The belief is that Colonel Buck had a witch put to death, right? Well, we just determined that a medicine woman would be the equivalent of a witch." Again I felt excitement trip across my skin. My heart began to pound a little harder and I knew that we were getting close to the truth of the matter. "Are there any other buildings around here that were still standing when Colonel Buck was alive?"

"Yes, several. Why?"

"Which ones?"

Rid laughed softly at my eagerness. "Well the most famous one is the Tenney house of course. It was an Inn back then and on a stagecoach route. But another house that factored pretty prominently in our town's history is Dawn Rowan's house."

My heart bumped in my chest and I coughed in response. Dawn Rowan? What an interesting coincidence. "Really?"

Rid tilted his head and looked at me with sudden, avid interest. "Do you know Dawn Rowan?"

"No, but I am having dinner with them this evening." I glanced at the clock on the fireplace mantel and realized with a bit of alarm that I was due to arrive there in ten minutes. "I told them I'd be there at six."

Rid glanced at the clock as well and pulled a face to show his disappointment. "This conversation is quite fascinating. I hate to let you go."

"Does the Rowan family know their house's history?"

"I would think they know more about it than anyone." Rid's answer was a bit stiff and it made me curious. Were there bad feelings between the two families?

Although I would have loved to stay a bit longer and probe for more answers, I stood up and smiled my thanks as Rid stood as well. "Thank you so much for your time and for allowing me to keep these." I held up the copper box. Rid waved away my thanks and motioned for me to precede him down the hallway to the door. He shuffled slowly behind. "I do hope we can get together again soon, Rid." Impulsively I leaned forward and wrapped my arms around his bony shoulders to give him a quick hug. "I'll keep you abreast of my findings."

"Thank you so much, dear, I would really appreciate that. And I very much would like to get with you again to talk some more." He helped me slip on my sweater then stood in the doorway and watched as I got into my car and pulled out of the driveway. He was still standing there as I drove off for the next part of this very exciting afternoon.

CHAPTER TEN

Barbara told me that Mary's family home was near the end of Bucksport's business district and across from the massive paper mill. It was on the same street as Rid's home but in the opposite direction. Barbara said the Rowans owned a large tract of land which sat pretty high up from the main street through town and had a great view of the river and the fort. Sympathetic as she was to Dawn's plight, Barbara's opinion on the matter was that they should have sold the house before getting to this point. It was worth a mint, she said, but the Rowans would end up with nothing and that was such a shame. Honestly, Barbara was a wealth of information and I felt rather guilty to learn as much as I did about the Rowan family's business. Barbara, however, didn't consider it gossip to share what she knew. To her way of thinking, she was doing nothing more than imparting facts. "The house is old as Hades, but very impressive. A beautiful Victorian. The upkeep is pretty extensive and the family just can't maintain it. Such a shame for it to go to waste but...well, you'll see."

Those words rang in my ears as I crested a hill and saw the house in question. Just as the case with Rid's house, there was no way I could miss it. The older homes around here, it seemed, had gone for size. It was a large three-story house with three chimneys. The rooftop was flat, its sides steeply sloped. A windowed cupola took up center stage and was surrounded by a decorative balustrade, which meant there must be access to the gated area within. I could just imagine myself up there in a comfortable chair, soaking up the sun, enjoying the view, feeling like I was on top of the world.

Another feature I found charming were the overhanging eaves edged with decorative brackets and cornices. The house was blue with white trim and in need of fresh paint. Still, it was a delightful house to look at. My eyes were again drawn to the cupola. They were, of course, a popular feature on homes built near the water. I could just imagine the view it afforded and thought if I owned the place, I'd be up there all the time. Although the mill property took up all the land across from the house, its large rambling structure was to the right of the house's location and in no way blocked the magnificent view. The lot directly across the street and edging the river contained rail lines and little else.

The driveway circled past the front steps of a wrap-around covered porch and ended at a two-car garage that was in pretty bad shape and probably no longer used for its intended purpose. Flower gardens that looked to have gone wild surrounded the perimeter of both the house and the garage. The lawn was in dire need of mowing. Though the front yard was somewhat limited, the back yard, from what I could see, looked quite extensive. Level with the house for maybe fifty feet or so, the lawn eventually sloped down and met up with the sidewalk edging Bucksport's Main Street. The lawn area to the right of the house ended at what looked like a little used side street. The property along that side was bordered by a dilapidated old fence that was missing slats in several places and sagging pitifully in others.

Slowed to a near stop as I was, I felt nothing but visual appreciation for the Rowans' home and anticipation for my visit with them, but when I pulled into the driveway I would almost swear I'd just entered a new dimension. My attention was immediately altered and I went on full psychic alert. Two vehicles were parked in front of the garage, an old Ford pickup truck, its green paint quite faded, and a shiny blue Volkswagen Beetle.

Although the air felt as though it crackled with excited energy and movement, it also seemed eerily still. My skin broke out in goose bumps and the hairs on the back of my neck began to stand on end. With my heart racing and pulse jumping with wild abandon, I had to catch my breath and consciously will myself to calm down. Was it just anticipation causing all this excitement? Ever since Rid told me the house was around during Buck's time, I couldn't wait to get here. Why that was the case, I couldn't say since Rid's house was around during Buck's time too and that hadn't yielded anything unusual. His wife's spirit being there was not unusual, not for me anyway, so that didn't count. No, what I felt now was significantly different.

I pulled in behind the pickup truck then sat for a moment to calm my skittering excitement. Senses heightened to an incredible degree, it was like I'd just plugged into some sort of spiritual energy socket, and as I stepped out of the car, I felt quite invincible. I wanted to run like the wind because I could. I wanted to jump for the clouds because I could. Was this how Superman would have felt had he been real? Truly, I felt as though I possessed unimaginable power. It was such an incredible feeling that I had to stand there a moment and bask in it.

"Tess?"

Startled from my sensual euphoria, I swung around and saw that I had something of an audience. Three people stood watching me, a guy about twenty or so, very tall, very muscular, barrel chest, huge; Mary, who stood in the middle and looked weak in comparison, and on the other side of Mary a tall thin woman who had to be their mother. She was not the white-haired, downtrodden woman I was expecting. Despite the impending loss of her home, she looked serene and unflustered. She was slightly taller than Mary, ramrod straight and thin but not in a frail way. Her brown hair was peppered with gray and looked good on her. Some women just looked good in gray. I hoped I'd be as lucky though I also hoped I didn't have to worry about it for a good long while.

Mary and her brother had the darkest eyes I'd ever seen. Dawn's were brown but more like a milk-chocolate brown. Although I noted Mary's strange eye color when I met her, it was a bit unnerving to have two sets of black eyes staring at me. Mary's gaze was welcoming, of course, and that put me a bit at ease but her brother looked distrustful. Considering everything, I felt as if I'd just stepped into some sort of bizarre paranormal novel. Good Lord, were they going to turn into wolves and eat me for dinner? The thought was absurd and I wanted to laugh except I couldn't seem to react. Frozen in complete stillness, I simply stared. Then Mary smiled and stepped forward.

"It's good to see you again." She turned and pointed her hand to the young man standing beside her. "This is my brother Adam."

At well over six feet and built solid, he looked as hard as stone when he stepped forward and offered his hand. Why I was reluctant to take it, I cannot say. His hand was large and firm, his fingers callused. Probably from all the weightlifting he obviously engaged in. His aura was like an impenetrable fortress around him. "Hi, Adam. Nice to meet you."

His dark eyes, like two obsidian pieces of rock, stared at me for a long quiet moment. I had the uncomfortable feeling that he was trying to read me in some way. "Same here." His voice was deep and husky. He let go of my hand and stepped back.

Relieved to get that particular introduction over with, I turned to look at Mary's mother and she stepped forward to shake my hand as soon as we made eye contact. "Hello, it's nice to meet you. My name is Dawn."

"It's nice to meet you as well. Thank you so much for inviting me over for dinner."

Dawn's eyes were not intimidating but they were very observant. Her hands were not soft, they were callused and firm. They looked like hands that lived a rough life. Work hands. "Please, come on inside." Dawn released my hand and turned toward the house. She glanced for a moment toward the mill and closed her eyes briefly. Wondering what she was doing, I pretended not to notice. After the slightest of pauses, she headed for the porch steps. Mary waved for me to follow ahead in front of her and I did so.

My back crawled with the knowledge that Adam was boring a hole through it. Never had I felt so intimidated by anyone in my life. He didn't seem threatening and yet I felt I needed to have defensive shields up.

We entered a spacious hallway with a staircase directly in front of us. Double doors leading into what looked like a sitting room was off to my right. Dawn led us through the open doors on our left. We entered a very spacious living room. A huge fireplace, built with a reddish stone that appeared to be granite, dominated the wall to our right and faced the row of windows overlooking the overgrown flower garden I'd noted earlier. Dawn walked to the black leather couch facing the fireplace and sat down. It was one of the longest couches I'd ever seen. It could easily fit six people upon it. It seemed silly to sit anywhere else so I sank down beside her. Adam sat in a matching easy chair near the right end of the sofa, facing us, and Mary sat next to me on my right. I felt surrounded and wondered about that. Where else did I expect they would sit?

The air continued to buzz with silent static. It was a wonder our hair wasn't standing up on end. The picture that brought to mind made me want to laugh but somehow I managed to stifle it. Instead, I turned to Mary. She didn't look as weighted down with problems as the last time I saw her but I knew the same feelings lurked within her. She was trying to hide them from her family. The serene look on her face looked practiced and I knew her mother and brother were not fooled.

Aside from the excitement I could feel swirling around me, I also could smell the aroma of baking bread and tomato sauce wafting through the air. "Dinner smells delicious, Mary. Thank you again for inviting me."

Mary waved away my thanks. "We don't get a lot of company so we should be thanking you for accepting the invitation." She tilted her head in a speculative look as she studied me, looking very much like I was something of an enigma. "We never got around to the reason why you came to Bucksport? Do you have family here?"

Adam leaned forward at this point, resting his forearms on his legs; his jeans stretched tight over massive thighs and clasped his large hands in front of him. "Mary says you are a ghost whisperer."

"Adam, if she wants to talk about that, we should let her introduce the subject." Dawn gave her son a sharp look and something passed between them.

Uncomfortable yet again, I shifted in my seat hoping to dispel my apprehension. I wasn't afraid of them, but something wasn't right here. "It's okay, Dawn. If it was a secret, I wouldn't have told Mary." I met Adam's eyes briefly before shifting my gaze to the fireplace. It was massive. I was using that word a lot. Massive. Everything just seemed so extraordinarily more here. The fireplace looked like I could easily sit in it without crouching. "I came to Bucksport because

I heard about the Jonathan Buck stone being cursed by a witch and wanted to check it out."

Dawn gave a thoughtful nod, looking like she wasn't surprised in the least at my reason for being there. "It's an interesting legend to be sure. When we were kids, we used to dare each other to go into that graveyard. We were all so sure the witch's spirit wandered around there."

"Why?" My interest was immediately caught as I wondered if perhaps the cemetery had mysterious stories attached to it.

Dawn laughed. "Because we were kids and we made up stuff to scare the heck out of each other. There were never any reports of anything spooky happening there but it didn't matter. The suggestion was made and that was all we needed."

"Do you believe in the legend, Dawn?" Considering her strong ties to the town, I was particularly interested in her views on the whole thing.

Dawn's thinly arched brows, still brown and nicely shaped, drew together as she gave the question some thought. "I don't know what to think." She gave a slight shiver and folded her arms in response.

Even as I noticed it, a chill passed through me as well. Somehow, though, I managed to control the shiver. The sudden drop in temperature was almost instant. A spiritual doorway had just opened and the cold it brought through slithered around us and stilled. I knew the other three in the room felt it but no one made comment. A light brush of cobwebs caressed my face and I closed my eyes for a brief grateful moment. Sheila's spirit was near and in protective mode. Although I was pretty occupied with what was happening in the netherworld, I knew I had to somehow keep up the appearance that all was normal. "I thought I'd stick around for a few days and check it out." It felt important just then that they know why I was here in Bucksport. All three of them looked at me speculatively and I wondered at the thoughts crawling through their minds.

"Why? What's to gain from that?" Adam crossed his big arms over his barrel chest and narrowed his gaze. Clearly he didn't trust me. I was pretty sure at this point that he'd be happy to have me get up and leave. I wondered why? Because I talk to spirits? Did he have a problem with that? A lot of people did. I thought of Modesta, the receptionist at Sea Willow Haven. She remained convinced I was in league with the devil. Even after everything that happened, she still didn't trust me.

"I'm just curious as to what started such a rumor. Have you never wondered about it?" Ignoring Adam, I turned to Mary then Dawn, but it was Adam, however, who responded first.

"I've never given that stupid legend any thought." He shook his head in a manner that said he thought the whole thing preposterous and it suddenly dawned on me that he and Mary had dark complexions. Either they tanned well or it was their natural coloring. I guessed the latter was the case considering they also had black hair and black eyes.

I turned to Mary. Her expression looked strained and I knew she was concerned by her brother's attitude and how it would affect me. I gave her a "don't worry about it" smile and her tensed shoulders relaxed a little. "It's just curiosity on my part. I've nothing else to keep me occupied these days."

"So what have you learned?" Mary asked.

"Nothing yet. Although, I am learning some interesting facts about Maine and the area." I leaned toward her, eager to share what I'd just learned but also hoping the conversation would lead to something useful. "Have you ever heard of the Red Paint Indians?"

Mary's dark brows, exact replicas of her brother's, arched high. "It sounds vaguely familiar." She looked at her mother, a question in her eyes.

"They used to live right here in the area," Dawn said. "But they disappeared and no one knows why. My understanding is their tribe was completely wiped out. Probably because we killed them all."

Adam scowled at his mother's choice of words. "We?"

Dawn waved a hand as if indicating an invisible crowd of guilty murderers. "When the Europeans came to America, the Indians either migrated elsewhere or stayed to fight. Not that it did them much good for we had the unfair advantage of guns."

"That's true, Dawn, but in the case of the Red Paint Indians, they disappeared thousands of years before our arrival on America's shores." Remembering my conversation with Rid, it seemed strange to be having it again so soon. "It was through the discovery of their grave sites that any knowledge of them came to light."

Dawn gestured toward the fireplace though her words indicated she was actually waving toward the area across the street. "One of those burial grounds was found right across from where we live as a matter of fact."

"I read that a burial site was located where the mill is now but you know where exactly, Dawn?"

"Not precisely no. My husband thought it was nearby though."

"Did your husband know anything about them?"

Dawn gave that some thought then shook her head. "Not much concerning the Red Paint Indians, no. I just remember him mentioning them and saying something about there being a gravesite across the street." She gave a small shrug. The matter to her mind was not all that important. "Perhaps other natives killed them off. Even the Indians fought among each other." She paused for a moment then indicated her children. "My husband believed he was a distant descendant of the Penobscot Indians. Though it was more a guess on his part. He just knew that somewhere in his family history, one of his relatives was a member of a local Indian tribe. Since the Penobscot Indians were pretty dominant in this area, he thought it might have been them. Whatever the tribe, their genes must be pretty dominant because he looked like a full-blooded Indian native even though his mother was Irish. My children all took after him in looks. None of them look like me."

Well that certainly explained their dark looks. Even so, they were still rather unusual. I attended some Native American festivals in my own state of New York and none of the Native tribesmen who participated had eyes as black as Mary's and Adam's.

Mary touched my arm to gain my attention. "What would that have to do with Jonathan Buck's cursed grave?"

"I don't know. Maybe nothing." For some reason, I didn't want to share with them my discovery at the Tenney house. Besides, I was too distracted by the shadows shifting just out of my line of sight. From the corners of my eyes, I could almost see them. It was hard to concentrate on the conversation and not look like I was noticing spirit activity going on around us. It honestly was beginning to feel like the room was literally filling up with spirits. Their energy was strong and it wasn't all good. Negative vibes mixed with positive. I mentally cast an image of white light around us but for some reason the image wouldn't hold. Even in my imagination I could see my light being pushed back and the darkness crowding in. For a moment panic raced through me and my heart jumped with nervous anticipation in my chest. Sheila! Help me.

A picture on the fireplace mantel suddenly fell to the floor and shattered. Startled, we all jumped at once. Mary shot off the couch, her face pale as she crossed the room and knelt before it. "What the hell?" She picked up the picture frame, its glass completely shattered out of it, and handed it to her mother who stood over the mess looking as shaken and pale as Mary. "I'll clean it up. Don't touch anything."

Dawn glanced down at the picture then looked at me. I had a feeling that other things of this nature were occurring in the house. Was this why they invited me here? "This is a picture of my husband Night and me on the day we got married." She handed me the broken frame and I looked at the black and white photo curiously. It was easy to see where Adam got his build and his coloring. Night Rowan definitely had Native Indian features. High cheekbones, high forehead, firm jaw, dark skin, dark hair and black eyes staring hard at the camera. He towered over Dawn by a good six inches and Dawn wasn't short by any means. He looked stern, his mouth held in a straight uncompromising line. If he was happy about the marriage, he didn't show it. Dawn looked happy though. She was smiling in the photo and looking very proud to be his wife. I wondered at the attraction. "He was a silent man, didn't talk much, but he was very caring. He was like a gentle giant and always serious."

I handed the picture back to her. "You made a very handsome couple."

Mary returned with a broom and dustpan and cleaned up the glass. "I wonder what made it fall?"

Detecting a movement out of the corner of my eye, I turned to look and saw a big gray tabby cat coming toward us from the hallway Mary had taken to get the broom. He walked in stealth mode, his tread slow and cautious. Soon as he reached the entrance to the room where we were located, he stopped. Suddenly his back arched and he let out a loud, teeth-baring hiss. In the next instant he was making a mad dash down the hall, moving so fast he didn't make the turn and slid smack into the wall. Without losing any momentum, he scrambled in place, gained traction then disappeared around the corner.

Mary, Adam and Dawn all turned to watch this odd little drama in speechless astonishment.

"What's got into Timmy?" Dawn glanced at Mary. "Maybe you should go check on him." She turned to me as her daughter left the room. "We named our cat Timmy because he was always such a timid little creature. We actually named him Timid but began calling him Timmy and so it seems he fits his name still. He hasn't acted up in days."

"Acted up?" Animals were a great indicator of spirit activity.

Adam went back to his chair and dropped heavily into it. I was amazed the legs didn't shatter at the impact. "That animal is crazy. One minute it's laying there happy as can be, purring away, and the next it's spitting mad and running around the room like its tail is on fire."

Dawn returned to the couch and perched uneasily on the edge of it. "All cats are a little weird. Lord knows what makes them act the way they do."

Too restless to sit, I walked over to the fireplace. "This is quite impressive."

Mary rejoined us, shrugging her shoulders as she did so. "Have no clue where the cat disappeared to." She sank onto the couch next to her mother and heaved a tired sigh. Obviously not wanting to talk about the cat, she waved toward the fireplace. "Back in the day, it was the only thing that heated this place."

It was the perfect opening for me. "Rid says your house has been around since Bucksport was first established."

"Rid? When did you see him?" Dawn's face looked tense and again I wondered if there were some bad feelings between the two families.

"Just before coming here. I stopped to speak to him about the Tenney house and he mentioned that yours was just as old."

"Older," Adam said looking rather proud of the fact. "Our house was one of the first built in this stupid town and it even survived the burning and ransacking the British did during the Revolutionary War."

I remembered reading something about that but I wanted to know what they knew. "The ransacking and burning?"

Dawn pulled a bit of a face and I got a strong feeling this was a long-suffering topic. "My husband was a history buff. He was obsessed with Maine's history but especially Bucksport's and the surrounding towns. He usually shared his knowledge and views of things with the kids." She shot Adam a sharp look. "Not that they cared much."

Adam shrugged in a 'who cares' manner. "Seriously, Mom? That all happened hundreds of years ago. What's it matter now?"

"The past matters, Adam. The past is what formed the life we now live."

Adam scowled, his hands tightening into fists. I had a pretty strong impression, though, that the emotions charging through him were not angry ones. He was doing his best to hold back his frustration. The internal struggle an easy read in his facial expressions. "Well it sure didn't do much for us did it?" he waved a hand around him. "Look at us, about to lose it all. The past has done nothing but bring us to complete ruin." He slumped back in his chair, his face scrunched in a scowl. He glanced at me and said, "We used to be considered a rich family. Back in the past. Now look at us. We have nothing. Our future doesn't look too bright either." He stood abruptly and practically stomped from the room. "Call me when dinner is ready." He disappeared down the same hallway as the cat.

A few seconds later we heard the decisive bang of a door. He didn't quite slam it but his displeasure was evident. We sat in silence for a moment and I glanced at Dawn and Mary, both women were looking at each other and in obvious silent communication. Feeling responsible for steering the conversation toward a topic that upset Adam like that, I returned to the couch and touched Mary's hand in a gesture of apology.

"I'm sorry. I didn't mean to upset him."

Mary gave me a faint smile. "Adam doesn't want to live here in Bucksport. He can't afford to leave because he can't get a job that pays enough to support his life and a savings account. You can't move anywhere if you don't have any money. Besides, he stays because..." Mary stopped in obvious reluctance to continue and Dawn picked up where she left off.

"He feels responsible for me. This house has been in my husband's family since it was built. Passing from son to son to son. Adam thinks he has to stay and carry on the tradition since his brothers have homes of their own."

"Although we're losing the house and it would give him his freedom, he doesn't want that to happen the way it is happening." Mary sighed heavily, looking very tired and worn down. "I love it here. I told him that I'd be more than happy to stay if he wanted to leave but..." Mary's eyes filled with tears. "He wants to find a job and help pay the back taxes and mortgage payments that we owe. But we owe so much, unless he lands a job that pays in six figures, he isn't going to make enough to save the day."

Dawn leaned over and patted her daughter's knee. "We must hold faith that something will happen."

Mary looked at her mother for a long quiet moment. Her expression was quite clear. She felt her mother was holding out hope for something that could never happen. She suddenly sniffed the air and stood. "I better check dinner."

Once she was out of the room, Dawn shook her head as if to dispel the doom and gloom hanging like a thick invisible cloud around us. "I didn't mean for the conversation to turn so bad. I'm sorry."

"Please don't apologize, Dawn. I'm sorry you are going through this. I wish I could help." It did flash through my mind that I had a pretty hefty bank account thanks to my husband's insurance policy and a settlement made on the accident that took his life. But even as I thought it, I knew they wouldn't accept my help and besides, it was too much of a financial risk for me to consider. I felt so helpless just then and I didn't like it one bit. "What did Adam mean that your family lost all your money?"

Dawn waved a dismissive hand. "He's talking way back into the family history. Back to when the Rowans first settled here. They were versatile traders from what I understand, getting their hands on things from the Indians that other settlers needed but couldn't get themselves. Night said that his family was even rumored to do some smuggling during the war. I guess those sort of activities were rampant along the coast of Maine at one time. With his family being connected to the Indians, the Rowans were privy to information and goods not available to the white settlers."

Dawn paused to smile at the memories floating through her mind. "Night's father was always telling us stories about his family. In fact, the one the kids enjoyed most was about one of his ancestors finding a treasure. Unfortunately, the treasure was lost and the family's fortune began to dwindle over time. Honestly, though, I think he told that story because of the excitement it generated in the kids. They were forever wanting to go treasure hunting." Dawn laughed softly, her eyes misting in response to the good memories of times past. She drew in a quick breath and visibly brightened, forcing her sadness away. "Randolph, Night's father, was quite a character, let me tell you. He nearly made it to his ninety-fifth birthday. I wish we'd paid more attention to his stories. I fear the kids have forever lost a lot of information on their family heritage. It's quite sad, isn't it?" Her tears back, she gave a discreet sniff and looked away.

Deciding a subject change was in order, I attempted to return to the topic we were on before Adam's outburst. "Your family name isn't mentioned in the initial listing of families that settled here."

Dawn gave a small nod as her brows arched with derision. "No, of course the Rowans wouldn't have been listed. As I told you, my husband's family is mixed with the Native Americans. His father's ancestors were here long before Buck landed and started staking claim. From what I can remember Randolph and Night telling me, the Rowan name became attached to Bucksport history when one migrated here from Canada and married a local girl who was half Indian and half English." Dawn's brow puckered in thought. "I'm not sure if that means her mother was from England or what. But anyway, I do know that her father was an Indian and so that made her a half-breed. A despicable name back in the day that was given to those of mixed races." Dawn waved a hand about her. "This house was initially built by them. The land coming to us through her family. Successive family members improved upon it over the years of course. I'm not all in the know on architecture but I do know that our home was originally built in the Georgian style and then it underwent a pretty massive reconstruction in the 1850s and is now considered early Italianate."

She glanced around her, the pride and love she felt for her home evident in her sad eyes. "The burning of the town that Adam was referring to was done by the British. They did it to punish the people of Bucksport for their part in the debacle in Castine." Dawn shook her head at the senselessness of it all and continued. "We tried to overtake a fort British troops had built there and drive them from Maine. Although, back then, you know, we were still part of Massachusetts." She shook her head sadly. "We suffered a terrible loss during that battle. Several of the men who participated were from Bucksport. Colonel Buck being one of the officers in charge. The British landed the day after our defeat and burned most of the buildings in town. They pillaged what they wanted and left those who remained with very little." She gave a small shrug, her expression almost apologetic. "More than likely, they didn't want to anger the Indians because they left this house alone." And then, remembering from where I just came, "Rid's house survived the British's retaliation as well."

I'd read about this incident in my research of Bucksport but Dawn seemed as knowledgeable as Rid and I found that admirable. "Your husband taught you well."

Dawn laughed softly even as her expression turned a little sad. I figured she was thinking about her husband and her next words confirmed it. "Night was obsessed with knowing everything there was to know about this area. I'm not sure why." Then, as an afterthought, "He was just as obsessively curious about his Indian heritage."

Adam returned at that moment. His body wasn't quite as tense so he must have worked off most of his frustration. He rubbed his mother's shoulder as he passed her and flopped back down in his chair. He must have been listening in the hallway for his voice was subdued, all his fight gone. "We've been here longer than anyone. You'd think that would count for something. We deserve that respect at least."

"Respect has nothing to do with this, Adam. You cannot replace money with respect and we need money. Lots of it."

Just like that, the tension was back, the air crackling with it. Adam stood and paced the room. I likened him to a great bear looking for something to maul. "Where will we go? When we lose the house, where will we live?" The sound of Mary coming back down the hallway made him turn to face her. He opened his mouth to say something but before he could utter another word the door slammed shut. And not by Adam's hand. Nor any hand that I could see.

Adam's dark eyes widened in disbelief. He turned and looked from his mother, whose back was to the door, and then me. "Did you see that?"

Mary pushed the door open and threw Adam a baleful glare. "Why did you slam the door like that? It nearly hit me in the face."

"I didn't do it!" Adam sliced a hand in my direction. "Ask her, she saw the whole thing."

Dawn stood and eyed her two children with concern. She lifted a hand and began to fiddle with her necklace in a show of nervous tension. It was, I noted, a small crucifix. "Oh dear, I just can't imagine what is happening."

Mary looked at me for confirmation of Adam's claim. I nodded to let her know her brother spoke the truth. Mary sighed heavily, her body deflating with her breath, her shoulders sagging. She gave me a tired smile. "Well, here you go, Tess. This should be right up your alley. We've been thinking for a while now that our house is haunted."

Adam swung around and looked at me, his belligerence gone. "Can you see any ghosts in the room with us?"

Another shiver passed through me. I couldn't see them, but I could feel them. Lots of them. "Have you always had trouble with ghosts here?" I wondered if I was perhaps stirring things up. Somehow the spirit world knew when someone was around that could sense them, hear them. Maybe they were here to communicate with me. The idea made me cringe inside. An unusual reaction to be sure. But I felt a lot of discontent coming from them and I wasn't sure I wanted to invite that into my life.

"It wasn't until after Night died that we started noticing things." Dawn gave a displeased frown. "If he's haunting us, I'm not very happy with him about it. He knows I don't like ghosts."

Adam shook his head. "We noticed things every now and then even before Pop died."

Mary's gaze did not leave mine and I knew she was looking for a sign in my expression that would confirm her question. "Do you think it's my father, Tess?"

If he was here, it wasn't him causing the stir. "He might be here more in a protective mode than anything because I assure you he's not the one shutting doors, scaring cats and breaking pictures."

Dawn moved close to her daughter. "Protective mode? Do we need protecting?"

"It's probable that he is concerned about the situation you are facing. If he is here, and note I said if, he is more than likely lending his support and doing his best to give you strength to get through this." But there was more going on here than a concerned father lurking in spirit with his family during their time of need. I could almost imagine someone shouting at me. I glanced around, eyes narrowed, and tried to pick up where the energy was coming from. The effort was a futile one because it seemed the other spirits surrounding me acted like a block. It was almost suffocating the way they crowded close. Something needed to be done.

"Excuse me a moment." I turned around, closed my eyes and focused in as vivid detail as I could imagine, my protective sphere of light surrounding us, forcing the shadows back. Though my thoughts were strong, the vision was not clear. Even in my imagination, they were a strong force to reckon with. I prayed for help and asked Sheila to join me. As the cobweb sensation swept gently across my face, the room began to lighten up. They were retreating. Thank God. Thank you, Sheila! They didn't go far however, for they hovered just outside the circle of my imaginary light, waiting. I turned to face the three people watching me. They were curious as to what I was doing but were respectful enough to stay quiet and not break my concentration. Once I felt in control of the situation, I smiled at them in an effort to relieve their tension. "I asked them to go and leave us in peace. Whatever they want, I'll communicate with them elsewhere."

Mary stepped close and touched my arm. "Are they our ghosts or did they follow you here?"

"Both I think but not to worry, Mary. They mean you no harm."

Adam pointed to the broken picture frame laying in guilty proof on the coffee table. "Then why break that picture and slam a door in my sister's face?"

"They were simply trying to get our attention. They have it. But I can work with them elsewhere. I don't think it should be here." I was rather fearful that inviting communication with them now would make them stronger and worsen the poltergeist activity that was occurring. This family had enough to deal with and I wasn't going to add a slew of spirits to the mix.

Mary waved a hand toward the hallway and touched her mother's shoulder to indicate she should precede us from the room. "Let's go eat. Dinner is ready."

The dining room was beautiful. Pine wood covered the floor and walls, the ceiling was high and beamed. Large windows looked out toward the river. It really was a nice view despite the hulking mill located nearby. The dining table could easily fit ten people. Mary set four places at one end. The lasagna, salad and garlic bread were already on the table. She and I sat next to each other, her brother and mother across from us. Conversation was stilted at first but after a while we managed to put the thoughts of ghosts and financial worries to the side and instead we discussed my vacation at Sea Willow Haven. They heard of the place and read about it in the papers and they wanted to know whatever I would tell them. Although I was happy to describe the beautiful resort and told them about Nancy and Jack. I didn't want to get into detail about the haunting that took place there. I felt it really wasn't my story to tell.

"It must have been hard to leave. It sounds lovely." Mary pushed her empty plate away and propped an elbow on the table, her chin resting in her hand. "You stayed a whole month?"

I popped the last bite of garlic bread into my mouth, chewed appreciatively and then sank back to relax. I was stuffed. "Yes. I was only going to stay until the end of the month but they talked me into staying through the Fourth of July weekend."

Kade told me the town put on a nice celebration and I shouldn't miss it. As I didn't want to celebrate the holiday with strangers, I happily stayed on a few more days. The cottage I was renting was booked during that time, however, so I had to move up to the main house. Nancy and Jack were kind enough to let me stay with them in their private quarters as their guest. Much as I appreciated the gesture, it became hard for Kade and I to spend much time together those last few days. While staying in the cottage it wasn't a problem because his cottage was right next to mine. Once I became Nancy's and Jack's guest, I didn't feel as free to run off and spend all my time with Kade, even though Nancy did encourage it. As Mary suggested, leaving there was hard. Leaving Kade even harder.

Once I left Bucksport, I would be returning back home to New York. It seemed like an ocean away. The thought made me sad.

"What's wrong, Tess?" Mary touched my arm. "Are you okay?"

Adam gave a smirk. "She left behind a boyfriend."

I glanced at him in surprise. He didn't seem sensitive enough to garner such a thought and I stared at him thoughtfully. Adam shifted uncomfortably beneath my stare. "Girls always look like that when they are mooning over guys." He nodded at Mary. "She looks like that when she's thinking about Daniel."

Mary gave a small gasp of dismay and Dawn sent her son a look of sharp reprimand. "Adam." Her tone was full of warning and Adam chose not to ignore it. Thank God.

He grabbed his plate and utensils. "Sorry, Mary. Dinner was great." He glanced at me and then dropped his gaze to stare at the table. "Sorry I've been such an ass. Seems I'm just pissed off all the time these days." He nodded toward the kitchen. "I'll just leave you women alone and let you visit without my sorry ass hanging around to spoil all the fun."

I stood up and held a hand out to him in entreaty. "There's no need to apologize, Adam. It was really nice to meet you."

Adam reached over and shook my hand briefly. "Same here. Enjoy the rest of your stay in Bucksport. If you figure out that old witch's curse thing, be sure to let us know."

I nodded to let him know that I would do so and he turned and walked from the room.

Dawn sighed tiredly. "Life is just so hard to manage these days. I don't know what's going to become of my children. I hate to even think how difficult the world is going to be for my grandkids. Life just gets harder and harder. Crazier and crazier." She stood and began to gather dishes.

Mary went around the table to her and gave her shoulders a squeeze. "Let me do this, Mom. You look tired, go relax."

I nodded in agreement to that suggestion. "I'll help Mary." And when both women began to protest, I held up a hand. "Please, I want to help. I haven't had any domestic duties for over a month and it's making me crazy."

Dawn looked from Mary to me then gave up the argument. She handed Mary the stack of dishes. "Okay, I'll leave you girls alone to talk. I am a little tired." She came around the table to give me a hug. "It was very nice to meet you, Tess. Please come visit us again. If you do manage to contact our ghosts, please let me know how that went. Promise?"

"I promise to keep you informed." Satisfied with my answer, Dawn gave a nod then left the room.

Mary filled her hands with more dishes. "You don't have to help. Just having your company is nice."

"Nonsense, I'm helping and let's not argue any more about it." I grabbed the remains of the lasagna and the empty basket that had held the garlic bread and followed her to the kitchen. Between the two of us, we managed to clean the table within a couple minutes and then I nodded to the sink. "I'll wash and you can dry. Since I don't know where anything goes, it makes more sense to let you dry and put away."

"I don't feel right having company do our dishes."

I rolled up the sleeves of my sweater. "I'm not company, I'm a friend and friends help friends do dishes."

Laughing at my determination, Mary gave in and handed me the dish soap. "Well then, have at 'er."

It was nice to be doing domestic duties again. I missed maintaining a household and thought how nice it would be to do so again. But then I thought of my empty house and some of my pleasure ebbed away. It was going to be hard to return home. My house was a reminder of a past life I no longer was a part of. And just like that I knew it was time to sell it. Where I'd go and live afterwards, I didn't know. But I wasn't going to stay there. Much as I loved the house, I felt no pleasure in the thought of returning to it. That home had belonged to Mike and me. There was no longer a Mike and me. Feeling a little sad, I dumped out the dishwater and wiped down the sink.

Mary sensed my change in mood and was silent for a moment. Then she said quietly, "I miss my family too."

I turned to look at her and saw that her eyes were filled with tears. I wiped my hands on her dishrag then gave her a hug. "I'm sorry, Mary."

Mary let her head fall on my shoulder. She hugged me back then pulled away. "My boys think I'm being too hard on Daniel, their father. And I suppose they are right. I just seem to be so angry all the time and I took it out on him. It wasn't right to do it but I couldn't seem to stop myself."

"Dealing with something we can't accept, it makes us angry and it's only natural to lash out at the ones we love. It's not right and doesn't make much sense but seems to be human nature for us to do it." I took her hand and led her back to the dining room. We sat in the same chairs we sat in during dinner and turned to each other, both of us resting an arm on the table and our heads in our hands. "I was so mad when Mike died that I was angry all the time. I was especially mad at God."

Mary sighed as if her very soul was a weight she couldn't maintain. "I'm just angry at myself."

I grabbed her hand and squeezed it. "The longer you hold onto that anger, the longer it will take to get your life back to where you want it. You have to make peace with yourself, Mary."

"How?" She squeezed my hand back, her tension evident in her hold. "How do I get over stuff that I can't accept happened?"

"You let God in. You have a heart to heart...you and God...and you let the peace in. When you let the peace in, the answers will come to you." I was experiencing happiness again and I felt now it was time to help Mary.

Mary's head hung low, her voice barely above a whisper. "I guess I feel ashamed to talk to God, Tess. I killed a man. I joined the military because I wanted to get out of Bucksport and see the world. I wanted to take advantage of their educational opportunities. I didn't think about the rest of it, what that actually entailed." She looked up at me, her black eyes two deep pools of hurt. "I didn't think about the fact that I might go to war and that we'd kill people."

Thoughts of Kade crowded my mind. An ex-Marine, Kade didn't question his military actions, but he did have a hard time dealing with the deaths of his friends and the troops that served with him. Sighing heavily but silently, I took both of

Mary's hands into mine and gave them a gentle tug to gain and hold her attention. "Listen to me. We didn't make the rules of this world. Most all of them were in place before we were even born. I don't know why we have to have such things as wars, street gangs, anger, hatred, hostility and all the rest of it but the fact is, it exists and we have to deal with it. Life is chaotic. It's good and it's bad and somehow we must try to survive it all. War is a fact of life in this world we live in. Our military is an honorable one. You may have joined to travel and for the educational benefits but you also answered the call when sent to defend what we stand for. Freedom, liberty, and the right to live with both."

Mary gave a small shake of her head. "We aren't defending our freedom and liberties when we are fighting wars on foreign soil, Tess."

"In a way we are, though. You think they would stop there if no one opposed them? Greed begets greed. Besides, we are fighting for the freedom of the people, the non-militia, from tyranny. We are the stronger people and it is up to the strong to defend the weak. You were there to protect them from terrorist factions. Maybe someday we can get past this having to kill to overcome but until that happens, that is what we have to do. You said it yourself, if you hadn't killed him, he would have killed your entire unit. You weren't there to seek and destroy, he was. His intention got him killed and now he has to deal with his actions in the afterlife."

"But let's say I didn't shoot him and we all died, would our death not be more honorable?"

"His intentions, Mary, were not honorable. He would take those dishonorable intentions and go kill more and more and more. When would he stop? He wouldn't until everyone who opposed him was dead. That is the law of our chaotic world. Is there honor in letting someone destroy and destroy and destroy? If we stopped fighting them, they would come here and wipe us all from the face of the earth. Your family, your children...everyone would die or live in misery under their rule."

Mary closed her eyes and thought about that for a long moment. Finally, I felt the tension in her hands ebb away and her bruising grip relaxed. "It's such a shame it has to be this way."

"It is. I wish for world peace the same as you, Mary, but letting the evil ones win is not going to give us world peace. Refusing to fight the evil is only going to spread it and until we can come up with a better way to deal with it, it's what must be done. It all gets sorted out in the afterlife." I pulled Mary into a hug and turned to whisper in her ear. "Thank you for defending our honorable country and for protecting those people in whose country the terrorists reign supreme. Thank you for being brave enough to shoot that man."

Mary began to sob softly. "Oh, God, Tess, it's just so sad."

"It is and now we will pray for his soul. You released his body from creating further torment, and now we will pray that he won't come back to do it again."

Mary pulled away and looked at me in confusion. "Come back?"

I gave her a small smile thinking maybe I should have just left that well enough alone. "You've heard of reincarnation, Mary?" At her nod, I went on to explain. "My belief is that reincarnation keeps the majority of the entire population from going straight to hell. Let's face it, most of us never achieve all the requirements for entry into heaven. I don't consider myself a terrible person but I'm no Jesus or Buddha or Krishna or ..." I waved a vague hand, "whoever else is considered an uber-great human above the flaws of sin."

Mary wiped her drying tears and smiled. "I haven't given it much thought but it's nice to think we might get another chance to become a better person. In any case, I do feel a little better and I will take up your advice and have a chat with God. Thank you."

We both stood up and I waved toward the living room. "I really should get going. A friend of mine is coming to stay at the B&B for a few days and I suspect he'll be here bright and early."

One of Mary's dark brows arched. "He?"

Smiling, I linked arms with her and we walked together down the hall, through the living room and toward the entry hall. "Yes, he. His name is Kade Sinclair. He's a painter, a very gifted artist. If you haven't seen his landscapes, you should, they are beautiful. I met him at Sea Willow Haven."

Mary patted my arm. "I hope it works out for you, Tess."

Laughing softly, I nudged her shoulder with mine. "Me too." We stopped in the entryway. "Is there no chance for things to work out between you and your husband?"

Mary's face tightened for a moment but then her eyes turned thoughtful. "I hadn't thought so but who knows. As you said, I haven't been willing to talk to Daniel because I didn't feel worthy but now...we'll see." She gave me another hug, holding tight for just a moment then stepping away. "Thank you, Tess."

"You're welcome. Thanks again for a delicious dinner." I stepped out onto the porch and turned to give her a quick wave before heading off to my car. It was quite dark, the moon a sliver in the sky. As I slipped into the front seat of my car and started the engine, I had the distinct impression that I was not going to be alone as I headed for the B&B. And I wasn't sure what to do about it.

CHAPTER ELEVEN

I drove all the way back to the B&B with the skin on my back crawling with the knowledge that many bodiless figures were following me home. They nearly bore holes right through me their focus was so intense and it was unnerving to say the least. I held tight to the vision of light surrounding my car and they hovered close in the dark edges beyond it. Dealing with one or two ghosts, that I could handle, having a whole league of them chasing me around was not quite my thing. I didn't like it. I didn't like that I didn't know what they wanted. Who the heck were they? Why so many? And just what were they so unhappy about?

I pulled into the same parking spot I'd had earlier. Thankfully, there weren't any houses on this section of the street so parking after business hours was not hard to get. Even better, it wasn't a metered parking spot so I could stay there as long as I wanted. I stepped out of my car then turned to look around. I couldn't see them, of course, but they were there. My imagination pictured hundreds of them standing like silent zombies in the street around me. It was a fanciful thought and I was sure that I was exaggerating. Surely there weren't that many?

Making my voice firm, I addressed the night air. "I'm looking for the witch that cursed that stone. That's it." Then, thinking my little pronouncement would look strange to onlookers, I glanced around to see if anyone else was about. I was quite alone. Or so it seemed, naturally, I was not. I had lots of company. All of it, for the moment, unwanted. "Sheila I need you!" After waiting a moment to see if the familiar sensation of cobwebs would brush across my face, and it did not, I again addressed her, "Keep them away from me, Sheila. Please and thank you."

Although I didn't feel her signature cobweb sensation, I did feel that she was near and some of my unease let up. I was safe for now. I could feel it in my all-knowing soul. It was the personality after all, the one presently inhabiting my body and better known as Tess Schafer, that didn't have a clue. A sad fact that, and one I was trying to overcome. Wishing I was better connected to my soul body, I walked up the short paved path to Barbara's B&B. The knowledge that they were all there behind me, hovering close, watching, made quivers shiver up and down my spine. I refused to turn around. I wasn't going to play the 'I feel someone right behind me' game.

It was a relief to open the door and enter the warm, glowing interior of the B&B. Barbara was in the sitting room reading a book. She glanced up as I entered but before she could give me a greeting, Max began growling low in his throat. He then bared his little teeth and went instantly on alert, his eyes latching onto something just beyond my right shoulder. The unexpectedness of it made me freeze for an instant but as I didn't want Barbara to get frightened nor give the spirit stalking me the satisfaction of rattling my nerves, I turned slowly and shut the door. It was a relief to see it hadn't materialized into visual form. I wasn't sure I could handle a face-to-face right now. Especially if it was covered in red.

I turned back around and took a cautious step toward Barbara, as I did so Max charged halfway toward me, both sets of teeth bared, the skin around them stretched back in a nasty snarl. Whoever was following me, Max didn't like him. I stepped to the side to see what Max would do. He did not follow my action. His eyes remained focused to my right.

Her face paling with concern, Barbara came to her feet and stood rooted to the floor. Her eyes wide with fright, she looked from her dog to me then back to her dog. "Max! Stop." When his racket didn't let up, Barbara looked back at me and shrugged helplessly. "I don't understand what's wrong with him."

Goosebumps broke out on my arms and I was glad to be wearing a sweater so Barbara wouldn't notice. But then her eyes widened with disbelief and she lifted a shaking hand to point at me. My heart thumped hard and painfully. What was she pointing at? And then I knew. She could see my breath frosting in the air. It didn't dissipate until it traveled beyond the frigid cold now surrounding me. Though I was unable to control my shivering, I clenched my teeth to keep them from chattering and fought to tamper my annoyance. Had I not told them to stay outside?

As I scrambled for ideas on how to handle this situation, Barbara took a couple of steps toward me. Max was a good three feet away from me at this point with hackles raised, teeth bared and his growls low in his throat. His eyes didn't look frightened however. No, Max was in full defensive mode and when Barbara took a step passed him, his protective instincts kicked in. He charged ahead of her but didn't get far. As soon as he hit the mass of cold air circling me, he let out a yip of surprise, his barking growls grinding to an abrupt halt. Instantly he dropped to a crouch and rolled over in submission. Barbara stopped her advance the moment her dog charged past her and when he dropped to the floor, she crouched down next to him. Although she intended to offer comfort to poor little Max, her hand halted above his quivering body and hovered there.

"My God, it's cold as ice!" Barbara glanced up at me, her pale face scrunched with near terror. Her own breath came out in spurts of foggy puffs and noting this, she gave another sound of distress. "What on earth is going on?"

I turned to my right in order to face whatever entity had followed me inside and closed my eyes to focus. The protective light I tried to imagine into being wasn't working. A dark swirling mass, agitated and determined to communicate refused to let me force its retreat. A little concerned about the unknown factors here and wondering whether I could trust this situation not to get out of hand, I decided to try and communicate.

As soon as my resistance to it caved, the bitter cold was gone. Max scrambled to his feet and scurried behind Barbara's chair. He peeked out just enough to keep an eye on us but stayed put and didn't make another sound. Barbara stood and took a step back. I didn't turn to look at her but spoke in as calm a voice as I could muster. I knew that if I appeared unnerved, she'd be much more so.

"It's okay, Barbara, someone wants to speak with me. Don't be afraid. Just give us a moment." I heard her retreat though she hovered protectively near. Or as near as she dared. I closed my eyes to better concentrate. "Okay," I said quietly, "What do you want? Who are you?" Nothing happened. I got no message, no sound, no visions, nothing. "You followed me here. What do you want?" Frustrated, I opened my eyes and found a huge bare chest, smooth of hair and covered in blood, a few mere inches from my face. My mouth dropped open in silent disbelief as my eyes moved slowly up and fixed onto the blood-covered face of the big man I'd seen at the Tenney house. It was so unexpected and far too real for my liking. He seemed as solid as anything else in the room and the shock of it frightened me. I took a hasty step back, tripping over the rug Max ruffled up during his charge and falling flat on my butt. Thankfully, the carpet cushioned the bone-jarring impact. During the whole thing, I didn't take my eyes off him. I didn't dare.

He had to be well over six feet tall considering his chest was at my eye level. He was massive, all muscle and power. And now I could see that he was completely covered in what looked like blood. The man had to have taken a bath in it. Not one part of his skin was visible beneath the red stuff covering him. His hair, the only thing not covered in red, was black as a moonless night. It was quite long and pulled into a high, tight ponytail on the back of his head. On any other man it would look ridiculous, not so on him. His arms, which were folded across his chest, would make Hercules look small in comparison. He stood like a silent, unmovable sentinel. At a distinct disadvantage, prone at his feet as I was, I remained as silent and still as he. The difference was I couldn't have moved if I wanted to. The only part of my body that seemed capable of movement was my eyes but I kept them firmly locked with his. Since he was looking down at me, the whites of his eyes didn't stand out in stark contrast to the red coloring like they did when I saw him at the Tenney house.

My scrambled brain tried to think though I had to work at it. Was it blood or paint? One thing for certain, he was definitely an Indian. As our gazes held, I had an uneasy feeling those black eyes of his were probing deep into my soul. What did he see there?

His arms dropped to his sides and that somehow helped me break eye contact, leaving me free to look him over. Every freaking inch of him was red, to include the form-fitting pants clinging to his muscular thighs and the boots laced half-way up his calves. The massiveness of him was overwhelming. What on earth did he do to get into that kind of shape? Surely they didn't conduct weight training back in his time? What would they lift? Logs? Boulders? Why was I thinking such mundane things when the strangest entity I'd ever come across was standing there looking at me? Again I took note of the red stuff covering him. Whatever it was it didn't appear to be wet. Now that I was free to look, it seemed that it was more like a stain. Did blood dry a bright red like that? I didn't think so, but I wasn't certain of much at the moment.

Now that I didn't feel so threatened, I calmed enough to really look him over. He wore a necklace around his trunk of a neck. The beads were red, which is why I hadn't noticed it at first. They were about the size of shelled peanuts. Several more strands of shiny black beads were wrapped around his wrists. They were much smaller, more the size of peas. A clear stone, flat and shaped in a triangle hung just above his forehead. I could now see that the dark strand it hung from was woven into his hair. It was hard to see at first. As I wasn't a rock expert, I couldn't be sure what sort of stone it was, a smoky quartz perhaps?

"Who are you?" I wasn't sure if I spoke the words out loud. Nothing felt like it was functioning quite right. I couldn't move, I could barely breathe. My heart was pounding out of control.

His response was to lift his hands and clap them together. The sound they made was like a booming crack of thunder. It made my teeth rattle and my ears ring. And then he was gone and Max was barking again. I turned my head to see that Barbara now stood next to her chair, having retreated as far as she could possibly go. She stared at me with wide-eyed fright, her mouth open in silent disbelief. She was clutching her necklace so tight her knuckles were white.

I glanced away and closed my eyes for a moment. I had to gather my wits and then somehow ease Barbara's fear. For the life of me, I couldn't say what just happened. The booming sound his hands made when he clapped them together was still ringing in my ears. Had Barbara heard it too? Max had.

Realizing that I was still sprawled on the floor, I scrambled to my feet and stalled for time by straightening out my clothes. Finally I turned to Barbara. She must have realized that whatever it was that just happened was now over for her knuckles weren't white any longer. Her hand, however, still clutched the crucifix dangling around her neck. "Did you see anything?"

Barbara shook her head. "No. But I heard that...that sound. It was like a clap of thunder." She glanced around toward the window. "Do you think anyone else heard it?"

"I have no idea. But it was loud."

"What was it?"

"You didn't see anything at all?" It was hard to believe she didn't see him as I had for he appeared as solid as the two of us. His image so clear, I was able to look him over at leisure, inspect him carefully. To think he could appear to me as clear as day, as solid as everything else in this room and yet Barbara hadn't seen him, was inconceivable to me. Did I imagine it all? If I did, what an imagination!

"I saw our breath. It was like a freezer in here." Then, before I could respond, she waved her hand to cancel out what she just said. "Well, it was cold over by you. When I stepped back, it wasn't cold anymore." She looked down at Max who was now sitting on his back haunches next to her feet, his nose in the air sniffing constantly. His ears were perked up and twitching. He wasn't quite sure our specter had left the building and was keeping his senses on full alert. "Max saw something." Barbara looked up, the lines in her face looking deeper than they had before. "You saw something too. What was it?"

I waved a hand toward the chairs. "Could we sit, Barbara? I really feel like I need to sit down."

Barbara nodded toward the chair next to hers then plopped down in her own as if her legs had suddenly given out on her. "I'm sorry, dear, of course we should sit." She glanced behind me. "It is really gone?"

I sank down into the chair with a grateful sigh and allowed myself to relax against the cushions. My bones felt like they had just turned to Jello. That encounter completely sapped me of energy. "It was the bl ... red-faced guy from the Tenney house."

"The Indian? Is he going to haunt me now?" Barbara's face paled even more than it already was. I worried she might pass out.

"No. He was here to give me a message. He's gone and I assure you, he's not going to hang out here at your inn."

"I should hope not. Poor Max couldn't handle that, not at all."

Max? I think she came out of this worse than he did but I didn't say anything. "I felt him following me. He was at Mary's house too." But not Rid's I noted to myself.

"What was his message?"

I pulled a "beats the heck out of me" face and shrugged my shoulders. "He didn't say anything. The loud noise you heard happened when he clapped his hands together. That's when he disappeared."

"But you said he was here to give you a message. If he didn't give you a message, then he will be back!" Barbara began fiddling with her crucifix again.

"Barbara, he wants my attention. I'm not sure why but I'll figure it out." I hoped. "In any case, he isn't dangerous."

"But why did Max react to him that way? I've never seen him snarl like that."

"He's a big man and he's powerful. By that, I mean his energy is strong. Max was reacting to the strength of his energy. It's rather overwhelming. Max took it as a threat."

"Why did Max go down on his back like that when he got close to you?"

"He was submitting to the energy. He recognized that the spirit was the Alpha Male and he bowed to it."

"Alpha Male?"

Maybe I used to watch too much of the Dog Whisperer back in the day when I was first training Tootsie. "The leader in a dog pack is called the Alpha Male. Dogs respond to the strongest energy that's around them. You are his Alpha Male right now. Gender has nothing to do with it when it comes to humans. In a dog pack, it's usually a male that leads. But as I was saying, you are in charge of him and he accepts your authority. He was protecting you from an unknown energy when the spirit came in the room with me. When Max got close to it, though, he recognized that the spirit was the stronger person in the room and he bowed to it."

"So it wasn't trying to hurt Max?"

"No. I don't even know if he realized Max was even here. He kept his gaze fixed on me the whole time. He didn't move in a threatening manner. I don't know what that loud clap was all about. Maybe he was trying to show me how powerful he is. I don't know, Barbara, but I hope to find out. I'm sorry it happened. I tried to make him stay outside." No way was I going to tell her that there was a whole league of spirits just beyond her door. I could still feel their presence. They expected something from me. But what? Was it because of the beads and the stone? My finding them might have got their attention. What was my keeping them going to do?

Barbara continued to fiddle with her crucifix, her expression troubled. "You said it was the man from the Tenney house. Now that you've seen him again, do you still think he's an Indian? Do you still feel that way now that you've seen him again?"

"Yes. He was covered in a red stain of some sort."

Barbara's brows lifted in interest. "So you think he was a Red Paint Indian?"

"I want to say yes but that makes no sense." I was really going to have to mull over this a lot more. Why would an Indian from a tribe that went extinct thousands of years ago suddenly start haunting me? Since he showed up before the beads were in my possession, I knew they couldn't be the reason he was bothering me. Besides, I truly believe he meant for me to discover them. But why? "Maybe he isn't a Red Paint Indian. Maybe he's from a tribe that copied that particular trait."

"Did he have any other marks on him?"

"No. But he was wearing a necklace made of red beads and he was wearing several beaded chains around both wrists. The chains were made of very small black beads. He had a clear stone, like a quartz crystal, shaped like a triangle here." I pointed to the center of my forehead just below the hairline.

"It was held there by a thread that was woven into his hair, which by the way, was the only thing on him not covered in red. It was black and pulled up in a ponytail." I yanked my hair up, pulling it near the top back of my head to demonstrate. "Rather strange place for a man to have a ponytail don't you think?"

Barbara looked fascinated. Scared too, but mostly fascinated. "What was he wearing?"

"Pants of some sort. They fit like a second skin and were as red as he was. He wore boots that laced almost up to his knees. They were form-fitting as well."

"I wonder why I couldn't see him? Was he hazy like a ghost?"

"No. He looked as solid as you and me. That's why I thought maybe you could see him."

"I'm thinking I'm glad I didn't." Barbara fell back against her chair. She looked very tired all of a sudden. "I think I would have fainted dead away if I'd seen him." Then she straightened up, looking at me with concern. "He didn't push you did he?"

"No. I was startled to see him looking so real and standing so close. I took a step back and tripped over the rug."

"Are you okay?"

"I'm fine." A yawn escaped me at that moment and Barbara stood up. "We should get some rest. You have your young man coming tomorrow and you've had quite the day. I wanted to hear how your visit went with Rid and with Dawn's family but we'll talk tomorrow."

Nodding in agreement with the plan, I stood as well and followed her toward the stairs. Since Barbara's room was on the first floor, she paused at the foot of the stairs to give me a hug. "We'll be okay tonight then?"

"We'll be okay. He's not dangerous, Barbara. But in any case, he's gone." She nodded acceptance of my assurance and smiled for the first time since I stepped through the door. "Try and have a good night then, dear."

"I will, Barbara, thank you." I started up the stairs then stopped. "Kade said he'd be here early. If I know him it will be near the crack of dawn and…"

Barbara raised a hand to stop me from saying anything further. "No worries, Tess. As I told you earlier, he can come anytime he wants. If he's early enough, he can have breakfast with us." She smiled like she hoped that was the case then added, "Ted is going to have breakfast with us before he heads out. His plane leaves at ten so I told him I'd have breakfast ready by seven."

Ted! I'd forgotten all about him. "Speaking of Ted, where is he tonight?" Surely if he'd been in his room, he would have come out when Max started all that racket.

"He said he'd be in late. One of his associates flew in at the Bangor airport this afternoon. Ted said they had a lot of paperwork to prepare for tomorrow morning." She looked excited. "The associate is here to close the deal on the Tenney house. They are going to buy it and I'm so happy about that." And then she smiled as the tension from the encounter we'd just gone through gave way to new thoughts. "The people here in this town will be glad to see it restored and in use again."

"That's wonderful, Barbara. I'm glad. It looks like it can be a grand house."

"Yes, well, let's hope it isn't chock full of ghosts. Especially big red ones that clap so loud it sounds like thunder!" We both laughed at that, relieving our stress. I waved a hand and trotted up the stairs. It was getting late, I was tired and drained, and I couldn't wait for tomorrow to arrive. Kade would be here in the morning. It felt like I hadn't seen him in ages. Two whole days. If two days felt so long, what was it going to be like when I went back to New York? My insides cringed at the thought and I pushed it from my mind. I didn't want to think about that right now. All I wanted was to enjoy the time we did have together. I had so much to tell him. Hopefully, between the two of us, we would come up with a good plan to solve this bizarre mystery. It seemed to be so much more than a cursed tombstone now. But what? Whatever it was, I had a very strong feeling it was going to be a doozy.

CHAPTER TWELVE

Although I had a lot to think about and mull over, I found I could hardly keep my eyes open when I finally fell into bed. I put my lethargy down to the strange encounter with the red man. I didn't know what to call him at this point. Maybe Kade could help me come up with a good name.

I had an uneasy feeling my dreams would be plagued with bizarre images throughout the night and I wasn't far off that prediction. I dreamed I was a bird soaring high over the land. Then I dove in the ocean and immediately merged with the water. As I flowed toward shore, I felt a rush of emotion so exhilarating I could barely contain it. I wanted to shoot like a geyser into the air but instead, I washed upon the beach and became one with it and the entire Earth. Solid and invincible, I felt sturdy and sure and nourishing. The wonder and awe of being part of everything was beyond description and before I could even try to put it into words, I began to shrink and burrow into the ground, deep, deep down until I became a tiny pod and sprouted, growing with a rush into a tree and bursting into the world of the sun with relish and vigor. The wind wrapped around me like a loving embrace and I suddenly was part of it. Not solid anymore and yet just as significant as when I was the water and the sand. I loved the freedom of movement and knew that I was invincible. A feeling like that took all concerns and fears away. With so much love around us, what was there to worry over? It truly was the most unusual dream I'd ever had and eerily similar to my meditation from the day before. Much as I loved the dream and the feelings it invoked, the entire experience wore me out.

I startled awake the instant my conscious brain suddenly remembered something important. The fact my room was bright with early morning sunlight made all my sleepiness and lethargy vanish with alarm. It was my intention to rise extra early so I would be showered, dressed, and ready when Kade arrived. A glance at my bedside clock told me I missed the boat on that ambitious plan. It was fifteen minutes to seven. Well, it wasn't too awfully late and at least I hadn't missed breakfast.

But then my heart started pounding with the realization that something was fundamentally different. There was a stirring of excitement in the air that made me quicken with a rush of adrenalin. At first I thought it was the aftermath of my strange dreams that had me feeling that way but then I knew it wasn't that. The prickling of my skin, like excited little zips of energy told me something important to my waking life was stirring up the stratosphere. I sat up and listened intently to the sounds around me then my pounding heart began to skip and race. Kade!

The faint sounds of voices, one lighter and one deeper, told me he had arrived already and was talking to Barbara. Of course I could be wrong and it might be Ted but the low timber of the male voice was unmistakable. It was Kade. I jumped out of bed and ran to my door, cracking it open just a tad to better listen. A soft masculine laugh floated up the stairs, followed closely by Barbara's high-pitched chuckle. I pressed my forehead to the door for a moment and closed my eyes. It was so damned nice to hear his voice and have him near again. Then I lifted my head with sudden impatience and shut the door quietly. What was I doing standing around?

I raced to the dresser and pulled open drawers. What to wear? Why hadn't I figured this out the night before? I pawed through my clothes, finally choosing a pair of snug fitting jean shorts and a yellow v-necked t-shirt with pretty embroidered designs on it. I wanted to look casual but nice and I knew Kade liked me in shorts. He told me I had nice legs and should show them off more often. Was it so bad to want to do that now, if only to please him? No, of course not.

I took a record-breaking shower and hastily dried my hair. Kade loved its length and although it usually got in my way when left to hang free, I didn't pull it back into a ponytail or pin it on the top of my head like I usually liked to do. After spritzing on a light floral scent that Kade particularly liked, I stepped back to survey myself in the mirror. My eyes looked especially blue today and I figured it was anticipation making them so bright. Not one to wear much make-up, I added a touch of eye-liner and some lip gloss then headed for the door.

It was quite the task to force a sedate descent down the stairs. My heart was nearly pounding out of my chest by the time I reached the bottom step. And then I saw him and came to a stop, completely arrested by the sight of him sprawled in the chair next to Barbara. He was facing me but looking at her. She was chatting about Max who was sitting beside Kade's chair enjoying his absent-minded chin scratches. Honestly, the man looked impossibly handsome and I drew in an appreciative breath. He was wearing tan khaki shorts and a black t-shirt. I loved how it stretched over his broad chest and accentuated his firm build. He wasn't beefed up like a weight-lifter (a fact for which I was glad) but he was solid and muscled and in great physical shape. It was nice to have a bit of time to admire him without his knowledge. Then he glanced over and our eyes met.

Kade had very deep blue eyes and I loved their appreciative intensity. His eyelashes were dark and long and half lowered. I found that particularly sexy. After an intense moment of mutual appreciation, his gaze left mine to sweep slowly down my body and back up again. The very air went still as anticipation built toward our next move.

Giving a lop-sided smile that made my stomach flip about crazily, Kade stood and started across the room toward me. Since I stood at the low end of average height (five feet four inches), his six foot frame was just right for me. The closer he got, the less I could breathe. And then his bone-melting scent wrapped around my senses. The faint musk of his cologne mixed with his body chemistry in so tantalizing a way that he oozed clean, sexy-as-sin masculinity. I wanted to close my eyes and breathe him in but I couldn't bring myself to break the hold his intent gaze held on me.

"Hi, Tess. It's good to see you again." His deep voice lowered to a soft rumble and it sent shivers through my entire body.

"It's good to see you, too, Kade." Those beautiful eyes of his narrowed in response to my hoarse reply (it was a wonder I could even talk) and then he was pulling me into his arms for a full-bodied hug and I closed my eyes to enjoy the contact. God, but he felt good. I buried my nose in his neck and took in a deep, quiet breath. Kade's head dropped to my hair.

"You smell good." He whispered the words next to my ear and a hot shiver raced down my spine.

I pulled my head back to look at him. "So do you." We stared at each other for a long moment, drinking each other in, then Barbara made a noise behind us and we pulled apart.

"Well now, you two probably have a lot to talk about. I'll just see about breakfast. Ted needs to be out of here before eight."

Kade turned to face Barbara while I stepped aside to give her a greeting. "Sounds great, Barbara, thank you."

Smiling, Barbara looked from me to Kade and then back to me. Her eyes twinkled with gentle amusement. "I make a pretty decent waffle. Got some fresh strawberries yesterday. How about we have waffles with strawberries and homemade cream?"

"Barbara, you'll never get rid of me if you feed me too well." Kade motioned for me to come into the sitting room and have a seat. He nodded to the coffee carafe sitting on the table between the two chairs he and Barbara were occupying. "She brought an extra cup for you."

While I busied myself in preparing a cup of coffee, Barbara lingered nearby. "Kade is going to paint me a picture while he's here, Tess. Isn't that wonderful?"

I glanced at Kade and he nodded to confirm her announcement. The pleasant thought raced through my mind that it would take him a few days to do that. So, maybe I'd have him for longer than I thought. Good. "That's very nice, Barbara. You are a lucky woman. Kade's paintings are superb."

"He's going to paint a picture of the new bridge that extends from Verona to Prospect and get Fort Knox in there as well. I'm going to hang it above the front desk for everyone to see."

Barbara looked quite excited. And so she should. Kade was in high demand, his paintings drawing large commissions. I thought it very nice of him to take on Barbara's request. I know he was looking forward to a bit of a break and now it seemed he wouldn't be getting one. Hopefully, it wouldn't take up too much of his time. It was a selfish thought but I was being honest. I missed him and the idea of having him to myself for a few days had me tied up in excited knots. "Well, I'll have to take you for a walk along the river so you can figure out the best viewpoint."

Barbara touched my arm to regain my attention. "I told him about our visitor last night." She looked at me with a touch of concern that perhaps I might not be happy about that. I gave her a smiling nod to let her know she was not to worry.

"Yes, sounds like you had quite the day yesterday. I can't wait to hear all about it." Kade poured himself another cup of coffee and eyed me over the rim of his cup as he took a cautious sip. "I want to hear all the details."

Barbara gave my shoulder a pat. "I'll let you two talk and will just go get that breakfast. Ted is packing up but should be joining us in a few."

I sat in the chair opposite Kade and smiled at him. It was so good to see him again. My eyes drifted up to his dark chestnut hair. He kept it short but not as short as it was when he was in the Marines. I loved that it was starting to grow out a bit. It flopped down across his forehead giving him a youthful look. Not that thirty-five was old. He was in prime shape despite the injuries he suffered in the bomb explosion that ended his military career. Although he endured painful spasms in his legs every now and then, Kade didn't let that stop him from staying active. He took long walks and worked out regularly. He enjoyed racquetball and tennis as well but participating in those activities usually brought on spasms. He was thinking about taking up bicycling for he thought it might help strengthen the muscles in his legs but had yet to do so.

"What are you thinking about?" Kade's quiet question brought me out of my reverie.

"You." Somehow I managed to throttle back my smile for I felt like I was going to start looking like a grinning idiot if I kept it up. Then he smiled back at me and I couldn't stop from returning it full force. He made me feel so good it was hard not to let that show all over my face. His eyes dropped down to my mouth, his lids lowering in that sexy way of his and my heart did a little flip as a prickle of heat spread across my face. I took a sip of my coffee to hide my reaction and over did it a tad as a dribble of it slid down my chin. Embarrassed, I wiped it away and tried to pretend I didn't notice his amused grin.

"Tell me about yesterday."

Yes, I'd do that and stop this silliness of acting like a teenage girl in the throes of her first crush. I told him about my visit with Rid and our discussion about the beads belonging to an Indian shaman. Kade listened thoughtfully and indicated he couldn't wait to see the beads himself. We then discussed the fact that the red-faced guy was an Indian though I had no idea from which tribe he hailed. Kade agreed that it didn't make sense for him to be a Red Paint Indian because they had been extinct for so long and wondered, as I did, if any of their kind had integrated with another tribe. "We need to come up with a name for him, Kade. I've a feeling I haven't seen the last of him and I hate referring to him as the big-red-faced-guy."

Kade gave me a lop-sided grin that made my heart knock around like an overexcited jumping bean and said, "How about we call him Red? Seems fitting."

I nodded. "Red it is." Before I could launch into my story about my visit with the Rowans, Ted came out of his room and made his way toward us.

"Morning, Tess." He gave me a friendly smile as I stood to greet him and turned his attention to Kade when he stepped forward to shake his hand.

"Kade Sinclair. Nice to meet you. Tess has been telling me about your adventures."

Ted shook Kade's hand then nodded toward the coffee carafe. "Any left?"

Barbara must have heard his arrival because she came up behind him with a fresh carafe of coffee and a full cup. "Here you go, Ted. Waffles will be ready in about five minutes." She turned about and bustled back out of the room.

Ted sat in the chair Barbara usually sat in and looked at me. "Speaking of adventures, any more ghost sightings?"

"Yes actually. The one that showed me that box of beads, well he was here last night."

Ted lifted a disbelieving brow. "No way. Why did he come here?"

I shrugged in response. "Just wants my attention I think. Though why he needs it, I don't know."

"We'll figure it out," Kade said, giving me a reassuring wink.

Ted gave us a knowing look and seemed to find our interaction amusing. He glanced at Kade speculatively and I knew he was curious as to Kade's thoughts on my talking to dead people. "So she told you about our run in with him at the Tenney house?"

"Yes she did. I haven't seen the box you found yet but I'm looking forward to checking it out. I haven't ever seen any homemade Indian beads before. The fact they are several hundred years old is pretty awesome."

"Did Rid tell you to keep them?" Ted finished off his coffee and poured another cup.

"Yes he did."

Barbara appeared in the doorway to the dining room. "Breakfast is ready."

In no time at all, we were enjoying Barbara's delicious waffles smothered in strawberries and cream and talking about the future plans for the Tenney house. It was going to be another up-scale inn that would also have a large open room to rent for special occasions such as weddings and conferences. "Always people coming to Maine. Artists flock here in all seasons. We are thinking of starting a yearly convention."

"Really?" I glanced at Kade. "Well there you go, Kade. You could be the first to sign up."

Ted's glance sharpened with interest. "Are you an artist?"

"You haven't heard of Kade Sinclair?" Barbara asked. She looked like she couldn't believe such a thing and I had to hide my smile.

Ted gave a thoughtful frown, thinking. "I'm not really into the arts all that much." And then he added quickly, "Not that I don't appreciate art. I do. But I don't follow the news about it or anything."

"He paints beautiful landscapes." I looked at Kade and felt such a wealth of pride for him that it brought tears to my eyes.

He was a very gifted man and I loved his creations. "Matter of fact, Barbara has commissioned him to paint a picture of the new bridge and the fort across the river."

"You should give me your business card, Kade, and we'll contact you if we ever put it all together. We need to buy the building first and conduct some extensive renovations so it might be awhile."

We continued to discuss the Tenney house for a bit longer and then Ted glanced at his watch. "Hey look, I'm going over there to get a few more pictures before I head out. You guys want to come with me?" He looked at Kade and grinned. "Maybe you'll have your own encounter with that ghost."

Kade's dark eyes gleamed with anticipation. "I'd like that very much, Ted, thanks."

"What time is your flight, Ted?" I wondered how much time we'd actually have. I was thinking it wouldn't be much and I didn't want to hold Ted up.

"It was at ten but I switched to a later flight. I'm now leaving at eleven-thirty." He glanced at his watch. "I have about an hour before I have to head to the airport and return my rental car."

Ten minutes later, we were standing in the foyer of the Tenney house. Although it was quite warm outside, it was cool and rather gloomy inside. I gave a small shiver and rubbed my bare arms while wishing I'd thought to put on a sweater. Kade moved close and wrapped an arm around my shoulders.

"You okay?"

A delighted shiver raced from my shoulders to the rest of my body, warming me up instantly. "I'm fine. Let's go upstairs. I'll show you where we found the box of beads."

Ted tagged along with us and snapped pictures as we made our way through the foyer and up the wide staircase. The door to the room we'd come to see was standing wide open. Ted, who was walking behind us, touched my shoulder to get my attention. "I was in here yesterday with Mark, he's one of the financers backing the purchase and flew in yesterday to close the sale. He wanted to see every room and I distinctly remember closing every door and locking them as we left each one. Mark was worried someone would break in and vandalize the place. I told him if vandals were going to break in, locked doors weren't going to deter them but he insisted we secure everything."

The three of us halted halfway down the hall. We stood looking at each other and then Kade grinned as our eyes met and held. He stepped in front of me and grabbed my hand to pull me along with him. "Well then, maybe I'll see my first ghost."

I immediately sent psychic feelers out in an effort to get a reading on the area around us but didn't pick up on anything unusual. I remembered how I'd felt the night before, like there were masses of spirits surrounding me and was somewhat relieved to feel nothing. When we reached the open door, Kade and I stood in the threshold and looked in. Ted peeked between us. The room was lit by the sun pouring through the three large windows. Warmth from their bright rays spilled into the cool interior of the dark hallway. I pulled my hand from Kade's and stepped into the room. "Nothing here." I motioned toward the fireplace. "The box was found over there."

Kade walked with me to the fireplace and crouched low while I showed him the etched arrow in the stone. We both crawled to the fireplace and leaned in while I showed him the small hidden compartment. Kade put his fingers inside the compartment and felt around.

"Just checking to be sure nothing was missed." He pulled his fingers away and the two of us gasped in surprise at the same time.

Kade held up his hand. The pads of his fingers were covered in a reddish stain. Faded to be sure but unmistakably red. He rubbed his fingers together. "Feels like a powder of some sort."

Ted leaned over to look. "Could be rust from the box."

Kade sniffed at it. "Doesn't have that rusty smell."

Ted gave a small shrug. "Maybe it's too old to have a smell anymore."

I shook my head. "It didn't come from the box. I've held it quite a bit and my fingers were not stained from handling it."

"Wonder what it's from?" Kade pulled his car keys from his pocket. His keychain held a small flashlight. He switched it on and we looked carefully at the place where the copper box had been hidden. What looked like specks of dust lined the corners and edges of the rectangular compartment. Kade gently blew on the dusty particles until it made a small reddish colored pile at one end. "Might have been something else was in here and over time it broke down. Ashes to ashes, dust to dust."

"That's what we say for bodies, Kade. This was no body."

He lifted a quizzical brow. "Might have been a body part."

"Ewww." Ted straightened so suddenly that he bumped his head on the mantel and rubbed it vigorously as he stepped back away from the fireplace.

"There are no bone fragments or anything so it can't have been a body part." I crawled backwards out of the fireplace and stood up. "It does make me wonder about the red stuff that covered Big Red."

"Big Red?" Ted took a picture of the fireplace, glanced in the review window to verify it was a good shot, and then turned to take a picture of the rest of the room.

"Kade suggested we call the guy I saw in here Red but I think Big Red suits him better." Even as I spoke, I felt a sudden chill skitter across my skin. Instantly on alert, I turned toward the fireplace half expecting to see Big Red staring at me. Behind me Ted made a choking sound.

"Holy sh...smokes!" Ted grabbed my arm to get my attention. "Look at this picture."

I looked at the review screen and waved for Kade to come see. "Ted got himself a ghost!"

Just to the right of the window furthest from us, Ted's picture captured a dark orb. A large one. Although there was a lot of controversy about orbs, I knew some of them were indeed the energy centers of spirit forms. Lots of people, however, believed they were nothing more than floating dust motes or insects caught in the flash. But Ted's camera did not flash and this orb was too big, too round, and too solid to be anything other than a spirit.

I stepped closer to the window where the orb was captured and put my hand out in front of me. The air temperature was definitely dropping. I stepped closer. It wasn't Big Red, though, for I was beginning to recognize his energy. I remembered sensing someone standing by this window the first time I entered the room yesterday. The energy seemed weak but stately. It was more like a ghostly imprint than a spirit. Residual energy. I closed my eyes and drew in calming breaths. It took some time to push bothersome thoughts away and still the mind chatter but I did eventually accomplish it. Then I waited. As always, I imagined my protective light surrounding me then asked for Sheila's help. Once I felt the light brush of cobwebs skitter lightly across my face, I asked the spirit who just joined us to communicate with me. Done with all my preparations, I stood quietly, focusing my mind on the spot by the window.

After a while, I began to hear voices whispering around me. Lots of them. They weren't spirits, however. Instinctively I knew I was tapping into the energy imprint of a time long past. People were frightened. I could feel their fear. The talk was subdued but full of emotion. It seemed they were having a heated discussion but were keeping their voices low so as to not be overheard. I couldn't make out anything they were saying. One figure began to form in my mind's eye. He was an older man, of medium height, his carriage straight. I sensed an air of calm authority around him. The last time I was in here, I sensed this same energy. On automatic pilot, I walked to the window. A throbbing pain shot up through my leg just as I reached the window and I leaned on the sill to alleviate some of the pressure from my right foot. Absently, I massaged the outside of my thigh in an effort to ease some of the pain and stared with wide-eyed wonder at the view outside.

The paved street was gone. That was the first thing that caught my eye. Mud was everywhere. The few buildings I could see were made of roughly hewn slabs of lumber. They were unpainted and simple in design. I could clearly see the river for there were hardly any buildings obstructing its view. Boats of all sizes dotted the waterway. Several wooden piers jutted out along the riverbank. More boats, different from anything I was familiar with, occupied some of the piers. I knew I was glimpsing into the past and I took in my fill, my eyes darting everywhere in an effort to see as much as I could before the vision cleared. It was moments like this that my gift awed me. How more fortunate could one be than to get a glimpse into the past?

One of my hands gripped the windowsill and as I became aware of this, I realized it was no longer my hand but his. Whoever he was, he was much older than me. His fingers were long and stiff. They were also cold and trembling slightly. Voices whispered behind us, some of them rising to a loud pitch before dropping to low murmurs. Haunting whispers. Though I tried to focus on them and tune in, I couldn't make out what any of them were saying, so I returned my attention to the view outside the window instead. As for those behind me speaking in agitation and fright, to the devil with the lot of them.

My eyes locked on to a boat anchored out in the widest and probably deepest part of the river. It was a long slender ship with two tall masts and complicated rigging. I would be hard pressed to describe more than that as I knew nothing about boats. A sense of pride washed through me as I looked at it and I knew instinctively that it belonged to the man with whom I was currently connected. And then it hit me who he was. In a flash of excitement, I knew, I just knew, I was connected to the energy imprint of Jonathan Buck. And because it was his energy imprint and not his spirit, I also knew I wouldn't be able to communicate with him and that was a bummer, but even so, I was still quite excited. I managed to do what I came here hoping to do and I found immense satisfaction in that.

The sudden flare of alarm that skittered across my back and up my neck made me swing around. Kade and Ted stood a short distance away. They both watched me in silence. Kade must have figured it out that I was in the throes of a vision and signaled Ted to be quiet. The vision gone, I met Kade's concerned gaze and smiled. Before I could speak, however, we heard the loud creak of the foyer door downstairs. Someone was about to join us. Whoever it was, he was quite noisy as he bounded up the stairs. The three of us waited curiously and Ted offered a possible identity.

"It's probably Mark."

The heavy tread of footsteps gradually grew louder as they came our way. Since we couldn't see into the hall from where we were standing, we merely looked toward the door and waited for whomever it was to join us. Although the footsteps came right into the room, we saw no one. Then the door swung shut with a decisive bang. Ted jumped and took a step back toward me.

Kade didn't even hesitate; he walked straight for the door and pulled it open. I could tell he was relieved that it did, in fact, open. I knew how deep that relief probably was. He'd had doors locked on him before. I pushed the thought away. I was not going to revisit what happened to us at Sea Willow Haven. I didn't want it to influence what was happening now.

Although an entity clearly came to the room, I didn't feel that anyone was with us. It was nothing more than a ghostly occurrence then. More energy of a time past recurring automatically because of strong emotion attached to it.

"What just happened? The door shut on its own, but no one is there!" Ted turned and looked at me for an explanation. Then, having a sudden thought, he turned back and took a picture of the open doorway. Kade stood just off to the side of it. Ted glanced at the review window on his camera and gave a sigh of disappointment. "No orbs."

"It was a ghostly event, Ted, not a spirit coming to speak with us. There's nothing here."

"But you had a vision?" Kade asked.

I nodded and turned back to the window. The paved street, busy with traffic, was back. Bummer that. "Yes. I think I connected with Colonel Buck actually."

Ted's eyebrows rose. "Really? I thought you said there weren't any ghosts here?"

"There aren't. I connected with an energy imprint of an event that took place here concerning him."

"What did you see?" Kade crossed the room and joined me at the window. He touched my arm in support, letting me know that he believed me and wanted to hear it all.

"A meeting of some sort was taking place. There were a lot of men in the room. They were quite agitated, very upset. I couldn't make out a thing they were saying but the discussion was heated and full of emotion. I think Colonel Buck was in charge, or at the least, a prominent authority figure. He was quite calm but annoyed with the talk going on around him. I think if he could have, he would have hopped on his boat and sailed away."

"His boat?" Ted stepped back and took a picture of Kade and me. He glanced at the camera's review window and shook his head with disappointment.

"He owned a sloop named Hannah but it was destroyed by the British when they burned and ransacked the town. Since I feel that the time period I tapped into happened after that event, I wonder if he'd built another ship?" I glanced back out the window and marveled at how different the scene was from moments ago.

"Maybe the meeting was about that attack?" Ted suggested.

I shook my head. "I highly doubt it." Filled with restless energy, I began to pace. "I feel pretty strongly that the scene I tapped into occurred long after the British attack."

"But how can you be sure?" Ted persisted.

"Because they wouldn't have had time to come back here to assemble and talk. When the battle in Castine ended, the men involved scattered."

Kade squeezed my arm gently. "Well, you came here to connect with him and you did."

I smiled at his comment. When Kade first learned about my ability to speak with the dead, he hadn't been sold on the idea. Now he took it at face value. He didn't doubt me. But then why should he after everything we'd been through? "I'm getting close. But all the Indian stuff that's coming through is confusing me. They shouldn't have anything to do with that cursed stone."

"Why not?" Ted asked. "Maybe it was an Indian who cursed him."

"I don't think Indians cursed people, Ted."

He waved off my protest. "What about the Medicine Men? Weren't they into all that stuff? Spirits and all that?"

"Being spiritual teachers and healers as they were, I don't think casting curses was part of their job description." Seeing that Ted reddened a bit, I hastily added, "But that doesn't mean they weren't involved in some way. Who knows, maybe the Indians killed the witch?"

"But why would that make Buck's stone carry the curse?" Kade shook his head. "I can't see a correlation."

"What if Buck was expected to protect her?" Ted suggested.

"Why would he be the one to protect her? He was an officer in the military but it was usually the lower ranks that carried out any specific tasks." Kade would know about how the military worked and his argument was sound but something niggled at me. We were on to something. But we didn't have it right. Not yet.

"I need more clues." And we weren't going to be getting them here. I headed for the door. "Are you done with your pictures, Ted?"

Not wanting to be last out of the room, Ted hurried along after me leaving Kade to fall in step behind him. "Yes. Thank you."

Once we were back out on the front porch of the Tenney house, we said our goodbyes to Ted. I reminded him to have his wife call me and after assuring me he would certainly do that, he hurried off. I wondered if I would ever see him again. He was a nice man and his wife sounded like someone I'd like to know. In any case, our meeting had served its purpose. He got me into the Tenney house. Twice.

Kade looked at me with a lifted dark brow. "What now?"

I reached for his hand. "Let's walk to the cemetery so you can see the stone for yourself."

We walked at a leisurely pace along the sidewalk. It felt nice to be holding his hand and to be close to him again. As we walked, Kade told me about the painting he'd just finished and filled me in on the happenings at Sea Willow Haven. Nancy and Jack were pretty well booked solid for the rest of the year. I was so glad to hear that for they were very worried their resort would suffer because of what happened while I was there. I knew the publicity would help. It didn't always matter if it was positive or not. Publicity was publicity. And they got a lot of it.

"So, is Modesta still spurting doom and gloom about me going to hell?" She was the receptionist at Sea Willow Haven and a firm believer that my communications with the other side was the work of Satan. Nothing I could say would persuade her to believe otherwise and after a while I realized that it didn't really matter to me what she thought. We are all entitled to our beliefs. If some new idea is brought to our attention and we chose to not accept it then that was certainly our prerogative to do so. Who was I to tell Modesta what to believe? Someday she'd know the truth. We all would.

"She doesn't hate you, Tess. I think she's praying for your soul now so that's a plus."

I laughed softly. "Yes it is. I can always use a prayer!" We finally made it to the cemetery and as we stood near the wrought iron fence looking in at the infamous stone, I felt no presence of a spiritual sort. Whoever the girl was that I'd connected to the last time I was here, she was not here now.

"Well it definitely looks like the bottom part of a leg." Kade pointed to the elongated heart near the top of the monument. "Does that have significance too?"

"I don't know. But I'm thinking yes."

"All I've heard about, though, is the booted leg." Kade slid an arm across my shoulders in a casual hold as we stood there together and stared with critical interest at the one object that was making my life very interesting of late. Had I not the excuse of coming here to investigate, I'd be back home in New York and I wouldn't be standing next to Kade. Maybe that heart was meant for us and anyone else who stood here staring at the stone.

"In Italy there is a place in Verona that is believed to be the home of Juliet, you know of the Romeo and Juliet story. Her bronze statue stands in the courtyard below the famous balcony from which Juliet is supposed to have spoken her famous, "Romeo, wherefore art though Romeo" speech. One of the breasts on the bronze statue is nearly worn down from countless hands touching it."

"Seriously?" Kade pulled away just enough to twist around and look me in the face to see if I was pulling his leg.

"Yes. The belief is that if you want true love to come into your life, you must rub the left breast, the one closest to her heart, and wish for true love. Everyone does it. As did I." Mike was with me at the time and I thought he was my one true love. Turns out, he was only one of my true loves. Seems we can have more than one. A month ago, I wouldn't have believed that.

"You don't feel that you were cheated? I mean, your husband is...well..." Kade turned away, his expression troubled. He was probably upset with himself for bringing it up.

I lay my head against his shoulder for a moment. "No, I don't feel cheated. I feel quite lucky. Mike was a wonderful husband for the time that I had him in my life. I don't regret that. I am grateful for it. And now I'm moving on with my life and getting my happiness back."

Kade's arm slid down my back and circled my waist. He turned to face me and brought his other hand up to cup my cheek. "I'm glad you are happy again, Tess."

I stared up into his blue, blue eyes, loving the way they peered at me through long dark lashes. The expression on his face made my heart thump hard and fast. Heat bloomed in my face and fanned out everywhere. "Me too, Kade."

He tossed his head to indicate the monument. "So why did you bring up that stuff about the Juliet statue? What's that to do with this thing here?"

"Well, I just wonder if that heart is there for another purpose. Maybe the stone isn't cursed. Maybe it's blessed with magic."

"What do you mean?"

Excitement skittered across my skin, touching everywhere at once. Maybe I was on to something here. "From everything I've read, Jonathan Buck was a decent man. He was very respected. He had a large family and a devoted wife. The whole family was upstanding. Why would someone like that be cursed? Maybe he was blessed. Maybe that heart is a reminder that love doesn't die, ever. Maybe if we stand here together and make a wish, we'll find true love...again."

Kade gave me a thoughtful look. "Is that what you are getting from the other side? Is your guardian angel telling you this?"

I laughed at that. It was really amazing how much he came to accept the things I told him about myself and my beliefs. "No, this just came to me and even if it's just a flight of fancy, who cares? Once it's out there, it becomes real. My suggestion has now made it a fact."

Kade nodded, accepting my explanation. "Okay then." He turned so that we were once again standing side by side and took my hand in his, raising it high. "Here's to finding love again." We both stood there staring at the heart shape stained into the stone and I couldn't get over the fact that we were staring at it and wishing for love. A thrill of excitement zipped through me from the inside out. Happiness had a way of blooming to a burst then flaring out into the stratosphere. After a quiet moment, Kade squeezed my hand and let them drop down between us. "So what's the foot represent?"

"It takes one leap of faith...one step in the right direction, to change your life."

"I like that." We both smiled at our fanciful thoughts and then Kade pulled me into his arms for a long, tight hug. I closed my eyes to enjoy it. I loved being close to him, feeling his strength, the warm glow of his feelings encompassing me. I snuggled my chin just under his and breathed in the scent of him. He always smelled so good. The slight musk of his cologne, the body wash he used, and a scent that was unique only to him. Everyone had their own smell and Kade's was bone-melting nice.

After a moment, I pulled reluctantly away and it was then, from the corner of my eye that I detected a shadow, a dark shape that was more than the natural shades cast by the tombstones and trees nearby. Dropping my arms from Kade's gentle hold, I stepped toward the wrought iron fence surrounding the cemetery and kept my focus just to the left of the shadow. There were a lot of theories as to why people were more apt to see a spirit or ghost from the corner of their eyes and I remember thinking they were logical enough to accept. Although I have seen spirits straight on, this one was elusive. I looked at Buck's monument, my gaze settling on the image of the leg and waited. Kade remained standing where I left him and did nothing to disturb my concentration. He was so great to have around, especially when something like this happened. I felt safe though I knew when it came to spiritual beings he really couldn't do much in the way of stopping anything from happening. What he could do was lend me the emotional strength and confidence I needed to deal with whatever was occurring. In this case there was no danger, but his belief in me helped to strengthen my own belief in me.

It was the girl I encountered the last time I was here. I could feel her anguish and wished she'd let me communicate with her. But she kept her distance, holding steady right next to the monument. She didn't trust me. She trusted no one. Even in death. It had to be a lonely place for her right now. My heart swelled with the need to help her. I asked Sheila to lend assistance and waited patiently to see what happened. Experimentally, I moved my gaze from the boot to the shadow hovering near and she vanished.

Although disappointed, I was not discouraged for I felt sure she was still around. I closed my eyes and cast out psychic feelers to see if I could locate her again. It's hard to explain how I did this casting of feelers. I imagined my consciousness expanding outward in an ever-increasing circle from my body. My hope was that as the circle grew, I would become aware of anything lurking nearby. Most of us did this on an unconscious level which was why we often became aware that we weren't alone even though we heard nothing and saw nothing. Aha. As I suspected. Her energy was weak but she was still here.

You don't have to fear me. I'm here to help. Even though it was a silent communication, I tried to inflect compassion and love into my mental voice. Her response was to flash close and enter into my awareness with sudden clarity. For a moment we mingled as one and everything about her entered my thoughts at once. Of course I couldn't process it. My conscious brain couldn't handle a sudden overload of information all at once. For just a brief instant, a second if anything, I felt I knew all there was to know about her then she was gone.

I sagged against the fence, holding the cool spikes between tense fingers as I drew in calming breaths to get my weakened state a moment to recover. It seemed that whenever I interacted with the spirit world, it sapped me of energy. Kade sensed the communication was over and came up behind me. He slipped his arms around my waist and pressed a kiss next to my ear.

"You okay?"

I nodded and leaned back against him. His strength seeped through me and I turned in his arms to give him a grateful smile. "I'm so glad you are here."

Kade's returning smile made my breath hitch. Every response to him was strong and exciting. But then it was usually that way for everyone when in a new relationship. It was because we were so positively focused on them. Feelings like that faded over time because the positive thoughts were often replaced with negative ones. As we stood there in mutual enjoyment of each other, I wished that these feelings would never fade. Somehow I needed to keep the negative thoughts that came to plague most relationships over time from entering my mind and coming between us.

"She was here again," I told him.

"Did she speak to you?"

"No. She doesn't trust me. She doesn't trust anyone. She's very sad, Kade. It makes me sad."

Kade kissed my temple. "You'll help her," he said, his voice confident. "We just need to figure out how. And to do that, we probably need to figure out who she is."

"I wonder if she's buried in this cemetery?" Even as I said it, I felt something was wrong about that. What could be wrong? Either she was buried here or she wasn't. I straightened and Kade stepped away, sensing I was ready to leave. He twined our fingers together and began walking back the way we had come. "Let's cross down to the river walk and return to the B&B from there. That way, you can find a spot to do your painting for Barbara. If you don't mind, once we get back to the B&B, I'd like to have some time alone. There's something I need to do." The story I'd started a couple days ago suddenly loomed strong in my thoughts. It was time to write again.

"Sounds good. While you are doing your thing, I'll go and do mine, get started on the sketch for Barbara's painting."

Each of us full of purpose, we hastened our walk and I thought again how lucky I was to have someone in my life who understood me so well and accepted me for who I am. As I had a feeling the following days were going to get weird, it was a darned good thing Kade no longer thought I was operating from left field of the Twilight Zone.

CHAPTER THIRTEEN

Once we managed to get Kade settled into his room, he came into mine to see the box of beads. He was quite impressed with the natives' handiwork and admired the smooth stone which he found equally interesting. After a short discussion on how they could have managed such artistry and I showed Kade the drawing of the necklace, he pressed a quick kiss to my mouth and headed for the door. He returned to his room for his sketch pad and once I heard him trot down the stairs, I ran to my window and waited for him to stride into view. No way was I going to miss watching him cross the street. He must have been aware I was doing so because he paused and turned to look up at my window. We stared at each other for a long moment and then he gave me a wave and continued on. I waited until he was out of sight then turned my focus to my laptop.

The itch to write was getting stronger. It seemed an age since I began Isi's story. When I told Kade about it, he immediately agreed I should work on it. "Remember what your story writing did for you at the resort."

Yes I did remember and with that in mind, I sat down and began to type. I could barely contain my excitement as I did so. It was time to learn a little more about our mystery.

They trekked through the woods at a quick pace. As the man was so much taller than Isi and the woman gripping her hand, it was difficult for them to keep up though they struggled to do so. Gasping for breath, Isi stumbled. The woman's hold broke and she stopped immediately to help Isi regain her footing. She called out to the man ahead of them and he turned to glare at them impatiently. When he pulled the magic stick from his shoulder, Isi froze in terror thinking he meant to use it on her. The woman touched her arm and shook her head, telling Isi in that simple gesture that he would not harm her. She pointed to a fallen log and motioned for Isi to sit. Not letting go of her hand, she sat as well. The man stood with his magic stick ready, his eyes moving slowly around the forest, alert to every sound and movement. Isi watched him curiously.

The woman squeezed Isi's hand to gain her attention. She gestured with her free hand and Isi understood. The woman wanted to let go of her hand but told her that if she ran, the man would point his magic stick and steal her soul. Isi nodded her understanding and the woman let her go. Isi rubbed at her arms where the man's fingers had bit into them earlier. The woman's eyes followed the gesture and leaned close to look. She saw the dark bruises and pressed her lips together. She turned and spoke in a sharp tone to the man. Isi marveled at her bravery for the women among her people would never speak that way to the men who cared for and protected them. The man answered back, his tone unpleasant and the woman's eyes narrowed on him. He moved uncomfortably and mumbled something that made the woman point at him. She spoke again and he turned away.

Isi watched the exchange and wondered what had just transpired between them. It seemed to her that although the man carried the magic stick, the woman had the upper hand. Was she the Chosen then? Was she like the Chosen among her people...the ones upon whom the Knowing One bestowed great power? But what of the magic stick?

The woman pulled something out of her clothing and handed it to Isi. Isi stared at it curiously. It was hard and shaped like a small rock. The woman had one too. She touched Isi's arm to get her attention and put the hard lump to her mouth and took a bite. She encouraged Isi to do the same. Cautiously, Isi did as the woman instructed. It was dry and hard but not bad to taste. Aware suddenly of her hunger, Isi ate the odd food and smiled her thanks to this kind one who must be of the Chosen. The woman smiled back. She pointed to herself and spoke slow and clear, dragging out the sounds she made. "Nee naaa." She pointed to Isi and gestured a question. Then she pointed to the man. "Giiii ells."

She was giving Isi their names. How odd. When the woman went through the process again, Isi decided to cooperate. For whatever reason, the Knowing One brought these strange people into her life and put her in their care. She was not to question this new fate no matter how sad it made her feel. Pointing to herself, Isi spoke. "Isi." She pointed to the woman. "Nina." Then she gestured to the man. "Giles."

The woman's smile was bright and warm. It eased some of the pain in Isi's heart. "Isi. Nina. Giles." She pointed to each in turn and then nodded her satisfaction. They were communicating. Hope surged within her chest. Maybe someday Isi might see her people again.

I stopped writing at this point and orientated myself back into my own life. While typing that story, it's like I am in another time and place. It was quite a challenge for me to write her story for Isi did not know things as I knew them. Though I found myself wanting to give name to the things Isi described, I let her control the writing to a degree. I was pretty sure Isi was referring to the dandelion flower when making a comparison to Nina's hair. I thought it curious how Isi used the world around her to describe things, such as the man's eyes being the color of the sea when angry and the woman's eyes being the color of the sky at dawn. Obviously shades of blue. Interesting. But even as I provided the words, I knew Isi didn't call the sky by the same name. Her thoughts were foreign and I interpreted them to my own understanding as I went along. It was an interesting process.

With my story focused on Isi and her plight, it made me think about America's history with the Native American Indians and it all made me sad. Their arrows were not as effective as our guns and so we won the land from them with a distinctly unfair advantage. History was full of much sadness.

Heaving a sigh, I stood and stretched. So, was Isi the girl at the cemetery? I didn't think so, it didn't sound right. But then why was I writing this story? Obviously Isi was an Indian Native though I had no idea what tribe she hailed from. I knew at one time that the colonists were under orders to shoot all natives on sight. All of them. Woman, children, even babies. The horror of it was beyond my comprehension. Why were we such a cruel species? How could anyone carry out orders like that? Obviously Nina and Giles were not as willing to comply. My impression of Isi was that of a young girl of about twelve. It was her young age that must have stopped Giles from shooting her on site. Either that or Nina hadn't let him. She obviously had some pull with the man. So who were they? Did the Indians have names like Isi? Of course, the names of my characters didn't always have any meaning. I learned that much from before.

Someone entered the foyer downstairs and then I heard the murmur of a male voice and knew that Kade was back. I saved my work, closed my laptop and hurried from my room. It was time to be with Kade again and find something to eat.

***

Kade and I had lunch at the town's one and only Chinese restaurant and I told him about my story while we ate. We both speculated over it and wondered if Isi was some sort of relation to Big Red.

"But Isi wasn't covered in red, Kade, and besides, she interacted with settlers and the Red Paint Indians wouldn't have done so since they died thousands of years before we arrived in the Americas."

"Maybe she's a descendent then? They might not all have died. Surely some of them would have integrated with other tribes?"

It was a logical suggestion and it had some merit but I didn't get a strong feeling that Isi's story had anything to do with Colonel Buck and his curse. I thought about the spiritual merge with the Indian girl that I experienced while holding the rock. The girl in that vision could possibly be an early ancestor of Isi's if Kade's theory was correct. But the question still remained, how did any of that have a connection to Jonathan Buck and his cursed monument? "I still don't get how these Indian clues have anything to do with Colonel Buck's curse."

"Well, it could be as you said earlier, it isn't cursed at all."

"True." I thought about our wishing upon that elongated heart stained into Buck's monument and hoped the wish came true...magical curses or not. I didn't want to spend the rest of my life alone. But I also wasn't sure I was ready to invite anyone into it on a permanent basis anytime soon either. Now, however, was not the time for thinking about that. "It seems the longer I stay here, the more confused I get." Before Kade could respond, my cell phone rang and I glanced at the caller

ID. It was Mary. Hoping everything was okay and she wasn't calling with more bad news, I hurried to answer. "Hi, Mary!"

There was a slight pause and then Mary spoke, her voice low and wobbly. "Tess? I just needed..." She drew in a ragged breath. "I needed to talk to someone." A choked sob followed and before I could respond, Mary rushed on as if she needed to get the words out quickly or not at all. "Mom received the final eviction notice this morning." Another sob escaped and then, "I don't know what we are going to do." She broke down then and I knew she wasn't going to hear a thing I said.

"Mary, I'll be right there." When she didn't respond, I repeated my intent. "Okay, Mary? I'll be there in just a few minutes."

"Okay." It was barely audible but at least she responded.

I stood and grabbed my sweater, looking at Kade and hoping he'd understand. "We need to get over to Mary's place. Her mother received the eviction notice."

Kade didn't hesitate. He called the waitress over and asked for the bill then handed her some money. "Keep the change."

We were out the door and on our way within a minute of Mary's call. It was a short drive to their house so I talked quickly, filling Kade in on the family. What little I knew. I also told him about all the spirits that had gathered there and then followed me back to the B&B.

"Well, you say the family is descended from a Native American tribe, surely it must have been some of them that you attracted there? They did have a pretty bloody ending to a lot of their lives, maybe they haven't recovered from that yet."

"Normally, Kade, I would agree with you, but I think there's more to it than that." I glanced at him briefly before returning my attention to the road. "Mary's father believed he was a descendant of the Penobscot Indian tribe. So, what does Big Red have to do with it? He's the one that chased me into the B&B after following me back from Mary's."

"It certainly is puzzling."

We pulled into the driveway of the Rowans' home and Kade looked appreciatively at the architecture. "Nice place. Big."

We stepped out of the car and stood for a moment in silence. The unreal quality I experience the last time I was here seeped back into my psyche. It was such an odd feeling. As goose bumps broke out on my skin, I rubbed at my arms and glanced around. Though I felt an energy spike, I didn't detect any spirits.

"You getting anything?" Kade glanced around, looking just a tad uneasy.

"Are you?"

He gave a shrug. "Yeah, the willies." He smiled to show he wasn't really all that scared but he did notice something. I took his hand and pulled him along toward the porch. Mary came out just as we started up the steps.

"Sorry to bother you, Tess, but I just needed a friend." She gave me a tight hug then pulled away and looked at Kade.

"Mary, this is Kade Sinclair. I hope you are okay with me bringing him along?"

Mary held out a hand to Kade in welcome. Her dark eyes shimmered with unshed tears but she managed to give a faint smile as they shook hands. "It's nice to meet you. Tess tells me you were in the Marines. Let me thank you now for your service to our country."

Kade nodded in acknowledgment of her thanks. "And I thank you. Tess tells me you retired from the Army recently."

Mary glanced back toward the front door then motioned toward a patio set not far from where we were standing. "Let's talk out here."

We sat down around the table and then fell silent as the three of us looked out over the flower garden. It wasn't a tame garden but I liked it. Once I felt Mary was ready, I turned to her.

"When do you have to move out? Do you have any idea where you will go?"

Her face expressionless, Mary's gaze remained on the flower gardens though I doubt she saw them. "Mom and Adam will probably move up with my sister until they can figure something out. She lives in a three bedroom house and has two kids of her own but they'll make it work somehow." She turned to meet my eyes. "I called Daniel."

Reaching for her hand, I squeezed it gently. "How did that go?"

Mary's smile was faint but at least she smiled. "Better. I didn't get all defensive and hostile like I've been in other calls." Mary rubbed her face with her free hand. "I've been such a mess but our talk last night helped." Mary glanced at Kade and then back at me, her brow lifted in question. "Does he know about the convoy?"

I nodded somewhat guiltily. "I hope you don't mind."

"You've nothing to be ashamed of, Mary. War sucks. Shit happens and none of us like it. Despite our moral belief that we 'shalt not kill', you did what had to be done." Kade gave her a decisive nod. "He came at you with hatred in his heart. You shot him with love in yours. Big difference."

Mary broke down at his words and buried her face in her hands. "I want to accept that, Kade, I do but love doesn't kill."

"Mary, you were just as much a victim as he was in that situation. Had you let him live, countless more would be dead." How to get her to see this?

"Did Jesus not say turn the other cheek? We shouldn't have been there in the first place. We were in his country, he was defending it."

Kade grabbed her hands and pulled them from her face. "No. The men that attacked your convoy, they were not defending their country. You were defending their country. They are trying to muscle into power to rule it with ruthless tyranny and hatred. Surely you understood that while you were over there? You were there in response to the masses, the general population who are all helpless from the onslaught of evil. He was the bad guy, Mary. There's no glory in war, there really isn't, but our society has made it a necessity and people like you are why our world is not overrun with evil."

I was quite impressed. Both Mary and I looked at Kade with wide, respectful eyes. Mary stared at his unwavering gaze for a long moment then nodded slowly, understanding dawning in the sorrowful depths of her dark eyes. "Yes. I hadn't thought of it that way. I just was so focused on what I did. I didn't think it right to rationalize away what happened."

"Stating facts is not rationalization, Mary. Now, that business is over for you, as mine is for me. We need to focus on what is happening now and see what can be done about it."

I loved how he said "we" and not "you". "Kade's right, Mary. The man for whom you mourn, he was part of a group that planted a roadside bomb that killed several men in Kade's unit. Innocent men who were not on a mission to kill. Where's the justice in that? The men that died in Kade's Humvee hadn't raised a single weapon to the men that planted that bomb. They were not in a kill-or-be-killed situation. Our troops aren't over there hiding bombs and hoping to kill whoever happens upon them. We aren't strapping bombs to innocent people and sending them out to kill crowds of people who have nothing to do with war. That is the kind of man you killed, Mary."

Kade leaned over and kissed me. It was so unexpected that I glanced at him in surprise. He gently ran a finger along my cheek. "You are pretty incredible."

Mary squeezed my arm. "Yes you are." She turned to Kade and touched his arm as well. "And so are you."

Kade sat back. "Okay, we have a mutual fan club going on here but what we need to do is focus on the situation at hand. Is there nothing to be done to postpone the foreclosure?"

"Daniel asked the same thing, we have some money put aside for the boys' college fund and he was willing to dip into it. But the amount we need is just more than we have."

"How much are we talking here, Mary?"

"Almost two-hundred thousand."

It was a surprising amount considering the house had been in the family for generations. Mary must have seen the question in my eyes and her voice sounded tired, weighted down with burden. "When my dad got sick, his medical insurance was not the greatest. It wouldn't pay for the experimental treatments he endured. They took out a loan against the house to pay the medical bills with extra to help with living expenses. The money has helped in the past five years but now it's gone. Unfortunately, the interest rate they secured is atrocious. We all knew mom wouldn't be able to handle the payments forever but we thought something would work out for her eventually. Then things happened that required money and suddenly we are out of time."

"What did you hope might happen to prevent this?" I know I was being particularly nosey but I really was curious. Maybe the answer to their problem could be found in the answer to this question.

Mary gave a short, sharp bark of laughter and ran a hand up through her hair. "I don't know...that one of us would win the lottery, or marry someone rich or land a great job...who knows what we thought. We were just living with blind hope."

"You are at the point now that you must pay the whole note? Can you pay a portion...?"

"Unfortunately it isn't just the mortgage payments mom fell behind on. She owes quite a bit in back taxes. One way or another, she's going to lose the house." Mary covered her mouth with her hand in an effort to stifle the sobs that rose in her throat. She made a choked sound and closed her eyes. "I just feel so bad for my mother. And I know Pop would be horrified to have his family home go to a stranger."

It was the most frustrating thing in the world to watch something happen that you wished you could prevent. If only I could do something. Much as I wanted to help her, that was a huge sum of money. With the family not having any possible answer to their financial woes in the near future, they were nothing but a huge financial risk. Even if they came up with the money to stop the foreclosure and pay off the taxes, how were they going to continue paying the high costs of living in and maintaining such a large home?

The three of us sat quietly, each lost in our own thoughts when we heard a crash from inside the house and someone screamed. We all jumped at once and went running.

When we entered the living room, we found Adam standing near the fireplace, a stricken look on his face. Dawn was kneeling next to him gathering shattered pieces of something on the floor.

"What happened?" Mary ran to her mother and grabbed her hand. "Mom! You're bleeding."

Dawn looked down at the blood dripping from a gash on the fleshy pad below her thumb. "I tried to catch it but it was broken before it even hit the floor." She brushed away Mary's gripping hand. "Leave it, Mary, I'm fine."

I knelt next to Dawn and looked at the mess spread everywhere. Whatever it was, it looked like it had literally exploded for it now lay in a million unrecognizable pieces. "What was it?"

"An Indian bust. You don't remember it from last night?" Dawn's mouth trembled as she surveyed the mess. "It's been in the family for ages. I think my husband's grandfather had it given to him as a gift."

"Don't touch anything, Mom. I'm going to get a broom and dustpan." Mary scurried away; sending me a look that clearly asked for my help in ensuring her mother obeyed her command.

I gently touched Dawn's shoulder. "What happened?"

"It exploded, that's what happened," Adam said, his voice high pitched with disbelief. "We were sitting here talking about what we could keep and what we could sell. Mom said that bust might bring in a pretty decent price and it freakin' exploded!" Adam ran an agitated hand through his hair. "But first it started vibrating on the mantel. That's when mom jumped up to grab it. Just as she went to reach for it, the thing literally exploded in air." He pulled his mother up and away from the mess. "Leave it, Mom."

"We should take care of that cut." The blood spurting from her wound was quite substantial. I wondered if she'd need stitches.

Kade stepped close to Dawn and held out his hand. "My name is Kade Sinclair, I'm a friend of Tess's. I used to be in the military and have had extensive training in first aid. Would you mind if I take a look?"

Dawn put her blood-covered hand in his. Kade bent over to get a better look. "I can't see the cut." He glanced at Adam. "Could you get me a clean cloth of some sort?"

Adam nodded and quickly left the room. Mary rejoined us and looked relieved that Kade was tending to her mom. She swept up the shattered pieces with disbelieving eyes. "That bust was made of granite. It was hand-carved and a family heirloom. Such a shame. What on earth would make it shatter like that?"

I was trying hard to think back to last night. Since we'd been talking about Indians, you'd think I would remember this bust...that it would have stood out somehow and caught my notice. Especially when the picture fell from the same mantel. Speaking of which, I saw it now sat on a small end table next to the easy chair Adam was sitting in last night. I looked from it to the mess now filling a large dustpan. Two things were thrown from the mantel. Two things. I walked over to the fireplace and looked around.

"What are you looking for?" Mary asked as she passed me to take the debris to the trash.

"I find it most interesting that two things have fallen from your mantel in the past two days."

Adam returned with a damp white hand towel. "Here." He held up a bottle of Peroxide. "In case you want to clean it."

I turned to watch Kade press the cloth gently to Dawn's palm. She didn't even wince. Her face was very pale, her eyes looking like she was not with us but lost in deep thought. She paid no mind to Kade and what he was doing.

Kade frowned. "I can't see a cut anywhere."

"It's on the fleshy pad below her thumb. That's where I thought I saw the blood coming from." The fireplace could wait. Dawn needed to be taken care of first. I stepped close to Dawn and gave her shoulders a gentle squeeze. "You okay?"

Dawn pulled from her thoughts and looked at me. "I think so. It doesn't hurt." She spread her palm wider so Kade could get a better look. "I can't figure what happened. Timmy was sitting on my lap. Just as the Indian bust began to shake, he hissed really loud, the hairs on his back going right up straight and then he scrambled off the couch and ran from the room."

"Maybe he scratched you?" It was likely the case especially if the bust burst before Dawn got to it.

Kade gently wiped away the blood. "That's about all I see, a surface scratch. How it generated this much blood I don't know."

We all leaned close to take a look and when Mary rejoined us I moved aside to allow her into our little circle. We stared at

Dawn's hand in complete amazement. As Kade stated, all we could see was a small scratch. It wasn't bleeding anymore. What the heck? How was this possible?

Dawn took the bloody white towel. "I'll just go wash up and be right back."

Once Dawn left the room, I pulled from my thoughts to look at Mary. "Where did your father get the bust?"

"I think his father, Grampa, had it gifted to him. I can't remember exactly." She glanced at her brother. "Do you know, Adam?"

Adam flopped down on the couch and heaved a huge, loud sigh. "No."

Kade was now examining the fireplace. "How long has this been here?"

"Since the house was built." Adam watched Kade with distrusting eyes. "Why?"

"Do you think you can get anything from it, Tess?" Kade waved me over and I immediately joined him.

"I don't know. I tried to pick up something last night."

"What are you talking about?" Adam asked.

"Sometimes things absorb energy from a past event and I can pick up on it." I put my hand on the cold, smooth mantel. It was made of wood and had an interesting shade of red, sort of like cranberries gone bad. Cherry wood maybe?

"What do you mean you can pick up on it? I thought you talked to ghosts?" Adam stood up and started toward the fireplace to join us but Mary grabbed his arm.

"Stay back, Adam, and let her do her thing."

Adam's eyes narrowed, his dislike of the request quite plain to see but he stayed where he was. "So what do you pick up?"

"I can sometime see visions of events that have happened. I can't always, though, so don't expect too much." I let my hands run along the mantel's smooth surface and closed my eyes. What happened next was so sudden I barely managed to gasp before the breath was stolen from my body. An invisible pair of hands took control of mine; making me grip the mantel so hard my knuckles turned white and my fingers went numb. I tried to pull away but couldn't. Cold air burst around me in a thick invisible mass, cocooning me in, muffling all sound. I heard sobbing, screams, chanting, gun shots, shouts. It all came at me in an instant. I tried to break the contact but whatever energy surrounded me, it wouldn't let me go. The cold got worse and my breath shot out in puffs of frosted air. I couldn't even close my eyes. It was an awful feeling. A helpless one. "Sheila, please help me! Please, God."

I managed to look at my hands and shock jolted through me. It wasn't my hands gripping the mantel. The hands I stared at were very male. Large, thick, strong. Deeply tanned. They held fast to the fireplace and I knew the owner of those hands was trying to control his emotions. He was trying...trying. I threw back my head and cried out in pain, for the pressure bearing down on me was too much to handle. Fighting it was worse but I felt I had to break free or be lost forever. As I struggled for control, I was sure my fingers were going to dent the wood or burst from the pressure.

"Tess! Dammit, Tess, can you hear me?"

Kade's frantic voice finally penetrated through the sounds of screams and sobs and anger. I focused on his voice, latching on to his words and using them as a beacon to safety from this nightmare.

"Tess, please answer me."

The pressure let up. Thank God. Oh thank God. As Kade's low murmurs continued from close by, I followed the sound. The grip on my hands suddenly went away and since I was pulling against a pressure now gone, I went flying backwards. Kade made a whoomph sound as I smacked into his chest but he held his ground as his arms went around me and steadied our balance.

"For the love of God, Tess, are you okay or not?"

I turned my face into his chest and listened to the frantic beating of his heart. My own was carrying on pretty well itself. "Yeah, I'm okay."

"It's times like this when I could really use a damned cigarette." Kade murmured the words next to my ear and I had to smile in response. We both quit smoking only a few weeks ago. Though I was glad to have kicked the habit, there were times, as Kade just said, when a cigarette sure would be nice.

Mary was beside us at once. "What happened? Are you sure you are okay?"

I forced myself to relax so Kade would feel reassured and let me go. His arms fell away reluctantly. "Yeah, I'm okay. Really."

"What's going on?" Dawn rejoined us, going straight to Adam and gripping his arm for support. "What's happened?"

"Mary's friend here just totally freaked on us."

I looked at him to see if he was kidding. He wasn't. "What did I do?"

"You were gripping that mantel so hard your hands were white. You were shaking all over and making strange noises." Kade ran an agitated hand through his hair. "I couldn't get close. It was like you had a damned force field around you. It was cold as hell and nearly blistered my hands when I tried to penetrate it."

Mary's hand fluttered nervously to her throat. I could see the pulse there pounding wildly. I reached out to touch her and she flinched. "My God, Tess, your hands are like ice."

They felt hot to me. I flexed my fingers several times and held them out for everyone to see. "They are fine. Really, it was just a vision. I'm sorry it frightened you."

"What was the vision?" Kade asked. He wasn't happy with the situation and I worried that he would decide this was all too strange and bizarre for him. What if he didn't want to be part of it anymore? My insides dropped like a rock and I actually bent over in response to it. "Tess, hey, are you okay?" Kade put an arm around my shoulders and bent low to look at my face. "Tell me what's going on."

I felt sick inside. The idea of him leaving me chased all other concerns from my mind. I pulled away from him so I could think. This was why I behaved myself and stopped a lot of my activities when Mike was alive. The world of the paranormal is a strange one. You can never know what to expect. Knowing Mike wasn't comfortable with it, I constantly worried something would happen to turn him off, make him stop loving me. Even though Kade was more open to it, I still worried that something like that would happen with him as well. I couldn't go through losing another love. Granted, going separate ways was not so final as a death but it was just as devastating. I know my own strength and I wouldn't be able to handle it. I wouldn't.

"Tess? What's wrong?" Kade wanted to touch me but since I withdrew from him, he held back. His hands clenched at his side and I knew he was holding in his frustration and worry.

"For a moment I was merged with a man. A very strong man. It wasn't Big Red."

"Big Red?" Mary frowned at the reference. "Who is that?"

"Just the name I gave to the Indian I've been seeing. The man who had a grip on that fireplace wasn't him, though. But it was a man nearly as big as him." I looked at Adam. "Was your dad your size?" From the shattered picture of him he looked like he might be.

"Dad was bigger than me. He was six four and weighed about two-hundred fifty pounds. He was solid muscle." Adam looked quite proud of this and I smiled in response. Such a shame that cancer brought him down. But then it was a shame when cancer brought anyone down.

"It might have been him but I don't think so." I thought for a moment then glanced at Dawn who was getting filled in on what happened by Mary. "You said this house has been in your husband's family since it was built, would you say that all the men in his family were large?"

"Yes, I'd say that."

I nodded thoughtfully. "Then it was one of his ancestors." I glanced at Mary and Adam and hoped that what I was about to share with them wouldn't add to their worry. Not that it should, but you never knew how people were going to react. "I heard a gunshot, shouts, crying. It had to have been from an event that occurred here a long time ago."

"You think someone was murdered here?" Adam asked. He didn't look too happy with that idea, but then, who would?

"I'm not sure, but something traumatic took place."

"Well, couldn't you just ask them?" Mary waved a hand as if a ghost was standing next to me and speaking to it was just a simple matter of ... well, just speaking to it. "If his ghost is still here, can't you still talk to him?"

"I wasn't in contact with his ghost. I somehow tuned into a past event. Maybe because I was standing in the very spot he had stood in, doing what he was doing. I don't know how I do it because it doesn't always happen at will." It was frustrating when visions came to me that I couldn't figure out. It was like handing someone pieces of a puzzle without showing them the picture they were meant to create with them.

"But what made the Indian bust explode? If not a ghost, what?" Adam scowled at the empty spot on the mantel where the bust must have been sitting. It still bothered me that I couldn't remember it.

Heaving a quiet sigh, I motioned toward the sofa. "Mind if I sit down?" I always felt weak after a vision. Kade started to take my arm but dropped his hand. He obviously wasn't sure if he should touch me or not because I had pulled away from him and hadn't looked at him since. I couldn't. The pain in my chest at the thought of losing him was too raw. He'd see it in my eyes, feel the tension in my body and want to know what was going on. I didn't want to talk about it.

Giving voice to fears often weakens them.

Sheila's voice popped into my head so strong and loud that I jumped and actually turned my head to look for her. Catching Kade's inquiring gaze, I shrugged to let him know it was nothing and turned to Mary who sank down beside me on the couch. Adam pushed himself up as we approached and returned to his normal chair of preference. He still didn't quite trust me. I couldn't blame him. It was all quite bizarre. "It could be that my being here is rousing up their energy. I'm not sure what these events are about...the picture falling last night and the bust today."

"Maybe Pop is trying to tell us something," Mary suggested. "I know you said he's not haunting us but could he show up just to give us some clues or something?"

"Clues to what?"

Mary gave a choked laugh. "I don't know, maybe he can tell us how to save the house."

Dawn sat down in the rocking chair facing us and shook her head sadly. "Nothing but money, and lots of it, is going to save us Mary. You know that." She glanced at me with a wry smile tugging at her lips. "Think you can conjure up some winning lottery numbers?"

Adam's head swiveled in my direction, a flare of hope in his dark eyes.

"I'm sorry, but I don't have that sort of ability. I don't know that ghosts can manipulate the machines that choose the winning numbers either. If it were possible, it would be happening a lot. You'd see it plastered all over the news." I splayed my hands as if giving a news flash. "Just in, 'Psychic comes up with winning lotto numbers!'" I gave a small sympathetic shrug. "Sorry, guys, but I've never heard of any such claims."

The light went out of Adam's eyes. He glanced away and stared into space. "We're done."

How to help them? I hated feeling this helpless. Faced with what they were facing, it all seemed so useless what I was doing. What did it matter if I uncovered the story behind a silly curse? The things that mattered in life were helping people like the Rowans. I wasn't even contacting any useful spirits for them. Instead I had a pack of Indians chasing me around. But why?

Mary touched my hand to gain my attention and I turned to her. "Would you and Kade like to stay and eat with us? My mom is making a boiled dinner. There's plenty. She always makes enough to feed an Army when she makes a boiled dinner."

"A boiled dinner?" Although I was pretty sure I knew what it was, I stalled for time as my eyes searched out Kade's to see what he wanted to do. He gave a small shrug to let me know it was my call.

"It's a ham boiled with vegetables. My mom puts potatoes, carrots, cabbage, turnips and onions in hers. The flavors blend very well together." Mary's fingers gently squeezed my arm. "Please?" And then, obviously remembering Kade had just arrived in town, her eyes widened in dismay. "Oh..." She looked at Kade then me then waved a hand to erase the invite. "You probably would rather spend some time alone together. I'm sorry..."

"Mary, we would love to stay and have dinner with you." I grasped her flailing hand. "Truly."

Mary's desperate eyes met mine and some of the turmoil in them lessoned. She gave me a ghost of a smile and nodded. "Okay. Great."

Dawn stood and started for the kitchen. "Wonderful. I'll just let you visit with each other while I go make a batch of biscuits."

Adam leaned forward in his chair and caught my eye. "Since you are going to be here awhile, do you think you could find out who is causing all the weird crap going on and put an end to it? If it isn't Pop, I don't want any ghosts hanging around blowing things up. At least not until we've managed to pack our stuff and vacate the premises." His expression hardened with contained anger. "Once we leave, you can tell every nasty ghost in existence to come hang out."

The room chilled in response to Adam's request and a shiver chased through my spine. Oddly, my scalp began to tingle with the rise of energy in the room and it was this that caught my undivided attention. A general belief, and one I accepted, was that our channel to the spirit world resided within the crown chakra, which was one of seven energy centers located within our bodies. The crown chakra resides just above the center of the forehead where the Third Eye, another chakra location, was located. A dear friend whom I'd met when I first started exploring my paranormal ability explained to me about these seven energy centers and though I didn't explore them as well as I should, I was aware of them and took note when one was activated.

I almost forgot about my chakra work during my two-year pity party. But now it was all coming back to me. The tingling in my scalp slowly moved down through the center of my body making me feel like my insides were speeding up with excitement. I cast my thoughts back to Shay's teachings and wondered what I needed to do to ensure I kept the channel open and do as Adam just asked.

Thinking of Shay, I felt a pang of regret for letting our communications dwindle to nothing. I met her when I was fourteen. My mother took me to one of her psychic seminars and she singled me out, sending a note requesting to meet with me when the seminar was over. Her name was Shay Storm, her true name, not a pseudonym, and she told me the spirits urged her to make my acquaintance. I was living with my parents in Virginia at the time. Shay, it turned out, lived in Virginia Beach only a short distance from Hampton where we lived. I spent a lot of time with Shay through my teen years, honing my ability and learning a lot about paranormal and supernatural phenomena. When I left to attend college in New York, where Mike and I met, Shay moved to Colorado and we lost touch. I hadn't thought of her in years. How strange. Considering the influence she had on my life, I wondered how it was that we drifted apart so completely.

It was obvious Kade noticed the drop in temperature for he rubbed at his arm as his observant gaze moved around the room. I could see his skin was broke out with goose bumps and hid my smile. A month ago, he wouldn't have thought twice about why a room might suddenly get cold. His deep blue eyes met mine and my heart gave a little lurch. He had quite the effect on me. Maybe when two souls meant to be together connected, our Heart Chakras (another energy center) recognized this and reacted? Or maybe it was because my eyes really appreciated what I saw. He grew more handsome the more I came to know him. Attraction and strong feelings did that. But now was not the time to think about it.

"Has Adam's invitation prompted a visit?" Kade's brows lifted in question and when Adam drew in a sharp breath, he winked.

Hiding a smile, I looked at Adam and gestured with my hand to gain his attention. He pulled his troubled dark eyes from an intent scan of the fireplace and met mine with an uneasy scowl. He was scared and worried and angry. It wasn't a good combination. "You didn't invoke anything, Adam. The spirits that have been active here lately are not haunting your house or trying to hurt you. I really think they might be trying to relay a message."

Mary gave a small shake of her head, disagreeing with me. "But something has been hanging around this house long before now, Tess. We've all noticed little things over the years.

You notice we don't have a dog? Every dog we've tried to have goes a little berserk. Our cats are more tolerable but even they get spooked as you've seen. It's just that lately things have become more active." She waved a hand toward the fireplace to make her point. "We've lost two things from that mantel in the past two days. That bust exploding like that isn't normal, Tess. Something more is going on."

"Maybe their energy is stirred up because of how upset you all are about losing the house," I suggested gently.

"But what do they care, Tess? They don't need to live here. They don't need anything anymore." Mary stood and paced the room. Her hands twisted together and knotted into fists. "Maybe Pop is upset with us for losing his heritage." Her eyes glistened with tears. "It doesn't seem right, losing this place. It should be ours forever, no matter what."

The energy in the room was increasing with each passing moment. I knew the emotions were so charged it was feeding that energy and I wondered if there was any way to calm it down before it got out of hand. If only I could figure out who was here and why.

Dawn bustled back into the room, a smudge of flour on her cheek. Seeing it, Mary walked over to her and gently brushed it away. "Mom, do you think it's Pop haunting us?"

Dawn heaved a sigh and patted her daughter's lingering hand before she walked over to the rocking chair she was sitting in earlier and sank into it. "No. But something is here. I can feel it." She gave an exaggerated shiver and rubbed her arms. "Is it chilly in here or is it just me?"

Adam's scowl deepened. "It's chilly."

"Okay, if you are all willing, let's try to contact it and see what it wants." I wasn't sure it was a good idea to invite this right now but something needed to be done. Especially as this family had enough to deal with already.

"It?" Mary's voice squeaked in alarm and I realized my mistake.

"Sorry, I just refer to spirits as an it sometimes until I know their gender." I smiled at Mary to ease her mind and gave a small chuckle in an attempt to lighten the atmosphere.

"Let's not go all Stephen King here and start imagining crazy and bizarre things."

Kade laughed softly and I turned to him at the sound. I loved his laugh. I loved his voice. I loved so many things about him. And that scared me more than whatever was making busts explode and the room go cold. "Are you game for it, Kade?"

He nodded in grave seriousness and that made everything seem so normal. Like what we were about to do was nothing out of the ordinary. "Whatever you think best, Tess. I'm with you."

I glanced at Mary who nodded at my silent question, then Adam who also gave a short nod of approval and finally settled my gaze on Dawn. I would let her make the decision. After a long hesitation in which I was pretty sure an intense internal argument was taking place, Dawn capitulated. She shook her head decisively and grasped the arms of her chair as if bracing for impact. "Let's do it."

Feeling somewhat apprehensive and trying not to show it, I gave a nod. "Good then. Let's prepare." I could only hope we were doing the right thing.

CHAPTER FOURTEEN

Everyone looked at me expectantly, awaiting instructions, so I stood and glanced around to see how best to do this. "Let's gather some chairs into a circle, close enough that we can hold hands." Everyone went into action as they grabbed five chairs that were easy to maneuver and situated them in the spacious area between the sofa and the fireplace. While the others arranged the chairs, Mary pushed the large easy chair where Adam always sat and a couple end tables out of the way. We all then sat down and linked hands. Kade sat to my right, Mary on my left. Beside Mary was her mother then Adam who sat on the other side of Kade. The circle was complete.

Because it was early in the day, there was quite a bit of light coming from the windows. Mary had pulled the curtains closed but it wasn't dark by any means. Not that having light was a problem because it wasn't, but it usually effected a better mood to have the lighting low. I usually liked to have a candle lit to give everyone something to focus on but decided to forgo that this time around. I had a feeling the entities hanging around us were strong enough to put in an appearance even if everyone's focus wasn't particularly strong.

"Okay, before we begin, I want you all to understand what we are going to do and what you might expect." Remembering the last séance I conducted, I was hoping to better prepare them for anything. "We'll begin with a prayer. I do this to ensure God is in control of any communication we may invoke. Just to be sure, I always ask everyone to envision a bright light surrounding our circle. I want you to think of this imaginary light as God's protection. When it comes to the spiritual realm, our imagination is as real as the physical world around us. This protective light acts as a barrier to negative entities, to anything harmful or bad that lurks on the other side looking for openings into our world. Séances are just such openings. Any time communication takes place between our world and theirs, a sort of portal is opened. We need to be responsible with this portal and not allow any old thing to come through it." I glanced at each of the four people around me. Their gazes were focused on me, trusting and unwavering. "You understand so far?" Everyone nodded except for Kade. He squeezed my hand and I turned to smile at him (we'd been through this before) and then returned my focus to the others. "Try as often as you can to focus on seeing the light surrounding us in your mind's eye. That keeps the energy we put into the light very strong. I will then ask for the spirits who have been trying to get our attention to come through. Again, we are allowing only those who are here for our well-being and theirs to come through and communicate with us. We are not inviting or allowing anything harmful or hurtful to enter our circle, so please don't be afraid."

"But what if it's a negative force that's been doing all the crap lately?" Adam asked.

"Then I'll ask for someone to come through that can help us understand who has been bothering you and why and ask for their help in sending the entity away so that it doesn't bother you anymore." Mary's cold hand trembled in mine and I squeezed it gently. "You okay to do this, Mary?"

Mary's dark eyes were apprehensive but determined as they met mine. "Yes. I trust you, Tess. I know we'll be fine."

I nodded my appreciation for her confidence in me then continued to explain what we could be in for. "You may notice the room drop in temperature. It's already done so as you've noticed but it could get worse. I am not sure why this phenomenon occurs. It isn't always the case. Sometimes people feel warmth. You might notice a rise in the energy around us...a sort of silent buzz in the air. The hairs on your arms and at the back of your neck may rise. You might feel chills down your back and get the feeling that someone is standing near you. Do not be afraid. If you feel something or hear something, tell me. Acknowledging what you feel often helps you to relax a little, especially if you share those feelings." I had to pause here to gauge everyone's comfort level. Although the Rowans appeared somewhat apprehensive, they also looked eager and excited. It was fear that I hoped to keep at bay.

"You all need to understand that this is our world, not theirs. We are in control here, not them. They only can come into control if you let them. I'm not going to allow that." I again let my eyes meet with each of the Rowans. Their trusting gazes did not waver from mine. Even Adam seemed enthralled and willing to trust me. "Sometimes they move things. Do not let this alarm you. They are just trying to validate their presence. It is something they are often compelled to do because the first thing we want to do is reason away what is happening and question whether or not we are really making contact with a spiritual entity."

"Has anyone ever been hurt from a séance?" Dawn asked. She didn't sound worried, more curious than anything.

Figuring she was thinking about the bust and how it exploded, it was a legitimate question. "No. Not during any of my séances and I've never heard of any harm that has happened to others either."

Satisfied with that answer, Dawn nodded and gave her children's hands a noticeable squeeze. "We are ready to do this."

"I need you to understand that often the communication with the spirits is largely through my thoughts. You probably won't hear anything. I can only tell you that I understand the difference between them and me. Their voice is a distinctly different one from my own internal voice." I tried to think how best to explain the process I went through. "Have any of you ever had a thought enter your mind that didn't sound like your voice and you actually wondered where the thought came from?" All four of my séance mates nodded their heads. I had to hide a smile that Kade had done so as well. We'd talked about this during our many discussions over the past couple of weeks. I figured he was participating to encourage the others to do the same. "Well that was probably a spirit guide talking to you or one of your guardian angels. It sort of works like that."

"So, we probably won't see anything?" Looking much relieved, Mary's tight grip relaxed a little.

"Most likely you won't see anything but that doesn't mean you won't." When Mary's hand tensed again, I squeezed it gently to reassure her. "There really isn't anything to fear." I glanced around the table, meeting everyone's eyes. "Whatever happens, do not break the circle. Keep a tight hold on each other. When a circle breaks, the focus usually goes away and that often severs the communication. Besides, we all draw from and give energy to each other while holding hands."

Satisfied that I had done all I could to prepare them, I closed my eyes and drew in a deep breath, letting it out slowly. Once I felt calm and centered, I opened my eyes just a tad and focused on the shiny wood floor in the center of our circle. "Okay, let's begin. I want you all to close your eyes and imagine a light glowing brightly just above our heads, bathing us in its brilliance. Again, I stress this to you because I want you to truly understand that this light is God's protective force and nothing negative can come through it." A quick glance told me that everyone seemed to be accepting my instructions without question. Good. After a moment of quiet, I spoke in a hushed voice. "Let us all say The Lord's Prayer together." I considered this particular prayer a powerful one and so included it in all spiritual communication attempts like this one. Once we finished reciting the prayer, the room went silent. The grandfather clock in the hallway next to the entrance sounded loud, its steady tick tock almost hypnotic in its monotonous litany.

I silently asked Sheila to help with our communication and almost instantly the familiar sensation of cobwebs brushed light as butterfly wings across my face. This signature sign of her presence always calmed me and filled my spirit with fearless confidence. Having her to oversee matters, I knew we'd be okay. Keeping my voice in a hushed tone, I spoke just loud enough for the others to hear.

"We are inviting the person (I didn't like to refer to them as "spirit" when speaking directly to them) that has been trying to get our attention to come through and speak to us." I looked to see if the Rowan family was still okay to proceed. Their eyes were open and when I glanced at each of them, they nodded in answer to my silent question. They were good to go. Okay then. After a slight pause, I again spoke out loud for the benefit of the others.

"We ask to speak with the person who has been trying to get our attention. We allow you to come through and speak to us only if you come in peace and will cause no harm." I was glad to note that Mary's hand, though cold, was much more relaxed. Kade's hand was firm and warm. I squeezed it gently and he squeezed back. "Try to keep your thoughts clear so as to not create any barriers to the communication. Keep your focus on the imaginary light surrounding us." Several minutes ticked by. Sheila's warm presence withdrew just enough that I no longer could feel the cobwebs. I knew she hadn't left me completely and I wondered if she was doing something on her end to help things along. The afterlife was such a mystery, though many claimed to know all about it.

The temperature in the room began to drop noticeably. Mary's hand trembled. I squeezed it gently. She squeezed back but did not turn her head to look at me. It dawned on me in that moment that the four people around me were focused with quiet intensity on the floor in front of us. And then I saw why.

Lost in my own internal wanderings, I'd missed it at first. A shadow danced in the spot of sunlight shining across the floor's smooth surface. I glanced to my right where the windows were located to see if a tree branch was perhaps creating the shadows. Mary had pulled the curtains closed but they parted just enough to allow a ray of sunlight to spike through. I could see nothing to explain the shadow. The sun's ray of light came into our circle between Kade and Adam. The shadow was faint at first, moving around as if it was indeed the result of a tree branch moving about in the breeze. Then it grew darker, forming into a circle about the size of a quarter. After a brief pause, it broke apart and formed into an ever expanding ring until it disappeared beyond the light. I glanced up at the others and found them all looking at me.

Adam broke the silence. "What was that?"

"I'm not sure." I felt a slight tremor at that moment and before I could say anything, Kade's hand tightened. The floor vibrated again. Remembering there was a train track across the street, I wondered if perhaps that was causing the vibration. Then my chair rumbled loudly in the quiet room as it moved slightly forward, scraping the floor in protest. Mary's and then Adam's did the same. Eyes wide with alarm, they both looked at me for reassurance. Then the floor shook again.

Earthquakes were not known in Maine and I'd never experienced one myself but the sensation was what I imagined it might be like. "The trains..."

"No," Dawn cut in, clearly fascinated. "We've never felt anything from them. They are barely moving by the time they arrive to the mill or pull out for departure." The fact she was more excited than afraid seemed to help relax her children as well.

"I think perhaps whoever is trying to communicate wants us to believe they really are here." Just as I said that, my chair moved back a couple inches and I clasped harder to Kade's and Mary's hands. The spirit wasn't done playing. Before I could try and reassure everyone that this phenomena was typical (not!), my chair began to rock back and forth, going up on the two front legs about a half inch, plopping down awkwardly and then propping up on the back legs in the same manner. These sorts of theatrics I could do without. "Stop." The rocking immediately stopped. Then the temperature dropped some more and a curious smell began to permeate the room. Even as I lifted my nose to the air, I noticed the others doing the same.

It was a sweet smell, almost like vanilla but that wasn't it...something else ... another pleasant scent similar to ... sage! The smell grew stronger and everyone was now drawing the scent into their noses, taking deep whiffs. "It's sage but something else..."

"Sweet grass." Dawn nodded with conviction as she took another big whiff. "Definitely sweet grass and sage. Possibly cedar as well."

I sniffed again and agreed that the distinctive smell of cedar could be detected now that she'd mentioned it. Of course it could be that suggestion was influencing our senses but it sounded right. Why these particular scents?

"Indians use sage for ceremonial rituals." Dawn glanced at me with wide eyes, comprehending. "It must be one of my husband's ancestors."

As soon as the words were out of Dawn's mouth the scent went away but the cold remained. I closed my eyes and waited to see if anyone would approach me for communication.

Expanding my focus on the room at large, I sent out psychic feelers in hopes of detecting the presence of unseen visitors. Someone was near the fireplace. I opened my eyes half expecting to actually see something but I saw nothing. My gaze dropped to the logs sitting in a neat stack in the grate and as I did so, they suddenly shifted making us all jump.

"Someone is here. I think you may be right, Dawn. I'm getting a strong impression of an Indian native." I could almost sense Kade's question and shook my head. "Not Big Red." But he was a big man, impressively so. A strange feeling passed through me, like another soul mixing with mine, and I had a sudden urge to call out in a guttural sound and flex my biceps. Of course, in truth, my biceps were nothing to be showing off despite the fact that they felt quite massive all of a sudden. My chest felt just as massive and I wasn't talking about suddenly sprouting big breasts. Male testosterone flooded my system. It was all I could do not to jump to my feet and start striking poses like the men on those Mr. Universe competitions. Okay, I get it. You are a big man. Tough. But what do you want?

The image of the witch's leg adorning Buck's monument flashed through my mind and then my foot stomped hard, jarring my knee bone. Mary gasped but I couldn't reassure her for this strong male entity had my complete attention. Another smell permeated the air around me. Some sort of flower but I couldn't place it. I am not a botanist. I need more to go on here. Why the smell? What is it?

The logs in the grate suddenly popped as if someone had punched them from beneath and they scattered on the floor next to us. Adam started to rise from his chair but I saw Kade's grip tighten and he relaxed back into his seat. "What the heck is it with the fireplace?"

The room was at once warm again. Whatever had joined us was now gone. Disappointed not to have made better contact, I looked around at the others to gage their reactions. The mood in the room was quiet and reflective. It wasn't until the entity left us that I noticed how dark the room had been while he was here. Concurrent with his departure, it was as if the sun had suddenly come out from behind the clouds although the windows were mostly covered by curtains. "He's gone."

Kade gave my hand another quick squeeze and let me go. He stood and went straight for the fireplace. "Do you think something is hidden here as well?"

A couple minutes later and we were all on our hands and knees scouring every inch of the fireplace, paying special attention to the hearth stones. We found nothing. Disappointed, I sank back on my knees. "He showed me the witch's leg on Buck's monument and right after that he made me stomp my foot and then the logs rolled out onto the floor. I thought for sure there was a connection somehow."

Kade straightened up and stretched, absently rubbing his leg as he considered everything he knew up to this point. "It's beginning to look like the witch's curse on that monument is tied to the Indians somehow."

He had a point. It sure was beginning to look that way. Logically I wanted to say it didn't make sense. Indians weren't known for making curses and part of a leg surely wasn't a symbol that would be associated with them. I knew better than to close my mind to any possibility so I shrugged in clueless bafflement. "Not sure, but I agree it's starting to look that way."

By silent agreement, we put the chairs back in their respective spots and returned to where we'd been sitting before the séance. All five of us sat in contemplative silence, each lost to our own musings.

It was Dawn who finally broke the silence. "I don't understand why everything has to be so cryptic." She shook her head, a small frown marring the area between her brows. "If they can communicate, why don't they just come out and tell us what they know or want us to know?"

Kade and I chuckled in mutual understanding. He'd asked the same question when we were investigating the haunting at Sea Willow Haven. In fact, everyone I've come into contact with concerning paranormal phenomena always wonders the same thing and asks that very question. Including me. "I think it has something to do with the fact that we learn more by searching for answers than what we do when they are simply given to us."

"But does everything have to be such a mystery?" Mary's dark eyes clouded with puzzled annoyance. "Why haunt us and not tell us why when we make contact and ask?" She touched my arm in sympathy. "You must get very frustrated."

I patted Mary's hand, noting that it didn't feel as cold as it had earlier. "Sometimes I get frustrated but mostly I just get more curious. It makes me dig more and search more and question more and through all that I learn more." I glanced at Dawn curiously as I remembered her recognition of the smells during the séance. "How did you know what those smells were? I'd heard of sweet grass being used in some spiritual rituals but I'd never encountered it."

"As I've said before, my husband was proud of his Indian heritage although he wasn't sure from which tribe his ancestors hailed. He studied all the different cultures and we attended a lot of Indian powwows."

Adam and Mary nodded their heads in fond remembrance and when their mother paused, Adam spoke up. "Pop dragged us to all sorts of Indian gatherings and celebrations. Not just here in Maine for we've gone as far south as Florida and as far east as Arizona."

Smiling, Mary looked more relaxed than I'd seen her. "We grew up having some of the best vacations."

Thinking about the beads I'd found at the Tenney house, I felt a sudden compulsion to share that with them and spoke up before I changed my mind. "You would probably love to see what I found at the Tenney house given your interest in Indians." That got the attention of all three Rowan family members.

Adam leaned forward, his expression filled with curiosity. "What?"

"A box of Indian beads."

Dawn was clearly perplexed by my announcement. "What do you mean you found them? And why would Indian beads be hidden in the Tenney house?"

"I made contact with a spirit who showed me where they were hidden which was in the fireplace. There was a secret compartment where a copper box was hidden. The box is filled with Indian beads and a smooth oval stone."

Clearly interested, Dawn motioned for me to continue with the story. "What do the beads look like? How do you know they are Indian beads?"

"I showed them to Rid since his nephew owns the property. Rid seems to be well versed in Indian history. He recognized them right away, but I also did some research on the internet." I paused for a moment then decided to tell them about my vision of the necklace. "I believe they used to make up a necklace. I saw it in another vision." Remembering the drawing I'd made to show Rid, I grabbed my sweater from the end of the couch where I'd tossed it after our mad dash into the house. "I drew a picture of it." I pulled the drawing out of my sweater pocket and handed it to Dawn. She stared at it for a long, thoughtful moment.

"This is a lovely design." She lifted her head and glanced at Mary. They exchanged a long look then Dawn gave a slight nod and stood up. "I'd like to show you something."

The rest of us stood at once and followed her out of the room. She went down another hallway that led in the opposite direction of the kitchen and opened a door at the end of it. Bright sunlight poured through several windows, lighting the cluttered craft room within. Dawn stepped aside so I could enter and I did so cautiously for most of the floor space was taken. Despite the chaos, there did seem to be some sort of order to everything. It wasn't messy, just very crowded. Craft supplies of every sort filled the floor-to-ceiling shelves. Drawers, bins, boxes, jars ... if it could hold some sort of supply, then it was present in this room. The workbench made it pretty obvious the craft of choice...jewelry.

Dawn glanced at my interested gaze and smiled. "I've been making jewelry for many years. Mary does as well. I think she's more talented than I, really, but I do enjoy it so much."

An assortment of jars and trays filled with beads were scattered around the large desk. I bent to look at them more closely. Glass beads, clay beads, rocks and gems...they had it all. "What a lovely hobby. I wish I knew how to do something like this."

Mary touched my arm to gain my attention. "Maybe you could give me those beads and I'll try to recreate the necklace for you."

My heart nearly stopped. It surely skipped hard. Excitement raced through me so fast my breath hitched and goose bumps broke out on my skin. I loved the synchronicity of the universe. How lucky was it to meet these people and have them be jewelry makers? I nodded immediately to show my approval of her suggestion. "That would be wonderful, Mary! Thank you so much."

Smiling wide for the first time that day, Mary nodded her own approval of the plan. "I'll come by later and pick them up. I've always wanted to see Barb's B&B. Mom is friends with her but that developed more after I left for the military."

Dawn was smiling as well. "Maybe I'll come too. I haven't seen Barbara in quite a while."

"Yes, please do. Barbara did tell me to extend her apologies for not visiting in so long and I'm sure she'd love to see you, Dawn."

Adam and Kade waited in the doorway since the room was too crowded for all of us. My eyes met Kade's briefly and I knew he approved of my decision to give the beads to Mary. He looked just as excited about that as I was actually.

Dawn glanced at her watch and turned to leave. "I better get those biscuits in the oven."

Once we were back in the living room, Adam walked over to the fireplace and looked at it thoughtfully. "So that's why you suddenly became interested in the fireplace earlier. You thought maybe to find another secret hiding spot?"

I gave a small shrug. "Well, I thought it couldn't hurt to look."

"I wonder who hid the beads and why?" Mary sank down on the couch and fell back against the cushions.

Kade and I returned to our previous spots as well. "I don't know, Mary, but I hope to find out. Maybe after you make that necklace, I'll put it on and see if it helps connect me to the events that led to those beads being hidden away."

Mary clasped her hands together in an effort to contain her excitement. I knew she couldn't wait to get her hands on those beads and bring the necklace into being. "This is all such a mystery. How exciting to be involved in it!" And then, remembering the stress looming over her life, some of the light went out of her eyes. "If only we could figure out how to save our home."

A pall fell over the room and we all sank into quiet contemplation. Dawn entered at that moment and pulled us from our disheartening thoughts. "Dinner is about ready. Mary, you want to give me a hand?"

I started to rise as well but both women waved me back down. Mary's eyes met mine and it was easy enough to recognize the plea in them not to argue with her. "No, Tess, please, let Mom and I take care of it. You relax here for a moment."

I couldn't argue with her after that. Besides, I had a strong suspicion the women wanted to talk in private. "Okay but call me if you need any help."

"I will." Mary wagged a finger at Adam. "Be a nice host." And then she and her mother hurried from the room.

Adam looked at me and then Kade and then back to me. "So was the Tenney house haunted too?"

"There was someone there but I'm pretty sure he's not haunting the place." I reached for Kade's hand because I liked having contact with him and he entwined his fingers through mine. It was so nice to have him near.

"So you are a painter?" Adam glanced down at our hands and then raised a smirking brow to me as if to remind me that he'd called it right the night before.

"Yes, I paint mostly landscapes but I do a bit of everything." Kade looked at Adam for a long moment, studying him. "What do you like to do?"

"I like to do landscaping." His tanned face actually colored a little. "I know that's hard to believe when you look at our yard but I didn't want to start something mom would expect me stay around and maintain." He shifted uncomfortably. "It was never my intention to stay in Bucksport."

"Where would you like to live?" I asked, curious.

"Pop took us to the Blue Ridge Mountains once to attend an Indian powwow there and I fell in love with the area. I've always wanted to go back." He gave a shrug and glanced away, his shoulders slumping, and I knew he felt that dream was completely unattainable. "There are a lot of rocks there. Just as there are here, of course, but there was something about that place..."

"Rocks?" Kade and I asked in unison and we smiled in acknowledgment that we were so in synch with each other.

"I love working with rocks to create stuff." He gave us a contemplative look and stood up. "If Mary and Mom can show you their stuff, then I might as well show you something I've done." He motioned for us to follow him. We went down yet another hallway and out a door that led to the back part of the porch. Both Kade and I had to stop for a quick moment to admire the view of the Penobscot River with Fort Knox gracing the opposite bank before hurrying after Adam who was stepping down onto the overgrown lawn. He pointed to the left of where we were standing and then began walking toward it. "I built that." It was a beautifully constructed fireplace.

Kade and I looked at each other and began to smile. I wasn't sure why this excited me but it did. "Wow, Adam, you made that?"

"Well, a crudely built fire pit has always been there. Pop said his family used it for Indian rituals." The glance he threw us was highly skeptical. "I wouldn't give much weight to that. He was always telling us stuff he thought us kids would get a kick out of. None of us believed him but we used to run around it like a pack of yahoos and make up stupid kid dances just the same." He smiled at the memory and then walked over to a wooden bench that sat facing the front of it. He plunked down upon it as if the weight of the world had suddenly become too much. "I decided after he died to honor his memory by building this."

Made entirely of rocks fitted closely together and secured with mortar, it was an impressive fireplace. The base of it was round, about two feet high with a pretty wide circumference. Seeing where my focus was directed, Adam explained its size. "I kept the original dimensions. I don't know what they did with it back in Pop's ancestors' day but they must have had a few bonfires here. Being this close to town, we could never get a fire permit to have anything more than a small campfire size blaze. We don't use it anyhow. Like I said, it's more of a memorial to my Pop."

The fireplace was built near the end of the flattest area of the lawn. A short distance behind it, the lawn sloped gently a short distance before dropping dramatically to another level area which eventually met the sidewalk edging the street below. Adam used the natural landscape to build a waterfall which followed a rock-lined stream to what looked like a small natural pond at the base of the hill. The waterfall, however, was not running and the rock basin from which it would spill from was partially filled with stagnant water.

Adam motioned toward it with his hand. "I built the waterfall for my Mom. I thought she would enjoy it from the porch but as you can see I've lost my ambition to keep it maintained." His voice turned bitter. "I didn't feel like keeping it in great working order for someone else to enjoy." He glanced at the fireplace and dropped his gaze. "No guarantee the new owners will even keep it."

As I stepped forward to run a comforting hand across Adam's taut shoulders, I noticed a scent in the air that I'd smelled earlier during the séance. Sniffing appreciatively, I looked around to locate the smell and knew it had to be the flowering bushes lining the edge of the property a short distance from the fireplace. Lilacs. Of course! But why was their scent brought through during the séance? Adam's shoulders tensed beneath my fingers and I gave him a sympathetic pat. "You did a lovely job, Adam. You are very talented. I'm sure your father would have loved it." I pointed to the lilac bushes. "Have those always been there?"

"Pop planted them when he and mom first got married. They are her favorite flower." Adam stood and walked closer to the fireplace. He stared down into its empty pit, his eyes almost as vacant. "Not only will mom miss her lilacs but we'll never get to use this fireplace either."

Not sure what to say, I dropped my gaze and noticed the area around the fireplace was nearly devoid of grass. The compact earth looked as if many a footprint had indeed surrounded it at one time. Several large flat stones were placed randomly in a semicircle fashion around the front of the fireplace, creating a natural patio of sorts. I pointed to them. "Did you put those there as well?"

Adam stretched his foot across one of the flat stones and rubbed a booted heel across its surface. "These are slate slabs. Pop said they've been there as far back as he can remember. They were probably put here to help keep the vegetation down."

"So here you all are." Mary stepped off the porch and came to join us. "Adam did a great job with that didn't he? He's an awesome landscaper but there's not much demand for it around here." She gave her brother a pointed look, "Not that he advertises himself or anything. Can't get any work if people don't know what you have to offer."

Adam threw his sister a scowl. "What does it matter? Looks like we won't be living here much longer anyways."

Mary gave him a quick hug. "I know and I'm sorry. Let's go eat, dinner is ready." Linking arms with her brother, Mary pulled him along with her and Kade and I fell into step behind them. As we made our way back to the house, I could feel their father standing behind us.

My back prickling, I turned to look. I could almost picture him standing near the lilac bushes; his feet planted firmly apart, his massive arms crossed and his face scrunched in a scowl of frustration because I wasn't getting his message.

Kade leaned down to whisper in my ear. "What? Do you see something?"

"I have a strong feeling their father is there. But it wasn't him who came through during the séance."

"You can't see him then?"

Smiling because Kade's belief in me was so strong he didn't even question my ability anymore, I squeezed his hand. "No, but I can imagine him pretty strongly."

"What's he doing?" We started up the steps of the porch. I glanced back again. "Standing there."

"Where?" Kade turned to look as well.

"Near the lilac bushes to the left of the fireplace."

Mary disappeared into the house and since Adam stood holding the door for us, I gave Kade's hand a quick squeeze to get his attention.

Kade looked back, saw Adam and stepped up our pace. "You really did a fine job with that, Adam. I'm impressed." He gave the younger man an approving pat on the back as we passed him to enter the house.

Dawn's New England boiled dinner was delicious, her biscuits to die for. Once again I ate way more than I should have and sat back to stretch when I was done. Oh how nice it would be right now to pop that button on my jean shorts. "I'm going to get fat if I keep eating like this."

Adam and Kade gave me a look that said I could probably use a few pounds and I laughed at their expressions, adding defensively, "I've gained several pounds since coming to Maine."

"And they look mighty fine on you too," Kade murmured quietly next to my ear.

Blushing at the compliment, I gave him a sideways look, telling him with my eyes to behave. Catching our glances, Mary said quietly, "Would you like to have some coffee out on the porch before you leave?" She waved a hand at the table. "Adam can help mom pick up the dishes and I'll do them later." She glanced at me firmly. "No arguments."

Adam readily agreed to the plan. "Deal. It's my turn to do dishes but if you want to do them, sister dear, I'm not going to argue."

Dawn stood and motioned for us to bustle along. "You guys head on out to the porch. I'll make us a pot of coffee and join you shortly."

Kade and I followed Mary out the door to the patio set we'd sat in earlier when we first arrived. The evening was warm, the air still, and we all sat back to enjoy the peace and quiet. "It's lovely here. Even though you have that big old mill across the street, it doesn't ruin the atmosphere in the least." I wondered about that as I closed my eyes to enjoy the moment.

"We don't hear the traffic as bad on this side of the house. Probably because we are so high up from the road." Mary touched my hand to get my attention and I opened my eyes to look at her.

"Thank you for coming over today. It's been really nice having you and Kade here." She looked at Kade and smiled, making sure he knew she was just as glad to have him there as she was to have me.

"I wish we knew what we could do to help you," Kade told her. His solemn voice was deep and soft and it made my stomach flutter in response.

"Crap happens." Mary gave a long sigh. "We'll live through it. Everyone does."

Dawn came around the corner with a laden tray and Kade hurried to help, bringing the tray to the table and setting it down carefully. Once we all had a cup of coffee in front of us, we sat in peaceful silence. Despite the bleak future looming before Dawn and Mary, we experienced a moment of contentment.

"So what are your plans for tomorrow?" Dawn asked.

"Well, I was thinking Kade and I would go check out Fort Knox. Then in the afternoon I imagine Kade will want to work on the painting he's doing for Barbara while I work on other stuff." I looked at Kade to see if he approved of the plan. His blue eyes met mine for a long moment and then he winked, making a rush of heat cross my face. It was so strange to be reacting to a man in such a physical way again. Although I still experienced a twinge of guilt, it was nowhere near as strong as it was when I first met him. I no longer thought it was a betrayal to Mike to be attracted to Kade, but since I never thought there would be anyone else, it still felt strange to be going through this again...with someone other than Mike.

"I think that sounds like an excellent plan," Kade said. "I've never been to the fort though I've passed it enough times during my travels."

"When would be a good time to come pick up the beads?" Mary asked.

"How about in the afternoon, around three or so?" Dawn and Mary both agreed to the time and then when we refused another cup of coffee, Dawn began to gather everything back on the tray.

"Well then, I guess we'll see you at three. I'm going to head in and catch the evening news." Dawn gave me a hug and then turned to give Kade one as well. He hid his surprise and hugged her back.

"Thank you for dinner. It was delicious." He gave Dawn and Mary one of those smiles I loved so much and my heart swelled in response. It didn't matter who the smile was directed toward, I still enjoyed it.

"You sure you don't want any pie or something?" Dawn glanced at both of us and when we nodded in polite refusal, she smiled in understanding. "Well, you two have a great evening." She picked up the tray and gave Mary a loving wink as she bustled away.

Kade and I looked at each other. We were ready to go. I turned to Mary. "We are going to head out now, Mary. Thank you for a great dinner. It truly was delicious."

The three of us stood, stretched, laughed because we had all done the same thing and then Mary followed us to the car. "Thank you again, both of you, for coming." Mary grabbed my hands and squeezed them gently. "Have a great day tomorrow." She pulled me into a hug and then turned to give Kade one as well.

She was still standing there at the edge of the driveway when we backed onto the street and pulled away. My last glimpse of her before we drove from sight was of her staring across the street toward the river. She looked so forlorn that I couldn't help but wonder what was going through her mind. The aura of sadness was back in place and my heart hurt for her.

Kade reached over and patted my thigh. "Things will work out in the end. Isn't that what you told me you believe?"

Smiling, glad for his reminder, I grabbed his hand and held it on the seat between us. "Yes, somehow things always do. You are right about that."

As I pulled into the parking spot in front of the B&B, I sent up a prayer for the Rowan family. Put the worry in God's hands and let it go. That's what my grandmother used to tell me all the time. Why didn't I think of those priceless nuggets of advice more often?

"Want an ice cream?" Kade waved a hand toward the ice cream parlor a short distance away. There were a few people in line and another couple walked past us licking ice cream cones as we stepped from the car.

"I shouldn't, considering how much I ate for dinner but a cone sounds like a great idea." Kade took my hand and tucked it into the crook of his arm, holding me close while we walked the short distance to the parlor.

As we stood in line, waiting our turn to order, I knew I wasn't quite ready to head back to the B&B. I glanced up at him. "How about we take our ice cream and walk along the river?"

Kade pulled his hand away so he could put his arm around my shoulders and hug me close. He dropped a kiss on the top of my head then bent to whisper in my ear, sending little thrills of excitement skittering across my skin. "You come up with the best ideas."

We walked from one end of the river walk to the other. Kade wanted to sit by the Veterans Memorial for a bit and we finished off our cones there. It was getting dark by the time we finally headed back to the B&B and the air was rapidly cooling. My sweater was no longer sufficient and Kade had only a t-shirt, though he didn't seem to be bothered by the cooler temperature.

Barbara was not in the sitting room when we entered the B&B and there was no sign of Max either. We went quietly up the stairs and by mutual agreement, headed to my room. As we paused in front of my door, Kade stood behind me and wrapped his arms loosely around my waist. "How about we snuggle for a bit and watch some TV and then I'll leave you in peace to get some sleep?"

I patted his linked hands and wondered if he could feel the butterflies pounding furiously against my stomach. "You come up with the best ideas." I giggled as he began to kiss my neck and I couldn't help but feel like I was in high school again.

A few minutes later we were snuggling on the bed and watching a sitcom. It felt so good to relax with him. "I really enjoy your company, Kade." He turned onto his side to look at me. Our eyes met and held.

Kade lifted a hand and ran a finger along my cheek. "I love your company too." He bent to give me a kiss and I readily lifted my mouth to meet him halfway. A small twinge of unease flitted through me as I worried that Kade might want more than what I was willing to give. He let his fingers flutter along my temple and thread into my hair and then leaned forward to deepen our kiss. Though I readily returned it, I held back just enough to let him know this was not going to go anywhere. Not yet. Kade's mouth let up slightly and I actually felt like chasing him for more when he lifted his head and pressed his forehead to mine. I knew he was exercising great control to keep our physical contact from getting out of hand and relaxed against him, grateful for his restraint and yet also wishing he'd push the issue.

After a long moment, Kade pulled away and looked at me seriously. "I want you so much, Tess, but I know you aren't ready. I'm willing to wait." He let his fingers run along my jaw and then up into my hair, fisting it there as he closed his eyes. "Just don't take too long or you are going to be the death of me." He smiled to soften the words and I laughed softly.

"Okay. I'm sorry..."

Kade put a finger on my lips. "Don't. No apologies. I'm happy to have what we have. And I'll be happy wherever this goes. No pressure and no worries. Okay?"

I nodded because I couldn't speak past the lump in my throat. Tears filled my eyes and spilled over. Kade caught at them with his thumb. "Don't cry, baby." He kissed me again and then stood up. "I'm going to head to my room and get a decent night's sleep. You do the same and I'll be expecting you to rise bright and early tomorrow morning. Okay?"

I followed him to my door and we exchanged another heated kiss. For a moment I think we almost gave in to the demands of our bodies but then I reluctantly let him go and stood back. "Sleep well, Kade."

He dropped another kiss on my forehead. "It might take me awhile after that kiss but I'll try. You too." And then he went across the hall and disappeared into his room. I shut the door and leaned against it for a moment, enjoying the warm feelings washing through me. A rush of joy filled my chest and

I had to draw in a deep breath and release it to ease the pressure. It was going to be okay. Everything was going to be okay. Now to get there...to that okay place.

CHAPTER FIFTEEN

Since I felt restless and edgy after Kade left and I knew it would be useless to try and go to bed, I headed for my laptop. My curiosity about Isi was now foremost in my mind and there was no way I could turn in without doing a little more writing. There must be a connection between her and everything else happening in my life. The only way to find out what it could be was to sit down and type out her story.

After a short rest period, Nina urged Isi to her feet and indicated they must hurry. Not sure why they were rushing or where they were going, Isi had to trust that she wouldn't lose her life when she got there. But why bring her along if they only intended to send her into the darkness? Would her soul be lost forever? This was her worry now that she was no longer with her people. When her time came to join the Knowing One would these people know how to prepare her for the journey? Isi closed her eyes and thought of her grandmother Mailee, a respected Chosen one. Isi was under Mailee's guidance and had been since her birth. Mailee said Isi would be a Chosen someday. Sadness washed through her as the realization sunk in that she would never be part of the Chosen. Her training was over. As she struggled to keep up with Nina and Giles, Isi vowed to never forget all she'd been taught. Her grandmother told her that everyone learned what they needed to know as they needed to know it. The Knowing One imparted information only when it was required. To Isi's way of thinking, the Knowing One had been preparing her for this event. She would use what she knew to survive and learn.

The trees suddenly gave way to a large open field. Two horses were standing near a strange object Isi had never seen before. Suddenly afraid, Isi stopped walking. Nina turned and spoke to her in a soft voice. Isi looked at her and wished she understood. If only she knew their language.

Nina motioned with her hand. "Come." She repeated her hand motion and said again, "Come."

The hand motion Isi understood. And now the word associated with it was understood as well. But Isi could not do as Nina asked because she was afraid. She didn't know what that thing was or what she was supposed to do when she got to it. Nina gently tugged on her hand. "Come."

As they approached the strange object together, Giles appeared to be attaching the horses to it. Nina stopped when they were close enough to touch it and waved a hand. "Wagon." She repeated the word slowly several times then motioned for Isi to do the same.

"Wa...gon."

Nina beamed at her and said something to Giles who merely grunted. That sound Isi understood. Even her people grunted. Nina jumped up on the thing she called a wagon and held a hand down to Isi. Obviously she meant for Isi to join her. Once again afraid, Isi held back. Giles came up behind her and lifted her into the air, settling her next to Nina. They sat on flattened wood and Giles motioned for them to make room. Nina and Isi moved over and Giles jumped up beside them. He grabbed the ropes attached to the horses and the next thing Isi knew, they were moving! Amazed, Isi watched as the land passed by. Were she not afraid of what was going to happen next, Isi was sure she would have enjoyed this new experience, even though it was terribly bumpy and uncomfortable on her bottom.

After a short time, Nina turned and crawled inside the large covered area behind them. She gently tugged Isi's arm and Isi reluctantly followed her inside. The interior was dimly lit but soon Isi's eyes adjusted. It wasn't long before Isi knew what Nina wanted her to do next. Nina held up some clothes and indicated Isi was to wear them. It took some work but soon Isi was wearing something Nina called a dress. Next Nina braided her hair and then covered her head with something Nina called a bonnet. It all felt restrictive and Isi didn't like it but Nina made enough motions to get the point across. They were hiding her identity. If anyone realized Isi was not one of them, the magic stick would steal her soul. Disheartened and homesick, Isi nodded sadly, letting Nina know that she understood. Nina made a sad face then pulled Isi to her.

"Isabelle." Nina spoke the strange word several times and then Isi understood again. She was now to use a new name. Her old life was quickly becoming a thing of the past.

They rode for hours and as the sun began to go down, Nina indicated Isi should lie down on the bedding spread out close behind the seat where Giles sat. Nina lay beside her and hummed softly. Lulled by the peaceful sound, Isi slept.

They traveled for several days and during that time Nina seemed determined to teach Isi as much of her language as she could. Isi learned quickly and that made things so much easier. Although Giles was rather gruff and had been rough with her that first time, he never touched her again or threatened her in any way. He seemed to care very much for Nina and Nina wanted Isi. Just so long as Nina continued to feel that way, Isi knew she'd be safe.

She learned very quickly how to wear their clothing. The food they ate was strange and after a few days of travel, Isi began to share with Nina some of the foods her own people enjoyed. Although Giles was skeptical at first, he finally started trying some of the items Isi prepared. Sometimes he nodded in approval and sometimes he would spit it out and make faces. Isi and Nina laughed when he did this and after a while he would join them, his laughter loud and booming.

They encountered a few people during their travels, men riding horses with furs bundled in stacks and hanging over the horse's sides. Isi always moved into the back of the wagon when others were around or she kept her head down, her bonnet hiding her face. During these times Isi's heart pounded as she worried that her identity would be discovered and they'd use their magic stick on her. How long could they keep her hidden? When they got to wherever they were going, what then?

A few days later, Isi found out. She was sleeping in the back of the wagon when it suddenly halted and Isi heard excited voices. Taking care to be very quiet, Isi crawled to the end of the wagon and peeked out. They were near a wooden structure that Nina called a house. They had passed a couple of these houses during their travel but never stopped at any of them. With a terrified heart, Isi knew that this was the end of their journey. They had arrived at their destination. Now what was to happen to her?

I stopped typing at this point and sat back to think. It was hard to try and stay true to Isi's viewpoint when I wanted to describe everything as I knew it. Since I was not privy to Isi's language, I had to interpret the images coming to me and keep it as true to Isi as I could. It would be so much easier to write Isi's story once she finally learned my language. Realizing how weird that sounded...my musing about a character whom I wished would learn my language so I could better write her story...well, it was rather amusing.

I couldn't help but wonder why Nina and Giles were out in those woods in the first place. And why did they feel they had to take Isi? My gut feeling was that Nina truly was trying to save her life. Once again I thought about the fact that there was a period in time when Indians were often shot and killed on sight. Perhaps Giles and Nina knew fur hunters were in the area and were afraid they'd come upon the young girl and kill her.

The only thing I couldn't seem to figure out was where the story was taking place and how long ago it happened. Was it before or after Colonel Buck's death? Did Isi's story have anything to do with him or not? It was frustrating to not have very many facts. One thing for sure, I was now quite caught up in Isi's story. Her references to the Knowing One which had to be the equivalent of God and the Chosen which had to be a reference to the leaders in her tribe made me even more curious. I was completely intrigued and would have loved to write more but I was getting tired.

Reluctantly, I powered down my laptop and glanced at my cell phone. It was nearing ten and too late to be calling anyone. I hadn't called my family or my friends since arriving here and I knew everyone was probably wondering why. I told them I was going to be conducting another investigation and to not call unless it was an emergency. I had to do that because otherwise they called me constantly. I picked up my cell phone and scrolled through all the text messages and checked email to be sure nothing important required my attention then fired off some quick replies. I told them I'd fill them in on all the details when I had time to talk.

As I prepared for bed, I wondered if I should open a Facebook account. My friends told me I was behind the times and needed to get with the program. Perhaps so, but how was I supposed to keep track of it when I didn't even keep up with my text messages?

It felt great to finally fall into bed and though I kept thinking about the fact that Kade was nearby, I still managed to fall asleep. My dreams were a jumbled mess. I dreamed about Indians and cowboys and gunfights. I dreamed about dancing around campfires and exploding fireplaces and beads raining down from the sky. I saw streams gleaming with gold and then turning blood red. None of it made any sense and when I finally opened my eyes to the gray light of dawn, I did not feel at all rested. Despite that, I couldn't get back to sleep because I knew Kade was nearby and I wanted to see him.

Eager for the day to begin, I jumped out of bed and headed for the shower, taking care to be quiet as possible when I entered the hallway so as not to wake Kade. The sun hadn't yet put in an appearance but I knew it was going to be a glorious day. One, I suspected, that would be full of surprises.

CHAPTER SIXTEEN

The sky was still in the predawn stage when I emerged from the bathroom. I couldn't stop myself from listening near Kade's door and though I couldn't be sure, I thought I heard movement. Since I didn't want him to find me standing in the hallway wrapped in a towel, I quickly hurried to my room. A glance at the clock on my nightstand said it was a little after five. Although I was a relatively early riser, it wasn't typical for me to be up before the sun. I glanced out the window at the quiet street below and had a sudden urge to walk to the cemetery. Without further delay, I put on a pair of jeans and a pretty blue knit top with floral designs embroidered into it. I pulled my hair back into a ponytail and grabbed a lightweight fleece jacket. One thing I learned quickly about Maine, the early mornings were usually quite cool. Finally ready, I headed for the door.

How I managed to stifle the startled cry that jumped into my throat I have no idea because when I pulled the door open and saw someone standing there, my first instinct was to scream. The realization that a man was standing in my doorway sent a spiral of fear zooming through my system in no time flat but before I could get a sound out, a finger gently touched my lips to stifle it.

"Shush, Tess, it's me."

Drawing in a much-needed breath, I grabbed Kade's hand and pulled it away from my mouth, though I continued to hold onto it if only to reassure myself it really was him. "You scared the crap out of me!"

"Sorry. I heard you moving around over here and I was getting ready to knock when you opened the door."

He was fully dressed in jeans and a long-sleeved gray flannel shirt which was unbuttoned and showing a black t-shirt underneath. His hair was still wet from the shower. Amazed that he was not only awake but showered and dressed, I glanced at my watch to double-check the time. Yup, five fifteen in the morning. "Up a little early aren't we?"

Kade leaned against the doorframe and let his gaze wonder over me, his eyes turning dark with appreciation as he took in my close fitting jeans and blue knit shirt. "Yes, we are aren't we? Going somewhere?"

Doing my best to ignore the heat rushing across my skin (it seemed I always reacted like that whenever Kade looked at me that way), I somehow managed to speak, though my voice was a tad husky. "I thought I'd take a walk up to the graveyard while it's relatively light traffic."

Like it was normal to get up at an ungodly hour and go traipsing to a graveyard, Kade nodded. "I'll get my jacket and come with you." He started to turn then stopped. "But first..." He leaned in and kissed me hard and quick. "You look great first thing in the morning." After a quick grin of approval, he strode to his room and I couldn't help but stand there, smile, and watch. He had a nice walk. And a nice backside. As soon as he disappeared inside his room, I shook my head to rid it of thoughts going places it had no business going at five dark thirty in the morning. Get a grip, Tess. Once again I found myself grinning like an idiot as I headed for the stairs to wait for Kade. Thoughts of him had that sort of effect on me.

Not a minute later, we were making our way quietly down the stairs. The foyer was dimly lit and quiet. Barbara obviously was not up yet. Taking care to make as little noise as possible, we opened the front door and stepped out into the cool morning air. It was blessedly still. Birds chirped cheerfully around the feeders Barbara kept filled next to the flower garden and I stopped briefly to admire them. Chickadees mostly, Maine's official state bird.

Kade's warm hand enveloped mine. "We better hurry or the traffic is going to get real busy real quick."

It took about ten minutes to walk there. A few more cars were beginning to traverse the main road but for the most part, it was very peaceful, the quiet disturbed only by the birds. We walked to the front of the cemetery facing the cursed monument and stood quietly. A prickle of chills skittered across my back. Someone else had joined us already.

Kade leaned down to whisper in my ear. "You feel something?"

I glanced at him in surprise. "How do you know?"

He indicated our linked hands. "You always tighten your grip when something's up."

"Someone has joined us. I think it's the girl." But then I knew right away it wasn't the same one I encountered before. No. This one felt different. Her sorrow hit me in the chest like an emotional club at full swing. I put my free hand there and closed my eyes, willing the pressure to ease off while offering support. "I'm here for you. Talk to me. Show me who you are." I preferred mental communication because I always felt silly talking out loud to what would appear as nothing to others. Someday I'd have to get over that, but today was not that day.

I pulled my hand from Kade's and clenched both of them into fists. Her frustration filled my psyche and I immediately surrounded myself with protective light. The unease her feelings generated eased off and though I was thankful to get some relief, my legs suddenly went weak and I couldn't stop myself from sinking to my knees. We were merging, she and I, and I allowed the process, though letting spirits take over my body was something I was not normally comfortable permitting. The worry was always there that they wouldn't want to leave.

Wrapping my arms about myself, I began to rock to the sounds of a chant. So clearly could I hear it that I wondered if Kade could as well. My hand played with something around my neck and a surge of recognition hit me like a mini lightning bolt. It was the necklace to which my newly acquired beads once belonged. As the whispered chants increased, I tilted my head back and waited. Then with sudden clarity, I knew she was about to die and welcomed it. My hands flung wide as I waited for the transition to spirit and then a sharp pain lanced through my head. The pain was only for a brief instant but I grabbed at my head and would have fallen backwards onto the ground if Kade's arms hadn't caught me.

"What happened, Tess? You okay?" He held me firmly and I welcomed his warmth, his strength.

"I'm fine. I'm not totally sure but I think I just experienced her death." Tears filled my eyes as I mourned her loss. Had she died? If so, who killed her and why? Who was she? Did she curse Buck's monument? The questions mounted and filled me with frustration.

"How did she die?"

"I'm not sure but she was either shot, beheaded or struck gravely." I touched the back of my head as tears fell in sorrow for her horrible demise. "She knew it was coming. I think she was praying to her God or whatever." I looked up at Kade, meeting his warm gaze and taking strength from it. "I'm quite sure she was an Indian native because I didn't feel like she was praying to God. Not as we understand him anyway. It wasn't the same girl I encountered here before. There was something...I don't know...different about her."

"What do you mean?"

"She seemed like one of us...you know, but it seemed to me in the brief moment I was merged with her that her beliefs were very different from what I am familiar with." I pulled away to think for it was impossible to do that while wrapped in Kade's arms. "I felt like she was wearing a dress, you know, like the Colonists, but she was also wearing a necklace." I glanced at Kade and met his inquisitive look. "Yes, that one."

"Wow, Tess. This is great."

Hands on hips, I looked to him for clarification. "How so? As I see it, all we have are more questions."

"Well, if she was wearing the necklace made from the beads you found then you also know she has to be linked to Buck here." He cocked his head toward the monument. "You said you sensed him in the room where the beads were found and now you sense them on a girl while standing here near his grave."

"But if Big Red is linked to those beads, as I suspect he is, how can Buck be involved as well? I don't get that connection at all because if Big Red is a Red Paint Indian, and I really think he is, then a connection between them makes no sense. They were wiped out thousands of years before Buck made his way here to Bucksport."

Kade gave it some thought. "Maybe she's a descendent of Big Red."

My heart gave a little lurch at the unexpected suggestion and I smiled thoughtfully. "You may be right, Kade. So, the thing to figure out is who is she, how did she die and did Buck have anything to do with it?" I couldn't help but needle him a little. "See? More questions."

Kade grabbed my hand and tugged me gently along with him. "Let's get back to the B&B and get some breakfast. We'll discuss it with Barbara and see what else comes up as the day progresses."

"It's one of the things I love about you, Kade. You come up with great plans."

Kade gave me a sideways look. "One of the things you love about me? There are more?"

I laughed as joy filled my being. "Yes, and I'm not going to share them right now." At his boyish pout, I laughed again. "Okay, I'll share one more. I love that you make me laugh."

Kade leaned down and pressed a quick kiss to my mouth. "I think I love everything about you, Tess."

Now we were moving into dangerous territory...for me anyway. I chose not to respond and though I sensed he was a little disappointed, Kade said nothing more until we reached the B&B. "I smell bacon. Barbara is up."

Max met us in the foyer and Barbara came bustling out from the dining room as we were hanging up our jackets. "I didn't realize you were up already. You guys sure were out early. Hungry? I've fixed a little of everything today. Rid is stopping by and he loves a traditional breakfast."

Rid was coming for breakfast? Perfect. He was knowledgeable about the area and we had a lot of questions. As we followed Barbara into the dining room, I told her about Dawn and Mary stopping by later to pick up the beads. "She's going to try and recreate the necklace. Isn't that thoughtful of her to offer?"

Barbara poured each of us a cup of coffee and sat down across from Kade and me. "I forgot about them making jewelry. I didn't hear you come in last night; I was in the back doing an inventory of my pantry. My daughter is going to come watch the place for a spell while I do some shopping." She took a sip of her coffee. "So, what did you learn yesterday? Anything good?"

"Well, we ended up holding a séance." I knew this would grab Barbara's attention and it did. Her eyes widened in surprise and then she leaned forward in anticipation of learning more. "Do tell."

I had to laugh at the breathy pitch in Barbara's voice but then sobered as I took a sip of my coffee and thought about yesterday. "We didn't talk to anyone so you might be disappointed in the story. But someone did join us. I'm just not sure who. I think a relative of Night Rowan's but that's about all I can say about it."

Kade took a drink of his coffee and with his cup still raised, tipped it toward me in encouragement. "Tell her about the chairs moving on their own steam and yours rocking back and forth. Or hey, she might like to hear about the strange shadows dancing on the floor."

Barbara glanced at Kade with an open mouth, her eyes narrowing in suspicion that he was pulling her leg. She turned to me. "Did that really happen?" She wagged a finger in warning. "Don't you dare leave anything out. I want to know it all."

"Theatrics. Spirits sometimes do those things and I'm not sure why but it does seem to generate excitement when it happens. Maybe they are hoping to validate their presence." I gave a dismissive shrug because it wasn't things like that which I found important. It was the message the spirits were trying to convey that interested me more. "I'm not sure what he wanted me to know and I only hope I can figure it out."

"Is this spirit someone different from the one at the Tenney house? It doesn't have anything to do with Buck's curse does it?" Barbara finished her coffee and pushed her cup to the side so she could lean on her arms. "You didn't get any message at all?"

"Well, I think the message is that there is a message and I need to keep trying to figure out what it is." I finished my coffee as well and pushed my empty cup towards Barbara. "Is there any more coffee?"

"Yes, of course. I'll bring out a carafe." Barbara stood up and then paused to wag her finger at me. "Don't think this conversation is over."

Barbara had no sooner disappeared into the kitchen when we heard the front door open and Max whine with excitement. A series of dog nails clicking on the floor and the jingle of dog collars told me that Rid had Teddy with him. A second later my suspicion was confirmed. Teddy waddled quietly into the dining room alongside Rid and Max followed close behind looking quite pleased to be having some company of his own kind.

Kade and I stood up as Rid entered and I gave him a hug as soon as he was close enough for me to do so. "Nice to see you again, Rid." I waved toward Kade. "This is Kade Sinclair. Kade, this is Rid Truman". The two men shook hands and then Barbara bustled back into the room, her face breaking out into a welcome smile.

"Good morning, Rid! Please, come around here and sit next to me." She glanced down at the dogs and then looked at us. "Do you mind if we break the rules and let them stay in the dining room while we eat? Neither of them begs so they shouldn't bother you."

"Of course we don't mind, Barbara. I always let Tootsie stay with us while we were eating. And she did beg."

Barbara smiled her thanks and patted Rid's shoulder. "Sit down here next to me, I'll bring in the food and we can eat in just a jiff." She waved off my offer to help. "Stay right there, this is my job."

Within no time at all we were enjoying a full breakfast of home fries, fluffy scrambled eggs, homemade toast, crispy bacon and corned beef hash, which we soon learned, was Rid's favorite. Conversation was confined to food at first but then once we were settled into our meal, Barbara wiggled her fingers for me to continue where we left off. "Please continue with what happened at Dawn's."

Rid looked up from his plate and met my eyes with concern. "Did something happen to Dawn?"

Barbara waved off his concern. "She held a séance and the ghosts moved their chairs around and made shadow dances on the floor!" Though Barbara was clearly in awe, I could also tell she would never agree to having a séance in her house.

One of Rid's bushy gray brows lifted. "Really? Was it Night Rowan?"

"No. Possibly a relative though." I wished I knew. Sometimes it was more than frustrating to get messages that weren't very clear.

"You don't know? Did Dawn have any idea?" Rid no doubt was thinking about his own experience with his wife. For him there was no question as to whose spirit was near when she was about.

"It's a big man and although I know that Dawn's husband was a big man, similar in build to Adam, it wasn't him. I had a strong impression that something unpleasant happened in that house many years ago." And just like that, like a sudden pinch to the heart, I wondered if the unpleasant thing involved the girl at the graveyard this morning?

Rid was thoughtful for a long moment. He concentrated on his corn beef hash and as if by mutual consent, we all remained just as quiet. Finally he set down his fork, rested his elbows on the table and steepled his bony fingers. "It could be that unpleasant things happened there. The house has been around a long time. A lot of unpleasant history has taken place in this town after all."

I wanted to know what Rid knew because I was sure he knew a lot more than Dawn. "You said that Dawn would know a lot of history about her house but it would seem that is either not accurate or she's forgotten. When we tried to think about who the spirit could be, she was as clueless as the rest of us." I thought about my experience at the fireplace when I was held in the grip of the spirit. Unease rippled through me at the memory. I could feel my back prickling and hoped that talking about this wasn't going to lure spirits into joining us. It would scare Barbara, upset the dogs and to be honest, I just wasn't up for it at the moment.

Rid gave a thoughtful frown, thinking. "It could be that Night didn't tell her everything." He gave me a considering look. "We were good friends, Night and I. Both of us went to school together and grew up here in town." He paused for a moment then sighed and I knew he was about to tell us something he hadn't planned on sharing. "I was sweet on

Dawn when we were kids but she had eyes only for Night. I think they were a match made in heaven because he never looked at anyone but her." Rid shook his head in obvious regret for his past actions. "I didn't care. I tried everything to woo her away from him. It nearly destroyed our friendship." Rid gave a heavy sigh. "I always thought Night was too big and silent for her but, well, I guess when they were alone it must have been different." Rid shook his head in a manner that said he still didn't quite understand it. "Night was such a serious person. I think he was born with the weight of the world on his shoulders."

"Do you know much of his family history, Rid?" Maybe if I knew more about Night and his connection to the town, I could figure out other things.

"Well now, the Rowan family history is an interesting one. Night's ancestors were actually already settled in Bucksport long before Buck and his cohorts laid claim to the land. Night knew that some of his ancestors were Native American but he never did learn from what tribe they hailed. He suspected it might be the Penobscot Indians but that was just a guess." Rid paused here to take a sip of his coffee and pull his thoughts together.

"What Night did know was that one of his great, great, heck if I know how many greats to add, grandfathers was a fur trader from Canada by the name of Pierre Rowan. He was French of course. It was he who brought Night's Indian heritage into his lineage for he married a girl who was half-Indian by the name of Meadow. Her father was a Native American, and it was him that Night thought might be from the Penobscot Tribe. He went by the American name of Rad Rivers and he somehow ended up marrying an English woman by the name of Ruth."

Rid glanced around at each of us. "You understand that sort of thing, settlers marrying Indians...it wasn't quite favorable back then?" He waved a dismissive hand. "I couldn't care less about that stuff but there were some powerful feelings towards the Indians back in the day. A lot of prejudice." Rid shook his head in obvious puzzlement for this sort of sentiment then waved a hand to dismiss his gloomy retrospection.

"Poor Night tried to trace Rivers' lineage but couldn't do it. There's nothing. So he took a guess that he might be from the Penobscot Indian tribe." Rid looked skeptical of that guess. "What he did learn was how Rad Rivers got his name. He was an advisor to the settlers and Rad is old English for advisor so it was a logical fit. Night guessed his last name came from his extensive knowledge of the all the rivers scattered around the New England territories. All we really know about them is that he and Ruth married in Massachusetts then traveled here to Bucksport and settled in the area shortly before Buck and crew arrived to survey it for development."

Rid paused to take a bite of his food, chewed it for a thoughtful moment then sipped his coffee to wash it down. "Rad laid claim to the land where the Rowans live and he was allowed to keep the property. Not sure if you know, but land was divided among the prominent folks who arrived with Buck. They had to fulfill certain requirements to receive the land, of course. One of them being they had to build a house and another to support the township. The Rowans' property has been passed from son to son to son until it landed in Night's possession."

"You said the town folk didn't like mixed races. Did that cause problems for the family?" Kade asked.

Glad to see Kade getting sucked into the story, I spared him a quick glance. Aware of my scrutiny, he glanced my way and offered a wink before returning his focus to Rid. Why is it that a wink can make someone feel so nice? As for his interest in what Rid was saying, well I could understand that well enough. History was fascinating. The good, the bad and all that resulted from both.

"Probably not at first. Rad Rivers became a valuable advisor to the new settlers and he was quite respected. Despite the initial peace, however, the Indians eventually began to stir up trouble as you can imagine. People were flocking to America and taking what they wanted. The Indians were given little to no consideration. I really don't know much about Rivers to be truthful. There is very little written about him.

Most of what I know came from Night and what he knew was passed down through his family." Again Rid paused to enjoy a few more bites of his food. The rest of us remained quiet so as to not interrupt his train of thought.

"The understanding back then was that the Indians would be allowed certain areas of property in exchange for their help. They knew the area well. Unfortunately, hostilities grew and peace broke down often between various tribes. Because Meadow's father was respected by Buck and the other men of the town, she was accepted to a degree. Some people, as you can imagine, probably had a hard time with it."

Kade leaned on the table and looked at Rid curiously. "How is it you know so much about the Rowan's family history?"

Rid lifted a gray brow, amused by the question. "I'm a history buff. I worked at the library here in town until I had to retire and I read a lot. I've read quite a bit of material concerning this town. In fact, at one time I was going to write a book but then decided to scrap the idea. Night found out about it and had a fit. Our relationship was already strained and I didn't want to make it worse so I just dropped it."

"Did Night know all that you know?" Dawn knew some of it, of course, but would she be interested in learning more? Would Mary and Adam? As for me, I would love an opportunity to learn about my family history. Something I actually knew very little about. A shame, that. I made a mental note to correct that oversight sometime in the near future.

"Yes he did. We discussed it many times over the years. Night was proud of his heritage. As for how much of it he shared with his wife and kids, I cannot say. Night was a very quiet, private man. Me, on the other hand, I used to talk his ear off about it. Especially as my family has been here among the town founders almost as long as his."

"So do you know of any tragedies being attached to the Rowan family?" Was it Meadow who I connected with at Buck's grave?

"There is tragedy in every family." Rid went silent for a moment and I knew that he was thinking, dredging up memories. "Meadow and Pierre had a son named Kip but their daughter became something of a mystery."

At this point, my heart started pounding like a mini-sledge hammer on overdrive. "Why is that?"

Rid shrugged and shook his head. "She just sort of disappeared. In fact, there isn't a lot mentioned about her at all. We know from the birth registry that she was the Rowan's first born and was several years older than her brother Kip. I don't know how old she was when she died or even how and where she died. As I said, there isn't much known and I'm not sure what made me think of it now."

Kade was trying to connect things as well. I felt him touch my leg under the table and turned to look at him. I could see the silent question in his eyes. Was she the spirit who came to me at the graveyard?

I answered in the same manner, telling him with a look that I didn't know. I leaned on the table toward Rid, fully engaged in the conversation and excited to learn more. "Do you know her name?"

"Now here again, I'm not sure but I think it was Isabelle."

The name was so unexpected that I couldn't stop the gasp of surprise as I felt the blood drain from my face. Kade grabbed my hand and squeezed it. "What?"

"That story I've been working on? Her name is Isabelle."

"What story?" Rid asked, his eyes sharp with curiosity.

"I've been writing a story that just comes to me as I type. I think it's a way for me to connect with past events. I've been writing about an Indian girl whose name was Isi but when she was taken by a couple settlers, they named her Isabelle." The problem here was that the Isabelle Rid was talking about was born to a French father and a woman who was only half-Indian. The Isabelle in my story was a full blooded Indian. That profile didn't fit my character at all. And yet, I knew there was a connection. But what?

Barbara was clearly interested in my story and I could see from her expression she wanted to know more. Her next question confirmed it. "What do you mean the story just comes to you?"

I shrugged in response because it was so hard to explain. "I just feel inspired to write and I sit down to my laptop and start typing. The story just comes to me as I go."

"So tell us about this story." Barbara urged, clearly fascinated.

"There isn't much to tell. This Indian girl named Isi is taken by a couple settlers by the name of Nina and Giles. She travels with them to their home...and where that is, I don't know...and that's as far as I've gotten with the story."

"Why did they rename her Isabelle?" Rid asked.

"Nina and Giles were hiding her identity because she was an Indian."

"So what happened to her?" Barbara asked.

"As I said, I've not written much. They have just arrived at the home of Nina and Giles. I have no idea what happens to her and won't until I write more."

"Fascinating." Rid looked at me as if I were an enigma. I took no offense. Sometimes that is how I felt too. I felt like an enigma.

"Do you think Isabelle's demise has something to do with Buck's curse?" Kade asked.

"There must be a connection." I looked at Rid hopefully. "Do you know anything more about her?"

Rid shook his head with regret. "I'm sorry but I don't. As I said, I'm not even sure what made me think of it now. All I know is that there was a lot of tension between the Rowan family and other town folks, especially after the fiasco with the British. When they came to burn down the town after the disaster in Castine, the Rowan's family home was not touched. That may have been because of their connection to the Indians but who knows? In any case, there was some resentment."

"But your home was spared too, Rid," I pointed out. "Were the town's folk upset with your family as well?"

Rid smiled. "Not that I'm aware of. My great-grandfather several times over was handicapped during the Revolutionary War. He couldn't participate in the Naval attack on the British in Castine and neither could his son for he was the only male in a family of five daughters. He was needed at home to help protect the family. When the British troops stormed the town, those who declared loyalty to the crown were spared. Since my ancestors couldn't move to safety as so many had done, they had to stay and hope for the best. Declaring loyalty to the British crown didn't seem too unreasonable a request especially as it was an empty oath." Rid shrugged. "One must do what one must do to survive."

"Do you think resentment towards the Rowan family was more geared toward their Indian ancestry?" Kade asked.

Rid gave the question some consideration and it seemed he was trying to decide if agreed with it or not. After a long pause, he finally shrugged his bony shoulders. "Although that sounds logical, I just can't say for sure. What I know has been gleaned from various documents and letters I've been privileged to read and from what my grandfather and Night's passed down to us." Rid gave his answer some more thought. "Night was determined to learn more about Isabelle and what happened to her but there's nothing written about it that he could find."

"His family didn't have any stories that they passed down concerning the matter?" Although I knew it wasn't typical for families these days to share information concerning their ancestry, I still hoped that maybe a rumor had survived. It would at least give me something to go on.

"Some things are left unsaid within family circles, especially if they are many generations removed. Lots of information gets lost over time. I don't know what happened to Isabelle but I've a feeling it wasn't anything good. There is no grave for her that I'm aware of."

That statement gave me a sudden, brilliant idea. "Where are the Rowans buried? Are they in the same graveyard as Buck and his family?"

"Good Lord, no. Despite the respect Rad Rivers held among the town folk, his family was buried outside town, near Silver Lake."

I knew that Silver Lake was not far from the town epicenter. It was the largest lake in the area. "Do you know where, Rid? Can I get to it? Are the graves marked?"

Rid scratched his balding head. "There's a graveyard located just before you get to the lake on the right. Just follow

Lakeview Drive and you'll see it. Where exactly the Rowan family is buried, I can't say for that is something I never cared to check out."

I looked at Kade and knew he interpreted my message without difficulty. We would be paying that graveyard a visit during some point of our day.

Barbara's eager gaze had focused on each of us as we talked. She paid close attention to what was being said and as soon as there was a lull in the conversation, she jumped in. "So tell me more about the séance."

"Yes, do. I'd like to hear more of that myself." Rid's gray brow lifted curiously. He glanced at me and then Kade. Judging by the look in his eyes, I'd say he was somewhat surprised that Kade would participate in something like that. Little did he know.

"As I said, there isn't much to tell I'm afraid." And when Barbara was about to protest, I raised a hand to staunch the flow. "Yes, yes, the chairs moved and some sort of strange shadow dance appeared on the floor but other than a few theatrics, I really didn't get much in the way of a message."

"Much? Then you got something?" Rid asked.

He was a shrewd one. That he was. "As I mentioned, I do know it was a male who came through. He was a big guy and I surmise that he was a relative of Night Rowan's. I felt…I sensed frustration coming from him. He wants to communicate but for some reason, he's having a hard time doing it. I really think that there's a lot of concern for the Rowans because they are about to lose their home." This statement put a pall on our mood and we went silent for a moment.

"Is there no way for them to avert the foreclosure?" Rid asked.

"Sure. If they can come up with the money, they could stop it. Otherwise, it's gone too far in the process at this point. They've already received notice of an auction date. Unless they can come up with the money by then, someone else is going to snatch up that house." I did want it to be me but at the same time, I knew I couldn't go around buying properties for people. At this point in my life, I had no intention of looking for a job.

Why should I when I had a tidy sum to support myself? I didn't dare jeopardize the security that offered me.

Rid shook his head. "It's a sorry state of affairs. Such a shame when that house has been in the family since before Bucksport's inception."

Again we went silent. I thought about all the information Rid had imparted and I knew, I just KNEW there was a connection to everything I'd been exposed to the past few days.

Kade glanced at his watch and tapped my arm to get my attention. "You want to head on over to the fort while it's still relatively early? I know you probably have another destination in mind before we head back here and I do want to get moving on the painting for Barbara. I imagine you will be itching to write some more on your story, too. Besides, Dawn and Mary will be here this afternoon and you'll want some time to visit with them."

Barbara stood up and began to gather the dishes. "You two go on and enjoy your day."

I stood as well and began to gather up our dishes when Barbara gently swatted my hand. "No you don't. This is my job. Yours is to be the guest."

Smiling, I relinquished hold of my plate and walked around the table to give Rid a hug. "Thanks for sharing so much great information, Rid."

Rid patted my hand. "It's my pleasure. I don't get to talk about my favorite subject often enough these days." With a twinkle in his faded blue eyes, he held my hand for added emphasis. "If you ever want to know about my peppered family history, just let me know. I've lots of skeletons in the family closet."

Laughing at his expression and intrigued, I gave him a decisive nod. "Count on it."

"Do you need directions anywhere?" Barbara asked.

Kade shook his head. "I think we can find our way around okay. Thanks. You two have a nice day."

It wasn't until we were crossing the bridge from Bucksport to the island of Verona that Kade, who had taken over the driving duties, reached for my hand and brought it to his mouth for a kiss. "This mystery of yours gets more interesting as we go along. I wonder if we'll be bombarded by spirits at this fort?"

I was admiring the view of the fort from the bridge and taking in the river walk along Bucksport's shores but I pulled my gaze away to meet his enquiring one. "Do you think the fort is haunted? Did a lot of people die there?"

Kade let our entwined hands fall to the gear shift, letting his hand rest atop mine in a firm hold. "Not sure. It was never used for the purpose for which it was built."

"To keep the British at bay? I think that's what I read."

Kade nodded. "Exactly. Ever since the disaster in Castine, the locals didn't quite trust the British. Since this was a strategic area and control of it was vital, they built the fort. Which, by the way, was never even completed. Nor was it ever needed for its intended purpose."

"Still, I imagine the undertaking to build something like that was dangerous. There are probably a few lost souls there." A shiver raced through me as I spoke and I knew I was right. Should I put up shields and try to keep them at bay or remain open to possible contact? Given that I was hoping to make sense of the cryptic messages coming from the spirit world the past few days, it would probably be best to take my chances and stay open to them.

That decision made me a little uneasy as we pulled into the fort's visitor parking lot. Oh yes, lots of paranormal activity going on here. Great.

CHAPTER SEVENTEEN

As Kade and I stepped out of the car, I could almost feel the spirits beginning to gather and look our way, their radar for people who could detect them on full alert. A cool breeze picked up and blew gently. A wild thought went through my mind that it was them, their curiosity and excitement stirred, brushing by for a closer look. Opportunity to interact with our world was rare for them and when it suddenly presented itself, they could be very persistent. I took a quiet moment to say a prayer for protection and envisioned my security blanket...my imaginary light...cocooning me in a tight, unbreakable circle.

I took Kade's hand and silently invited Sheila to join us. When her tickle of cobwebs brushed my face, my anxiety melted away. If she was near, I had extra protection. Not that I was really worried about that because I didn't get any uneasy feelings of negative energy. No, it was excitement that buzzed in the air and although it could get annoying, it was certainly not dangerous.

Kade and I walked at a leisurely pace down past the visitor's center, which we decided to check out later before leaving the park, and continued on around the fort's outer wall which, of course, faced the Penobscot River. The view across to Bucksport was spectacular. The quaint town spread out along the gently sloping shores of the river's opposite bank was quite picture worthy and Kade stopped to snap some photos. The retaining wall leading up to where we were standing was an impressive show of workmanship. I couldn't even imagine all the work that had gone into building it. Mid-sized blocks were layered in a style that reminded me of the outer walls of the great pyramids (something I hadn't seen personally but hope to remedy in the not-too-distant-future). After admiring the view a little longer, we entered the fort's interior through the arched granite entryway Kade told me was called the Sally Port (he was reading the brochure we were given when we paid the entrance fee). We came out into the fort's interior open space.

"Oh, it's a bailey. Isn't that what they called these open courtyards within the fort boundaries?" I hadn't ever seen a castle in person either but the historical romance books I used to read so much when I was a teenager always made me feel as if I had.

Kade grinned and shook his head. "This area is called the parade grounds but if you want to call it a bailey, go right ahead."

I gave him a playful swat. "Same difference, Kade. I'm sure the architects of the day were operating on knowledge garnered from the fortifications of castle structures."

Kade draped an arm about my shoulders and steered me toward a row of vaulted rooms. Though they stood open to the parade grounds, their outer wall faced the river and was made of huge granite stones. For that matter, so were the dividing walls and arched ceilings. I saw narrow slotted openings in the wall facing the river and wondered if they were windows.

"Those vaulted rooms are called casements. The cannons were housed there." He pointed to the highest casement in the row and I saw it still housed a single cannon. It faced the narrow slotted opening and I realized it wasn't a window. It was where the cannon balls were shot from. "They never used it so don't be thinking of its murder rate." Kade dropped a kiss on my brow and let his arm fall down until our hands met and held. "Let's go look at the spiral staircase. This fort has two of them. There are only five such staircases in our humble country."

The stonework involved to create the spiral staircase leading to the upper levels of the fort was quite impressive and Kade took more pictures. The entire fort was such a feat of workmanship and skill that we marveled over and over everywhere we went. I could well imagine the blood and sweat suffered by the workers as they labored day in and out, shaping and placing the massive granite blocks.

The inner walls of the officers' quarters were mostly constructed of brick. How tiring it had to have been to place each one. The task must have loomed before them in a never-ending cycle of repetition. What did they think about as they layered all these bricks and stacked those massive stones? Were they too tired to think? Did any of them die during this massive undertaking?

Even as I thought the question, a shiver crawled along my spine until it reached my scalp and made my head tingle to the point that I wanted to run my hands though my hair to rid it of the feeling. I let go of Kade's hand and slowly circled about. "Someone's here."

Remaining respectfully silent, Kade moved away to give me space and pulled his sketch pad from his knapsack. He nodded toward an outside wall. "I'll just go and make some sketches while you, ah...do what you do."

Smiling at his quick understanding, I blew him a kiss and turned away to concentrate. Now that I was focused on the energy around me, I realized there was more than one. Several men from the feel of it. Not sure why they were here, wandering the fort in their bodiless world, I silently told them they should look for the light and move into it. Whether they took my advice or even heard me, I couldn't say.

What did I really know of the afterlife? Maybe they liked hanging out in this drafty old fort of brick and stone. How or why it happened, I couldn't say, but it did seem that some people, once in spirit, became confused about where they were or what they should do. Some of them were afraid to move on and so lingered in what I considered "limbo". Though I was pretty sure my idea of limbo wasn't quite the same as what they actually experienced. I came to understand through my interactions with spirit that those lingering in the Tri-State do not have any sense of time. For them there is only awareness of being. To my mind, it was the quality of that being that mattered. Spend it hanging around this world, or spend it on other adventures. I did hope I would pick other adventures when I finally crossed over.

The room's temperature began to steadily drop causing me to shiver slightly and wish I'd remembered to grab my sweater from the car. The interior of the fort was considerably cooler than the outside because the thick granite blocks were quite effective in holding off the sun's warmth. The structure was designed, after all, to sustain direct hits from cannon balls. The steadily dropping temperature was getting uncomfortably frigid. I mentally invited the spirits surrounding me to come along as I moved out of the officers' quarters and headed across the parade grounds (personally I preferred to call it a bailey) for the fort's kitchen. I felt like a teacher shepherding her herd as I entered the large vaulted room.

Not feeling as cold as I was moments earlier, I decided to give the fort some attention before I gave it all to the spirits crowding the room around me. A plaque told me that the deep square holes built into the wall were the kitchen's ovens. I took a moment to peer into them. They were nearly big enough to crawl into. Were they ever used? (Kade had the brochure so I couldn't check to see). It was hard to imagine anyone actually cooking something in there.

My back literally began to twitch with the feeling of someone standing close. I could almost imagine them breathing which was a silly thought because of course spirits didn't breathe. Still, many of them mimicked habits long held while alive. I turned and faced the room, glad as I did so that none of them appeared before me as solid as Big Red had done a couple nights back.

Straight ahead was a long tiered corridor where the Enlisted Quarters was located. Each open vaulted room was built slightly higher than the one before it. Kade mentioned earlier that the idea was for the heat of the kitchen ovens to float up along the open corridor and fill each of the rooms with heat. The room at the end, from what I could tell, was a considerable distance away. I couldn't imagine any heat generated from the kitchen making it that far. Good thing none of these quarters were ever used. The poor souls assigned to the rooms farthest away would have frozen in their beds during Maine's bitter cold winters. My understanding was that most of the troops who stayed here (some regiments were actually assigned here for a time) all slept in tents. Supposedly there were other buildings around the fort at one time but they were all gone now.

I walked up to the next vaulted room which was the first of the Enlisted Quarters and stopped in a spot of sunlight coming through the windows facing the parade grounds. It felt quite lovely to bask in some warmth. Luckily there were few people about so I could make the attempt to communicate.

"Who are you? What do you want from me? How can I help you?" I spoke each question quietly and at some space apart, alert for any mental or emotional response. Often when conversing with spirits, their voices filtered through my mind as sudden foreign thoughts, all of which were spoken in a tone different from my own internal voice. I knew the difference.

It took a moment for me to quiet my own thoughts and as soon as I did, I sensed concern and confusion. These poor lost souls. What to do? Could they even hear me?

Eyes closed, I lifted my head until I was nearly facing the ceiling. I envisioned myself as an open channel, allowing energy from spirit to flow down through me even as I filtered some of my own outward. Mentally I cast a psychic line and tried to locate the spirits hovering near. They maintained a respectful distance, their curiosity about me drawing them like the proverbial moths to flame. And in truth, the cliché fit for I was indeed like a lighted beacon to them. Their world was shrouded with darkness and confusion. I invited them into my light and felt a couple of them draw near.

"You understand you are dead? Your body has died and now you must move on. Go without fear. Accept that you are in spirit and fear not. The light will encompass you and peace will come. I promise." It was a typical speech for me to make when conversing with spirits. Oddly enough, many of them did not realize they were dead. A strange thought, I know, but a fact nonetheless. Another thing that held spirits back from moving on was fear. Perhaps they had it in their 'head' they were destined for hell. I could only imagine the life of a soul trapped in this limbo world I called the Tri-state. It had to be so confusing for them.

Someone tapped me on the shoulder and I swung around, startled. No one was there, of course. Clever. "Yes, I know you are here. I am aware of you. You are real." I sensed sometimes that these disembodied spirits wondered if they were 'real' anymore. It had to be a frightening state to be in when stuck between worlds...not of this one and yet not integrated into the next either.

I tried to bring the restless spirit seeking my attention into mental focus, expanding my energy to encompass him and inviting him to enter my light. I could feel his essence as he drew closer and then our spirits, for a brief moment, intermingled and I was at once part of his memories and his confusion. Communications with the spirit world are often done entirely through emotions rather than words. Words are restrictive, emotions are not.

I 'talked' with the spirit of a young man for only a few seconds and yet I shared all I knew in that brief moment of time, and he shared all of himself with me. It's a strange feeling to be two people at the same time. And then he was gone. Hopefully, he had moved on in his spiritual journey. I could only hope this was so since I felt nothing more of him. Perhaps the other spirits hovering near witnessed our exchange and learned something from it. None of them, however, came near though I waited to see if they would. After a short while, I sensed the charged energy in the room dissipating.

I spent a few more quiet moments sending loving energy to the confused and frightened spirits still hovering near then turned and headed for the parade grounds, the sunshine, warm air, and Kade. I found him perched on a parapet wall in the upper most tier of the fort sketching a cannon located on the grounds far below. It faced the river like an old forgotten dog gazing with forlorn sadness at the world passing by. Once a proud member of an impressive Battery, it now was the sole remainder of a bygone era.

Kade glanced up and gave me a questioning look and when I nodded that I was fine, he bent his head and continued with his sketch. These silent communications spoke volumes to me. We were bonding, growing close and understanding each other. I had that with Mike to a degree. But not in the same way I shared it with Kade. I headed for the area above the bastion. It was such a great view. Bucksport was a nice location. I liked it here. Perhaps I'd stay longer.

Kade eventually joined me and we made a leisurely stroll back to the car, stopping briefly to check out the visitor's center before continuing on our way.

Once we were belted in our seats and the car was started, Kade looked at me. "Where to now?"

"I'd like to find the cemetery where the Rowan family is buried. Do you know how to get to Silver Lake?"

Kade nodded. "I think so. I have a map of the area and studied it last night. Besides," he pointed to his car's GPS system. "This thing can get us just about anywhere."

"The convenience of modern invention." We shared a smile, a look that quickly heated, and then I turned away to gaze out my window because I was afraid. Afraid of this amazing relationship building between Kade and myself. Really, what was there to be afraid of? What were the chances of having two men snatched from your life? It wasn't a fair question and I couldn't go through life thinking that way...but there it was. Feeling a little down at the thought, I let out a sigh loud enough that Kade heard.

"What's wrong?" He pulled onto the road and glanced my way with concern. "Did something happen back at the fort? Did you get in touch with anyone?"

"Nothing's wrong and yes I did." Glad to latch on to any topic that didn't meander into the area of our relationship, I went on to tell him about my experience in both the Officer and Enlisted Quarters. "There were several spirits there. I'm not sure if they died there or were lured there because of me. I did get the impression that some of them at least, died there. I imagine it was dangerous, backbreaking work building that fort. Deaths were bound to occur. I think I may have helped at least one of them move on but I can't be sure."

"So no big reveal or anything?"

"No." Smiling, because it seemed that people always thought the dead wanted to share secrets when mostly they just wanted to make contact with someone who could acknowledge their existence, I shook my head with regret. "Sadly, no one there could offer me anything of any use in this world. I think most of them were confused about where they were though some were content with their situation." I just couldn't understand why people who passed on into spirit would want to hang out here any longer? Surely there was another whole realm of existence to explore? But then, people did the same in life...never exploring the world around them. Sad.

Kade turned off the road onto the new expansion bridge that spanned across the Penobscot River to Verona Island and I gazed up at the tall observation tower. Someday I might attempt to go up there but since I was somewhat afraid of heights, I wasn't sure about it actually happening. The bridge sported two towers, one at each end, but only one of them had an observation deck. The old bridge stretched alongside the new one though lower down and looking decidedly smaller. Barbara said it was scheduled to be dismantled sometime in the near future. Time marches on. I'm sure that poor old bridge was quite the thing in its day. What would future bridges look like? Would we even need them?

As we made our way along the main route through Verona towards the bridge that led back into Bucksport, I felt a distinct chill race through me. Instantly alert, I looked slowly about and wondered where this new energy was coming from. Another spirit lingered here. A troubled one. I glanced at my cell phone to check the time and decided to let it go since we had a lot to accomplish today. I sent out a silent promise to come back another time and make contact then let it go. I couldn't answer every call though I wished that I could.

As soon as we left the island and entered the bridge crossing to Bucksport, another chill, much more pronounced than the last one, began to seep through me. Standing up ahead on the bridge's sidewalk was a young teenage girl. She stood with her back to the bridge's rails, her dress and long hair blowing in the breeze. It seemed her dark gaze was latched onto me and I met it curiously. Was she alive or was she a ghost? Funny how I couldn't always make that distinction anymore. I closed my eyes for a second and when I opened them she was gone. It happened so fast I couldn't be sure it actually happened, but my gut instinct told me I had not imagined it. Oh yes, for sure I would have to come back here and try to find her again. But not today. As we passed the spot where I saw her standing, I promised her I'd return and then gave a long sigh. Spirit work was never done.

It wasn't long before we were making our way along a quiet country road leading out of Bucksport's town center. The day was sunny and warm, pleasant and peaceful. It was a good day to visit a graveyard. The energy was good.

We didn't have to go far when we saw a glimpse of Silver Lake and just before it, a graveyard off to the right and built on the rise of a hill. Kade pulled up into it and parked about midway in. It was a pretty good-sized graveyard.

As we stepped out of the car, Kade quirked a questioning brow (I loved it when he did that). "So, any ideas on how we are supposed to find the Rowan family?" He swept his hand about him. "Seems to be a rather crowded place."

I stood for a quiet moment then turned. "This way."

CHAPTER EIGHTEEN

Kade followed quietly along as we moved among the graves, pausing every now and then to admire a gravestone's engraving or special carving. It was always a risk for someone like me to visit graveyards but then it also amused me that many people assumed all graveyards were haunted. More often than not, a person who has crossed over and plans to stick around will linger around the area where they died or lived. Some of them attach themselves to something meaningful or to a person close to them, but rarely did they hang around their graves. That being said, people who visit these places are often focused on someone buried there and that focus alone can pull their spirit near.

Spirits wanting to make contact with the physical world were especially attracted to people like me. I wondered how it was they knew I could do that? Was my energy different than others? Perhaps it was just the fact that I often walked around in a state of awareness and it was that alone that pulled them to me? I didn't know the answers, but I knew this much, some of the people buried here were beginning to amass. I put up a protective shield and silently let them know I was not open to communication. I was here for the Rowan family. If any of them were present, I'd surely appreciate them stepping forward and making themselves known.

Finally we came upon some old grave markers that bore the name Rowan. How we managed to find them, I don't know, perhaps they helped. However we did it, I was quite grateful. I stared at the typically shaped tombstones, arched at the top, their engraved lettering faded into near obscurity. I didn't care about that; I was hoping to make contact with their spirit, not read their grave markers.

"Are you getting anything?" Kade glanced around and as he did so I saw him reach for the pocket of his t-shirt and feel around. I grinned when I caught his eye and he realized what he was doing. He was looking for a cigarette. Old habits are hard to break. Obviously, he was a bit antsy.

"Why don't you walk around, Kade? Graveyards, especially old ones, are so interesting to explore."

His blue eyes met mine, looking serious and sexy and it made my heart pound looking into them. "You sure?"

I nodded in response. "It's probably better I be alone."

He stepped forward to press a kiss on my forehead then turned to head back up the hill. Something must have caught his eye earlier because he looked like he knew where he was going. Curious, I watched him for a moment then turned away to focus on my own agenda.

"Okay, if any of you Rowans are in the area, I'd like to talk." I spoke quietly, almost under my breath, and laughed softly at myself. Sometimes it seemed so silly what I did. Until things grew serious. I thought about my time at Sea Willow Haven and quickly pushed the thoughts aside. No, I couldn't allow what happened there to interfere with what I wanted to happen here. After a moment of calm silence, the graveyard really was in a peaceful state, I asked Sheila to give me a hand. Can you see if any of the Rowans will come talk to me?

While I waited, a movement caught my attention and I turned to see someone disappear down an embankment and through a copse of trees which led, if I wasn't mistaken, back to the main road. I stood for about one full minute, if that, and headed for the trees. My senses were heightened, on alert, and I wasn't sure if it was because of all the spirits I was attracting or if it was because of the person whom I wasn't even sure I'd seen. Was she a ghost?

As I started down the hill and neared the trees, it looked like a mound of some sort was present there. Upon closer inspection, I knew it was the roof of a vaulted tomb. There was something of a path beside it and I made my way carefully down to the even ground below. A woman was sitting on the granite edging that jutted out on each side of the tomb's main structure. They sloped from the top front corners to the ground. It appeared to be some sort of support. Probably a retaining wall to keep the earth cover from eroding away. Why I was thinking about walls when an older lady, perhaps in her mid-sixties, was sitting a few feet away I don't know.

She wore a simple white-buttoned blouse and a dark unpleated skirt which I found somewhat odd but then women her age wore whatever they felt like wearing and opinions be damned. Her graying brown hair was pulled back into a loose bun behind her head. Her hands were folded in her lap and she appeared to be lost in thought, unaware of my approach though I know I was loud enough to wake...well, the dead!

I stood for a moment, uncertain if I should bother her and looked around for her car. There wasn't one. She was wearing a pair of black shoes that looked comfortable enough to walk in. So, did she walk here? Was someone buried in the tomb that she knew? Did they still bury people in tombs?

Suddenly she looked up and gave a small smile. I think she was well aware of my uncertainty on approaching her. "Hello."

"I'm sorry. I didn't mean to disturb you..."

The woman waved her hand to dispel my protest. "You are not disturbing me, I assure you. I come here sometimes to think." She looked around and settled her gaze on the lake located a few feet away and obscured somewhat by a growth of trees. "It's always so quiet here. Very peaceful."

"Do you live nearby then?"

She nodded and waved a vague hand. "Just up the road a ways. It's a good walk but I don't mind. I enjoy walking and do a lot of it."

I perched on the edge of the granite support wall on my side of the tomb and fell into silence with her. Since it appeared she had once again lapsed into her thoughts, I took the opportunity to covertly study her. She looked real enough though her skin was somewhat pale. Then again, she probably didn't stay out much in the sun. I felt no indication that she was a ghost. Even my buzzing excitement from moments ago was gone. Was this what I've come to? Not knowing who is dead and who is not? Geez.

Finally the woman roused herself from her deep reverie and looked at me curiously. "You aren't from here are you?"

"No, I'm just visiting."

"So what brings you to the cemetery? You have family buried here?"

"No, I'm just..." Well, how to answer? "I like to visit cemeteries." Did that sound any better than "I'm looking for spirits?" To some degree it did or so I thought. I figured since she asked, I could do the same. "Do you have someone buried here?" I indicated the tomb.

The woman's eyes widened slightly and I wondered why she was surprised by the question. Blue eyes. Pale like the rest of her, though some color was beginning to show in her cheeks. Of medium build, she was a sturdy woman, not thin, not fat. She looked like someone who stayed busy but who also enjoyed a good meal. Happily, the two things balanced each other out.

"I don't even know if they use this anymore to tell you the truth." She gazed at the front of the tomb like the thought never occurred to her that people might be in there. "They don't keep people in there for long, in any case. Just until they can bury them."

"Have you lived in Bucksport long?"

The woman considered the question and I had to wonder what she needed to think about. "A fair amount I'd say."

Which meant she wasn't of the Bucksport-born-and-raised variety. Bummer. I was sort of hoping fate brought us together because she could offer some useful information on my investigation of Buck's supposed curse. Well, I'd just throw it out there and see what came of it. "I came to check out that curse made on Buck's memorial."

Lips pursed, my new tomb-lady friend (what else was I going to call her?) chewed on my announcement for a moment then gave me a sideways glance that had my heart pounding again. Hard. She was going to do it. She was going to offer me something useful.

"Seems one can make a mountain out of any old molehill. It just depends on perspective."

Nodding quietly as if I understood the correlation between that profound bit of wisdom and the Buck curse, I urged her on. "That's quite true."

"Every rumor exists for a reason. But then that's true with anything isn't it? Everything in existence is created for a reason."

I totally agreed with that statement and enthusiastically nodded my head to let her know it.

"That leg appearing like that...even if it isn't a cursed image, it has to mean something, right?" Tomb Lady (I really needed to ask for her name) cocked her head to the side and waited for me to challenge her statement.

Since I had no intention of doing that because I wholeheartedly agreed with her, I gave her a wide, approving smile. "Yes, I suppose so."

The old woman's pale blue eyes studied me for a few quiet seconds. Finally she smiled back, her eyes gleaming with approval. "There's a lot that's happened here. Who knows if our town founder was involved in something that resulted in that leg appearing on his monument or not? The fact is, the image is there and God put it there for a reason."

"Have you ever heard of that cemetery being haunted?" I don't know what made me ask the question, especially as I hadn't bothered to ask anyone else but it popped into my head and now it was out there waiting for an answer.

Tomb Lady started laughing. Just a low one, more an amused chuckle, but it went on longer than what I thought was necessary. I didn't quite get the joke. "Well how I see it, there's ghosts roaming all over this poor town. It's seen a fair share of tragedy after all." She pointed a finger at the tomb. "Wouldn't be surprised if this old chamber was involved a time or two with some of those tragedies."

I glanced at its smooth granite front covered in moss and lichen and wondered. There were no markings on the tomb that I could see. The door was barred shut. Its construction was simple. Surely it had been here awhile? It looked like it had. Was this my message? Was I supposed to focus on the spirits of those who had come through here on their way to their final resting place? Not wanting to intrude any longer on her quiet time, I stood and motioned toward the cemetery. "I probably should go and not bother you any longer."

Tomb Lady glanced at me for a long considering moment. "That you most certainly are not doing. I don't get much chance to talk to people these days. Everyone's too busy with their lives." She glanced off into space as if her thoughts had just drifted into unpleasant territory and she wasn't sure how to find her way back again. "Sometimes people want to know all your business and other times, they look the other way because they couldn't care less."

She looked so sad sitting there that I wanted to give her a hug but offered her a sympathetic smile instead. "It's been that way since the beginning of time I think."

Tomb Lady laughed softly, the sound a shade raspy. A smoker? "You are right about that. Yes indeed." She stood up slowly as if her joints had frozen in place and she had to urge them into action. "I suppose I better start the trek home." She waved a hand. "Nice to meet you, yes indeed. Enjoy your stay here in Bucksport. It's a pretty decent town for the most part." She took a step and paused. "If it's ghosts you are looking for, I'd say you wouldn't have to go far. Poor souls are everywhere."

"You speaking from experience?" I wanted her to stay a bit more, see if I could get any more useful information out of her but she seemed determined to be on her way.

"Well, I 'spose I've encountered one a time or two over the years." She turned from me before I could respond, effectively shutting off further conversation, and shuffled off toward the road a few feet away. Once she reached it, she turned left toward town.

"You want me to give you a lift home?" I didn't feel right to not at least give the offer but she waved a hand up in the air to let me know she appreciated the thought but no thanks. She didn't even turn around to look at me as she did so. I watched her for a few moments. She looked like a woman with purpose, striding with confidence despite the struggle to rise from her seat. She said she walked a lot; one could see her and easily figure that out.

"What are you doing down here, Tess? I've been everywhere looking for you."

Surprised that Kade had come down the rough path without my hearing him, I swung around to look at him. "Sorry. I saw that woman come down here and had to investigate."

Kade glanced around. "What woman?"

I waved toward the road. "Don't know her name. We've been chatting for a bit and..." I turned to point to her and she was nowhere in sight. No way! I ran to the road for a clear view. Nothing. There were no houses nearby so she couldn't have possibly left the road. Even if she'd stepped off the road for a shortcut home, I should still be able to see her. A shiver raced through me as the implications set in. A ghost? Really? But, she seemed so real. And though I knew this shouldn't have surprised me, it did. Why couldn't I tell when I was speaking to a dead person?

"Don't tell me...she was a ghost?" Kade grinned at my incredulous expression. "It's not like it hasn't happened before." He shook his head. "I don't know how I'd feel if I were you. I can't imagine speaking to someone who is dead and not even know it."

Well this was interesting. Her appearance had to mean something. I began to think about our conversation, wishing now that I had written it down. Which was silly because of course I wouldn't have done anything like that.

Kade glanced at his watch. "We need to get going. You said you wanted to work on your story for a while and I need to finish up my sketch for Barbara's painting. We've a few hours before Mary and Dawn stop by for the beads and I'm getting hungry."

I took his hand and headed for the path back up to the cemetery. "Well, let's go find something to eat then. I'm hungry too." I could almost feel the Tomb Lady's gaze follow us back up the hill.

As our car pulled onto the road a few moments later, I glanced to my right and found myself looking for her. She was nowhere in sight. But she was here...somewhere. Who was she and why in the heck hadn't I asked her?

Kade glanced at me. He knew what I was doing. "Do you think she was a relative of the Rowans?"

"No. I don't think so." Heaving a frustrated sigh, disappointed with myself for not asking her identity, I shook my head. "I don't know why I didn't ask for her name."

Kade reached over and patted my leg. "She might not have given it to you anyway. I haven't noticed that any of these ghosts of yours are very helpful with their information."

True. "Well, let's just find something to eat and I'll ponder it later." But it weighed heavily on my mind as we entered town and stopped to grab a subway sandwich from one of the local stores. I'd just stumbled onto another mystery to investigate. It was looking more and more like a longer stay in Bucksport was in order.

CHAPTER NINETEEN

After an enjoyable lunch eaten down at the river walk on one of the picnic tables scattered about, we parted ways when we returned to the B&B with the promise to meet at the ice cream parlor in two hours' time. We wanted to enjoy our treat and have a few moments reprieve before Mary and Dawn arrived to get the beads.

I could hardly contain my excitement to get back to Isi's story. I hoped that something would come out of today's writing to help me figure out just where she fit in to the mystery of the cursed monument. If she even fit in at all. What if she was yet another mystery to solve? The idea bummed me out a little for I truly wanted to bring this thing to a conclusion. Then I could concentrate on Tomb Lady and the girl on the bridge. I was determined to find out who they were. Whatever their stories, they had to be pretty good.

As curious as I was about them, I pushed those thoughts from my mind and sat down to my laptop. Right now I wanted to find out what Isi was up to and prayed that a clue to who she was would come through.

It was a strange world Isi found herself living in. She learned their language rather quickly and was glad about that because it made her life so much easier. Her new 'family' was kind to her and as much as Isi liked Nina and Giles, she could never forget the fact that it was they who snatched her from her people and thrust her into this new life. She didn't belong here. Their ways were so different from those of her people and she missed her family. Did her brother survive the fever? How was her grandmother handling her disappearance? Perhaps she had known this would happen. Her grandmother knew things were going to happen before they happened. There were times, Isi remembered, when she caught her grandmother staring at her, her eyes sad. She started missing me before I even left, Isi thought.

The teachings of her people Isi kept to herself. She did as her new family showed her but at night, lying under the cover of darkness and safe from their watchful eyes, Isi would recite the words her grandmother taught her and go over every lesson she could recall in her mind. She was determined to never forget who she was and where she came from.

Despite the longing for the return of her own life, Isi did care about these people. They believed they had saved her. Now that Isi understood their language, Nina often tried to explain.

"You do understand, Isi? We had to bring you with us. There was a group of men...they are bad men to your people. If they had found you..." Nina's eyes would tear up at this point and she always hugged Isi close to her. "When we found you that day, we were so frightened. For you and for us. We want you to be happy, Isi. Just tell us what you need."

As time went on, Isi did come to understand what was happening. Nina's and Giles' people were taking land and making homes. They planted large fields of crops and they hunted the animals. Their respect for the world was not the same as Isi's. They took more than they gave and Isi wondered how the world could survive this and for how long? The tension between the settlers and the Indians (the nicer of the words she heard to describe her people) grew over time. Isi's looks were passed off as French. Giles claimed she was a niece from his French connections. It was explained that her family were dead. Isi hoped that wasn't true and knew over time that it was not. They lived.

Sometimes, when Isi was alone, she would fly off like a bird and see them. What a delight it was to learn this new skill. Her grandmother had told her about it but Isi had never been able to do it until a few months after her abduction. Oh how glad she was to learn that her brother lived.

During these bodiless visits, her grandmother always acknowledged her. Though Isi understood that her mind was free from the physical body and could roam at will, she didn't understand how her grandmother knew when she was near. But every time Isi visited her, she would raise her graying head and look up, her eyes staring directly into Isi's soul. They mingled for a moment and enjoyed the love they shared then Isi would come back to her bed, silent tears coursing down her cheeks. Only in death would they ever reunite once and for all.

Hidden Voices

This ability Isi had to loosen free of her body and fly to wherever she wanted to go was something she kept to herself. Her new family wouldn't understand and it would frighten them. Many things, she discovered, frightened them. Church was a fearsome time for Isi. She didn't understand why it was all so horrible; this fear that was preached to them every Sunday of a God whose wrath knew no bounds when his will was not obeyed. Horrible things would happen. Isi was glad that their God was not hers, though she pretended that he was. She played their game well. But then, she did love her new family after all.

Nina, Isi learned, could not have children. She managed to birth one daughter who lived for nearly seven years. It had been almost a year since her death when they had come upon Isi in the field gathering medicine for her brother. Nina, in her deep sorrow, had convinced Giles to take her home to her own family in a place called Virginia. They stayed until Nina felt healed enough to return to their own home once again. It was during their return home that they found Isi and decided to "save" her.

Nina and Giles lived with Giles' mother and father. He had two younger brothers, twins (a rarity to Isi's people) Phillip and Paul. They were, Isi was sure, a little older than herself. The boys were curious about her and she remembered when Giles first told his family who she was they were frightened. An argument had ensued until Nina spoke up. Isi was so sure at the time that they were discussing ways to be rid of her. That hadn't been the case at all. Gile's parents wanted them to return her to her people. If only Isi had understood that at the time. But, as Nina explained to her over the years why they could not do that, so she had done that day to her husband's parents.

"If anyone discovers Isi is one of them, they will kill her. She's a child. Her chances are better to live with us. We can give her a life."

It wasn't until Isi was in her womanhood, two years since the time of her first bleeding, that she witnessed Nina's dire prediction during one of her nighttime travels. Her family's village was raided and burned. Those who had not managed to escape were killed. Nina's grandmother had foreseen the gruesome events well in advance and her brother was spared. He went deep into the woods as he'd been instructed to do a day before the raid. When he returned, Isi felt his pain though she'd been in the fields at the time helping to harvest the corn.

His sorrow and horror had reached out to her and Isi had gone to him at once. She remembered standing still as a tree in the fields, her mind flying through space until she found him, his pain burning bright in the ether of the universe. Isi's spirit wrapped around him in an effort to comfort. He murmured her name then he stood up from where he'd fallen prostrate on the ground and walked away.

Often Isi wondered why her grandmother hadn't saved more. Why not her parents or herself? Others had lived but Isi connected only with her brother and followed him as he went deeper into the woods, away from the coastal areas because the raiders from over the big water used the waterways to conduct trade and get around. He lived a lonely life but he learned to survive. Just like Isi.

More time passed as Isi struggled to live in two worlds. The one with Nina and Giles, his parents both having passed to their new life with the Knowing One, or God as Nina and Giles called him and the life she lived at night in her mind. The boys grew and married and moved to settle on their own land. Isi stayed with Nina and when Giles died in an accident while building a neighbor's barn, Nina slowly withered away. Isi sat with her during every available moment.

"Isi, what is to become of you? Who will take care of you? You must go to Paul or Phillip. They love you." And as tears flowed down her face, she had said softly, "I love you. That day in the woods, you saved me, Isi. It wasn't me saving you. It was you saving me. You are the daughter I couldn't have and I'm so sorry to leave you."

But Isi felt her grandmother near and spoke softly for the first time of things she never dared share before. "You are not leaving me, Nina. You are going to pass through the dark into a new life with the Knowing One. You call him God. My grandmother will show you the way. She visits me often, Nina, and I know this is true. You have nothing to fear. She tells me that Giles is there too and he is waiting." And then after a long pause. "There is a beautiful young lady with him, she was little when she went to live with the Knowing One but now she waits for you to join her at last."

At this, Nina wept for a long time and Isi held her sobbing body close. "Oh, Isi, do you know how special you are? Do you have any idea?"

"I know that the Knowing One wanted me to come with you that day. My grandmother prepared me. I'm glad you found me, Nina. I love you too."

"I hope you find a husband who is good to you, Isi. A kind loving man like Giles was to me. And I hope you have a beautiful daughter, one as beautiful as my little Ruth."

Isi could not speak for the emotion clogging her throat. But she managed to nod and then buried her head in Nina's soft hair. That night Paul and Phillip arrived with their wives. The five of them sat vigil over Nina's fading life and two days later, she crossed into the dark where Isi watched her grandmother take her hand and guide her away. Just before fading from view, Nina turned, her face radiant, her beaming smile reaching into Isi's aching heart and easing the pain settled there. She waved once then turned away, eager to be with her family once again.

As they stood over her grave and spoke the words of their God, Isi remembered that radiant look and knew that someday she too would make that journey and she would once again see her own family. For now, though, she had to live out her life here. As the Knowing One intended.

It was decided that she would go live with Paul and his wife Cassie. Their home could easily accommodate Isi living with them and Cassie, admitting to loneliness, begged her to come. It was close to the Canadian border and far from civilization according to Cassie. But, Paul was doing well cutting the trees and hunting the animals.

Isi knew it was the right choice to go with them. And a year later she met her husband, Clay Rowan.

As soon as I typed that name, a shot of surprise raced through me and I stopped typing. Lost as I was in Isi's story, I finally realize my cheeks were wet with tears. It truly felt, while writing her story that I lived it with her, so connected to her did I feel.

A surge of restless energy race through me and I stood to pace the room. Isi was an ancestor of the Rowan family! Not only that but she was special...she had the gift of sight and she obviously could conduct astral travel as well. Who exactly were her people that she could do those things? Much as I tried to come up with an Indian tribal name, I could not. Was she possibly a descendant of the Red Paint Indians? It was a natural assumption to make considering they kept popping up in thought and conversation all the time. The only problem with that is Isi never mentioned anything about red ocher. Nothing. So what did this all mean? Why was I being shown Isi's story?

A light tap sounded at my door and I swung around to glance at the clock on the nightstand. It had to be Kade. I was late for our meeting at the ice cream parlor by fifteen minutes. "Coming!" I rushed to the door and opened it. Kade was leaning against the door jam licking an ice cream cone and holding out another in offering to me. "For you, my lady."

Grinning with relief that he wasn't upset with me for missing our appointed meeting time, I graciously accepted the cone and took an appreciative lick. "Kade, you are a man after my own heart."

Kade's eyes met mine and for a long moment we stood there and stared at each other without saying a word then Kade finally spoke. "Yes indeed I am."

Heat suffused my face as I stepped back and waved him in. How to respond to comments like that? One part of me wanted to jump him and devour him, the other wanted to run. What if I let myself love him and he left me? What would I do then? "Come in, I've got a lot to share."

Kade indicated the sketch pad under his arm and this time when his eyes met mine they were dark with a significance that made me at once impatient and excited to see what he had. "Yes, me too."

We walked over to my bed and sat down. Kade set his sketch pad on the mattress between us and nodded toward my open lap top. "Did you get anything from your writing?"

"Yes, you'll never guess!" And then because I wanted to hurry up and get my news done with so we could move on to his, I rushed on before he could say anything. "Isi was Night Rowan's grandmother several greats removed. She married a man named Clay Rowan. He was a Frenchman from Canada. Remember, Pierre Rowan came to Bucksport from Canada…well, now we know who his ancestors were." It seemed that now the floodgates of knowledge had opened, thanks to Isi's story, I knew far more than I realized. "Pierre Rowan was Isi's grandson. With that being the case, it means Pierre was also half-Indian." And then in a flash, I understood the rest of the story. "Kade!" I looked at him in surprise and wondered how it was that I came to be so privileged to learn such things. "Isi had a brother who escaped the massacre of their village. She kept tabs on him because she had the gift of sight that developed stronger as she grew older. I think it runs in the family actually." I looked at him and wondered how he would take the next bit of information. "Isi often conducted astral travel. It's how she managed to keep watch over her brother."

Kade's dark brow puckered. "Astral travel? As in leaving her body and flying around in spirit form?"

Smiling because it seemed Kade was always having to suspend disbelief when dealing with me, I patted his leg. "Yes! How she knew to do it, I don't know but I've a feeling her grandmother may have taught her. She hadn't actually done it though, until after she was abducted by Nina and Giles." I waved my hand to get past this part of the story. We had more important things to talk about. "I've a very strong feeling that her brother was the father of Rad Rivers, Meadow's father."

"And Meadow married Pierre Rowan." He frowned with realization as he put it all together. "So Meadow and Pierre were cousins."

"Well, second cousins. And I'm also willing to bet that Isi and her brother were only half-brother and sister so even that relation was weakened. Though you know, Kade, back in the day it wasn't frowned upon for cousins to marry. Besides, they didn't even know they were related."

"This is pretty extraordinary, Tess. What are the odds that you'd come to Bucksport, randomly meet someone whose family history you..." he twirled his hand in the air as if I'd conjured things up with magic, "You did your...thing...and voila, you know the Rowan family ancestral line. Or at least part it."

"Yes, it's pretty extraordinary, but it doesn't help me solve the mystery behind Buck's cursed monument or the ghost girl hanging out at his cemetery."

"Or how Big Red fits into the picture."

Good point. That part really had me stymied. "Maybe Isi's family is a descendant of the Red Paint people? That would make the Rowan family a descendant of them as well." It sounded right even as I said it though I hadn't yet figured out the connection.

"So what do you think the beads have to do with all this?" And then his eyes widened with the suddenly remembrance of something. "You better take a look at this." Kade opened his sketch pad and turned it around to face me.

I stared at his penciled drawing and gasped in awe. Aside from the fact that Kade's drawing skills were pretty amazing, the picture he drew was even more so. Standing on the paved path of the river walk, the paper mill rising behind him as a backdrop, was a large Indian man. He looked huge, the bushes and trees Kade roughly sketched next to him helped to scale his size. He wore buckskin pants and calf-length moccasins. His chest was bare except for strings of beads and...were they claws? Teeth? Then I looked closer, picking the drawing up to better study it. Kade shaded him quite dark but not too much to cover his features or his body adornments. The necklace around his neck held the same design as the one I'd seen the beads create in my vision.

"I think he's covered in red though I only had a pencil so I couldn't add color but that's why his shading is so dark."

His strong facial features were heavily lined, the whites around his irises clearly visible and contrasting sharply to the dark shading of his eyes. His long hair was pulled up tight in a high ponytail toward the back of the head. He stood with his arms resting at his sides, his feet planted firmly apart. His stance was one of power. "It's Big Red." I spoke softly, in awe of the aura his picture evoked. I could only imagine what sort of force he would have been to reckon with had we met him in person. Was he a shaman?

"I was wondering about that, if this was Big Red or not." Kade scratched the back of his head and shrugged. "I didn't see him, of course, the way you do. I just started drawing him. I couldn't stop until I was done and then I came straight here to show you." He grinned at this point and nodded toward the last of our cones. "After stopping for these that is."

It wasn't surprising that Kade would do this. He'd done something similar while we were investigating the haunting at Sea Willow Haven. Kade connected with spiritual forces through his art. I looked at him, watched as he studied the picture critically, his expression thoughtful, and my heart felt it would burst with feeling for him. We were such a great match for each other.

Kade's eyes lifted and met mine. "What?"

I pulled my gaze from his, uncomfortable with the rush of emotion racing through me and stood up. I needed to move, do something. I walked over to the laptop and shut it down then glanced at the clock on my nightstand. "Mary and Dawn should be here any minute." I snatched up the box of beads and nodded for Kade to grab his sketch pad. "We'll show them your drawing. He's probably a distant relative of theirs and I want them to see the necklace."

We were halfway down the stairs when the two women arrived. Barbara greeted them in the foyer, hugging Dawn tightly for a long moment before waving us all toward the small parlor. "Let's get cozy in here shall we? I've made iced tea. Anyone thirsty?"

"That sounds lovely, Barbara, thank you," I threw Barbara a grateful look as she bustled away for I was indeed thirsty, especially after eating that ice cream. I waited until Mary chose a seat then sank down on the stool next to her chair. Kade and Dawn took the two chairs facing the window, leaving Barbara's rocking chair free for her to reclaim when she returned.

Mary nodded to the copper box clutched in my hands. "Are those the beads?"

I handed her the box. "Yes, I hope you can string them together okay. I can't tell you how much I appreciate the offer."

Dawn leaned forward to have a look and both women exclaimed over them, their appreciation for the workmanship and beauty of the beads exciting them and making them eager to work on the necklace. They ran their fingers through the beads then Mary gave a small shiver. "Oh wow, I felt a sudden rush of cold go through me just now."

Dawn nodded wisely, her eyes almost reverent as they looked at the beads. "Someone just turned in their grave."

Smiling at the old wives' tale, I said, "You could be more accurate than you think, Dawn. I've a suspicion these beads are actually from a distant relative of your husband's."

Mary gave a small exclamation of pleasure and surprise. "Really, Tess? Why would you say that? Have you learned something else?"

Kade opened his sketchpad and handed it to Dawn.

Dawn drew in her breath, clearly moved by the drawing. "Oh my, Kade! You drew this? You are so talented." She stared at the picture for a moment then said softly, "He looks an awful lot like Night." She ran a finger near the edges of the Indian figure so as not to smudge it. "He's a lot darker of course. Night looked like he had an all-year tan but he wasn't that dark." Then she looked closer, her eyes squinting a bit. "Is this the necklace, Tess?"

"Yes it is." Mary and I both leaned forward to study the picture with Dawn. "Kade was inspired to draw this while he was working on a sketch for Barbara. He's shaded dark because he's covered in red paint...or more accurately I should say ocher. I really think he's a distant relative of your husband's, Dawn, though I'm not sure and haven't made any connection other than having the thought pop in my head."

Kade touched my arm to get my attention and murmured in my ear. "Tell them about Isi."

Once I told them Isi's story and saw the amazed expression come across Dawn's face when I named the man Isi eventually married, I knew that my reason for coming to Bucksport was to help this family. How finding their family history was supposed to help them I didn't know but the Universe did and that was enough for now. The more I thought about this, the more sure I became. I was here for them. Did that mean then that I wasn't going to get the mystery of Buck's curse figured out?

"This is all quite fascinating, Tess." Dawn handed the sketchpad back to Kade. "You really do have an amazing talent, Kade. That drawing is exquisite."

"Thanks, Dawn." He put the sketch pad aside and pressed his hands together. "Now if we can figure out why all this is coming to light, that would be great."

Dawn looked at me and I could see she was trying to puzzle it all out. "So if this Isi of yours married Clay Rowan and they lived up near Canada, it must be their...son?...who came to Bucksport and married the half-Indian girl." Before I could answer, her eyes widened and she rushed on. "You said Isi was an Indian and if it was her son who came to Bucksport then he was Indian too!"

I nodded; excited to see how everything was beginning to make sense. "Yes, that's right but I think he was Isi's grandson. Although I don't know the dates when everything took place, I believe Isi's timeline is too far back for him to have been her son. His name was Pierre Rowan and the girl he married was named Meadow."

Dawn's brow raised in surprise. "How do you know their names?"

"Rid told us all this at breakfast this morning. Meadow's parents were Rad and Ruth Rivers. Rad was an Indian though Rid had no idea from which tribe. Your husband thought his Indian heritage came into the family line through Meadow but in fact, it came into the family through both Pierre and Meadow."

"Who was Meadow's mother?" Mary asked.

"Her name was Ruth and she was English. I'm pretty sure Rad continued to live among his own people so Ruth must have joined him."

"Her family probably disowned her anyway if she married an Indian," Mary muttered, her face scrunched in disapproval. "People are so darned...prejudiced...and it's all such a shame."

Nodding in agreement with Mary but not wanting the conversation to go off on a tangent about the unfairness of society, I continued with my story. "After she and Rad married, they moved here and were already settled in the area when Buck arrived to conduct his land survey."

"Well, now it seems we know the whole story," Dawn said, smiling with satisfaction. She looked at her daughter and patted her hand. "You really should record your father's family history. It's all quite interesting."

I stood up because there was too much energy racing through me to sit still. "There's a connection between your family and the Buck curse. I'm sure of it. The beads I found belonged to someone of the Red Paint people. I feel that quite strongly although I'll probably never be able to prove it. It's something I just know. I found the beads in the Tenney house and Buck was present when they were hidden."

"He was?" Kade quirked up a brow. "You didn't tell us that before."

"That's because I just thought of it." I began pacing again and stopped when Barbara came back in the room. "Sorry, the phone rang, had to take a couple reservations." She set a tray laden with five tall glasses of iced tea, a plate of lemon slices and a sugar bowl on the table between Mary's chair and her own. "So, what did I miss?" Before we could answer, she picked up the first glass. "Mary? Would you like a lemon slice? Sugar?"

Once we were all settled with our drinks, Barbara sank in her chair, took an appreciative sip then waved a hand in the manner of a queen giving her minions permission to speak. "So, bring me up to date."

Dawn did the honors while I continued pacing. My mind was racing with too many crowded thoughts and the result was mass confusion. Somehow I needed to sort them all out and then connect them properly together. But how?

"So, lots of revelations it seems!" Barbara nodded her head as if all was going according to plan. When the conversation quieted, she waited a few moments before looking at Kade, her expression curious. "Not to change the subject but did you visit the fort?"

"Yes we did and Tess connected with some spirits there," Kade told her.

Mary turned her head to follow me as I paced from the front entry hall to the sitting room and back again. "Do tell, Tess."

"There's not much to tell. I think some of them are there because they want to be there for whatever reason and some are confused about where they are. I think at least one moved on though." I finally returned to my stool and dropped down onto it. "On our way back to Bucksport, as we were crossing the bridge into town, I saw a woman, a spirit. She was young...maybe late teens." I glanced at Dawn since she'd been here the longest. "Have you heard of the bridge being haunted?"

Dawn's forehead puckered as she lapsed into thought. After a moment, she shook her head. "No, I've never heard of anyone seeing a ghost on the bridge."

"Has anyone ever jumped from it and died?"

Again Dawn shook her head. "I think I remember there being someone but if so, it was a long time ago and I don't remember the details. I'm sorry I'm not much help."

Kade made a slight sound and I turned to look at him. His eyes met mine, a question in their depths. "You didn't say anything to me about it."

"No, it happened so fast. I just got a glimpse of her and no more."

Although I could tell it bothered him that I kept the incident to myself, he chose to let it go. At least for now. "And then there's the woman at the tomb."

"What woman? What tomb?" Mary asked.

"We went to the cemetery out by Silver Lake...to look up your family's gravesites actually. There's a tomb located just off the main road and on the outskirts of the cemetery. I met a woman there and we chatted for a bit. I thought she was real...alive. But it turned out she was a spirit."

Dawn, Mary and Barbara all gaped in surprise. Barbara splayed a hand across her ample chest. "You didn't know she was a ghost?"

"No. She seemed as alive as you and I."

Mary leaned forward, her elbow propped on her knee, her chin in her hand, and her eyes fastened on me with fascination. "Amazing. Tell us more. What did she say?"

"We just chatted a little bit but she didn't tell me anything useful. I'm not sure why she's haunting that area but I'll bet that tomb has a hand in it."

"That tomb you're talking about has been there quite a long time, Tess. Lots of bodies have passed through it." Barbara sank back in her chair and began to rock as if she too had a lot of pent up energy to expel. "You were a busy one today. I had no idea Bucksport was so full of ghosts."

"Yeah, me neither. I'm thinking I might stay longer actually."

Barbara's eyes lit up. "That's wonderful, Tess. You can have the room as long as you like."

Smiling at her enthusiasm, I said gently, "I do appreciate that, Barbara, but I'm thinking I might look for a place to rent for a few months." I thought about my friends back in New York and knew they would be disappointed to hear this hasty decision. I'd have to go home to pack my things, of course, and sell the house. No reason to tell them anything until I was there to break the news in person. Maybe I'd finally set up a Facebook account so I could keep in touch with them. They'd love that. So would my parents. Or my mother in any case. She spent a lot of time on the computer but then she would. She used to be an editor for a major magazine and now free-lanced out to whomever she chose to help.

"I know a place perfect for you, Tess!" Mary touched my arm to get my attention. She had it.

"If you want to be close to the tomb and make contact with that woman again, there's a house out near there that is perfect for you. It's supposed to be haunted and no one will touch it."

"Haunted?" I started laughing. "Just what I need, a house full of ghosts."

Dawn nodded in enthusiastic agreement with her daughter, her excitement over the idea gaining ground as she talked. "The old Baker house is a lovely old house, a Queen Anne design, you'll love it. It was built in the mid-eighteen hundreds I believe. It's old but well-maintained. Harold and Mavis Baker died a few years ago and left the house to their children but none of them will live there. The kids put quite a bit of money into it hoping to attract a buyer but so far no one has even made an offer." She glanced at Mary with a slight frown. "Are you sure they'll rent it?"

"Well, at least they'll get some rent money instead of having it sit there empty earning nothing. Why not? Doesn't hurt to ask." Mary stood and motioned for Kade and me to do so as well. "Let's go out there now and take a look. If it interests you, Tess, I'll take you over to the realtor's office handling the property."

"What's the hurry, Mary?" Dawn stood up and glanced at Barbara apologetically. "We don't mean to run off on you so quickly, Barbara."

Barbara waved off her apology. "No worries. If Tess likes the place, we'll have her around a little longer and that will be exciting for all of us."

Laughing at their enthusiasm to keep me around, I gave Barbara a hug. "We'll chat some more when I get back."

A few minutes later, we were all piled into Mary's Volkswagen Beetle. Kade and I squeeze into the back seat, the small space bringing us close together. He grabbed my hand and held it firmly in his own and I scooted a bit closer in response. A few minutes later we were on the road to Silver Lake. Again.

Mary took a dirt road off to the left just before the short stretch to the cemetery. The road curved through the woods and around to a clearing. A glimpse of marshland and some open water could easily be seen behind the house. As for the house, it was a tall structure of various symmetrical proportions. It had one of the most interesting designs I'd ever seen. In all honesty, it was way too big for me and yet I fell in love with it on sight. Three stories high, the third floor looked more like attic space, though, for the rooms within would be affected by the roof's inclines. A couple of the roof top areas were flat and one such area in the center had a widow's walk enclosed by a decorative balcony. Even the roofing tiles were interesting, sporting a geometric design. Decorative gables added a picturesque flare to the areas where the roof was steepled and the dormer windows on the second floor looked like they opened to the most interesting of rooms. My favorite feature, though, was the rounded turret built to the front left of the house. It put me in mind of Sea Willow Haven. The resort's turreted towers, though, were more medieval looking than this one. I couldn't wait to see what rooms it held. A wrap around porch with pretty spindlework was an added bonus to an overall beautiful piece of architecture. Put together, it oozed an aura of mystery and adventure.

The lawns around the house were well maintained and azalea bushes were in full bloom on both sides of the wide porch steps. Tall pines shaded the outer limits of the yard and their needles blanketed the ground. Haunted or not, I couldn't believe the property hadn't been snatched up already by some lucky buyer. Just looking at it made me feel urgent to secure it as my own. "What's the asking price?"

Dawn and Mary both shrugged, indicating they had no idea. Mary twisted around in her seat to grin at me. 'You like it don't you?" She looked at the house then back to me. "Does it feel haunted to you?"

I stepped out of the car and stood for a moment to absorb the energy around me. It was calm and pleasant enough but there were undercurrents I couldn't readily identify. It discomfited me a bit but also excited me. The place definitely was home to a spirit or two. I could sense them in the outer edges of my perception, keeping their distance while checking me out. As I looked around, I felt a growing attachment to the place begin to form. The sights and smells only tightened the bond. Fresh pine, azalea flowers, roses from the climbing vines that grew on part of the porch and turret wall, recently cut grass...they all permeated the air with a natural perfume I would dearly love to bottle. It smelled clean and fresh and wonderful.

"You want to go peek in the windows?" Mary headed for the porch and the large bay window that protruded outward. I wondered if it sported deep windowsills for if it did I could load them down with plants. The front door to the left of the bay window was a delight. Made of polished oak, it was deeply inset within an arched entryway decorated with carvings I couldn't quite make out from where I was standing.

Dawn made a motion for me to follow her and took off after Mary. Kade came around the car and stood quietly beside me. "That's a lot of house."

"I love it."

He looked at the house then back to me then the house again. Finally he nodded. "It suits you." He gestured toward the body of water we could glimpse through the trees. "That must be part of Silver Lake."

Kade put his arm around my shoulders and hugged me to him. He dropped a kiss on the top of my head then sauntered off to join Dawn and Mary who were peering through the bay window and exclaiming excitedly on the house's interior. Obviously it met with their approval. I took one step in their direction and stopped – frozen to immobility, unable to move so much as a muscle. Alarm pumped through my system and I closed my eyes to better imagine my protective light. A quick prayer for protection and a plea for Sheila to join me went a long way in calming my panic. Whoever was demanding my attention didn't mean any harm.

I turned away from my intended path to the porch and allowed myself to be guided along. We went around the house toward the marshy area behind it. I walked across the expanse of lawn in a semi-conscious state, stopping when I reached the area where the lawn met the marsh. My hand lifted and pointed toward the body of water just beyond the marshland. I then turned and pointed behind me, just to the right of the house. What in the world?

"Tess?"

And just like that I snapped out of my intense focus inward and became once again part of the world around me. Kade, Mary and Dawn all stood a short distance away, their expressions that of curiosity and anticipation. No doubt they thought I'd just connected with the ghosts inhabiting the property and couldn't wait to hear what I had to share with them. If only I could give them more than what I actually had.

Heaving a sigh, I began walking toward them. Why couldn't these things be clearer to me? "I don't know what that was about but I think one of the spirits was trying to tell me something."

"You think?" Kade started laughing and I could see that he was greatly amused. His laughter grew to the point that he had to lean forward and rest his hands on his knees. His mirth grew to gut-wrenching laughter.

I had to laugh too because his laugh was infectious then I really saw the humor in the situation. Who but me would walk like a zombie across the lawn, point like some ominous scythe holder of death and proclaim I was perhaps being given yet another cryptic message from beyond? It was too much. Before I knew it, we were all laughing so hard we were holding our stomachs and gasping for air.

When we finally had control of ourselves, I headed with purpose back across the lawn. "Let's get to the realtor's office before it closes."

Mary caught up with me pretty quickly. "Don't you want to look in the windows?"

"No, I'll look around properly when I have a key."

* * *

The realtor was with clients when we arrived so we settled down in the waiting room. A map of the area was on the wall. I glanced at it, looked away then glanced again. An idea was beginning to take hold. I stood up and walked closer to the map to get a better look.

"What's grabbed your attention so much?" Kade came to stand next to me and studied the map along with me. He pointed to one of the small stickpins stuck into it. "That's where your house is. Looks like that body of water we saw beyond the marsh is the tip of the lake."

I grabbed Kade's arm and jabbed a finger on the map. "Kade, look at the lake! Do you see its shape?"

"Yes. Why?"

"Well, if you use your imagination a bit...it sort of looks like an old fashioned shoe. You know the kind? Ankle length with big buckles on the front and thick heals?"

"Yes, I suppose." He stood back and gazed at it for a moment, twisting his head this way and that. Finally he gave a nod. "Yes, I see what you mean."

"Well think about it, Kade! The lake is shaped like a shoe and Buck's tombstone has a leg marked on it. Some say it's a booted foot but it looks more like a bare foot as viewed from the side...pointing downward. The shape of this lake is like that of a shoe and its toe...where I stood earlier today...points toward..." I followed from the tip of the lake in a straight line across the map with my finger. In doing so, I crossed over where Dawn's home would be and ended in the area where...I was willing to bet...the Red Paint Indians' burial ground was located. I jabbed the area triumphantly. "How much you want to bet the Indian burial ground is located there?"

Kade quirked a brow, his entire look that of skepticism. "Stretching it a bit here, don't you think, Tess?" He waved a hand at the map. "And what's the significance?"

I looked at him, incredulous. "What's the significance? What's the significance in anything we've uncovered? By themselves, nothing, but...you don't think this is a rather strange coincidence?"

Mary and Dawn were now standing with us listening. They both looked at the lake, their heads tilting this way and that just as Kade had done. "Tess, is right, Kade. The lake does sort of look like one of those old fashioned shoes and the toe points right to our house." Mary looked at me with expectations I was sure I couldn't fulfill. Not yet. "But the booted foot...or the bare foot as you claim it to be...on Buck's monument doesn't point to anything but the ground."

I began to pace. I needed to think and it was hard to do when energy was zipping through me like an internal whirlwind. My poor mind was buzzing with information overload. I knew the answer to this. I did. I just needed to pull it all together. Something happened that involved Buck. His son was the town's Justice of the Peace, a magistrate if you will, and the men in that room at the Tenney house were arguing over a serious issue. Something happened. Something unpleasant and they were upset, scared, angry.

I walked the perimeter of the small waiting room in a rapid circle, the faster my mind began to work, the faster I walked. "The necklace belonged to someone important and was more than likely symbolic of something significant. It was hidden away because no one dared destroy it and yet they had to hide the fact it was in their possession." I closed my eyes and thought back to when I was in the Tenney house hearing that ghostly argument take place. Mostly it was emotions that I remembered more so than actual words. Buck was upset, the men with him angry and frightened. Images floated into my mind of the necklace being shoved into a box sitting on the desk. They rushed from the room and went...where? To the Rowans?

The only way to get answers was to stop thinking and allow the images to come without comment. And come they did. I was now in the Rowan house. There was arguing, sobs, voices raised. A shot fired. Silence. I waited for more to come, my heart pounding loud in my ears. Nothing.

The door next to us opened and a woman came through it followed by a young couple, both of whom were smiling broadly. The couple waved at us, shook the older woman's hand, thanked her for all her help then hurried away with excitement stamped all over their faces. Obviously they just had their offer on a house accepted. Hopefully it wasn't my house.

The woman looked at us expectantly. "Can I help you?"

"We're here about the Baker property." Mary waved a hand toward me. "She's interested."

The realtor, a woman in her mid-fifties I'd guess, her short hair permed in a neat style around her face, glasses hanging from a chain around her neck, looked at me with sudden acute interest. "Have you been out to see it?"

"Yes, we went out there and looked at it before coming here."

"And you are still interested?" She glanced curiously at Kade then turned to indicate that we should enter her office. "Come on in and let's talk."

We all filed into the spacious office. Mary and Dawn sat on a small sofa near the door. Kade and I headed for the two chairs in front of the desk and waited before sitting down. The realtor held out her hand.

"I'm Sandra Reilly. Everyone calls me Sandy."

I took her hand, taking care to note the long thin fingers and how cool they were to touch. Her handshake, though, was firm. "I'm Tess Schafer and this is my friend Kade Sinclair."

Sandy waved to the chairs. "Please have a seat."

We sat. I was feeling quite anxious at this point. I wanted to get this situation all settled so I could head over to Dawn's house. I was hoping I'd be able to follow that scene I'd just witnessed in my head through to its conclusion. Not wanting to waste time on small talk, I decided to launch right into business. "What is the asking price?"

Sandy's thin brows, outlined with dark brown liner, rose until they disappeared beneath her bangs. "There's just over six acres of property with the house. It's been newly renovated...the heating and wiring updated. A new kitchen and bathroom were also installed. It's in great shape..."

"So how much are they asking?"

Kade touched my knee to gain my attention. "I thought you wanted to rent it?"

"Rent? Well...." Sandy shook her head as if uncertain about that idea.

I interrupted her before she could continue. "I've changed my mind. I think I might be interested in buying it. I'll want to see it first and of course it depends on the asking price?"

"It's listed for $149,000 but if you agree to a quick sale, they'll take $120,000 for it."

"What does that mean?" I glanced at Kade and he gave me a cautious shake of his head. He obviously was somewhat suspicious of the deal.

Sandy glanced at Kade then settled her gaze on me. "There is no mortgage on the property. The house is owned equally between three adult children and they have given legal jurisdiction to the oldest of the three to handle the sale. None of them want to deal with the property..."

"Why?" If it was because of ghosts, I could handle that. If there were other factors involved, well I wanted to know.

Sandy looked down at the papers spread before her. Finally, after a short pause, she looked up and met my eyes. I think she was expecting me to be put off by her answer but was just as determined to be honest. "The house is haunted. The family moved there when the three kids were all teenagers. Their father inherited the place from his grandfather. Two of the kids moved out shortly after moving in...they went to live with their mother's parents. The other child stayed for a while but he was...unstable."

"What's that mean?" Kade asked.

"He tried to make friends with the ghosts and it nearly drove him mad. He's fine now, from what I understand, but he was committed for a while up at the Bangor Mental Health Institute. Unfortunately, he was quite vocal to the locals about the ghosts in his house and word spread pretty fast. The place already had quite a reputation and this just made it worse." Before I could question that statement, she rushed on, "The house and the property are worth much more than the asking price. The family had the place appraised and inspected about two months ago. If you accept their reports and not go through the inspection process, they are willing to bring the price down for a quick sale. Of course, to do this, unless you pay in full, you'll need to get a bank to agree and to do that you'll have to put a substantial amount down. If you have the funds to do that, I don't anticipate the banks having a problem with financing because the house's appraisal came in at just over $190,000. It's quite a good deal."

Yes it was, if the house was sound. "I'd like to see it."

The realtor glanced at her calendar. "How about tomorrow morning? I have another house to show in about an hour. By the time I'm done with that, it will be getting dark and the electricity is not on out at the property."

"Tomorrow is fine."

Sandy smiled, looking quite pleased. "The ghosts don't concern you then?"

"No they do not. In fact, most of the time they are chasing me around so it wouldn't matter anyway."

Sandy's eyes widened and she looked at Kade to see if he would confirm it was a joke. Kade shook his head at the silent question. "She's a medium."

"Oh. Oh!" She looked at me with renewed interest. "Well then...tomorrow should be very interesting. I don't know if I believe the stories or not but I do know the place makes me uncomfortable. I always put it down to my being influenced by the rumors."

"Can we do it around nine?" I asked.

"Yes of course. I'll meet you there at nine." She handed me a folder. "Here's all the information on the property."

As we stepped out of the office, I couldn't shake the excitement racing through me. I was about to become the owner of my second house. I just knew it. And then chasing that excited thought was my doubts. What was I doing?

"So, you want me to take you back to the B&B?" Mary asked.

"No, Mary. I'd like to go to your place. I think we need to have another go at contacting the spirits there. I know a bit more now and I think our questions might get answered this time."

Dawn's eyes lit up. "Oh this is going to be fun!"

I didn't know about that but it sure as heck was going to be enlightening. We were close to cracking this mystery. I just knew that too. And about time–seemed other mysteries were stacking up on me. The tomb lady and the girl at the bridge needed to have their stories come to light. First, though, to get this blasted curse straightened out.

CHAPTER TWENTY

When we arrived at the Rowans' home, the air was crackling with excitement, the energy around the house stirred to a near frenzy. I stepped from the car and the hairs on my arms stood in response to the buzzing anticipation. Shivers raced along my spine and I knew something amazing was about to happen. I could feel it as surely as the pounding of my heart.

Kade came around the car to join me. He looked about then lowered his head to whisper close to my ear. "Something's up. Can you feel that? Weird."

Mary and Dawn looked oblivious to the static in the atmosphere as they motioned for us to follow them, looking for all the world as if we'd just come for tea. Did they really not feel anything?

We stepped into the house and Dawn glanced around, rubbing her arms as she did so. "The house is awfully cold don't you think? Wonder why...?" She headed for the living room as if she'd find the answer to that question there.

Mary grabbed my arm and drew me close so she could speak without her mother overhearing. "Something doesn't feel right. I mean...something's..." Her voice trailed off and she shrugged, at a loss to explain how she felt. She looked at me with wide, confused eyes. "It's like I'm high right now and the last time I felt like this, I was in the dentist chair huffing laughing gas."

I laughed at Mary's expression and gave her a quick hug. "Don't worry. I think this is a good thing. I think we are about to get some answers."

"Why now?"

Good question. Persistence? Was my brain finally putting the pieces together? Who knew, I sure as heck didn't. Rubbing my hands together in anticipation, I nodded toward the living room. "Let's see what we can find out."

Adam was standing next to his mother and both were very still and focused. They were as aware of the quiet buzzing in the air as I was and trying to figure out where it was coming from. Amused, I walked over to them and touched Dawn's arm. "The spirits are ready to talk, I think."

We stood in a spot where the late afternoon sunlight poured through the windows. Oddly, the sun's rays offered no warmth. It was nearly cold enough to frost a glass. I didn't understand the phenomena of having the air temperature drop when spirit activity was occurring. There were lots of theories but no one really knew for sure. When it came to the paranormal, it was anyone's guess. I was sure it had to do with energy being affected somehow but as I wasn't a physicist, I couldn't even begin to try an explanation. Did the why of it matter? No. The end result mattered. We were about to communicate with the other side of life and I was most impatient to get on with it.

Mary looked as eager as I felt and I wondered why she wasn't as fearful about this anymore? "Well then, let's see what they have to say." She and Dawn started gathering chairs and putting them in a circle like we'd done the last time we did this.

A sudden surge of energy gripped me, rooting me to the floor and making it impossible to even breathe. When I finally managed to draw air into my lungs, I got the oddest sensation, like I was drawing in a swarm of miniature bees. The strange feeling zipped through my body making me tingle. It wasn't a comfortable feeling but it wasn't altogether unpleasant either. It was just so strange and I didn't know what to make of it.

A humming noise started in my ears and though I wanted to ask the others if they heard it too, I couldn't even open my mouth to speak. Neither could I look at them. Instead, I turned about and walked down the hall to the back door, the one Adam used when he took us outside to show us the fireplace. And then I knew that was exactly where we were going this time too. Someone from 'beyond' was controlling the situation and for the moment I allowed it.

Having an entity take possession of my body without permission was not a happy circumstance for me but I knew if I wanted it to end, it would. It was a male energy. He was very large, his presence filling my space and more. I knew the others would follow and that was the last I thought of them as we stepped off the porch and made our way across the lawn.

When I reached the fireplace, the male energy released me and I collapsed from the sudden loss of support. As soon as I connected with the ground, I instantly merged with someone else. A girl. Several emotions spun through my system but the one I felt most was panic. Her panic. Though I knew instinctively this was not going to end well, I decided to go with it and let it all play out. I needed to know what she knew and the only way to do that was to be her. It wasn't going to be easy, though, for she was in great peril.

Settling quickly into her drama, we glanced behind us to ensure there was no immediate danger of discovery then turned back to dig with frantic vigor at the ground before us. Our nails broke and the tender skin on our fingers became punctured with small stinging cuts. Tears mingled with mucus and dripped down our chin as the pain in our heart filled every part of our being. I couldn't help but wonder if this was the girl from Buck's graveyard?

The fact I could still think as me even as I remained merged with her was quite fascinating. Though I didn't like merging with another and going through their horror, my fascination with the whole process ensured that I did not stop it from happening. My need to know urged me to continue though I knew I wasn't going to like the experience one single bit.

Behind us was chaos, fast approaching. A gunshot rang loud in our ears. We flinched at the sound and froze, unable to move or suck in a breath. Echoes of shouting and sobs filled the air, sounding as hollow and mournful as a cold winter wind. A renewed sense of purpose filled us and our breathing ability returned, though it was labored and ragged. We continued our digging efforts at an even more frantic pace. Our fingers worked feverishly, desperation spurring us on despite the sharp stings of pain. Finally we uncovered a rectangular piece of metal and it didn't take me long to realize it was the lid to a box. It was slightly larger than a cigar box and made of thicker material than the copper one I found at the Tenney house. We pried the lid open and grabbed a soft pouch lying on the ground beside us. I had no time to wonder at its contents before it was shoved into the box and the lid closed over it.

The understanding that we had little time had us quickly reburying the box. Once we were satisfied it was aptly covered, we grabbed one of the flat slabs of slate lying loose upon the ground and slid it atop the freshly dug dirt. Dried leaves and pine needles were scattered everywhere and we grabbed handfuls of them to toss above and around the slab. We did our best to disguise the fact that the dirt here was recently disturbed.

As soon as she was satisfied that her hiding spot was safe, we crawled away, stood and stumbled forward, catching our fall on a pole lodged in the dirt a few feet away. Carvings on the pole caught my attention for a brief precious moment and I glanced at them curiously. They looked like hieroglyphics though I couldn't be sure. My curiosity aroused, I looked around and the area where the lilac trees had been now appeared to be a small graveyard and an odd one at that. Mounds of rocks were piled there. The thought chased through my mind that they might be the same rocks Adam used to make his fireplace! I had no time to ponder this revelation however for we were suddenly grabbed from behind and crushed against a hard male body.

The girl's screams of terror filled my ears and my soul. As her tears fell, so did mine. A man's arm held us so hard he cut off our breathing and we had to struggle for every little bit of air we managed to draw in.

"Where did you hide it, witch?" Sickened by his voice, we twisted in a frantic effort to free ourselves but his arm tightened more and breathing became impossible. "You will tell me."

We pawed at the arm imprisoning us and managed to do nothing more than choke out noise. His hold eased up and her raspy voice sounded foreign and rough, totally unrecognizable though it came from me. "There's nothing to tell you."

His response was to jerk hard and we choked out a plea for mercy as he dragged us without any consideration across the ground. We dragged our heels to hinder his progress but all that managed to do was pry our shoes loose, losing one and then the other almost immediately. Sharp rocks dug into our skin and we had to stop resisting because the pain became intolerable.

The sounds of horses, their nervous snickers and restless hoofs clopping the ground, echoed impossibly loud in our ears. Terror raged within me and I had to remind myself that I was only having a vision and could pull away from it whenever I wanted. Calmed by the reminder, the spirit with whom I was joined calmed as well. For a wondrous moment I almost believed she was aware of me. In the next instant we were hoisted roughly upon a horse, slung across the front of it like a sack of potatoes, the saddle horn digging into our stomach. A flash of fear of a different sort charged through us and when I realized what it meant, I almost threw up. Oh God! And then we lifted our head and met the terrified eyes of a young boy crouching in the thick brush a short distance away.

Terrified as we were, we did our best to convey reassurance while at the same time urging him silently to stay where he was. The girl's feelings for him were strong and filled with love. It made my eyes water to experience the tender connection between them and the sorrow they both felt for what was happening.

It was all too much to deal with and for a moment I had to pull back from it to get my bearings and to remind myself that what was happening was only a vision playing out in my mind. I took just long enough to know that I was crouched on the ground, my forehead resting on one of the slate slabs, before I closed my eyes and gave myself up to the girl's horrific drama once again.

It took a moment to reconnect and until I did, I floated in limbo, the world dark and silent around me. There was no light, no awareness of anything. Nothing. Though it felt like the valley of the shadow of death, I did not fear any evil. I waited. And then the voices came...soft at first then louder.

"Get up you evil daughter of Satan!"

What? I opened my eyes and found we were surrounded by three men. One of them she knew well. It was the same man who grabbed us from behind and dragged us away. It was too dark to see their faces and I knew it was best this way. The looks in their eyes would not have offered any comfort. A feeling of betrayal surged through us and I knew that most of her suffering was coming from that bitter fact. Although I felt one with the girl, merged with her in every way, I was determined not to lose my sense of self and this helped tremendously as the next few moments played out. Part of me didn't want to go on, didn't want to see what was about to happen. Another part of me knew that I had to continue with it. This story needed to be told, people needed to know.

"What did you do with it?" The man she thought she knew so well and who now betrayed her so horribly grabbed our arm and twisted it painfully behind us. We couldn't speak from the sheer agony that ripped through our body when he did so. It honestly felt as if our arm was being torn from its socket. I had to separate from her in order to continue with the vision. The pain was just too much to bear.

How could people do this to others? How can people inflict pain like this on another human being? Or any other living soul for that matter.

"Tell us now or we'll rip you to pieces and feed you to the dogs of Satan."

Tears fell in silent succession, one faster than the other and though I knew the outcome of this vile scene, I could do nothing to stop it. She was not going to give them what they wanted and she accepted the conditions of that decision. I could do nothing but watch it happen. Indeed, even if I had the power to change the outcome, I knew that I would not go against her wishes. But please, God, let it be quick.

"Someone's coming!" One of the other two men whispered loudly, urgently. "Hurry up."

The man holding her arm put his mouth to her ear, and though I had become an observer, I could feel his hot breath against her skin as his voice seared a path into our souls. It was vile and disgusting and I wanted this to end. "You think this will matter? We will find it, witch."

Her legs buckled and she sagged against him in a near faint. Giving a snarl of disgust, the man let go of her arm and she fell to the ground in sobbing relief. After dragging in a few breaths, she struggled to rise into a kneeling position and once she did she raised both her arms high, opening them wide to the sky and to the Knowing One.

She knew what was coming. So did I. The blow when it came was mercifully quick. As soon as she slumped into darkness, I came out of the vision and gave in to my own tears. God, it was all so sad and senseless. Life just totally sucked sometimes.

Feeling sluggish, as if waking from a nightmare, I slowly became aware of the world around me, flawed though it may be, never so welcome as now. My hands which were spread out in front of me curled around the clumps of grass that I could feel beneath them. I needed to get a grip and ground myself back into my own life. As I did this, I realized that my cheek was resting on a piece of slate and I turned my head to allow the tears streaming down my face to fall onto the warm stone. After a few quiet moments, the turmoil I'd just witnessed began to fade from my psyche and become a distant memory. I lifted my head and immediately was drawn into a firm but tender embrace.

"Tess? Jesus...you'd think I'd get used to this but Christ...you don't know what it does to me when you go off like that." Kade rocked me in his arms and ran one of his hands repeatedly through my hair. "You okay?"

Still too overwhelmed to speak, I could only nod and bury my face in his chest. The whole story, or a good part of it, was now part of my knowing. I had to process it all and make sense of it before I could tell the others about their good fortune and the tragedy that led to it.

"I'm okay, Kade. Sorry about that." Although I wanted to stay there in his arms until the horror of what just happened faded completely away, I reluctantly pulled out of his warm embrace. I was practically freezing to death. It was a reaction to what I just experienced but knowing that didn't make it feel any more bearable.

After a quiet moment of deep breathing to help calm myself, I glanced around to again get my bearings. Kade and I were kneeling near the center of all the slate slabs embedded into the dirt. Dawn and Mary stood to our left, Adam to our right. The women looked concerned, Adam fascinated. I wiped at my tears and sat up a bit straighter. "I had a vision. Hope I didn't scare you." I pushed to my knees and brushed the leaves and dirt from my hands and clothes. I could feel the sting of heat fill my cheeks as a surge of embarrassment flooded my face. What did I look like to others when in the throes of a vision? No doubt if I had lived a hundred years earlier, I would have been burned at the stake. Shivering in response to that thought, I combed my hands through my tangled hair and pushed it all behind me.

"What did you see, Tess?" Mary sank down to her knees beside me.

I looked at her and began to smile. In fact, I was smiling so wide I figured it looked unnatural and tried to rein it in. "Mary, Dawn, Adam...you guys are not going to believe this." I looked at the slate slabs around me and closed my eyes to think. Stretching out my arms, I let my fingers land where they willed and when they came to rest on one of the pieces of slate, I opened my eyes and looked at it. Nodding with conviction, I glanced around for a stick or something sharp. We needed to get that slab moved. Realizing that the others didn't know what I was doing, I tapped the slate in front of me then looked at it more closely. No way! I began to laugh because the irony of it was just too much.

"What's so funny?" Kade asked.

I pointed at the slate. "Look at it, does the shape look familiar?" As everyone leaned in to look, I said, "It's similar to the same shape as the witch's leg on Buck's monument." And it was, a little fatter perhaps, but similar. "We need to get this stone up."

Adam pulled a small metal lantern stake out of the ground and began to poke at the dirt around the edges of the rock. "Why?"

"I think something is buried beneath it."

Within minutes we were all eagerly digging at the dirt. The slabs had been in the ground so long they were all tightly embedded. The one we were trying to pry loose was almost dead center of the others. Funny how I got nothing on it when I'd come out here...when was it? Yesterday? "Something did happen here. Something very sad." I sat back and let the others work so I could focus on the story I was about to relay. "Rid told us this morning about two of your father's ancestors, Kip and Isabelle. They were the children of Meadow and Pierre Rowan. We were just talking about Meadow and Pierre earlier at the B&B if you remember."

"What about them?" Mary's eyes latched on to mine and I could tell she got it that what I was about to tell her was going to fundamentally change their lives.

Giving Mary's shoulder a quick reassuring squeeze, I looked at Dawn. "Well, it was Isabelle with whom I just connected. Rid said there wasn't a lot known about her, that she just sort of disappeared." I glanced from Adam to Mary, wanting to impress upon them the wealth of information Rid contained concerning their family. "He shares your father's love for local history. You really should talk to him, he knows a lot." I glanced at Dawn wondering how she felt about that considering their history but she merely smiled and nodded for me to continue. "There's not much known about Isabelle because she was part of something that happened here which her family," I glanced at Adam and Mary, "Your family, tried to keep quiet."

Here I had to gather my thoughts. It was all there in my head but I had to bring it out slowly and make sense of it as I went along. "I just went through Isabelle's experience with her and what I'm about to tell you came from that vision."

Dawn stopped digging and stood out of the way while Kade and Adam finished the task. "But what does Isabelle have to do with digging up this rock?"

Smiling, because I knew they were in for the shock of their lives, I shrugged my shoulders in a teasing 'haven't a clue manner' and Mary laughed, swatting my arm playfully. "Stop being a tease and tell us what you know about Isabelle and why we're digging up an old rock that's been there for ages." Mary waved a hand toward the guys who were now the only two working hard to loosen the slab from the ground.

"Isabelle hid something here just before she was taken away by three men. One of whom she knew quite well. In fact, she was in love with him and carrying his child." I remembered the fear Isabelle felt when she worried how that man's rough treatment might harm her baby, their baby, and forced the bile that rose in my throat back down. It all was so sickening. "The man Isabelle loved called her a witch. I'm going to guess he did that because she had the gift of sight just like her great-grandmother Isi." I glanced around to ensure everyone was still with me. "You remember how we established that Isabelle's father Pierre was Isi's grandson?" Since Adam was busy digging, it was Mary and Dawn who nodded that they did indeed remember and waved for me to continue. "I'm thinking that's how this Isabelle got her name. She was named after Isi who was renamed Isabelle by the people who took her."

"Got it!" Adam pulled the heavy slab out from its resting spot. Beneath was more dirt. The men looked at me and I waved my hand.

"Keep digging."

"I'll get a shovel." Adam started to walk away but I touched his arm to stop him.

"Adam, it's not that far down. Isabelle dug the hole with her hands." Speaking of which, I glanced at my fingers as I remembered the stinging pain we suffered while frantically digging at the dirt. They looked fine. No residual injuries thank God.

"What are we looking for? Did you see what it was that she buried?" Mary asked.

Smiling broadly because I couldn't wait for them to discover what I just learned, I gave Mary a "just you wait and see" wink. "Yes, but let me tell you the whole story." I paused again to gather my composure then continued. "While Isabelle was out here burying what you are about to find, there was an argument going on in the house. I heard a gunshot but I don't think anyone was killed because it would surely have become public knowledge if that was the case."

"But how do you know that whatever Isabelle buried is still here? Wouldn't she have come back for it later?" Dawn asked.

I turned my head to look at Dawn and pain stabbed through my heart as I answered her. "She didn't. After they dragged her away and couldn't get it out of her where she'd hidden what she did, they injured her pretty badly." Here I paused as an emotional lump lodged in my throat. It took effort to speak. "As I said earlier, she was carrying a child and the man who hurt her was its father. He didn't kill Isabelle but she ended up dying a few months later while giving birth to her baby."

Mary covered her mouth with her hands. "Oh my, God."

"But if Isabelle lived, even for a short while, why didn't she tell her family about what she hid?" Dawn asked.

It was a good question and I could only make an educated guess as to the answer. "I'm not sure, to tell you the truth though I have my suspicions. I can only tell you that I know it's still here. I feel it."

At that precise moment, Adam exclaimed loudly, "We found something!"

We all leaned forward to watch as Adam and Kade dug faster, brushing dirt off what looked like a rusty piece of metal. I couldn't contain my little squeal of excitement. "It's the lid to the box!" Seeing it again, as I had a short time earlier in my vision, was quite thrilling. I could barely contain myself as Kade sat back to allow Adam the honors of pulling the box free from its hiding spot.

For a moment he went completely still and so did the rest of us. It was a momentous occasion. The last time this lid was opened, a frantic young girl put something in there then later lost her life because of it. In silent agreement, we bowed our heads and said a prayer for poor Isabelle. In truth however, she wasn't such a poor thing at all. Not anymore. She was quite radiantly happy.

"Open it, Adam," I urged softly.

Adam nodded. He lifted the lid. Inside was a dark lumpy mass. The remains of the leather pouch. Adam touched it and the mass disintegrated. Beneath it was what looked like grains of yellow sand mixed with small shiny chunks of the same stuff. Adam brushed the disintegrated pouch out of the way and scooped up some of the sand. It gleamed gold in the sunlight. Although I knew what it was, I gasped right along with everyone else. It was an amazing discovery. A true treasure and no mistake about it.

"Oh...my...God!" Mary stood up. She covered her mouth with one hand and grabbed her mother with the other. "Is that...is it real?"

Kade took one of the small chunks of gold out of Adam's hand and held it up to the light. "Looks like gold to me. If it was hidden at the risk of death, I'd say it must be real."

"I don't understand." Dawn sank to her knees as the implication of our find began to sink in. "Why?"

"If anyone knew where to dig for this stuff, it would have been your husband's family, Dawn. The Indians knew the entire region. They knew the land. It was tough times here while America was at war with the British. As I mentioned, there was a lot of smuggling going on." I thought about the cave I'd found back at Poke Harbor while staying at Sea Willow Haven. It hadn't harbored any gold but it harbored a precious love a time or two. I pushed the thought from my mind as I sat back and watch the Rowans look over the answer to their troubles. Life for them was about to undergo quite a drastic change. And they didn't know the half of it. Not yet.

"How did you do this, Tess?" Dawn looked at me, her brown eyes shimmering with tears.

"You said that Isabelle was called a witch. Is she the witch that cursed Buck's monument?" Adam asked.

"She wasn't really a witch, Adam." I sank back on my knees and gave everything some thought. I had a basic understanding of the whole story but I hadn't put it all into logical order yet. "While I was merged with Isabelle, all her memories were part of me as well. At the time I was going through the vision, I couldn't really focus on them because of what was happening to her."

I sank back on my knees and struggled to recall the memories that floated through Isabelle's mind while I was merged with her. "Isabelle was upset because she had a pretty good idea that something must have happened to her grandfather Rad Rivers. Since the men were at the house demanding the gold Rad recently delivered to her mother and father, she knew they must have caught up to him and that they wouldn't be bothering her if he was still alive." I took another minute to think things through because I knew it was going to get messy. Honestly, it was hard enough to recall my own memories let alone someone else's.

"You see, Rad was worried about the smuggling activities that Pierre was engaging in and so he went hunting for gold. He, of all people, would know where to find it. Somehow or other, Isabelle's boyfriend found out what Rad was doing. Maybe she mentioned it to him for she did love and trust him." Confused by all the visions running through my head, I closed my eyes and tried to bring it all into clearer focus. "Once Rad delivered this gold, he left to return to his village." I waved a hand through the air. "Or wherever it was that he lived. Anyhow, Isabelle's boyfriend went after him. When he realized that Rad no longer possessed the gold, he came back to get it. Somehow, Isabelle knew he was coming and managed to hide the gold here in the family's hiding spot."

"If this was the family hiding spot, then even if she was too badly injured to tell the family where the gold was, they should have known anyway," Adam pointed out.

"True but I think only a couple people actually knew about this. After Isabelle was hurt, she was taken away and cared for. She was not married, she was pregnant and she was injured. Not a good circumstance to be in, especially for the times. Unwed pregnancies were really frowned upon and Isabelle had a tough time as it was because of her Indian heritage."

I paused again to gather my thoughts and let all I knew sink in and make sense. "I really believe that the family was afraid to use the gold because the men who came to their home and injured Isabelle were never captured. They especially didn't want to use it when they found out Rad was dead for they worried that more family members might die." I stopped here to give a snort of disgust. "People act stupid when gold is involved. Ever read about the furor that took place during the California Gold Rush?" Everyone nodded that they did indeed understand how the gold could create further dilemma for Isabelle and her family. "When Isabelle died, her parents didn't want to risk more heartache and decided to leave the gold right where she buried it."

"The entire family just let it sit here?" Adam looked incredulous at the very idea. Obviously, he didn't agree with their decision.

"Kip knew about the gold but he didn't know about the hiding spot. It might be through him that your family's stories of hidden treasure were first told."

"Do you know who these men were that attacked Isabelle?" Dawn asked.

I shook my head, frustrated not to know more. "I only know that Isabelle was seeing one of them in secret. He knew about Isabelle's visions. In fact, I think he was probably using her visions, to some extent, for his own gain. Don't ask me how, it's just the impression I get because Isabelle felt so betrayed by him and she kept thinking over and over how he had used her for his own good, and then she would berate herself for not seeing it." It was all quite sad and I wanted to weep again just thinking about the heartache that occurred. I waved a hand toward the gold the Rowans were holding. "She was determined he wouldn't have it and she was willing to die to make sure that he did not. In the end, she did."

While the Rowans examined the small gold chunks and sifted their fingers through the golden flakes in the box, wondering at its value and discussing the matter with Kade, I thought about the beads and how they ended up where they did. "You know, I think that necklace made from the beads I found belonged to Rad Rivers. I'm not sure if I told you that I suspect he was the son of Isi's brother." When all three Rowans frowned because they couldn't remember if I'd said as much either, I went on with my thoughts. "I'll be willing to bet he got the necklace from his grandmother. Isi called her one of the Chosen, meaning she was a spiritual leader among her people. In any case, regardless where Rad got the necklace, it was taken from him and somehow ended up at the Tenney house where it was shown to Buck's son. He was serving as Justice of the Peace at the time and the only law the town had immediately available. I think the argument I heard take place in that room was concerning the men who killed Rad Rivers. Buck and the others must have surmised, as I have and as Isabelle did, that Rad was dead. There is no way those men would have got hold of the necklace otherwise. I'm sure they were being detained while a decision was being made on what to do about them but they got away and high-tailed it here to your house."

"So, Isabelle's scumbag boyfriend came after her," Adam frowned. "I hope he's rotting in hell right now."

"I don't know anything about the other two men that was with him. It was her scumbag boyfriend as you so aptly named him, Adam, who struck her down. I get the impression that he didn't have time to stick around and finish her off. The fact there isn't anything known in Bucksport's history about gold being hidden or any stories about an Indian guide being murdered; I am guessing that everything was hushed up. Maybe in part to protect Isabelle but also to keep the peace. I'm sure if the circumstances behind Rad's murder had come to light it would have angered a lot of people."

"So, those three men got away with murder?" Adam's face scrunched in anger. "They hushed it all up and let three men go free?"

"They probably left town and never looked back, Adam. It would have been hard to find them anyway. Besides, I'm pretty sure they wouldn't have been hunted down in any case because Rad was an Indian and I'd be willing to bet people weren't held accountable for killing Indians. Not during that point in our history anyway." To be fair to the Buck family, I felt it only right to continue voicing my impressions on the whole matter. "I really believe Buck, his son, and any of the other men in that room were afraid of stirring up more trouble if word got out about what happened. That's why there's nothing written anywhere concerning the whole incident. The necklace was hidden away and eventually forgotten. I truly believe that Buck's son would have seen those men punished in some way for what they did but they managed to escape their confinement, as I said, and made their way here to your house. Their plan, of course, was to take the gold and flee."

"But how did this all lead to the curse?" Kade asked. Everyone was now sitting on the grass around me, the gold for the moment, temporarily forgotten.

"Well, as to that, bear with me, I'm still piecing it all together." Tears gathered in my eyes as I recalled everything that happened in my vision. "Isabelle's brother Kip was quite young at the time of this incident. He saw them take her away." I couldn't stop the tears that chased down my cheeks. No one spoke. After a moment I managed to continue though my voice wobbled considerably. "Her shoes came off as they dragged her away."

Dawn gave a small gasp. "Her shoes? Do you think that's a coincidence? You know, her losing her shoes and there being a booted foot on Buck's monument?"

"A shoeless foot, remember Mom? Tess says that the foot on the monument looks more like a shoeless one." Mary's eyes practically glowed with inner joy. Realization of what this all meant was beginning to sink in.

Kade shook his head, clearly confused. "But what's the correlation? What does any of this have to do with the curse?"

"Ah, but there's more to this puzzle. Hang tight and I'll try to explain." Excitement raced through me as the realization struck that I was about to solve the mystery of Buck's curse. "Remember that I told you Kip probably knew about the gold but not the hiding spot? Well I'm willing to bet that after his father died, whom I suspect was the only other person who knew where the gold was hidden, Kip tried to find it. Of course, he never did but he probably mentioned it to other family members which is how you ended up getting stories told by your grandfather about hidden treasure." I tapped Adam's and Mary's hands, both holding some of the gold. "As time went on, it all just became a fun story to tell." I had to pause here to take a breath. My heart was pounding so hard I wondered if they could hear it. My knees were beginning to protest at the continued crouching and I slowly straightened up and moved to the bench a couple feet behind me. Kade looked relieved at the change in seating arrangements and joined me. I saw him rub his leg and touched his arm in concern. "You okay?"

Kade nodded. "Sure but I don't mind telling you, I could use a cigarette about now." He sighed with the acceptance that it wasn't going to happen and waved for me to continue. "Please tell us how that monument became cursed."

Though I hated to admit it, I pretty much felt the same way. A few drags of a cigarette sounded good and I wondered when that urge would go away once and for all? Echoing Kade's sigh, I continued on with my story. "Well, here's what came through as I was merged with Isabelle. Remember I told you she had a baby? Well, she gave birth to a daughter. The name that comes to mind for her daughter is Isidora." I glanced around at everyone to see if they made the connection to Isi. They did. "Because she died giving birth, no one from town ever saw her again. They certainly didn't know about Isidora." Again I paused as I remembered how it felt to be merged with Isabelle's spirit. Because I was privy to her life, I could also glimpse into the life of her daughter. "I'm pretty sure Isidora inherited her mother's special gifts."

Here again I had to pause. There was so much injustice in the world and I was uncovering quite a bit of it in the telling of this family's history. "You know those sorts of things were often thought of as witchcraft back in the day." I waved a hand for them to give me a moment. There was so much to explain.

"I just don't see how the curse comes into play?" Mary said. "Is it Isidora then who cast the curse?" Clearly enthralled with the story, I could see her brain trying to make connections and reason it all out.

Impressions were filling my mind and I had a strong suspicion Isidora was connecting with me. Things were coming through like they did when writing Isi's story. "Isidora came to town when she was fully grown. She settled in the area and I think she was considered by some of the locals to be a witch because of her psychic gifts. I'm pretty sure no one knew her connection to your family. Since I keep getting visions of plants, I am willing to bet she was a knowledgeable herbalist as well."

Once again I had to pause to let Isidora's memories fill my consciousness. "Now here the story is a bit sketchy and I'm relying heavily on my psychic ability to make sense of it." I truly believed Isidora was connecting with me and bringing this information through. Otherwise, where did it come from?

"I don't know if you realize there was a strong Spiritualist community here at one time but there was."

"Spiritualist community?" Adam asked, the term obviously unfamiliar to him. Dawn and Mary nodded that they heard of them. Kade certainly knew.

"Spiritualists believe in life after death and they also believe that you can and should keep in contact with those who have crossed over. Or, as they call it, gone through transition. Part of their church service is dedicated to allowing messages from departed loved ones to come through via a medium."

"Cool, are there any Spiritualists around today?" Adam's eyes met his sister's and I figured the church was about to get a couple new members.

"Yes, they are still going strong though not so much in this area like they were back in the late 1800s when Spiritualism was sweeping across Europe and the United States." I closed my eyes at this point and tried to concentrate on the impressions filling my mind. I could feel Isidora's spirit and was glad she was helping me with all the details for I was as curious to know as the Rowans. "Buck's monument was erected in the mid-eighteen hundreds when Spiritualism was at its height and as I said, there was a strong community of them right here in Bucksport. Now, the rest of this story I can't confirm. I'm telling you as it comes to me and I haven't verified any of it." The Rowans all nodded in understanding and gestured for me to continue while Kade took my hand and held it firmly in his. "Well here I keep getting the name Clayton and I'm not talking about the Clay Rowan that was married to Isi."

Dawn nodded as if that made sense. "One of Night's distant grandfathers was named Clayton. I remember that name because we considered naming one of our sons after him."

Smiling because I loved it when things came together, I continued on with even more enthusiasm. "Well Clayton believed the story passed down about hidden treasure and he hooked up with a friend of his to find it. I'm pretty sure this friend was a distant relative of Colonel Buck's. The name Elijah comes to me on this." Since no one here knew any of

Buck's family history, I didn't figure the name would ring any bells. "Isidora came to town round about this time. I am almost positive it is her who I keep encountering at Buck's monument. I get the feeling she fell in love with Elijah." A little stab of pain pierced through my heart at the precise moment I mentioned Elijah's name and I knew I had it right. "Isidora knew where the gold was hidden, its hiding spot revealed to her by her dead mother. Not such an amazing feat as I've just done the same thing. Right?" I laughed here because it was all so strange and joyous. Sometimes this bizarre gift of mine was quite wonderful.

"But if Isidora knew where the gold was, why didn't she just tell her family and dig it up?" Kade asked.

"I'm not sure she knew the Rowans were her family. And maybe she didn't think it was her secret to tell. I don't know her whole story but obviously she died and her death was...well it ended sadly. I think Elijah betrayed her somehow." I had to take a moment to think about this because once again images were crowding my mind. I also had to deal with the emotions that accompanied them. This poor family sure did suffer a lot of betrayal. Maybe it was their family karma, something they needed to work through. "I can see quite clearly in my mind's eye a young man, Clayton I think, kneeling before a dying Isidora." I paused for affect then delivered my little bombshell. "She's the supposed witch in the Buck curse. Although really, she was not a witch and she most certainly did not cast a curse. In fact, I think she was using her gift of sight when she spoke to Clayton of Buck's monument and the image that would appear upon it."

"What do you mean?" Mary asked.

"The monument hadn't even been placed on Buck's gravesite at this point." I paused to clarify the words ringing like a distant echo in my brain. "She tells Clayton that the Buck family will suffer and the Rowans will prosper when a sign is given for all to see on Jonathan Buck's grave marker." I glanced at the three Rowan faces staring at me with rapt attention. "Clayton knew about Isidora's affection for Elijah and his subsequent betrayal, and please don't ask me for that story, I don't know it. He must have believed she was cursing

Hidden Voices

the Buck family when she told him her vision. She was doing no such thing, of course. She was simply predicting the images that would appear on Buck's monument. She knew a negative legend would be spurred from it marring Buck's good name. She also knew that the Rowans, you guys, would eventually prosper from the image. The foot, as you can see, is a clue to the gold." And something else I had yet to tell them.

Mary's forehead puckered in confusion. "I still don't get what that image really has to do with this even though you somehow managed to put it all together? In all honesty, it just doesn't make sense."

"The world works in perfect synchronicity. All events affect other events and so on and so on until everything is related somehow. The chain of events set in motion when Rad was killed, the necklace taken, the discovery of it and subsequent argument at the Tenney house, the eventual hiding of the necklace which I would find and set in motion my own investigation...well it all comes together. I learn about Isabelle losing her shoes, the lake is shaped similarly to the type of shoe she would have worn, a leg image appears on Buck's stone, a witch legend is born, the foot points down toward sacred ground." I waved my hand toward the fireplace. "Your father told you his family used to dance around the fire. They conducted spiritual rituals out here." Now I glanced at the lilac trees and began to get excited all over again. "This whole area is probably considered sacred and believe it or not there's an Indian burial ground right there." I pointed at the lilac bushes.

That little bombshell caused quite the commotion. Everyone began talking at once and I raised my hand to quiet them. "I saw it in my vision. There's a burial site right where your father planted those lilac bushes and I'm willing to bet you'll find some interesting treasure hidden in those graves."

Adam stood and grabbed his head, incredulous to this new bit of information. He walked over to the bushes. "No freaking way."

"Where did you get the rocks to build this fireplace, Adam?"

He swung around to look at me, his expression guarded. "There used to be a rock wall along here and I dismantled it. Why?"

"They used to cover the burial mounds."

"Oh God. Seriously? Oh man." Adam glanced around nervously. "Are the spirits pissed about that and that's why they are haunting us?"

I hurried to calm his fears. "No, of course not. I think they like what you've done actually."

"What should we do about this, Tess? You said there might be interesting treasure in the graves but wouldn't that upset them?" Dawn asked, waving a hand to indicate the spirits she thought must be surrounding us.

"No, they won't mind. In fact, I think it's what they want."

Kade shook his head in amazement. "This is just fantastic, Tess. You are awesome. You know that?"

Although I was as fascinated with the idea of an Indian burial ground being right next to us as they were, I wanted to get on with the rest of my story. "You will need to decide what to do with that knowledge later but right now I want to share what else I know." Adam came back to join us, flopping down on the ground at my feet. Mary and Dawn did the same. They waved for me to continue and I took some time to gather my thoughts. Somehow I needed to put all the images and the bits of knowledge rattling around in my brain into some sort of coherent story. "I just don't believe all these things are a coincidence." I pointed to the slate slab we just removed from its resting spot of countless years. "Even that slab has a similar shape to the leg image on Buck's monument. The universe works in a synchronistic way that is beyond our imagination. Everything ties together in some way. It's in being unaware of the connections where we often come up short. In any case, as soon as I saw the map of the lake and the outline it made, I connected it to the foot image on Buck's monument and now I'm linking it to the incident with Isabelle and the loss of her shoes. Everything came to me as soon as I stepped out of the car when we got here to the house. Isabelle, and now Isidora, have showed me everything."

My little audience was quiet with eager anticipation for the rest of my story. "You understand that when I am merged with a spirit, we do not communicate in the same way that you and I communicate. I don't have a conversation with them. It's more like I am filled with their knowledge and just suddenly know what they know. It all comes to me at once. It's only later, after the vision is over, that I can sort it all out and put it into logical thought. Or at least, into something I can understand. Which is what I am trying to do right now."

"But what does any of that have to do with the Spiritualists?" Dawn asked.

"Well, Buck's monument was erected in 1854, the Spiritualists were, as I mentioned, very active here in Bucksport around that time or shortly after. When the images appeared on Buck's monument, everyone wanted to know what they meant. A lot of speculation arose from it. The stone, when it was placed, was blemish free. Natural flaws in the stone, which some claim those markings are, wouldn't suddenly appear after a period of time, they would have been there when the monument was made. Their sudden appearance, therefore, sparked a lot of stories and fired up a lot of over-active imaginations."

Curious as to how Mary and Adam were taking everything in, I stopped to look at them. Their expressions were open and accepting. Thank God. "I think some of your family members tried contacting either Isabelle or Isidora during a séance. Something Spiritualists do often. Whatever came through during that séance, they incorrectly put it together with what they already knew. I'm sure Clayton must have shared Isidora's prophetic visions with his family." I again closed my eyes to concentrate on the knowledge buried within my brain.

"It was Isidora who came through during the séance, though the medium conducting it didn't know that. Isidora said her heart lay broken and since Buck's monument also has an image of a heart lying sideways, it was thought that she must have been a mistress of his. The other part of the message that came through was that a family in turmoil would remain so for many years until their agony was over." I looked, smiling, at the Rowans. "She was talking about you guys, of course, but the medium thought she was referring to the Buck family. Isidora, speaking through the medium, knew the gold wouldn't be found for many more generations and she also knew it would be her own family that would find it. But as word got out about the séance and what was said, the town folks just assumed the message was a curse on the Buck family."

I looked at the faces around me and could see that they were finally pulling it all together in their minds and making sense of it. "You know, it was a reporter who made the rumor into an infamous legend, coming up with a fabricated story he printed in the paper about Buck having a mistress whom he eventually had burned as a witch."

Dawn shook her head sadly. "After your visit the other night, I went on the internet to look up the curse and I read that ridiculous story printed in the paper. For some reason, people took it at face value."

It was funny the things people would believe or not. "Buck's monument is a prominent landmark and I really think that's why it was his stone the universe chose to leave its clue. It's made the town somewhat famous after all. Really, if you think about it, it's been a pretty positive thing for Bucksport, something to brag about in any case."

"Not sure I'd call a legend about having a woman burned for witchcraft a positive thing but I do see what you mean. It's all pretty fascinating the way it fits together." Kade dropped a kiss on my temple and put an arm around my shoulders. "You did it. You solved the mystery of the curse."

Smiling at Kade's admiring glance, I felt my cheeks sting with heat and glanced away. "Obviously the universe gave up its secret to us in order to help you. You are not meant to lose this house. This property belongs in your family and now with that gold and whatever else you find in those graves, you are going to be able to keep it." I couldn't help but marvel at the utter synchronicity of it all. "Honestly, the more I think about it, the more I believe it was the best way to get all the secrets out in the open. It's not just about this gold here but about so much more–your Indian heritage, Isabelle's and Isidora's story. Those graves."

Adam stared at the gold in his hand then looked up at me, his black eyes gleaming with unshed tears. "I wish someone in our family had figured it out before now."

"All things are revealed when the time is right. God wants you to have that gold. I now know it's been your ancestors bugging me since my arrival, trying to get me to put the pieces together and figure it out." I smiled, quite pleased with myself and the spirits who helped uncover this mystery. The Rowans just had the impossible happen. They found their pot of gold and the answer to their financial problems. How cool was that?

Kade patted my back. "Well done, Tess."

I put my hand on Kade's thigh and squeezed it in response. "Thanks. But the real reward is that the Rowans now have the money they need to keep their home."

Mary, Dawn and Adam looked at the gold they were holding, their expressions that of incredulity. "What if we are accused of stealing it?" Adam asked. "No one just suddenly finds gold like this." Adam shifted nervously and glanced at Kade and I. "Will we be able to keep it?"

"It's your gold. Why wouldn't you? It was found on your property." And as it all truly sunk in, the Rowans burst into whoops of joy, tears and lots of laughter. We all did. After much hugging and excited talk and more laughter, we finally headed for the house for a celebratory drink. Dawn had some wine she'd been saving, very old she said, and now was the time to drink it.

Kade leaned close while the Rowans talked about their future plans and said softly, "Remember when we were standing in front of the monument and we said that the heart was there for new loves to find their way to each other by taking a step in the right direction?"

I nodded, my heart pounding in response to his softly whispered words.

"I'd say that you just gave all these people a step towards a very bright future and a heart full of joy. That's the message on that tombstone now. Finding love and joy. It worked for you and me too, don't you think?"

I met his eyes and became lost in them. We stared at each other for the longest time then Mary tugged on our arms. "Come on, it's time for some toasts!"

As we toasted to the Rowan's happy future, Kade and I looked at each other again. So much was shared in our glance. More than I can put into words. Promises. A beautiful future. Love. Everything looked so wonderful right now. I had a possible new house (though I truly knew it was mine already), some more spirits to help and a future with Kade to explore. Life was good. And I couldn't wait to get on with it.

The End

Historical Note - Sorting Fact from Fiction

Since the town of Bucksport, Maine, truly exists and the legend of Colonel Jonathan Buck does as well (though it's 'truth factor' is quite nonexistent), I thought it only fair to set the record straight as to what is fact in Hidden Voices and what is fiction. I tried to keep true to Bucksport's actual history since I found it colorful enough to add flair and credibility to my fictional story. Colonel Buck has earned, unfairly and unjustly in my opinion, a smudged reputation due to a stain that appeared on his graveside monument.

Since I grew up in Bucksport and was always fascinated with the eerie legend, I thought it would be pretty cool to put my own creative spin on it. None of this legendary story is grounded in fact. If Buck's monument is cursed, there is no documentation anywhere to suggest why this would be the case. Colonel Buck was a devoted husband and father and he was highly respected among the citizens of Bucksport and the local area. His children grew to become just as admirable and respected. My story is a complete fabrication other than the specific historical data given here. I took creative liberty to reinvent the legend and use historical facts and actual historical figures, such as Jonathan Buck and the Red Paint Indians, to make it more interesting. I do want to make clear, though, that none of the other characters (save the mention of Buck's son Jonathan Buck, Jr.) actually existed. Although it's a shame to have one's name so unjustly tarnished as Buck's has become, the legend has given the town of Bucksport a distinction from others. Who knows why that stain appeared on the monument like it did. God put it there and since ALL things happen for a reason...maybe Tess's conclusion is more accurate than not! I mean...I got the idea from somewhere? Right? Perhaps spirit inspired me to write something that has more foundation than a witch's evil curse! In any case, I like my version of the legend much better.

So, to help sort the facts from the fiction, here is a brief history about Colonel Buck and the town of Bucksport, Maine. I used information gathered from various sources on the

Internet and scored some great data in Emeric Spooner's books. Emeric is a local author who has written 13 books on various subjects, to include Bucksport and her mysteries. I am sure I'll be using more of Spooner's books to gather information for future stories! So, without further ado, here is a brief recap of Bucksport's history:

First, I must talk about the Red Paint Indians for they truly were believed to have existed. They were thusly named because of the red ochre found in their gravesites. Several of those gravesites were in fact found in Bucksport and Orland (the two towns border each other). Since these Indian natives went extinct several thousand years ago, there's not much left in their gravesites to garner information concerning them. Some historians have speculated their connection to the Beothuk of Newfoundland because of their shared interest in red ochre (the Beothuk covered themselves in the stuff) but that is as much argued against as for. Who knows for sure? No one. And because of that, I can make up whatever I want concerning them, right? That's what writers do...they take creative license to make up stories and use actual data sometimes to do it!

So now I'll move on to Colonel Buck's true story. He sailed into the Penobscot harbor in June of 1763 on his sloop named "Sally". With him he brought his family as well as a few other determined settlers and they all got to work forging a life and building a town, then called Plantation No. 1.

In 1779, the Revolutionary War came to the area when the British began constructing Fort George in the Penobscot Bay vicinity of present-day Castine (then called Plantation No. 3). The fort was intended as a stronghold for attacking American privateers operating against British shipping. Their naval blockade effectively shut off communications and supplies to the settlers of Plantation No. 1. Short of food and powder, facing almost certain extinction and losing several of their children due to starvation, town authorities sent off a message to the General Court of Massachusetts seeking aid.

Massachusetts sent a fleet of ships and a force of over 1000 men to dislodge the British from the fort. Colonel Buck took part in this effort along with other volunteers from the surrounding local area. The 21-day battle that followed resulted in one of the greatest fiascoes in US military history. Until Pearl Harbor, it remained the largest naval defeat. Survivors, to include Colonel Buck, were forced to flee for their lives. A quick return home to pack up what possessions they could carry, Buck and his family, along with many other citizens of Plantation No. 1, left their homes.

The day after the naval disaster ended, the British sloop NAUTILUS dropped anchor in the harbor of Plantation No. 1 and the crew went ashore to pillage and burn the properties of the departed patriots. The few settlers who remained, by pledging allegiance to the crown, were spared. Colonel Buck and his family did not return until a treaty was signed with the British in 1783.

In 1789, the people of Plantation No. 1 petitioned the Court for permission to incorporate Plantation No. 1 as the town of Buckstown- honoring by its name, Colonel Jonathan Buck (in 1817, the town was renamed Bucksport). Jonathan Buck, Jr., was named the first Justice of the Peace for the Penobscot area and so reigned a just and righteous family, respected and admired, their reputation unblemished until a stain appeared on a graveside monument.

Jonathan Buck died on March 18, 1795. In August of 1852, his grandchildren, thinking this prominent member of their family, the founding father of Bucksport, Maine, should be honored for his contributions and importance to the town's existence, erected a monument near his gravesite. Shortly thereafter, a weathered image in the form of a woman's leg and foot appeared under the Buck name. The image of a heart also appeared near the top of the obelisk. The actual monument appears on the cover to this book.

Although their appearance sparked intense speculation and rumor, the first record concerning it didn't appear in print until March 22, 1899. The Haverhill Gazette's article recounting the Buck legend has become the more popular version although there are certainly many variations on the theme.

Briefly restated, the tale runs: Jonathan Buck was a Puritan to whom witchcraft was denounced. A woman was accused of witchcraft and he sentenced her to be executed. Then, according to the Haverhill Gazette, "the hangmen was about to perform his gruesome duty when the woman turned to Col. Buck and raising one hand to heaven, as if to direct her last words on earth, pronounced this astounding prophecy: 'Jonathan Buck, listen to these words, the last my tongue will utter. It is the spirit of the only true and living God which bids me speak them to you. You will soon die. Over your grave they will erect a stone that all may know where your bones are crumbling into dust. But listen, upon that stone the imprint of my feet will appear, and for all time, long after you and your accursed race have perished from the earth, will the people from far and wide know that you murdered a woman. Remember well, Jonathan Buck, remember well."

None of that, of course, actually happened but the tale was now in written form and that's as good a truth. Right? Whatever caused the images to appear, the fact is they do exist. Although it is rumored that attempts were made to remove the images and failing that, the stone was replaced several times, there is no official record of that actually happening.

Over the years, geologists have explained that the "stains" are the result of a natural flaw in the stone, perhaps a vein of iron which darkens through contact with oxygen. The problem with this explanation is that any flaws in the stone would have been present at the time the monument was made. The family was insistent to use the cleanest, most flawless of stones. So, who knows why those images are there. God did it. That is the only reasonable explanation (unless, of course, you are an atheist and in that case, well, you are welcome to come up with your own explanation). I took fictional license to make up my own story, and I think it's a pretty good one...who knows, maybe I've channeled through bits of truth. Or not.

I think it's sad that this legend has unjustly tarnished the excellent reputation of an upstanding citizen. Jonathan Buck was respected and admired. His extensive family was model citizens and many of his sons became prominent members of society. Most of them were devout Christians, were hard-working, honest, charitable and caring. They persevered during trying times and because of that, we now have a solid community in which to live and grow. Although I've written a story that puts the legend back in the limelight (however small that may be!), I do hope that I've given better credit to Colonel Buck's memory. May he rest in peace!

About the Author

Deborah J. Hughes was living a normal, happy life when, at the age of seven, she moved into a haunted old farmhouse. Suddenly she was sharing space with dead people and experiencing the bizarre world of the unknown. An over-active imagination did not, at first, serve her well for she feared what she did not understand.

Learning to read opened her to the world of books and they became her escape from a life that was, at times, frightening. When she was older and understood the strange things happening in her house weren't "normal", she began to read everything she could find about supernatural and paranormal phenomena. The more she read, the more she learned and the more she realized how little she knew. This has led to a lifelong search for knowledge. It has also sparked many a story! In fact, she wrote her first one at the age of eight and hasn't stopped since.

Although determined to grow up and become an author, her sense of adventure led to a career in the United States Air Force. Despite a busy and demanding life, Deborah continued writing the stories that streamed like movies through her mind. She also continued her quest for knowledge.

Her military career behind her, she is now focused on her lifelong dream of being an author. She loves the stories she feels so compelled to write and hopes her readers enjoy them too.

Contact Information

Deborah welcomes all comments and/or questions you may have, please email her: deborah.hughes@rocketmail.com or visit her blog at http://www.deborahjhughes.com.

If you are on Facebook, then check out her Author page and stay in touch!
https://www.fb.com/AuthorDeborahJHughes/

She is also quite active on Twitter so if you want to connect there, please do (and yes, she always follows back!)
https://twitter.com/DeborahJHughes

Subscribe to her blog to stay informed of upcoming book release dates and tidbits of information concerning her stories. She loves to hear from readers and interact with them on her various posts. Her blog is not just a platform for sharing her stories, interests and experiences but also provides a place where others can do the same in return.

Other Books by Deborah J. Hughes

Tess Shcafer-Medium Series

Be Still, My Love
Hidden Voices
Vanquishing Ghosts
Rosemary's Ghosts
Ghost Trouble
Haunting Ground

Paranormal Thriller

No Matter What

Romance

Tangled Up Hearts
Moments in the Moonlight

Made in the USA
Columbia, SC
13 February 2025